THE CHOCOLATE
LOVERS' CLUB

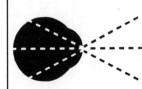

THE CHOCOLATE LOVERS' CLUB

CAROLE MATTHEWS

THORNDIKE PRESS

A part of Gale, Cengage Learning

GALE
CENGAGE Learning™

Detroit • New York • San Francisco • New Haven, Conn • Waterville, Maine • London

GALE
CENGAGE Learning

LIBRARY OF CONGRESS CATALOGING-IN-PUBLICATION DATA

Matthews, Carole.
    The chocolate lovers' club / by Carole Matthews.
        p. cm. — (Thorndike Press large print laugh lines)
    ISBN-13: 978-1-4104-0648-4 (hardcover : alk. paper)
    ISBN-10: 1-4104-0648-2 (hardcover : alk. paper)
    1. Female friendship — Fiction. 2. Chick lit. 3. Large type
books. I. Title.
    PR6113.A88C47 2008b
    823'.92—dc22   2008000933

Published in 2008 by arrangement with St. Martin's Press, LLC.

Printed in the United States of America
1 2 3 4 5 6 7 12 11 10 09 08

The research for this book has been very taxing — all that chocolate, so little time! A big thanks to all the people who have helped me with my quest and who have turned a passion for chocolate into a major addiction. And to Lovely Kev for carrying out the arduous task of helping me eat all that chocolate with his usual verve.

CHAPTER ONE

"Hit me again," I say.

Eyebrows are raised. "Are you sure?"

"I can handle it."

"You can overdose on this," he warns. "Even you, a hardened user."

"Never."

In times of crisis, my drug of choice is single plantation Madagascar. There is nothing — absolutely nothing — that it fails to cure. This is the remedy for anything from a broken heart to a headache — and I've had plenty of both in my time, I can tell you.

"Bring it on, boy." I nod solemnly and my dealer hands over my drugs, making me sigh with relief. Chocolate. Mmm. Mmm. *Mmm!* Lovely, lovely, creamy, sweet, delicious chocolate. I just can't get enough of it.

Taking my first bite, I feel its warm, comforting taste start to edge through my pain. There are times when chocolate really is the answer to all of your prayers.

"Better?"

"Getting there," I say with a wan smile.

"The posse will be here soon and then you'll be okay."

"I know. Thanks, Clive. You're a savior."

"All part of the service, dear." He high-fives me in a very camp way — but then he's gay, so he's allowed.

Taking my stash, I find a sofa in the corner and sink into it. My weary bones start to relax and, breathing in the strong vanilla scent, I feel my head starting to clear too.

I'm not alone in my desires. Oh no. I'm part of a small but perfectly formed sect that we've christened the Chocolate Lovers' Club. We have just four members in our guilty gang, and we meet here at Chocolate Heaven as often as we can. This place is an addict's paradise — the equivalent of the opium den for the chocoholic. It's tucked away in a cobbled back street in a smart area of London, but I'm not going to say where, because then my secret would be out and hordes of wide-eyed, craving women would descend on our special place and spoil it. It's like when you discover a great holiday destination — miles and miles of deserted, white beaches, intimate little restaurants and nightspots — then you tell everyone about it and how fabulous it is and next year it's been swamped by people on EasyJet flights, and you can't move on the beach for bloated bodies in beaded sarongs from Matalan and ghetto blasters. All the intimate little restaurants now serve sausage and chips and the nightspots offer half-price drinks and have foam machines. For now though, Chocolate Heaven is the haunt of the chosen few and long may it remain so.

I let my head drop back and score once more, popping another divine chocolate into my mouth with yet another heartfelt sigh.

I'm Lucy Lombard, and I suppose I'm the founding member because I'm the lucky soul who found Chocolate Heaven first. Today, an ad-hoc meeting of the Chocolate Lovers' Club has been hastily convened. If any one of us texts CHOCOLATE EMER-GENCY, we all try to drop whatever we're doing and run for our sanctuary. It's the equivalent of telling an on-call doctor that his heart patient has just flatlined. This time I'm the one who's called the meeting. Wait until I tell my best girls what's happened — they won't believe it. Or maybe they will.

Autumn is the first to arrive. As I finish my last chocolate, she bursts through the door. "Are you okay?" she asks breathlessly. Autumn Fielding is one of life's carers.

"Marcus. Again," I offer. Marcus is supposed to be my dearly beloved boyfriend — but more of that later.

She tuts sympathetically in return.

Many moons ago, I used to come in here alone and skulk in the corner. I don't really like eating in front of other people and I particularly don't like to be watched when I'm eating chocolate. I suspect druggies don't like to be watched either as they tuck into a crack pipe or mainline their heroin. There's something slightly sleazy about being observed while taking part in your particular perversion. (Unless your particular perversion is being watched, I guess.) I don't actually drool, but I feel that I look as if I do. And, I think you'll agree, drooling is best done in private.

It was during one of my many solo visits that I met Autumn. There wasn't a spare seat in the place except the one next to me, so she plonked herself down and we hit it off immediately. But then I don't think anyone would *not* like Autumn — as long as you don't mind people who can't help being constantly nice. A small word of caution though. Parents, be warned: If you're going to call your daughter Autumn, she will inevitably grow up to have curly red hair and will vote for the Green Party — just as this one does.

Autumn is a dark-chocolate person. In the world of chocolate psychology — and I'm sure there is one — this may indicate that she's hiding her dark side. Autumn nibbles her chocolate — eking out each piece with a thousand tiny tasting bites, which I think makes her feel less guilty about the poor people. She suffers terrible guilt when she feeds her chocolate habit. The rest of us agonize about the number of calories we're consuming and how long they're going to sit on our hips. Autumn agonizes about the starving children who have to survive on a bowl of rice every day and can't have chocolate — not ever. I don't worry about starving children — I try to block them out of my vision completely as, quite frankly, I have more than enough stuff to worry about at home.

"We need hot chocolate to give us a lift," Autumn says as she unwinds her scarf — no doubt hand-knitted by some poor Mexican teenager earning a quid a year in a filth-ridden slum.

"Clive," I shout over at the counter to our friend and supplier. "The others will be here soon. What about getting some hot chocolate on the go for us?"

"Will do," he says, and bustles into action.

Then Nadia arrives. She comes and gives me a hug and looks deeply into my eyes. "He's not good for you."

"I know." We all know. She didn't even need to ask who was the cause of my crisis. It's always Marcus. "I've just ordered hot chocolate."

"Fabulous."

Nadia Stone was the next person to come along to take our cozy couple to the realms of a gang. She arrived one lunchtime at Chocolate Heaven looking stressed and tearful, before ordering a wide selection of goodies from Clive's business and life partner, Tristan, with more haste than good taste. Both Autumn and I empathized with that as we have been there a million times ourselves. It was only right that we took her under our wing there and then.

Autumn and I had already slipped into the habit of meeting up at least once a week — twice if our stress levels warranted it. Now we all have a sort of rolling arrangement.

Nadia is the only one among us who is a mother. She has a demanding three-year-old — aren't they all? Her son's called Lewis, and night after night without proper sleep was the main reason for *her* tears, but things are better now. Lewis sleeps through on enough occasions to allow Nadia to function in the real world.

Nadia is not discerning in her choice of chocolate. She says it's her only respite, but she seems to wolf it down without tasting it. A sin in my book. If you have an addiction, you should at least be able to savor it. Nadia eats her chocolate for comfort — along with 99 percent of the female population, I should imagine. Like me, she is on the comely side of size ten. She blames it on never regaining her figure after the birth of Lewis. I'd blame it on the fact that she snaffles all of her son's chocolate before he can get near it. She even admits to licking the chocolate off his digestive biscuits when he's not looking.

"I *hate* the British weather." The final member of our foursome to arrive is Chantal. Flopping into her seat, she shakes the rain from her glossy hair.

Originally from sunny California, Chantal Hamilton, like Nadia, is also married. She has a fabulously wealthy husband, Ted, who is some kind of financial genius in the City. Chantal is the oldest among us — pushing forty — but is by far the most gorgeous and glamorous. She's tall, slender, always immaculately groomed, ridiculously beautiful and talented. If she were a horse, she'd be a thoroughbred. Her hair is cut into a sleek, dark bob by one of the top stylists in London — one of those who's on the telly all the time. There's never a hair out of place. Chantal is invited into the VIP room and gets complimentary champagne with her hairdo. How the other half live! She wears the kind of shoes that make my feet hurt just looking at them, and frequents the type of designer boutiques where you require appointments and have sales advisors who would terrify punters with bank accounts within the normal range. Yes, Chantal Hamilton has everything in life.

Everything but a husband who wants sex with her.

It's true. In this day and age, when we assume everyone is mad for it, Chantal and Ted make love about once a year. Twice, if she can get him drunk at Christmas on the lethal combination of vodka and something she calls "egg nog." Sounds hideous. Either Valentine's Day or her birthday can be counted on as a cert — but the rest is in the lap of the gods. Chantal wishes it was more to do with Ted's lap.

Despite her good breeding and high-class image, Chantal is also an indiscriminate chocolate eater who refuses to admit that she is an addict. Our American friend simply insists that she has "a sweet tooth." I'd call that deep denial.

"So why are we here?" Chantal wants to know. "You should have seen the butt on the photographer I just had to blow off." Chantal has ways other than chocolate of dealing with her husband's lack of desire to exert his conjugal rights. Not to put too fine a point on it, she prefers to *blow* her photographers rather than blow them off. "It had better be good."

"It's not," I say morosely.

Clive brings over a tray laden down with four glasses of steaming hot chocolate topped with whipped cream and shavings of milk chocolate. He puts it down on the low coffee table in our midst. A curl of steam rises into the air. It looks just the thing to warm our cold toes — and the cockles of my broken heart.

"I've made some *feuillantines,*" he tells us with a dramatic raising of his eyes heavenward, indicating bliss. "Thin slivers of wafer flavored with ginger, clove, nutmeg and cinnamon." We coo our approval. "You *have* to try them."

Quite frankly, who are we to argue?

"Here we go, ladies." There is a collective

sigh of anticipation as I hand out the glasses.

My fellow club members and I snuggle down into the soft, deep sofas. We sip the hot chocolate in unison and there is a second collective sigh — of appreciation.

"Well?" Chantal says.

Autumn already has a ring of chocolate round her mouth and is wide-eyed with expectation.

I look round at the circle of my good friends. "Are you sitting comfortably?" They all nod at me and we simultaneously reach for a thick, chocolaty *feuillantine.*

"Then let me begin . . ."

CHAPTER TWO

She who eats chocolate must work out — it's one of the first rules of the universe. So, on Tuesday evenings I go to a yoga class. I finish the last bite of my Mars Bar and throw the wrapper in the bin. It's six o'clock and I'm hauling my gym bag from under my desk with the hope of making a prompt escape.

I'm currently working at Targa, a computer company that specializes in data recovery — whatever that might be. All I know is that I work here more frequently than anywhere else in my role as a temporary secretary, thoroughly wasting the degree in Media Studies that I struggled so hard to get — despite the fact that everyone views it as a "nonsense" qualification. Targa has endemic levels of stress, sickness and the deployment of duvet days. I think some of my colleagues would benefit more than I do from going to my yoga class. Whenever

17

anyone falls pregnant they seem to find a reason to sack the poor, unfortunate woman — which can take some time and creativity. So, I've done more than my fair share of extended maternity cover over the last few years. Employment legislation means nothing here.

One of the few reasons that I like working at Targa is that it's perilously close to Chocolate Heaven and, if I'm brisk, I can nip there during my lunch hour. My current job is to cater to the wide and varying whims of six assorted salesmen, under the eagle eye of Sales Manager, Mr. Aiden Holby.

"Hi there, Gorgeous," Aiden Holby says as he passes my desk. "Off to put your legs behind your neck tonight?"

Targa is a very politically incorrect company too. Sexual harassment and general abuse of the staff is encouraged — mainly because it's the only form of relief from the constant stress. An ability to flirt outrageously and a wide vocabulary of offensive language are both necessary requirements of recruitment.

"Yes. Yoga beckons."

"What I wouldn't give to see you bending over in one of those tight little Lycra leotards."

"Yeah?"

He holds up his hand. "Don't interrupt me. I'm having a male moment."

"Dream on," I tell him as I head for the door.

"I'm having a drink later with the guys at the Space Bar," he says, turning up his 100-kilowatt smile. "Join us."

"Can't. But thanks."

"I'll buy you some of that chocolate vodka you're so fond of."

It's tempting. There's only one thing that can count as better than chocolate and that's a chocolate-alcohol combo. "I'd better give it a miss," I say, trying to be virtuous.

"I was hoping to get you drunk so that you'd seduce me."

"You couldn't afford that much vodka."

He laughs softly. "Goodnight, Gorgeous. See you tomorrow."

Aiden always addresses me as Gorgeous, but I'm not sure whether it's because he does, in fact, think I'm gorgeous, or because they've had so many temps through the office that one generic name fits us all. Saves all that pesky remembering. I don't, however, call *him* Gorgeous — even though he is.

Aiden Holby is possessed of a rare charm.

19

All the female members of staff, particularly those of a certain age and of an impressionable disposition, think he's fab. He's tall, dark and ridiculously handsome. The fact that he's got an irrepressibly cheeky smile and naughty twinkling eyes hasn't exactly escaped my attention either. I do occasionally find myself talking in glowing terms about Mr. Aiden Holby at the Chocolate Lovers' Club and the girls have duly nicknamed him Crush. Not that I do have a crush on my boss — not really. Besides, while Mr. Aiden "Crush" Holby is a resolutely single man, I am a woman in a committed, long-term relationship. I'm loyal to Marcus to the nth degree — even though my friends at the Chocolate Lovers' Club quite often point out that my loyalty is entirely misguided.

CHAPTER THREE

I join the throng heading down into the Tube and scoot along a few stops to my health club where the yoga class is held. This isn't a particularly salubrious club, but it's just about within my meager budget. Actually it's beyond my meager budget, but I'm not about to split hairs. There are no gleaming chrome and frosted-glass surfaces here. Despite the constant smell of cheap disinfectant in the locker rooms, it's not as clean as it might be, and you don't catch me lingering in the showers — and there's a faint odor of stale sweat in the workout studios. The air-conditioning never works properly either and it's been a very warm day — the sort of day when Toffee Crisps go all soft and chewy in your handbag. I know because that's what I'm going to have for dinner on the way. But if I come here to punish my body on a regular basis, then it can just about keep pace with my calorie consumption.

I conduct a continuing battle with myself not to blossom into the more rotund side of chubby. I'm short, a natural blonde and not *too* much of a heifer considering my addiction — although I probably would be described as "ample" or "curvaceous" should I ever find myself the subject of a tabloid scandal. Luscious Lucy or Juicy Lucy would be my red-top moniker. I'll stop short of Lardy Lucy.

I used to have ambitions, but I'm not sure that I do anymore. I only know that I don't want to spend the rest of my life filing papers and fetching coffee for people who don't even bother to get to know me because I'm not going to be around for long enough. After all these years, I'm still mired in student debt, but one day I'll stop spending all my money on excess calories and start saving up for sensibledom. Even though I'm tipping the scales at the wrong side of thirty, I'm very comfortable with it.

I'm neither a sad single nor a smug married. I have a permanent boyfriend — sometimes. Marcus Canning is the man who adores me and wants to marry me. Eventually. We've been together for five years and he's currently edging further toward a "commitment," which is a good thing.

As I get nearer to the health club my heart starts to sink. I do yoga to help reduce my stress levels, but I'm not sure that it works as I invariably lie there, fists curled into tense balls, thinking, Get a move on! when everyone else is seemingly lying contentedly on the floor listening to some kind of twinkly birdsong and the droning low-level voice of our teacher, Persephone. I also struggle to get my knees to comply with the leg-mangling Lotus, and my Half-Plough position is distinctly halfhearted. My dedication to my spiritual side also means that I don't usually see Marcus on Tuesdays.

Occasionally Marcus calls me and begs me not to pursue my quest to get fit and lures me round to his place instead by offering copious amounts of chocolate and large quantities of red wine. Call me weak, but I always capitulate — even though I sometimes try to make a fuss about not going. Marcus rarely buys into my reluctance as he knows that he can twist me round his little finger. Besides, a glass of wine is good for the heart. Though I'm not sure about the other four that invariably get necked as well. Two squares of dark chocolate a day are also beneficial for your health. They boost your levels of endorphins and antioxidants, and that has to be good. How often are scientists wrong? Huh? So, actually, by staying in and drinking wine and eating chocs, I'm probably doing myself a lot more good than risking injury in my yoga class. And, let's face it, whether it's a scientific fact or not, booze and a box of chocs will always win over health and hatha yoga for the majority of people, and I'm no exception.

My boyfriend knows that I can't resist the lure of chocolates, or him. But, despite me staring at my phone for lengthy periods throughout the day and willing him to save me from torture by the Triangle pose, Marcus hasn't called at all. I phoned him a few times — about ten times or so — but then I thought I was obsessing. And, anyway, each time his mobile went straight to voicemail.

I unwrap the Toffee Crisp from my emergency stash in my handbag and tuck into it. Exercising on an empty stomach — even yoga — always makes me feel faint. Frankly, I'm a recent convert to the delights of pure plantation chocolate. I adore chocolate in all its many forms, but my current passion is couture chocolates made with the selected beans from single plantations all around the world — Trinidad, Tobago, Ecuador, Venezuela, New Guinea. Exotic locations, all of them. They are — out and out — the best type of chocolate. In my humble opinion. The Jimmy Choos of the chocolate world. Though truffles are a fierce competitor. (Strictly speaking, truffles are confectionary as opposed to chocolates, but I feel that's making me sound like a chocolate anorak.)

Another obsession of mine is Green & Black's chocolate bars. Absolute heaven. I've turned Autumn on to the rich, creamy bars, which she can eat without any guilt, because they're made from organic chocolate and the company practices fair trade with the bean growers. Can't say I'm not a caring, sharing human being, right? When my friend eats the Maya Gold bar, she doesn't have to toss and turn all night thinking about the fate of the poor cocoa bean farmers. I care about Mayan bean pickers too, but frankly I care more about the blend of dark chocolate with the refreshing twist of orange, perfectly balanced by the warmth of cinnamon, nutmeg and vanilla. Those Mayan blokes certainly know what they're doing. Divine. I hope they have happy lives knowing that so many women depend on them.

So as not to appear a chocolate snob, I also shove in Mars Bars, Snickers and

Double Deckers as if they're going out of fashion. Like the best, I was brought up on a diet of Cadbury and Nestlé, with Milky Bars and Curly Wurlys being particular favorites — and both of which I'm sure have grown considerably smaller with the passing of the years. Walnut Whips are a bit of a disappointment these days too. They're not like they used to be. Doesn't stop me from eating them, of course — call it product research.

Hastily munching the last bit of my Toffee Crisp as I swing through the doors, I offer a cheery, "Hello," to the receptionist, a young slip of a thing called Becky who looks as if the temptation of chocolate never darkens her doorstep, and breeze through to get changed.

"Oh, Lucy," she shouts after me. "The yoga class is canceled tonight. Persephone's put her back out."

That's not a very good advertisement for yoga, is it? "Damn," I say. "I was so looking forward to getting all my knots unkinked." Call me a liar — see if I care.

"You could squeeze into the FitBall class instead," Becky suggests. "Or there's always the gym."

Both of which sound too much like hard work. I like yoga because you can pretend

26

to be working hard while actually doing very little. If you stop jogging in an aerobics class, everyone knows. Fall asleep in yoga and everyone just thinks you're great at meditating. "Maybe I'll give it a miss tonight," I say, as if I'm disappointed. Cobblers to the Cobbler position, I think with a surge of glee. I make my voice fill with empathy. "I do hope Persephone's okay."

"She should be back in a few days."

So, now what? I could shoot off to the Space Bar and join the guys for a drink. The offer of chocolate vodka is very appealing. The thought of a little socializing with Crush isn't deeply repellent either, but then I'd have to listen to a whole litany of yoga-type jokes from him and the other reps. Maybe Crush would try to get me drunk and maybe — just maybe — I *might* try to seduce him. Can't go there. Targa is very keen on team-bonding exercises, and sometimes they involve alcohol and invariably end in shame, sackings and sexual harassment lawsuits. I'd have to face Crush in the office tomorrow and am also full-time girlfriend of wonderful man already.

Alternatively, Marcus's place isn't too far from here. I could jump on the Tube again and go to give my man a lovely surprise. Weighing up the possibilities, I decide I should definitely run to the warmth of Marcus's arms. Much more sensible. The thought of seeing my dearly beloved puts a spring in my step again and I decide that's exactly what I'll do.

CHAPTER FOUR

Marcus has a great flat on the top floor of one of those grand Georgian buildings in a really trendy area of London. He only bought it last year and that worried me slightly, as I had hoped that we'd move in together when Marcus outgrew the place he was sharing with three other guys, but he said that he didn't feel ready for that. He did, however, give me my own key, which I always think is a crucial extension of trust in a relationship. Besides, he assured me, this flat would be a good investment for our future. When we do live together — which I'm sure we will one day — then Marcus will have accumulated some equity in this property and we can use that as a deposit for our own home. Marcus is very good with investment planning. Like Chantal's husband, he works in a terribly high-paid job in the City and is a complete workaholic. His job is his life. And me, of course.

Marcus is beautiful. He's a blond bombshell and I feel so lucky to have a boyfriend like him. Sometimes, when I'm feeling a bit insecure, I can't help but think that really he's out of my league. For a girl who grew up with the nickname Chubby Cheeks, it always feels strange, having a boyfriend like Marcus. He only has to walk into a room and all female heads swivel in his direction — sometimes male ones too. My looks are of the more ordinary variety — not too shabby, but put it this way: I'm never going to be talent-spotted in the street by the Elite Agency looking for a more mature and fatter brand of model.

Marcus and I met in a bookshop, which I always think sounds terribly romantic. I was buying a copy of *Pride and Prejudice* to replace my much-thumbed one, and he was buying a copy of *Crap Towns: The 50 Worst Places to Live in the UK*. It was love at first sight. Well, for me, at least. Marcus asked for my phone number, but it took him over a month to ring me, even though I willed him to do so, every day. He confessed later that he stumbled across it accidentally while flicking through the contacts list in his mobile phone, and that when he did find it, he'd forgotten whose number it was and just called it out of curiosity. I guess it was my lucky day.

Putting my key in the lock, I call out as I do so, "Hi, honey, I'm home!" It's our little joke.

The fabulous scent of something spicy greets me. "Mmm." I didn't realize how hungry I was. All I've had to eat today is chocolate, chocolate and more chocolate — no change there, then. As I go into the living room, Marcus comes out of the kitchen. He's wearing an apron and is brandishing a wooden spoon.

"What are you doing here?" he says.

"Is that the same as 'Hello, darling, I love you'?" I say as I drop my gym bag on the floor and go over to kiss him. "That smells delicious." I snake my arms around his waist and give him a squeeze. "I'm very impressed. You should do this more often. What's cooking?"

"Oh, not much," he answers distractedly.

"Mmm." I trail one of my fingers along his spoon, scooping up some of the delicious sauce, and then lick my finger. "Is there enough for two?"

"Yes. Just enough."

"Ooh, good."

He unpeels my arms from round his waist with his free hand. "Actually, I'm expecting someone." *And it wasn't you,* his tone says.

"Oh?" Trying to hide my disappointment, I follow Marcus as he retreats into the kitchen. This is a great room, all stainless steel and frosted glass — just like my health club should be. Much too sophisticated for Marcus's usual ready meals and takeaways. He has cupboards with nothing in them, lots of boy gadgets that he's never used. I'm glad to see that he's discovering the joys of cooking. While he fusses with dinner, I delve into the fridge. "Who?"

"An old schoolfriend," he says.

"Mmm. My favorite." Two small pots of dark chocolate mousse are sitting there, looking very alluring. "You made this all by yourself?"

"Well . . ."

"A man of hidden talents," I tease him. "Any to spare?"

" 'Fraid not," Marcus says.

There's also champagne chilling. A very nice bottle. "Is it someone special?"

"No." He shakes his head vigorously. "Just a mate. No one you know. I thought Tuesday was your yoga night."

"Canceled," I say, as I spy a bottle of red wine on the counter that's already half drunk. "Teacher's hurt her back."

"That's not a great advert for yoga."

"That's exactly what I said." Sometimes

Marcus and I are so in tune, I'm sure that we read each other's thoughts.

"Couldn't you have done another class?"

"Too tired," I say. "Besides, I wanted to see you." I lean my head on his shoulder as he stirs his sauce. My eyes rove over the kitchen counter to the open recipe book. "Moroccan chicken with olives. Wow. Chocolate mousse too? You're pushing the boat out."

"I thought I'd make a bit of an effort. I like cooking." The cookery book is one that I bought him for Christmas two years ago. *How to Be Her Kitchen Love God.* Funny that he's never tried out any of the recipes on me.

"What's this?" I lift the lid on another pot.

"Saffron-scented mashed potatoes," he says, somewhat reluctantly.

"Yum. That sounds glorious. I hope your friend isn't a hamburger and chips chap."

He eases away from me again. "Let me just make a phone call, see if I can cancel."

"Don't cancel on my behalf. I'd like to meet him. Are you sure there isn't enough to go round? There looks to be plenty." I'll fight Marcus for the chocolate mousse.

"It'd be better to do it another time." Marcus picks up his phone and flicks up a number. "We'll be joshing about old times.

You'd be bored."

The bowl in which Marcus has made the chocolate mousse is discarded by the sink. Picking it up, I run my finger through the remains of the rich sauce and then stick it in my mouth, sucking greedily on the chocolate. This is good. I'd probably get my tongue in and lick the bowl out if I were alone, but I don't want to appear too skanky. "Are you saying that I'll be in the way?"

"Well . . ." Marcus says and then lets it hang in the air.

"Okay." I can't help feeling a bit miserable that Marcus doesn't want me around. He's very funny about things like this. We hardly ever socialize with his friends or family. He prefers it to be just the two of us. I should like that, shouldn't I? But sometimes it makes me feel as if he thinks I'm not good enough for him. Silly, I know. Marcus tells me I'm a twit all the time. "I'll only stay long enough to say hi and then I'll disappear. I shouldn't just have dropped in. I thought you'd be kicking around."

"Normally, I am," Marcus says. "But this has kind of been organized for a while."

"You never mentioned it."

"I didn't think you'd be interested." The phone continues to ring. "Voicemail," he

34

says with a tut. *"Hi, this is Marcus. Can you call me back? Urgently."*

"You shouldn't put it off. I'll go if you want me to." I try not to sound petulant. "Can I do anything to help before I leave? Shall I set the table for you?"

"It's all done," he says. "There's really no need for you to hang around."

"Oh." I haven't even had a chance to pour myself a glass of wine yet. "Okay. There are a few bits in the bedroom that I want to take home to wash. I'll go and get those then vamoose."

"Great." Marcus gives me a peck on the cheek. "I'll see you tomorrow. Maybe we can catch a film."

"That would be nice." Even though we have to watch far too many movies starring Angelina Jolie.

I leave the kitchen and go through to the bedroom. Wow. It looks as if Marcus has had a spring-clean in here. Everything's spick-and-span. There are none of his clothes draped over the bed as there usually are. Even all the dirty washing is in the laundry basket. And there are candles everywhere. Lovely tall church candles in stainless-steel holders. Very classy. I root through the laundry basket and pull out my few bits and pieces.

"The bedroom looks great," I say when I return. "Love those candles. What on earth made you buy them?"

Marcus flushes. For a straight guy he's very into home furnishings — he just doesn't like to admit it. His apartment is immaculate. There are expensive white leather sofas highlighted with red cushions, set perfectly on dark wood floors. His artwork is color coordinated and contemporary. "I was passing a shop the other day and saw them in the window," he says. "I thought they'd look cool."

"They do," I agree as I stuff my washing into the now groaning gym bag and heave it onto my shoulder. "Very romantic." I put on my most seductive pout. "I can't wait to try them out."

Then I notice that the dining-room table is set for two and that's also looking rather romantic. There are even more candles and a small arrangement of red roses that Marcus has clearly picked up from another little shop. I can't think of a time when he's cooked me dinner that he's ever put flowers on the table — not even on Valentine's Day. Beside the roses there's a small box of chocolates and I recognize the packaging so well. "You've been to Chocolate Heaven," I say in surprise. Marcus never goes to

Chocolate Heaven; he knows that's my place, the place I go with my girls. Suddenly my heart is in my mouth.

And that's when the doorbell rings. Marcus freezes. As do I. "That must be your friend," I somehow manage to say, even though my throat is trying to close.

Marcus is clearly torn between remaining immobile and opening the door. The bell rings again.

"Want me to get it?"

"No," he says. "No."

I stand, not knowing what to do while he slowly swings open the door. Not surprisingly, Marcus's old schoolfriend is a petite and extraordinarily pretty brunette. She steps into the apartment and kisses Marcus full on the lips. "Hello, darling," she says.

Marcus recoils slightly and casts a worried glance in my direction which his friend follows.

"Hi," I say, extending my hand as I try to force my face into a smile. She takes it. Her hand is cool and delicate, as slender as the rest of her. "I'm Lucy," I continue brightly. "Marcus's girlfriend."

Now it's her turn to recoil.

"This is my friend, Joanne," Marcus says tightly.

I look at my lover. "An old *school*friend.

That's what you said, isn't it?" I turn back to Joanne. "Which school did you go to with Marcus? Primary? Grammar? Or maybe it was the harsh school of life?"

His old schoolfriend looks at him blankly. "I don't know quite what's going on here, Marcus," she says. "But I don't think that I want to be part of it." She turns away from him, spinning on her heel toward the door.

"Jo," Marcus pleads as he catches her sleeve. "Don't go."

And I think that's my cue to leave. "Oh, Marcus," I say sadly. "Do you have so little respect for me?"

"I can explain," he says, and I notice that he's still looking at Jo rather than at me.

"You're welcome to stay and listen to it," I say to Jo. "I'll be the one to leave." Marcus does nothing to stop me, so I hitch up my gym bag once more and move toward the door. "It's been nice meeting you," I say to Marcus's new love. "You'll enjoy your dinner. It smells wonderful. It even covers the smell of a rat. The chocolates are great, by the way. I hope you both choke on them."

Then I hold my head as high as I can while I walk away.

CHAPTER FIVE

My flat is less glamorous than Marcus's — but it's home. I live in Camden, in a teeny-tiny place above a hairdressing salon that was once run by my dearly departed mother, years ago, when she herself was a stylist. I call Mum "dearly departed" not because she's dead, but because she's moved to Spain. Mum — long since divorced from my fickle father — has remarried, an older and richer man, and now doesn't work at all but spends all her time lounging around at their sumptuous villa on the Iberian peninsula and having her hair done by someone else. Frankly, I see so little of her these days that she might as well have croaked it. She still owns the Camden property and I stay here because she gives me a cheap deal on my rent and doesn't stress too much if I accidentally forget to pay her sometimes. In return I don't burn the place down or leave the bath overflowing like most tenants would.

Now the salon is run by a really flamboyant guy called Darren who gives me a free cut and blow-dry every now and again as I keep an eye on the place for him out of hours. I guess if I moved I'd have to start paying for hairdos, too. He gives me one of those funky, chippy cuts favored by children's presenters on the BBC and I like to think that it keeps me looking young. Gamine. But maybe it just emphasizes my chubby cheeks. I really should introduce him to Clive and Tristan one day. Those boys might make fab chocolates, but they could both do with a revamp in the hair department. Their current styles favor an overindulgence in hair gel and some unfortunate bleached highlights. They would love Darren. Darren is skeletal — the bitch. He weighs about nine stone and has hips like a twelve-year-old girl. Clive and Tris would fatten him up a treat. Anyway, back to my family. Dad, conversely, is now married to a much younger woman who's also a hairdresser. She has failed to do much with my father's combover, but there's a spring in his step which I put down to something other than her skill with scissors. Dad lives on the south coast and I see even less of him than I do of Mum.

Unlocking the door, I throw my gym bag on the floor and head for the fridge without turning the kitchen light on. Sitting on the cold tiles with the fridge door open, I reenact the scene from *9 1/2 Weeks* all by myself. A tub of Ben & Jerry's Phish Food Ice Cream from the freezer compartment is the first to go. I don't even bother with a spoon, I just claw it out with my fingers and cram it into my mouth. All the way home on the Tube, I managed to stop myself from sobbing, but now fat, wet tears roll down my face and into my chocolate ice cream, making all the little chocolate fish and the marshmallows taste salty. When that's gone, I start on the stash of Snickers Bars and devour three with as few chews as possible. A milk chocolate Bounty Bar is the next to go. Normally, I ponder on the fact that Bounty is missing a trick by not putting one dark chocolate and one milk chocolate bar in each wrapper, to save all that troublesome choosing — but tonight I don't care what color they are as I guzzle the sweet coconut down. I have a box of pure plantation chocolates from Chocolate Heaven in there too — though Clive would pass out at the thought of me eating their chocolates at anything other than room temperature — and, despite my pain, even I realize that they

41

would be wasted on me at this moment. So, I opt instead for a bar of Cadbury's Dairy Milk, three Green & Black's white chocolate bars, and a box of Celebrations which I can hardly unwrap quickly enough.

All the time that I'm eating, I hardly think of Marcus and how shabbily he has treated me — once more. For now, it's just me and the comfort chocolate. In the Celebrations go, one after another with no discernible gap — orange, coconut, caramel. I hardly taste them. But when I stop gorging, I feel sick. Sick to my stomach. So I stagger to the bedroom, strip off my clothes and head for my bed, where I lie on my back and wait for morning.

CHAPTER SIX

Next morning, I'm as white as the driven snow when I look in the bathroom mirror, apart from the dark plugholes of my eyes. I lean heavily on the edge of the sink, feeling disgusted with myself. This is not the first time that Marcus has treated me so badly — it's just the first time that I've actually been confronted with him in the very act of infidelity.

I've given five years of my life to Marcus Canning. Five of my very best years. And I feel so stupid that I've squandered them on him. I keep hanging on in there because he insists that I'm the only woman in the world he couldn't live without. Then, every now and again, he meets an obliging girl in the local wine bar or somewhere — someone thin and pretty like Jo — and decides he'd better check if I *really* am the only woman he can't live without . . . or whether he's mistaken. So, off he trots into the wide blue yonder without a backward glance. Until he decides that he *can* live without *her,* but not — after all — without little old *me.* Then he comes back. It involves begging on his part — and more each time — but invariably I cave in and take him back. It's what keeps my consumption of single Madagascar chocolate on the excessive side. Well — no more! This time, Marcus and I are through.

After a shower, I scrub at my teeth, letting the harsh mint hit take away the sour taste in my mouth. Why the hell don't they make toothpaste in chocolate flavor? That would be so much better. Why can't we have women toothpaste designers, then we'd get it in yummy tiramisu or fudge brownie flavor, not poxy spearmint. Yack. I get dressed, pulling on the clothes that I'd discarded on the bedroom floor last night. I forgo breakfast as I can't bear to open the fridge again, and then head out of the flat, waving with forced cheeriness at Darren the hairdresser as he arrives for work. Then, instead of taking my usual route to the office, I jump on the Northern Line and head back to Marcus's flat.

Before I let myself in the front door, I take a very deep breath, but there's no sign of Marcus or his paramour, Jo. As I hoped, he has already left for the day. The man is a complete workaholic and likes to be in the office at 7:30 a.m. He hates to think that his colleagues might arrive earlier than him and get a head start. Marcus's morning begins at 6:30 a.m. prompt with a run and a cold shower, and neither I — nor, I suspect, a new lover — would make him change that routine.

There are signs, however, that a good time was had by all last night. Jo might have found herself caught in the middle of a love triangle, but she clearly didn't mind staying around when she thought that one of the angles had been dispensed with. The remains of dinner still grace the table — dirty dishes, rumpled napkins, a champagne flute bearing a lipstick mark. There's even one of the Chocolate Heaven goodies left in the box — which is absolute sacrilege in my book, so I pop it in my mouth and enjoy the brief lift it gives me. I huff unhappily to myself. If they left chocolate uneaten, that must be because they couldn't wait to get down to it. Two of the red cushions from the sofa are on the floor, which shows a certain carelessness that Marcus doesn't normally exhibit. They're scattered on the white, fluffy sheepskin rug, which should immediately make me suspicious — and it does. I walk through to the bedroom and, of course, it isn't looking quite as pristine as it did yesterday. Both sides of the bed are disheveled and I think that tells me just one thing. But, if I needed confirmation, there's a bottle of champagne and two more flutes by the side of the bed. It seems that Marcus didn't sleep alone.

Heavy of heart and footstep, I trail back through to the kitchen. More devastation faces me. Marcus has made no attempt to clear up. The dishes haven't been put into the dishwasher and the congealed remnants of last night's Moroccan chicken with olives and saffron-scented mash still stand in their respective saucepans on the cooker. Tipping the contents of one pan into the other, I then pick up a serving spoon and carry them both through to the bedroom. I slide open the wardrobe doors and the sight of Marcus's neatly organized rows of shirts and suits greet me. Balancing the pan rather precariously on my hip, I dip the serving spoon into the chicken and mashed potatoes and scoop up as much as I can. Opening the pocket of Marcus's favorite Hugo Boss suit, I deposit the cold mash into it. To give the man credit where credit is due, his mash is very light and fluffy.

I move along the row, garnishing each of his suits with some of his gourmet dish, and when I've done all of them, find that I still have some food remaining. Seems as if the lovers didn't have much of an appetite, after all. I move onto Marcus's shoes — rows and rows of lovely designer footwear — casual at one end, smart at the other. He has a shoe collection that far surpasses mine. Ted Baker, Paul Smith, Prada, Miu Miu, Tod's . . . I slot a full spoon delicately into each one, pressing it down into the toe area for maximum impact.

I take the saucepan back into the kitchen and return it to the hob. With the way I'm feeling, Marcus is very lucky that I don't just burn his flat down. Instead, I open the freezer. My boyfriend — *ex*-boyfriend — has a love of seafood. (And other women, of course.) I take out a bag of frozen tiger prawns and rip it open. In the living room, I remove the cushions from the sofa and gently but firmly push a couple of handfuls of the prawns down the back. Through to the bedroom and I lift the mattress on Marcus's lovely leather bed and slip the remaining prawns beneath it, pressing them as flat as I can. In a couple of days, they should smell quite interesting.

As my pièce de résistance, I go back to the kitchen and take the half-finished bottle of red wine — the one that I didn't even get a sniff at — and pour it all over Marcus's white, fluffy rug. I place my key in the middle of the spreading stain. Then I take out my lipstick, a nice red one called Bitter Scarlet — which is quite appropriate, if you ask me — and I write on his white leather sofa, in my best possible script: MARCUS CANNING, YOU ARE A CHEATING BAS-TARD.

CHAPTER SEVEN

"And then I called you." My lip is wobbling now that I've brought my dear friends up to date with the latest installment in the soap opera that is my disastrous love life. When I pick up my hot chocolate, my hands are shaking. I hold the mug tightly until the warmth starts to relax my fingers.

"Goodness me," Autumn says, wide-eyed.

"Bloody well done," Nadia chips in. "Bloody well done to you. What a git Marcus is."

The revenge-by-prawns felt like a perfect touch when I did it. Now I'm not so sure. "I don't think he'll ever forgive me for this," I mumble.

Chantal snorts. "Why should you think about *him* forgiving *you!* He's the one who put you in that terrible situation. He's the one who should be looking for forgiveness. Toughen up, Lucy. It's time you stopped being his doormat."

"What if he has me arrested for criminal damage?"

"He wouldn't dare," Nadia says.

Clive and Tristan have joined us at the table and nibble furiously at their own *feuillantines*. There's nothing they like better than a good gossip.

"What do you think, boys?"

"You did great," Clive assures me with a pat on my hand. "Sublime blend of drama and outrage. You could be an honorary gay."

Tristan and Clive watch over their most precious clients with a proprietorial air. They regularly chip in to help us solve our problems, but as they are both campier than Eddie Izzard, I'm sure that their advice is sometimes skewed. Plus, it wouldn't do if they solved all our relationship dilemmas anyway, because then they'd both be out of business. Their profits would drop by a minimum of 50 percent if I didn't come here for a week. But then that's a stupid thought. I couldn't *last* a week without coming here at least once.

Tristan, a former accountant and fully practicing chocoholic, is supposed to be the entrepreneur. He's aiming for a chain of Chocolate Heaven cafés reaching across the land, nudging their elbows into the ribs of Starbucks. Clive is the master chocolatier, having started his career as a pastry chef at one of the top hotels in London, indulging his lifelong passion for chocolate in fabulously exotic desserts. When he and Tristan got together, they both quit their day jobs and set up Chocolate Heaven. Clive now spends his time creating the most exquisite concoctions known to man — or should that be woman? And although both of these guys are as gay as they come, they both know *exactly* how to keep a girl happy.

"Did you phone Crush?" Chantal wants to know. "If you haven't been in to work yet, they'll all be wondering where you are."

"No," I say with a tearful sniff. "I didn't even think about the office."

"Give me your phone," she instructs. "I'll call and say you'll be in at lunchtime." Which she does. As I listen to Chantal's earnest and evasive explanation of my absence, I try to blank out thoughts of this story doing the rounds of Targa when it gets out, as these things always do. "He's worried about you, Mr. Aiden Holby," Chantal says when she hangs up. "He sounds cute."

Chantal thinks that everyone under forty, who is breathing, sounds cute. But in this case she's right. Hang on — how can I even be thinking that, when I'm so recently devastated? I force myself to say brightly,

51

"He *is* cute."

"Good girl," Chantal says. "There *is* life after Marcus. Just hang on in there. Hey, Clive, we need more chocolate."

Autumn and I nod our agreement.

"Truffles," he says wisely, a finger stroking his neat goatee. "That's what we need. Ideal for a crisis." He scuttles off to replenish our stock.

"Not for me," Nadia says, standing up. "I've got to go and pick Lewis up from nursery. My freedom for the day hath ended." She throws up her hands in a resigned gesture.

The rest of us, never having had much to do with kids other than going to school with them when we were kids ourselves, simply nod in the right places when Nadia pours out all her concerns about her shaky parenting skills. Getting Lewis onto solids was a particularly lengthy topic — although we did point out that chocolate is a solid, and who could resist that? Now he'll happily eat pizza, sausages and chocolate — good boy! These days, Nadia comes to our regular get-togethers whenever possible to try to stop her brain from rotting. Her words, not ours, although we do agree with her. Sometimes she forgets herself and starts telling us about how her son likes to explore the contents of his nose — a topic of conversation that we're very quick to knock on the head. But we have weaned her from her worse excesses and keep her conversation in the world of grown-ups as much as we can.

Nadia is only my age, but she seems so much older. Her responsibilities sometimes weigh heavily on her. She has a lovely home, a lovely husband and a lovely baby, but to be honest — as she is with us — sometimes she's bored to tears with her life.

The main fly in the ointment is that Nadia is Indian and her husband isn't. Her family disowned her because she shunned her arranged marriage to her third cousin Tariq, or something like that. She was cast out of her cozy, extended family and, to this day, she's never clapped eyes on any of her relatives since. Which means, on the upside, that she's been spared a thousand visits by sundry well-meaning aunties bearing Tupperware containers filled with onion bhajees, but it also means, on the downside, that she has to cope with everything pretty much alone.

When Nadia became pregnant she hoped that it would, at least, spark a reunion with her two sisters to whom she'd been so close. But it never happened and I guess we, the Chocolate Lovers' Club, have become her surrogate sisters.

Having wanted to escape a traditional Indian marriage, she now seems to have found herself lumbered with a man who's regressed fifty years. After the baby was born, Toby insisted that he didn't want any wife of *his* working, and now Nadia stays at home with Lewis — which is a luxury they can barely afford. Toby has his own plumbing business and we all know how lucrative that can be, but children — like good chocolate — are extremely expensive. Nadia has complied, but it means that she's given up a career as a publicist for a trendy publisher which she thoroughly enjoyed, and I can't help but feel as if there's some resentment simmering there. I try to console her by convincing her that her job was "*so* last year." But, secretly, she knows that I'd saw off one of my arms for a gig like that.

Nadia kisses me on the cheek and grabs the last chocolate from the plate. "Maybe I'll catch you later in the week."

"Thanks for coming." I do appreciate it as I know how hard it is for Nadia to get time by herself.

Autumn works weird and wonderful hours, so she can normally duck in here for an hour or so when required. She "does good" as a job, working in a rehabilitation center for young druggies — I'm sure there's a more politically correct term. The program's called something trendy, like KICK IT! or STUFF IT! or FUCK IT! — something like that, I can't remember. She teaches creative glass techniques, which I'm sure must come in terribly useful when you're trying to quit heroin. But I shouldn't scoff, she's very earnest about it all and cares about all her charges — probably far too deeply. Having been blessed with the name Autumn has somehow landed her with an overactive-conscience gene — something normally missing from the upper classes, I find. We all love her, despite her eccentricities, because we are bonded together by our shared addiction.

Autumn is the archetypal English Rose and she's a lovely, warm human being. Her only apparent flaw is that she thinks cheesecloth is a cool fabric. I'd describe what she's wearing, but I couldn't bear to. It's dreadful — all sort of hippy and mismatched. Floaty chiffon skirt with denim jacket and . . . well, cheesecloth. That's as far as I'm going. We may be joined by our mutual appreciation of all things chocolaty, but we certainly don't share a fashion sense. I, being a secretary-aspiring-to-be-an-executive, wear smart clothes — suits and tailored dresses.

The fact that I buy them all from Primark is neither here nor there. At least I'm not at the charity-shop level that my friend prefers. Autumn is also the most principled among us. She recycles things (other than her clothing), and she rides a bike in preference to driving a car and not because she can't afford one. Autumn also favors scuffed Dr. Martens boots over Jimmy Choos, and she can afford those too. You can tell she's not normal. I keep trying to convince her that she should buy Jimmy Choos and then pass them on to the less fortunate when she's worn them a couple of times — like me, for instance. Autumn uses Eco washing powder and environmentally friendly bleach and has been known to shun Dr. Hauschka's Rose Day Cream in favor of washing her face in her own urine. It was, thankfully, an experiment that didn't last long because it made her smell funny — even though she denied it. There'll come a time in our lives when we'll all smell of wee, and my view is that it's best not to hasten the process.

Autumn is young — twenty-eight in physical years, but somehow much younger emotionally. She seems to have led a sheltered life — she was educated at a top-notch boarding school followed by a red-brick university, but still has a lot to learn about life. She's from what's called a "well to do" family — in other words, seriously loaded. This woman is as posh as they come, probably ninety-seventh in line to the throne or something like that. And I'm sure her life would have followed its destined path if she'd been called Fenella or Genevieve or Eugenie.

Autumn never has a boyfriend, partly because she is too busy doing good to have time to meet men and partly, I think, because who would want to go out with her while she's dressed like that? She also likes to have long discussions on the merits of wind turbines as a source of sustainable power, and most normal men don't. Her sole comfort is chocolate and for that, and many other things, I applaud her.

I, technically, work a nine-to-five job, but have a reckless disregard for the terms of my employment contract and simply disappear whenever I feel like it. I'm a temp — we're supposed to be unreliable and who's going to sack me? Crush, thankfully, seems to agree and gives me a large amount of leeway when it comes to my work ethic.

Chantal is the luckiest among us as she works for herself, even though she doesn't need to as she is fabulously wealthy without having to lift a finger. So, like me, she is fairly disdainful of regular working practices. Whereas my friend's disdain is founded in some sort of reality, I mistakenly live with the fantasy that I don't need to work. Chantal's husband, Ted, is from "old" money. They have a wisteria-covered pile in Richmond just near Mick Jagger's old house — Chantal often bumps into "Jerry" at the local florists. They have a boat moored on the Thames which they never use, a villa in the South of France that stands empty for the majority of the year and a weekend retreat in Cornwall — which they do occasionally visit. How flash is that? Ted is astonishingly good-looking — not the usual chinless wonder who normally graces the upper echelons of our society. (I speak as if I have a lot of experience in this area, but I don't.)

Chantal works as a freelance journalist, employed mainly by an American magazine called *Style USA* which features the homes of our American cousins in different countries throughout the globe. Chantal covers England, which means she gets to swan around the country, photographer in tow, interviewing people who are keen to have their homes spread-eagled on the glossy pages. She's been living in England for ten years now and has even swapped her coffee-drinking habit in preference for a nice cup of tea. *And* she takes it with milk, not lemon. There's someone who's really abandoned their American roots.

Chocolate might be a well-known aphrodisiac, but nothing Chantal has tried reaches Ted's nether regions. Even a night with a chocolate body-paint concoction that Clive lovingly hand created for her was a failure. It seems incredible that a wife who wouldn't look out of place in a Hugh Grant film has a husband who can't raise a glimmer of interest in his missus. Chantal has to beg her husband to shag her. Sorry, that's not polite but I can't think of any other way to put it, and *she* puts it that way in her frequent downloads about the state of her nonexistent sex life. He blames pressure of work, pressure of golf, pressure of everything. We discuss all of his excuses in minute and rather exacting detail during our chocolate-and-counseling sessions — a fact that I'm sure would make him even more reluctant to sleep with his wife if he only knew about it. So, I guess we all have our troubles, is what I'm saying.

"Just call me if you need me, Lucy," Nadia instructs. "I mean it. Chin up. You did great with Marcus."

I give my chin a defiant little tilt in response. But I know that I *didn't* do great. None of my friends have to know about my solo eating orgy. We're all entitled to have our secrets, aren't we? This is what Marcus has reduced me to. I've done so well to control my binge-eating recently, but one tiny bit of emotional turmoil and my self-esteem is dragging its belly on the ground again and I'm back on the gorging band-wagon. This is another legacy of going through my school years as Chubby Cheeks. Why couldn't I have been Lucy Lastic? Because I had chubby cheeks rather than boys clamoring to get in my underwear, I assume.

Speaking of underwear that will come off at the drop of a hat, I thought that Marcus might have called me this morning — to say something, *anything* about this latest development, perhaps even proffer an apology . . . but he hasn't. When he gets back to his flat tonight, I'm sure he'll be straight on the phone, but I imagine that I'm not going to like what he says after he's seen my customization of his wardrobe, his sofa and his rug.

The boys return with the truffles and we duly tuck in. Autumn is supposed to be a vegan, but her diet seems to consist entirely of chocolate. She believes that vegetables have feelings too. Though how sensitive spinach is or how caring cabbage might be, I don't know. Chantal likes to use chocolate as a sex substitute, but currently it isn't working.

"How are things with you, Chantal?" I ask, wanting to deflect the attention from my own relationship shortcomings.

"Oh, you know," she says breezily. "Nothing that a good night in the sack wouldn't cure."

"Still no action from Ted?"

"We're both so busy that we're never in bed and awake at the same time. Let alone anything else. I'm away for three nights each week. When I'm there, Ted rarely gets home before midnight, by which time I'm asleep. I leave the house before seven, when Ted's still out for the count. Even if we didn't have problems, it wouldn't make for great marital relations."

"Chantal," Tristan says. "Even *I'd* consider sleeping with you."

"That's so sweet." Chantal kisses him on the cheek. "Until we can sort it out, I have to find other ways to scratch my itch." She gives me a wink, but in my current mood my heart sinks. I know that the desperate state of Chantal's marriage isn't entirely her fault, but I can't think that it helps when she jumps into bed with every available guy. Maybe I'm still smarting too much over Marcus to find my empathy button.

"Speaking of which," she says, "I have a very hot photographer waiting for me and I don't want him to go cold. I'm outta here. Are you sure you're okay now, Lucy?"

"I'm fine. Really."

"I'll call you tomorrow." She picks up her Anya Hindmarch bag and leaves.

"I'm teaching soon," Autumn says with a glance at her watch. "I'd better make a move as well. Don't forget that this might all be for the best. The universe might have something better waiting for you just around the corner."

I like the fact that Autumn believes the universe has everything mapped out for us and that this isn't simply down to my boyfriend's inability to stay faithful.

"Big hug," she says, and then gives me a big hug.

I sigh and pop another truffle. One day I would like to have some sweetness in my life that isn't a direct result of chocolate consumption. "I'd better head to work too." I sound about as enthusiastic as I feel. "I'll take the bill, Clive." I feel it's my turn to settle as it was my emergency.

"Wouldn't hear of it, darling. You're

traumatized enough. Have this crisis on the house, courtesy of Uncle Clive."

"You're both angels," I say. "If either of you ever get fed up with men, I'm very easy to love."

Clive gives me a hug and a kiss. "Someday you'll find someone straight who's as sexy as I am. Someone who loves you just as much as you love him."

"I think it'll be a long day coming," I say with feeling.

CHAPTER EIGHT

Nadia decided that her front door needed painting. The house was starting to look really shabby and, although her husband Toby had been promising to get around to doing it, he wasn't showing any signs that he was in imminent danger of picking up a paintbrush. Though, to be honest, the peeling door now blended in perfectly well with the rest of the street. This was an area of London that was still waiting for the development boom to hit. Estate agents kept promising it, but the majority of properties remained down-at-heel, shunned by renovators and young professionals alike. The chichi wine bars and cafés opened — giving brief hope that a resurgence was just around the corner — but they closed again within months when the customers failed to come. It did mean, however, that she and Toby could afford to live here rather than heading out to Northampton and Peterborough as so many of their friends had done, wandering further and further up the M1 in search of cheaper house prices, a better quality of education and cleaner air. As she looked at the litter on the pavements and the graffiti on the brick walls, she sometimes struggled to remember *why* they actually wanted to live here. Toby said that it was better for business, but she doubted it. Wasn't there a shortage of plumbers everywhere these days? The good people of Northampton must have leaky taps like everyone else.

Nadia had collected Lewis from his nursery school and now had a day of housework to look forward to. A small mountain of ironing awaited her. She had shopping to do too as there was no food in the house for the rest of the week. As she approached the house, Nadia noticed that Toby's van was parked outside and her heart sank. It was just after midday and he should have been out on a job. If he was home at this time, there was only one thing that it could mean.

Opening the front door, she called out as brightly as she could, "It's me, Toby!" Slipping off Lewis's coat, she said, "Come on, sweetie. Let's go and say hello to Daddy."

Lewis raced up the stairs ahead of her as

she shrugged off her own jacket. She felt dowdy in her worn clothes. Long gone were the smart business outfits she used to wear; nowadays her fashion sense had "mumsy" written all over it. She'd long given up her colorful saris and embroidered shalwar kameez for the lazy comfort of Western clothes. Anything that said "easy care" or "non-iron" on it was a surefire hit. Style came a poor second. Glancing in the mirror, she vowed to do something about her hair. Her once lustrous chestnut mane had lost all of its shine — probably due to using the cheapest supermarket own-brand stuff that she could find — and spent most of its time scraped up in a ponytail for low maintenance. This was the only way she could ensure that she didn't go out with bits of Lewis's lunch stuck in her tresses. It hung to her shoulders when loose and badly needed cutting. Perhaps she should consider a close crop and sell her hair to those who made hair extensions — but who would want it in this condition? It wasn't only the front door that needed a total revamp.

Trying to force some lightness into her footsteps, she climbed the stairs after Lewis. Sure enough, when Nadia followed her son into the tiny spare bedroom that served as an office, Toby was sitting at the computer looking guilty. Nadia's guilt would have centered on the plate of chocolate digestives that sat next to the computer. She'd spent — wasted — a couple of pounds of their rapidly dwindling funds on some biscuits, trying to convince herself that they were for Lewis, when she knew that they were really intended for her. Toby had no such thoughts. His guilt was for an entirely different reason.

"Thought I'd pop back and get some invoices out of the way while I had a bit of a gap," her husband said.

If only she could believe him.

"Come and give your dad a big kiss," he said and Lewis flew into his arms. Her son certainly wasn't disappointed to see his dad sitting at home during the day.

Nadia tried to look over her husband's shoulder to see if there were, indeed, any invoices on the screen, but he flicked the mouse and nothing more incriminating than the screensaver appeared. Goodness only knows, he needed to send out some invoices. The bills were piling up and there wasn't enough money in the account to pay them.

"I thought you were working flat out this week," she said, quoting him.

"I left Paul in charge for a while. He can manage."

She stifled a sigh. "Do you want some lunch with us?"

"A quick sandwich would be great."

"A quick sandwich is all it can be," she said, more sharply than she intended and he looked up at her. "I need some money, Toby. There's not a scrap of food in the cupboards. I've got to go to the supermarket today."

Toby raked his hands through his hair. "Love, what on earth do you do with all the cash I dole out?"

"You didn't give me any housekeeping last week," she reminded him. "I've got five pounds in my purse. That's it." She'd felt dreadful in Chocolate Heaven this morning as she knew that she didn't actually have enough money to pay her part of the bill. In her heart, she knew that she shouldn't go along so regularly to meet the girls, but the Chocolate Lovers' Club was proving to be her sanctuary, her only respite in what seemed to be an increasingly mad world. It was the one place where she could share her problems — but even then, the others didn't know the half of it. Sure, her friends knew that her life wasn't a bed of roses, but they didn't know the full story. Still, none of them minded paying her share of the bill — even when, on the rare occasion, she did have the cash to spare.

"I'm a bit tight this week, love. Put it on plastic."

She had a raft of credit cards. All of them maxed. "I can't keep doing this, Toby. We can't pay our bills. You really *do* need to be sending out some invoices."

"I'm on to it," he snapped. "I said I'm on to it."

"Lewis," she said, "go and play with Bob the Builder for a minute. I need to talk to Daddy."

Her son unwound himself from Toby's lap and raced off into his bedroom to find his beloved toy.

She knelt down beside her husband and rested her hand on his thigh, stroking it absently. "I'm scared, Toby," she said. "This is getting out of hand." She flicked her eyes at the computer.

"I can handle it," he replied tightly.

"But *I* can't."

Until he'd gone to his best friend's stag weekend in Las Vegas, her husband's only experience of gambling had been buying a weekly lottery ticket for a pound. If it was a rollover week, he might splash out and spend a fiver. That hardly made him a high-league player. But on that trip he'd won a thousand dollars — and something had pushed the buttons of a latent addiction. It was "easy money," he'd said. Since then, he'd been hooked on the online gambling sites. For three years he'd ploughed all their income, their savings, into trying to win "the big one." Every roll of the dice, every flip of the cards, every spin of the slot machines was pushing them further and further into debt.

Nadia had always thought that the stereotypical gambling addict was a big, fat man with an equally big, fat cigar gracing the casinos of Europe, risking his yacht, his Roller, his Rolex, his reputation at the roulette wheel. She didn't think that gambling addicts were home-loving family men — ordinary men with hair that needed cutting and mischievous eyes, hardworking plumbers who spent their evenings locked in front of a computer monitor risking their sanity, their happiness, their marriages . . . to feed their compulsion. Now she knew better.

"I want you to stop this, Toby. I want you to get help."

He clutched her arms. "I don't need help, Nadia. I'm *that* much away from a big win." He showed her a fraction of an inch with his fingers. "It could all be ours. A big house, a big car. Designer clothes. Fabulous holidays. We could take Lewis to Disneyland. Every year if we wanted to."

"I don't want all those things," she said. "That's not real life. I want you. I want my husband back, not sitting in front of a computer every waking hour squandering everything we've ever worked for."

His jaw set and his eyes darkened. "I could remind you that you don't work, Nadia."

"I could," she said. "I could try to get a job again. That would help to pay some of our debts."

"I want you here for Lewis," he said. "You know that. Look at all the stories you see in the newspapers about kids getting neglected at their nurseries. A couple of mornings is bad enough."

"That accounts for a tiny fraction, I'm sure. Lewis loves his nursery. They're really good with him."

"I don't want him looked after by strangers."

"But there isn't enough money, Toby. We can't go on like this."

He stood and pushed her away from him. "Don't you think I know that? That's why I'm doing this." He banged his fist on top of the computer. "I'm doing it for us, to bring us a better life. I don't want to be a plumber for the rest of my life. Tied to a

71

phone twenty-four hours of the day, seven days a week. I want to live. This could give us that chance. Do you have any idea how much I could win?"

"But you don't," she said. "You don't win."

"I can't discuss this with you, Nadia. You just don't understand. Oh, what the hell. I'm going back to work." With that he slammed out of the room, his feet thundered down the stairs and the front door banged behind him.

Her son appeared at the door clutching Bob the Builder. "Has Daddy gone?"

She nodded as she slid onto the computer chair and pulled Lewis to her.

"He didn't say goodbye."

"Daddy's got a lot on his mind," she said as she ruffled his hair.

The sad thing was that she fully understood the pressures on her husband. He'd taken it upon himself to be the sole breadwinner and Nadia could appreciate how difficult that must be. She would dearly love to go back to work to help them out, but the truth of the matter was that even if she got a job again, the cost of paying for a fulltime nursery would just about eat up her salary and, given the situation with her family, it wasn't as if she could rely on any of her relatives to help with her child care. It wasn't only the cost of a day nursery that was sky-high. The price of everything today seemed to have rocketed. Normal families were almost bankrupted simply to provide a roof over their heads. Clothes and shoes for Lewis cost just as much as they did for adults. Even before this addiction had really started to take hold, Toby had been working longer and longer hours simply to keep their heads above water. Her heart went out to him, but she just wished that her husband could find another way to deal with it.

Nadia flicked the mouse over the screen. Sure enough, the gaudy, flashing site of an online casino sprang to life — the Money Palace. It glittered in front of her. Here was the temple at which her husband worshiped, and where he could ruin their lives without ever leaving the house. Lights sparkled, huge sums of money blinked on the screen — money, cash riches beyond compare. A treasure trove of temptation, luring you in with its promises of wealth, fortune, the easy life. Promises that were never, ever fulfilled.

CHAPTER NINE

Chantal slipped into the photographer's car. It was a big, black Mercedes four-wheel drive, sleek and luxurious, loaded up with the very latest in camera gear. She'd worked with this guy once before and he'd been good. She also seemed to remember that they'd enjoyed a mild flirtation. That had been a quick day shoot, so it would be interesting to see if he lived up to the potential she'd seen in him. Now they had a long drive up to the Lake District ahead of them — four, maybe five hours, depending on how much he adhered to the speed limit — and she hoped that he had good taste in music and a sparkling line in repartee to pass the journey. All she'd had to do was bring herself and some chocolate along for the ride. She'd chosen a thick slab from Chocolate Heaven, studded with crushed coffee beans — one of Clive's many specialities. It smelled divine and the coffee beans would certainly help to keep them both awake.

She should have phoned Ted to tell him that she was leaving on an assignment and wouldn't be back until tomorrow night, but she was pissed with him. Again. Let him stew. If she wasn't there, maybe he might, *might,* just miss her. Fat chance. It had been months since she'd tried to interest him in lovemaking, but last night she'd gone to bed naked and had pressed the length of her warm body against him, circling her fingertips over the fine, soft hair on his tight butt — and he'd stiffened. But not in the way that she'd hoped.

"Leave it, Chantal," was all he had said to her, and it had taken her every ounce of willpower not to cry with disappointment, hurt and frustration. They'd been married for fourteen years. Some of them happy. They'd survived the seven-year itch, but Chantal wasn't sure that they'd survive it the second time around. She still wanted her husband and wanted him to love her — and he, quite clearly, didn't. If they couldn't resolve this fundamental difference between them, was it worth keeping on with this loveless marriage? Except that it wasn't exactly loveless. It was simply sexless. They'd once been the best of friends. They liked the same foods, shared a love of good wine and champagne, enjoyed the same music, both loved the theater, laughed at the same jokes. Ted was handsome, clever, witty and rich. He was a catch. When she'd first met him at a friend's weekend party at the Hamptons, he'd taken her breath away with his vitality. And virility. She'd slept with him the very first night. They made love time after time, until they were sated, bruised and in love. What had gone wrong in the intervening years? Why did he now find the sight of his naked wife repellent? Why did he recoil from her touch?

Most of their friends and acquaintances would have no idea that there was anything wrong in their relationship. To the outside world, they had a match made in heaven. Yet sometimes it felt like a living hell. She'd lost count of the nights that she'd lain awake, her body aching with desire, next to a fabulous man who had no urge to satisfy her. Only the girls at the Chocolate Lovers' Club knew her true situation. If she didn't have them to talk to, she felt as if the facade of her life would come crashing down around her. They listened to the lurid stories of her infidelities without judging her. They didn't know Ted, either, so she felt it was part of her life that she could keep separate.

A lifeline. If they did meet him, they too would fail to understand why he wasn't a hot stud in the bedroom. She'd tried to discuss their lack of sex life a million times, but it was something Ted just didn't want to face; he seemed happy to hide behind lame excuses — too tired, too busy, too much work. Didn't all couples have these constraints? Somehow, most people seemed to rub along okay — why were they unable to do the same thing? His parents had never been a particularly affectionate couple and she wondered if that had shaped him — but then when they were first together he couldn't keep his hands off her. So what had gone wrong in the intervening years? Chantal only wished that she knew.

To her it was a fundamental part of being a woman, a wife. To be loved, desired. Could Ted truly love her if he never wanted to be intimate with her? She wasn't sure when the rot had set in. Over the years she'd given up a lot to be with him. Chantal had been an ambitious young magazine journalist. If she'd stayed in the U.S. she could have been Anna "Nuclear" Wintour or her equivalent by now, heading up one of the major glossies. Instead, she'd given up her career for his. Ted, a thrusting, financial whiz, had been promoted to head up a division of Grenfell Martin investment bankers. The downside was that his post was in London. So, saying goodbye to friends and family and a glitzy career, she'd willingly followed. The job she now had on *Style USA* magazine wasn't nearly as high-powered as she was used to, but with the decline of her sex life it had provided her with a certain number of perks over the years — which were almost a compensation now that Ted's desire to thrust had all but died and her marriage had gone ass up.

This shoot was of a sprawling pile nestled on the edge of Lake Coniston. It was owned by a couple who'd moved over to England from Boston twenty years ago. He was a well-known travel writer. She was an accomplished horsewoman. According to Chantal's brief, they'd spent the time restoring the home to its traditional Georgian splendor. Her fellow Yanks would go wild for it. Chantal could see the pages already — sumptuous colors, mellow lighting . . . the article would write itself. Giving her time for plenty of other distractions. The magazine was generous, both with its salaries and its expense accounts. Tonight she and the photographer would be staying in a swish country-house hotel, complete with four-poster beds, jacuzzis and Dom

Pérignon chilling in the mini-bar. All the things you needed for a romantic tryst. Chantal grinned to herself.

She pulled down the vanity mirror in the car and checked that her dark bob was sitting smoothly in place. There was no way that she looked all of her thirty-nine years. Her makeup was immaculate and her most seductive smile was in place. If her husband didn't want her, there were still men who did.

The photographer, Jeremy Wade, slid his long frame into the driver's seat next to her. "I think we're all set," he said.

"Great," she said, flashing her colleague a warm smile. "Let's go check out all the delights the Lake District has to offer."

CHAPTER TEN

"Night, Autumn." Addison put his head through the open door and gave her a wave as she was tidying away the remnants of colored glass for the day.

"Oh," she said. "Good night. Nice to see you again." She tucked her hair behind her ear, trying in vain to smooth it down. Why did she suddenly wish that she was wearing something nicer today?

Addison Deacon was an enterprise development officer who'd recently started to come into the Stolford Centre, where she worked, to help the center's clients get involved with local businesses and, hopefully, find a way of breaking the cycle of crime that most of the kids found themselves in. It was an uphill struggle for him, but he never lost the wide, white-toothed grin from his black, beaming face. He was tall and handsome, and muscular — certainly no one could ignore Addison when he came into the room, herself included. His head was shaved and he permanently wore sunglasses — it made him look more like the kind of guy that their clients would deal with rather than someone from social services trying to help them. But it was his kind, easy way with the damaged kids that she admired most of all.

"Working late again?" he asked.

She shrugged. "You know how it is." Autumn didn't like to tell him that there was no reason for her to go home and that she was happier here among the rejects of society and their artistic efforts than she was alone in her comfortable flat.

"Maybe one night you'll let me take you out for dinner?"

"I . . . er," she said. "I . . . er."

"Think about it," Addison said with a smile. "No pressure." Then he glanced at his watch. "I have to dash. Funding meeting with the Council."

She managed to spit out, "Good luck."

"I'll need it." Addison waved again and ducked back out of the door.

"Bye," Autumn shouted after him. She sighed to herself and forced her attention back to her chores. "You idiot! You complete idiot!" she muttered to herself as she put the glass back into the relevant boxes. "Why didn't you just say, 'Yes, dinner would be nice'?" Why did she always have to be so ridiculously shy in his presence? This is why you don't have a boyfriend, she thought. This is why you're going to be a sad and lonely spinster when everyone else is happily married with children, and all you'll have is a box of bloody chocolates for company.

She looked at herself in the mirror on the wall — the one that some of her students had made that was bordered by colorful pansies and a slightly cross-eyed cat. Sometimes the truth could hurt.

When Autumn got home from the rehabilitation center she was exhausted. All she wanted to do was sink into a nice hot bath with a bar of her favorite dark chocolate and let the water and the sugar hit soothe her cares away. It wasn't difficult teaching the young people the basic crafts such as mosaic or stained-glass techniques that formed part of the KICK IT! program. It was mainly girls who attended the sessions, and most of them grasped the craft quite readily, grateful for a few hours of normality when they didn't have to think about the horrors of their daily lives. But some days it was difficult to look at their hardened, careworn faces — faces that showed how emotionally scarred most of them were. Their bodies were marked with cuts, sometimes from self-harm, and bruises from fights that had occurred while under the influence of drugs, along with the scars from needles that were the legacy of their addiction. And those were only the marks that showed.

It distressed Autumn to see the capacity that human beings had to be cruel to each other and to themselves. Most of the youngsters who came through their doors had managed to escape from their difficult domestic situations, the situations that helped to keep them hooked — but she knew that some of them would go right back to the men or the families that they had fled from, just as soon as their marks faded, the memories of why they'd left disappearing as soon as the drugs left their systems. She'd been working here at the center for four years now, and saw the same faces return time and time again. It seemed that, no matter how hard they tried to extract themselves, the kids' lives somehow stayed the same. That was the really difficult part. It was mentally draining to watch teenagers she had grown to like and care for get repeatedly burned, drawn to their addictions like moths to a flame. She knew that Addison felt the same too.

Autumn chained her bike to the railings outside her apartment building. It was always slightly incongruous, seeing her scuffed old cycle amid the Mercedes and the Porsches that were the more usual mode of transport in this area. She climbed the stairs. When she got to the door of her flat, she saw that her brother was sitting outside, two large holdalls at his feet.

"Hi, sis," he said.

"Richard? What are you doing here? Is something wrong?"

"A temporary embarrassment," Richard said ruefully. "I was wondering if I could camp out here for a while."

"Here?" She unlocked the door and he followed her inside. "What's wrong with your own place?"

"Gone," he said flatly.

Autumn threw her bag down on the sofa and turned to her brother. "Gone? How can it be gone?"

Richard kicked his bags to one side and sank into a chair. "I owed a man some money and . . . well, let's say he took the apartment as a down payment."

"Your flat has got to be worth half a million pounds, Rich! That's one hell of a debt." She felt wide-eyed with shock and yet her brother was sitting there apparently unconcerned about his situation. "Technically, you don't even own it." Like she didn't own this place. All of it was bought and paid for by her parents. How else would she live just off Sloane Square on the salary they paid to a part-time arts and crafts teacher? She might be uncomfortable with her parents' rather obvious form of wealth, but there were times when it came in extraordinarily handy.

"So? Can I move in?" her brother asked.

There was no reason why Richard couldn't stay here for a while. She didn't have a boyfriend to consider — more's the pity. She didn't even have the wherewithal to bag herself a great dinner date when it was on offer. The flat had two bedrooms, albeit small ones. All she'd need to do was move her clothes around to find him some wardrobe space. Though judging by his sparse luggage, he hadn't actually brought that much with him. He looked for all the world like a man who was running away.

She sighed. "Are you in trouble again?" She knew that he'd indulged in drugs in the past. Two expensive sojourns in an upscale rehabilitation clinic were supposed to have cured Richard's dependence on recreational drugs; it was a world away from the center she worked in. Richard didn't know just how lucky he was. He'd owed money to shadowy men then — often resulting in black eyes and broken limbs. Autumn wondered if he was using the hard stuff again. A bit of marijuana was hardly going to cost him his flat, and she was concerned about what Rich had got himself involved in this time.

"Not really," he said, massaging his temples. He avoided her gaze. "Nothing I can't sort out. Just don't tell Mater and Pater that I'm here."

That wouldn't be difficult. Her parents had such busy lives that neither she nor Richard saw that much of them. They weren't the sort of people who would drop in unannounced. Their parents were both barristers in very busy chambers. Their parental duty ran to remembering their offspring's birthdays and Christmas, and picking up the tab for everything else in between. Not that Autumn had anything to complain about. Both she and Richard had enjoyed a privileged upbringing. She'd excelled at the viola and dressage. Richard had played rugby and polo. Every year they'd gone on exotic holidays round the globe with their parents — to Monte Carlo,

Montserrat, Mustique. Compared to the desperate teenagers she worked with, she had so much to be thankful for.

She and Richard had both gone to the same boarding school — a strict and outmoded place where boys and girls still wore frock coats — but they'd had each other, and as the elder by two years, she'd made sure that her little brother had gone through his years there relatively untroubled. She was the one who'd always looked after him, and it seemed as if that wasn't going to change as they grew older. Richard had always been the wild child, while she'd been the sensible one. But no matter what he did, he was her little brother and she loved him. It was a closeness she hoped they'd maintain, but there were areas of Richard's life that she knew he kept secret from her. Autumn knew very few of his friends. She wasn't even sure that he had any. He had a constant parade of well-heeled girlfriends, but again she rarely met any of them. Not that they lasted long.

"You would tell me if it was bad, Rich?"

"Of course I would. You're my darling sister."

"You're my pain-in-the-neck brother and I worry about you."

"I love you. And I'm fine. Really. I'm fine."

If he was fine, why was he here and homeless? Autumn sighed to herself. No doubt she'd find out in due course. When Richard was ready to tell her, he would, and not before. "I'll make up the spare bed for you."

"I promise I won't be a nuisance, Autumn. You'll hardly know that I'm here."

"Do you need money?"

"Well . . ." He gave a shrug of his shoulders. "A few quid wouldn't go amiss. If you can spare it."

"I'll see what I've got." Autumn always had a few hundred pounds put away for a rainy day.

She glanced over at her brother and he gave her one of his charming, sheepish smiles. Looked like that rainy day was here.

CHAPTER ELEVEN

When I finally turn up at the office at lunchtime, Crush immediately comes out of his cubbyhole to talk to me. "Everything okay, Gorgeous?"

"Not that you'd notice," I sigh.

He waits patiently while I huff about a bit, taking off my coat and opening and closing my desk drawers for no good reason. Even a glimpse of the stash of chocolate I have in there fails to lift my spirits. It doesn't go unnoticed by Crush either. "Mmm," he says, smacking his lips together. "Green and Black's bars."

"Hands off," I warn him. "They're mine and I'm going to need them all to myself today."

"Give me a bite," he pleads. "You know you want to."

I reluctantly hand over a mint chocolate bar. "If I run out of chocolate later and go all funny, it will be your fault."

He takes the chocolate anyway, unwrapping it straight away. I have no choice but to join him and unpeel the other bar so that we take our first bite in unison. "Sorry I was late in today," I mumble.

As he chews, Crush does have the good grace to look concerned. "Problems?"

"Man trouble," I explain. "I'm having a crisis. Last night I had a traumatic experience with Marcus."

"Mmm. Kinky?"

"No, not kinky. Horrible. Very horrible." I get a hideous flashback of Marcus's new love breezing through his door with her beautiful smile and her perky tits. Grrr. I bang papers about on my desk. It took me half an hour in the ladies' loo at Chocolate Heaven to patch up my face enough to disguise my puffy, crying-induced eye bags before I was fit to face the world.

"Want to tell me about it?"

"Not particularly." I shake my head. "But I think it's fair to say that my relationship is well and truly over."

"I'm sorry to hear that," he says, but he's smiling.

"What are you grinning at?"

"I love it when you're angry," he says. "You get two little pink spots on your cheeks."

"I do not."

"They make you look like a Cabbage Patch Kid."

"Fuck off, Aiden," I say to my boss. Which may not be the typical form of address for one's superiors, but I don't care. It's not very politically correct to tell your personal assistant that she looks like a Cabbage Patch Kid.

"Look on the bright side," he continues. "I can make a pass at you now that you're single again."

"Try it and you're dead meat," I mutter at him.

He laughs out loud. "Not all men are crass idiots."

"No?"

"Some of us are compassionate and caring."

"Yeah?"

"You need someone to look after you."

"I need no one," I tell him. Especially not some smarty-pants, smoothy sales manager. "I can manage perfectly well alone."

Crush shakes his head. "He must be an idiot if he's dumped you."

"I didn't say that he'd dumped me."

"If *you'd* dumped *him,* you wouldn't be so upset."

I hate it when men come over all logical,

so I scowl at him.

He looks completely unperturbed. "I suppose that amidst your trauma, you've remembered that it's the monthly sales meeting this afternoon."

"Oh bugger," I say. Now I'm wishing I'd taken the whole day off. I'll have to sit there all afternoon and take notes, which I can never read back. I hate it when I have to do real work. Normally, I try to make the proceedings bearable by buying one of those great big boxes of scrummy chocolate biscuits from Marks & Spencer which I charge to the company, but today I've completely forgotten. We'll have to do the meeting completely treat free. Oh poo. Even that small crumb of comfort vanishes — no pun intended.

"We'll be starting in about five minutes," Crush says. "The guys are already in the conference room."

I tut loudly. Stress at home, stress at work. I wish I was dead. Or, at least, at a health spa.

"Sure you're up for this?"

"Of course. Of course. Why would a little thing like my life crashing around my ears mean that the sales meeting should suffer?"

He puts his arm round me and gives me a hug — and in a very familiar way for a boss,

I can tell you. "Come on," he says. "No one can tell that your heart is breaking. Your secret's safe with me."

I give him a weary smile.

"With all that makeup you've put on, they won't guess that you've been crying."

I hate men. All of them.

CHAPTER TWELVE

The sales team is, indeed, all waiting in the conference room by the time I arrive. So I bustle to my seat and try to look deeply efficient. God, I should get an Oscar for some of the performances I put on in this place. The guys are all sitting around in an informal circle with Aiden at the head near an easel complete with crisp white paper. That means it's going to be a gentle pep-talk meeting and I relax a little. I don't think I could have coped with a table-thumping target-achieving tactical roustabout today. If they've noticed the lack of treats, no one complains.

Then "Where are the biscuits?" one of the sales team pipes up.

I hate him.

"No biscuits today, chaps," Aiden intercedes. "Cutbacks. Targa's thinking of your waistlines — as you should be."

There's a bit of disgruntled tutting. Aiden

can be very sweet sometimes. I've had bosses in the past who would have blamed me. I make a smile come to my lips and aim it in Crush's direction and he smiles back.

While he starts the meeting, I gaze out of the window, looking over the rooftops of London toward the City. The City, where my ex-boyfriend is busy doing what he does best. It's nearly two o'clock and I've heard no word from Marcus yet. Nothing. If I'd broken someone's heart so spectacularly, at least I'd have had the decency to ring them up the next day and find out if they were okay, or offer some sort of apology for my appalling behavior. I guess it's just another indication of how little he cares for me.

Aiden Holby is standing up and is waving his arms around as he talks. I remember that I'm supposed to be writing all this down to circulate to the sales team later, and so I scribble furiously on my notepad until Aiden shuts up and takes his seat again.

Crush winks at me and gives me an encouraging smile. Mr. Aiden Holby has very nice eyes, actually. Now that I'm a single person again, I'm going to have to reacquaint myself with this flirting lark. I cross my legs and try to think seductive thoughts.

A little fling might be just the thing to get over Marcus. I don't normally agree with office relationships, primarily because I've never had one and I hate those bitches who shag their bosses and thus look forward to going to work every morning. That can't be right, can it? But I might make an exception, just this once.

One of the sales team is on his feet telling us all we need to know about some new software product that's coming onto the market. Blah, blah, blah. I try to give his spiel my full attention, but I can't concentrate. He uses all kinds of technical terms and I've no idea what he's talking about. Crush looks over at me again and smiles. I wonder if anyone else in the office has noticed that there's a certain chemistry between us? Not that I ever gave him any encouragement when I was with Marcus. I know what it's like to be on the receiving end of infidelity and would never put anyone through that. But now I'm single . . .

I swing my leg a little jauntily and wet my lower lip with my tongue ever so slightly. An amused smile plays at my mouth. Crush meets my eyes. He raises his eyebrows and directs his gaze to my leg. I have on killer heels and maybe Crush has a foot fetish, because he's certainly giving them a lot of attention. His eyes have gone all saucer-shaped. My smile curls further. I'm glad I've got trousers on as I do believe that my boss, Mr. Aiden Holby, is mentally undressing me. I have to say there's a certain frisson running down my spine. This is a wonderful tonic for the brokenhearted. I angle my body toward Crush and mirror his position. Isn't that how you tell someone you fancy them? Not that I do. This is just a bit of fun to liven up a dull sales meeting.

The sales rep is droning on . . . I know I'm going to regret this later, but I lean back in my chair and give a flick of my cute haircut as I let my leg swing higher. And then I see what Crush is smiling at. But it's too late. I put on my trousers in such a catatonic state this morning that I didn't notice that yesterday's knickers were stuffed down my right trouser leg. They're now around my ankle, draped over my shoe, but the pendulum is already in full motion and there's nothing I can do to stop it. With a final swing of my leg, my lilac lacy knickers fly off my shoe and sail across the room, stopping the sales rep right in the middle of his pitch.

Crush dives out of his chair and catches them before they hit the floor. "Howzat!" he shouts in the style of ace cricketer Freddie Flintoff. A deadly hush falls across the meeting. "Nice shot."

Every ounce of blood in my body rushes to my face.

"Thank you, Lucy," he continues. "Your enthusiasm is much appreciated. I thought it was only aging rock stars who had knickers thrown at them."

The sales team erupts with laughter and I know that the best way to diffuse this would be to laugh myself, but I can't as I'm perilously close to crying. Crush winks at me again and then stuffs my knickers into his jacket pocket and gives it a pat. I could die. If the sales team giggles any more, I *will* die.

After that, the meeting descends into chaos as no one can concentrate. I hang my head in shame and pretend to be taking copious notes so that I can let my hair fall forward and hide my humiliation behind it. Fifteen minutes later, and Aiden gives up on trying to get sense out of anyone.

"Let's call it a day," he says. "I'll give the rest of the notes to Lacy . . . sorry, I mean *Lucy* . . . to circulate to you all."

More sniggering ensues. My nickname in the office will now surely be Lacy Lucy. I almost want to tell them to call me Chubby Cheeks. This day cannot get any worse. I'm going to go to the top of the building and hurl myself off.

Everyone else makes toward the door as I pretend to be tidying things up. Perhaps I could stay in here for the rest of the afternoon if I tried. Perhaps I could stay in here for the rest of my contract with Targa. Perhaps I could just leave and never have to face anyone ever again. Risking a glance up, I see that everyone has now left the room. Everyone but Crush. I ignore him and carry on doing nothing. Eventually, he clears his throat. "Ms. Lombard."

When I force myself to look up at him, he's holding my knickers in his hand. "I believe these are yours." He holds out my underwear. And not in a discreet bunch. Oh no. He holds my knickers out by the sides and dangles them right in front of his face like one of those masks worn by Arabian women in harems. He flutters his eyelashes at me above them. "This doesn't mean we're engaged," he says coquettishly.

"I have knickers on," I tell him curtly.

He shrugs. "Shame."

My jaw tightens further. "That's last night's pair."

"Good. Care to offer a more detailed explanation?"

"No. I just wanted you to let the sales team know what the real story is."

"If only I knew," Crush says with a grin. "But you can be safe in the knowledge that we'll be discussing your frilly bits on many and varied occasions in the future."

I flush furiously and snatch at my underwear, grabbing it from his hands. It feels warm from his touch. "That's the closest you're *ever* going to get to my knickers," I tell him.

Aiden walks away, laughing softly. "Hey, Gorgeous," he shouts over his shoulder. "Those pink spots are back."

CHAPTER THIRTEEN

The Keating House Hotel stood in its own grounds by the edge of Lake Coniston, nestled deep in the surrounding woods. The journey had been hell due to a proliferation of roadworks and "sheer weight of traffic" as they kept announcing on the radio bulletins, and they'd arrived much later than Chantal had imagined. Jeremy had been good company on the way up, gossiping with her, regaling her with stories of previous jobs that he'd undertaken for the magazine, other journalists that he'd worked with. He hadn't eaten more than his fair share of the chocolate slab, which was a good quality in a man. She'd also found out that he wasn't married, but he was living with a younger woman who already had a child from a previous relationship. Doomed to failure, obviously. Jeremy Wade would do very nicely for tonight, she'd decided. Very nicely indeed.

It was gone seven in the evening by the time they found the hotel and checked in. Chantal failed to persuade Jeremy to join her in the hotel's pool for a quick dip before dinner. He had e-mails to attend to, he'd said. So did she, but they could wait. It was harder to stay slim as she got older and she had to put the work in to make sure that she kept pace with her chocolate consumption. They'd agreed to meet in the bar for a drink before dinner at 8:30 p.m. So Chantal had taken herself off to the spa to swim alone. There was plenty of time for them to get it together. After all, they had all night.

The pool was quiet. A couple of overweight businessmen ploughed through the water, panting heavily as they completed their laborious lengths. A young, giggling couple were making out in the Jacuzzi. One guy sat alone on one of the loungers reading a copy of the *Financial Times,* a white towel slung round his neck. He was handsome, toned, and he looked up as Chantal came in and gave her an appraising smile. She returned it and then dived in, arms high, slicing through the water. A dozen lengths of front crawl later and she knew that he was still watching her, could feel his gaze on her bare skin. If strangers like him couldn't take their eyes off her, then why was it so hard for her own husband to appreciate her sexuality? Chantal shook the thought away, along with the drops of water on her skin, and levered herself out of the pool. Taking her time to dry herself, she looked over again at the guy on the lounger.

He lowered his newspaper. "You're a strong swimmer," he said.

"Used to be," Chantal conceded. She'd been on the swim team at high school. "Not anymore. Don't get the time to practice."

"You looked good to me."

"Thanks."

"Are you here for a few days?"

"Just tonight."

"Business or pleasure?"

"Business," Chantal answered.

"Me too," the guy said. "Are you dining alone?"

"I'm here with a colleague."

"Shame," he said with a smile and a shrug of his shoulders.

"Yeah," she agreed. "Shame." But it wasn't a shame, not with what she'd got planned for Jeremy Wade.

Now she was dressed and ready for dinner. She'd packed a slinky black dress in her overnight case. Low-cut, backless, slit to the thigh. A little obvious, but she only had tonight. This wasn't the time for a slow seduction. It was going to be a wham-bam-thank-you-ma'am opportunity. She'd brought all her jewelry too and took time to clip on her sparkling one-carat diamond earrings — a present from Ted at Christmas. He'd probably sent his assistant out to buy them. But that was being ungrateful — he was a very busy man and she loved them anyway. Next, she slipped on her bracelet — another row of twenty-six diamonds. Her watch was a gold Rolex. The pendant she finally fastened at her neck was a solid gold ingot set with diamonds. All of them presents from her husband. She couldn't fault his taste or his generosity with money. It was only his body that he rationed.

The only jewelry that she did remove was her wedding and engagement ring; the latter was a sizable rock too. She slowly slipped them off and put them on the dressing table. Call her old-fashioned, but it didn't seem right doing the dirty deed with her rings on her finger. Okay, so it was a token nod toward morality, but it was better than nothing, she reasoned. The bed had already been turned down for the night and there was a gold-wrapped chocolate lying on the pillow. She tore off the foil and popped the chocolate into her mouth. Bland, minty, but who cared? It was chocolate nevertheless and she didn't want to see it go to waste.

Chantal regarded herself in the mirror. Brittle and beautiful, she concluded. A lethal combination. Still, she was ready for some action — so she picked up her purse and headed down for dinner.

Jeremy was already at the bar when she arrived. "Wow," he said as she approached. "You look fabulous."

"Thanks." She slipped onto the bar stool next to him.

"I feel a little underdressed."

Chantal took in his black jeans and his gray cashmere sweater. The scent of his aftershave was sharp, like freshly cut limes. He looked like a man who'd made an effort. "You look just fine to me."

"I took the liberty," he said, holding up a champagne flute. She was beginning to like this man more by the minute.

"Perfect." The bartender poured her a glass.

"To *Style USA*," Jeremy proposed.

She clinked her glass against Jeremy's. "To us."

"We don't have to be at the house until ten o'clock tomorrow. I thought we could let our hair down a little tonight."

"Funny," Chantal said. "That's exactly what I had in mind."

The dinner was sublime, the company all she could have hoped for. They'd finished their coffee and though she was in a hurry to get Jeremy into her bed, she'd still taken the time to nibble her way through all of the delicious after-dinner chocolates — a few more minutes would hardly make a difference — and now it was crunch time.

"Let's go through to the bar for a nightcap," Jeremy suggested.

"I have a bottle of champagne chilling in my room," Chantal said. "We could go there and be more cozy."

There was a moment of hesitation in Jeremy's eyes, then he said, "Right. Let's do that."

She left the restaurant and he followed. They waited for the elevator, standing self-consciously in Reception. Once inside, Barry Manilow treated them with a serenade of "Copacabana" and she pressed the button for her floor. Chantal reached out and took Jeremy's hand and drew him to her, feeling the heat of him through her thin dress. His heart was banging against his chest. She tilted her head and searched for his lips.

Jeremy drew away from her. "You know,"

he said, "I don't think that I can do this."

Chantal felt panic rising in her. Don't let this be.

He let go of her hand. "I'm in a relationship."

"So am I," she said. "I'm married."

"Then it's not right."

"No one will know."

"I will," he said. "I'm sorry, Chantal. You're a very attractive woman, but . . ." Jeremy chewed at his lip.

The lift stopped and the doors opened. "Well," she said, "I guess this is good night then."

"If this were a different situation," Jeremy said, "if I were in a different place, then I wouldn't hesitate."

"Fine," she said tightly. It was hard not to show her disappointment. The evening had all gone according to plan. Until now.

"We had a wonderful evening."

"It didn't need to end right now."

"Good night." Jeremy gave her a peck on the cheek.

"Good night."

She stepped out of the lift and stood forlornly in the hall. Jeremy pressed the button for another floor and the doors started to close. He gave her a small, uncomfortable wave.

Chantal walked to her room and unlocked the door. She could look at her e-mails and have an early night, she supposed. Her laptop sat on the coffee table — difficult when she'd been planning on giving another kind of laptop some attention. She took off her earrings and bracelet, putting them on the dressing table next to her wedding and engagement rings. Then, taking off her necklace, she massaged her neck as she paced the floor. There was no way she could sleep in this state of sexual arousal. The anticipation of a night with Jeremy had really got her motor running and she could not be content with satisfying herself. For a thirty-nine-year-old woman with a rampant sex drive, masturbation was *the* most depressing of pastimes. She'd tried it enough times to know. That was *so* not going to happen. She wanted sex. Hot, hard sex. It was as simple as that and, to be honest, she didn't really care who with.

Chantal sighed to herself. Looked like she was going to have to put Plan B into action.

CHAPTER FOURTEEN

The guy that she'd met by the swimming pool was sitting in the corner of the bar as she hoped he'd be. Chantal ordered a cosmopolitan from the bartender and then turned and flashed him an open smile. He took the hint and, picking up his drink, he came over to her.

"So what happened to your dinner date?"

"That was business," Chantal said. "This is pleasure."

The guy's glass was nearly empty. "Can I get you another drink?" he asked.

"Well, you could," Chantal said. "Or we could go back to my room and drink the champagne I have waiting there."

He grinned at her. "I'd always heard that American women were very forward."

She didn't bother to tell him that she'd been ten years in Britain and that some of the nation's eccentricities had become embroiled in her psyche a long time ago.

Now she felt like some sort of mid-Atlantic hybrid.

"You heard right," she said. Chantal didn't want small talk, she didn't want to know whether he had a wife, kids, a dog. She didn't care whether he sold software, hardware or peddled drugs. She wanted him in her bed tonight and to say good-bye to him in the morning. Plus she wanted to prove to herself that she could pick up any guy. She hated to admit it, but Jeremy turning her down had been a blow. It had felt like being rejected by Ted all over again. What if she was getting to the age where she couldn't find strangers who wanted to sleep with her? What would happen then? Some women could dress up in a killer outfit, flirt all night with the hottest studs in the bar and still go home unlucky. Was she going to turn into one of those poor, unfortunate bitches?

He shrugged his shoulders and put his glass back on the bar. "Then let's go."

A feeling of relief and elation flooded through her. This was a kick that she couldn't get, no matter how much chocolate she consumed. Chantal downed her cosmopolitan — a drink that she hadn't wanted. She didn't need to be drunk to do this. She preferred to be stone-cold sober to enjoy her conquests.

They went to the elevator, but this time there was no discomfort between them as there had been with Jeremy, just a bristling of electricity. This time they both knew exactly what they wanted.

Inside, Chantal pressed the button for her floor. As soon as the doors closed, he was upon her. He pulled her to him roughly, his mouth crushed against hers, his hand went inside her low-cut dress, baring her breast and she gasped as his mouth traveled to it, his teeth grazing her nipple. His fingers slid up inside her thigh, inside her panties, inside her. And she was ready and wanting him.

The lift doors opened and they staggered out still entwined, fumbling together until they got to her room. With shaking hands, she let them both inside. He pulled her to the bed, undoing his trousers and hitching up her skirt as he did. Dragging down the top of her dress, he feasted on her breasts again, entering her with her thousand-pound dress tangled all round her waist. He thrust into her frantically and she came fast and furiously. They lay together breathing heavily and then she felt him harden again. Peeling her dress from her, he then lifted her from the bed, bending her over the chair by the dressing table. He came into her from behind, rutting like a dog, where she could see herself in the mirror, legs trembling, her breasts squeezed tight in his hands, being fucked by this handsome stranger. Lifting her again, he sat her on the dressing table, pressing her thighs around him as he pushed into her. She laid back, grasping at the table, scattering her jewelry to the floor, knocking over the table lamp, and came again.

"Better now?" he said, with a smile.

"Yes," she breathed. "Yes."

He took her hand and led her to the bed. "Want to open that champagne?"

"No." She curled up on the bed. This was what she'd wanted. Anonymous fucking with no chitchat, no foreplay, no commitment. It would be better now if he just left. "I'm tired." The truth was, she was exhausted. Physically and emotionally spent.

He lay down beside her, still stroking her butt. "You're one hell of a sexy woman," he said.

This is what she wanted to hear. This is what she wanted to hear — but from a different man. Chantal bit down on her lip. She wouldn't cry. She would never cry over this.

"I don't know your name," she said, and

she turned to face him. But he'd already
gone to sleep.

CHAPTER FIFTEEN

Chantal forced herself to open her eyes. She had a headache from too much champagne and her limbs ached. Her thighs and her insides were sore. She'd got what she wanted last night, but somehow it always left a bitter taste in her mouth the next morning. Now she'd have to face the guy again in the cold light of day. She always hated this part.

Turning over, she found that the other side of the bed was empty. There were no obvious sounds from the bathroom. Sighing with relief, she thanked her lucky stars that he'd got up and left before she'd woken. She liked guys who did that. The ones who wanted to stay for breakfast were the real pains in the ass. It had been good last night, but it had been reckless. He'd been on her so quick, had fucked her senses so much that she'd forgotten to ask him to use a condom. She'd have to take herself off to the chemist tomorrow to get the morning-after pill. The fear of pregnancy wasn't a problem these days, but it wouldn't be so smart to contract AIDS or some other sexually transmitted disease. That had been a stupid thing to do. She shook her head ruefully. Next time she'd have to be more careful.

Chantal looked at the clock. It was just before seven. That would give her time for a long, hot bath; she could then do her e-mails and still have time for a quick breakfast before meeting Jeremy. Only chocolate croissants and strong, hot coffee were going to be enough to revive her today, and she hoped they were on the menu. It was a shame that Jeremy hadn't been on the menu last night as she'd planned, but hey, never mind. If they had to work together today, maybe it was better that they hadn't woken up together, but he'd sure missed out on a wild night. Chantal smiled smugly to herself.

She stretched out in the bed, arching her back. Perhaps she should check her mail first before she did anything else. Chantal glanced over at the coffee table, but her laptop wasn't there. Strange. And then it hit her. Suddenly she was wide awake. She scanned the room. Not only was her laptop missing, but her handbag had gone too.

Shooting out of bed, she went over to the dressing table, crouched on all fours and examined the floor where she had scattered her jewelry just a few hours earlier. Sure enough, it had all gone.

Chantal sat back on her heels and hugged herself. The bastard had robbed her. He'd fucked her and then robbed her. There had been at least five hundred pounds in her handbag in cash, and all her credit cards. She'd have to phone the companies and put a stop on them right away. If he managed to get into her laptop, he'd find all her PIN numbers stored there — then couldn't he have some fun?

Chantal rubbed at her eyes. This was a nightmare. A first-class fucking nightmare. But that wasn't the worst thing. The jewelry was worth thousands — thousands and thousands. All of the pieces were high-grade diamonds. She tried to remember how much they'd been valued at, at their last insurance assessment. Was it thirty grand? Surely not. Christ, it didn't bear thinking about. Would she even be covered if he hadn't broken into her room, but was there at her request? All that he'd left was her watch, which she was wearing. She supposed she should be thankful for small mercies. God, that scamming bastard must be smiling to himself.

How was she going to explain this to Ted? How was she going to explain it to anyone? She could hardly go down to the hotel reception and ask them to call the police and report that she'd been robbed by one of their hotel guests that she'd invited back to her room to screw. Instead, she was the one who'd been screwed. And royally. His name? Oh, she had no idea. But he was handsome. Tall, dark and handsome — more your romantic-hero type than the average burglar. And he was great in bed. But what a price to pay.

Chantal closed her eyes and wished it would all go away. So much for an uncomplicated fuck.

CHAPTER SIXTEEN

I'm sitting in Chocolate Heaven. It's lunchtime and I've eschewed the healthy option of a Pret a Manger sandwich in favor of some hot chocolate and a large slice of Clive's chocolate gâteau. It's busy in here today and there's only a window seat left, but that suits me fine. I can gaze out into the melee of shoppers passing by and try not to dwell on my woes. Shopping doesn't do it for me — which is probably just as well as I have more than enough addictions already, like chocolate, Marcus and humiliating myself publicly, to mention a few of them.

This morning, following the knicker-kicking incident, I asked Crush to accept my resignation. Technically I don't need to give him my resignation as I'm a temp and could simply phone up the agency and get them to move me to another office. He laughed his head off and said I was too much fun to have around for him to ever consider letting me go. I'm trying to work out if that is a good thing.

Coming here was a last-minute decision, so I didn't have time to text any of the other members of the Chocolate Lovers' Club to see if they could join me. I could do without solitude today, but I'm not "in" with the crowd of girls at the office. They never invite me to go to lunch with them. Partly, I think it's jealousy because I work for Crush and he's the office heartthrob. If I were them, I'd do it the other way and I'd get "in" with me to get close to him. Clearly, they are low-level manipulators. I've still heard nothing from Marcus and that's giving me a stomachache that just won't go away. Perhaps this chocolate cake will help. I need to go back to the office buzzing with sugar if I'm to have any hope of getting through the afternoon.

The door opens and one *gorgeous* guy comes in. All the gorgeous guys who come in here are usually gay because they're all mates of Clive and Tristan, but it would be a sin against humanity if this one turned out to be interested only in boys. He gets a cappuccino and selects a plate of Clive's pure plantation chocolates — a man after my own heart! — and then he looks round for somewhere to sit. As luck would have it — *my* luck — there is nowhere else to sit except at my table. A couple of girls on the squashy sofa look as if they're about to start rearranging their shopping bags with a view to leaving and I will them to faff about for a bit longer which, obligingly, they do.

"Is anyone sitting here?" he asks me.

"No." I try not to look too agog. Over at the counter, Clive is trying to catch my eye, but I ignore him.

"Mind if I join you?"

"Please," I say magnanimously, and gesture at the empty chair.

"This is a great place, isn't it?" he says as he settles himself. "I can't get enough of their chocolates. I've only just discovered it, but now it's my favorite haunt."

"Mine too." Already, I am in love. Call me fickle, but I could really forget all about Marcus with a guy like this. He's got that great dirty-blond, mussed-up hair — and eyes the shade of a summer sky. And he's a chocoholic. I feel this is a match made in heaven. Most probably I should stay away from blonds, but what's the saying about one bad apple? Quickly, I check out his ring finger before I'm hopelessly smitten by someone else inappropriate. No wedding band. Looking good.

"At the risk of sounding corny . . ." He laughs at how corny he *is* sounding. Self-deprecating — I like that. ". . . do you come here often?"

"I do," I say. Oh my word, how great does that sound? *Do you, Lucy Lombard, take this man as your lawful wedded husband? I do.*

"I'm Jacob," he tells me. "Jacob Lawson."

Jacob. *Do you, Lucy Lombard, take this man, Jacob Lawson, as your lawful wedded husband? Oh yes! I do!*

"Lucy," I breathe. "Lucy Lombard."

"Nice to meet you." He reaches over and offers me his hand to shake. I take it, hoping that I've not got smears of chocolate icing all over mine. Jacob smiles at me and I smile back — open, warm, accepting — hoping that I'm giving off all the right signals. Formalities completed, Jacob then turns his attention to devouring his chocolates. "Do you work round here?"

Glancing guiltily at my watch, I realize that I should be back at the office by now. One of these days Crush is going to chew my ears off for my tardiness, but I hope it's not today. I'll give him some old tat about having to rush into Boots to buy tampons — that always makes male bosses back off. "Yes. I temp in one of the offices just down the road. Big IT company."

He nods as if he's impressed.

"What about you?" He has on a great suit and is carrying a stainless-steel attaché case.

"I freelance in the entertainment business," he says.

"Wow," I say. "Wow." I could sound more like a complete airhead, but I'm not quite sure how. Reluctantly, I check my watch again. "Look, I'm sorry, but I really have to be going."

His face registers disappointment. "Why don't we meet up again?" he suggests.

Now I'm so flustered that I can hardly speak. One day as a single woman and I'm being asked out on a date! "That would be lovely."

"There's a chocolate and champagne evening coming up at the Savoy Hotel next week — do you fancy it?"

Do I fancy it! I want to throw myself at his feet and weep with joy. He's rescuing me from becoming a lonely and morbidly obese spinster. "That would be lovely." Someone needs to jog me, my record's stuck.

"Here's my card." Jacob slides it over the table to me. It's a plain white card with just a mobile phone number on it. How flash is that?

"Thanks," I say, then root round in my

handbag for a pen and a scrap of paper. Settling on the back of the Chocolate Heaven bill, I scrawl out my name and number.

"See you, then," I say and then I bolt for the door, giving Clive a theatrical wink as I leave. Jacob waves at me as I walk past the window. My fingers curl round his card in my pocket. I do hope he calls me. You don't know how much I hope he calls me.

CHAPTER SEVENTEEN

"Hi, Gorgeous," Crush says as I hurry to my desk. "Good of you to join us."

"Sorry, sorry," I mutter. "My life is one big crisis. Live with it. I have to."

I could tell him about my good fortune in getting the offer of a date, but as I can't quite believe it myself, I choose — for once — to keep my big, fat mouth shut. Aiden Holby comes and perches on the edge of my desk. It makes me hot when he sits so close to me, and I put up little barricades of files, pen holders and even my pink plastic pig, which holds my paper clips, around my desk to try to thwart him in his attempts to cozy up to me. But it all fails. He just sweeps aside my defenses and crashes on in. His firm, tight buttock is right next to my arm.

As if I wasn't flustered enough, he asks, "What are you doing this weekend?"

Oh my word. Crush is asking me out too! Twice in one day! I must be giving out loads of pheromones or whatever they are that make men fall at your feet. And here was me thinking that he only sweet-talked me because of all the chocolate supplies I keep in my desk. "I'm not sure." I might just have to hedge my bets here. "Why?"

"The Sales Department has got a team-building exercise this weekend. We're going whitewater rafting in Wales. Up for it, Gorgeous?"

Oh, so not a date. "Whitewater rafting? Why don't I know about this?"

"Because it's in your files and you never look at them," he explains patiently. "Tracy or whateverhernamewas organized it before she got sprogged and left."

This is the sort of sharing, caring company I work for.

"The guys all want you to come along."

My heart lifts despite the fact that it isn't a romantic tryst that's on the cards. It's nice to feel loved by anyone. Even if it's the sales team. "They do?"

"Yeah," Crush says. "They want to make sure that there's someone really crap there who's going to make them all look great in comparison."

One balloon. One pin. One pop. "Cheers," I say miserably.

"It'll be fun."

My idea of fun is a chocolate and champagne evening at the Savoy Hotel with a hot date — not getting soaking wet in Wales.

"We'll pay you," Crush says. "As an extra incentive."

That does it, really. I have my price — and it usually involves money of any description. It wouldn't be too bad to get wet in Wales and be paid for it. "I'll check my diary," I say coolly. "I'm seeing someone at the moment and we might have plans."

Now it's Crush's turn to look miffed. "I thought you'd only just been dumped by Marcus?"

"Women like me don't stay on the open market for long," I say smugly.

Crush huffs.

I feel I have the upper hand here. "Double time and I'll do it."

"You drive a hard bargain, Lucy Lombard," he says with a shake of his head. "Be here at six o'clock on Saturday morning. We've got a minibus coming to collect us."

Six o'clock on Saturday morning? I didn't know such a time existed.

Now Crush is the one wearing a smug smile. He disappears back into his office and I swear there's a bubble above his head with "Hee-hee-hee" written in it.

I try to make up for my lengthy lunch

126

hour by working hard. I try, but somehow concentration evades me once again. After I've fiddled about with some sales figures and have done a bit of filing, I eat a Daim Bar, or Dime Bar as they used to be called — a perfectly adequate name that didn't need changing in my humble opinion — that I have in my desk with my cup of vending-machine tea and then stare into space for a while. Then, at four o'clock, when I am rapidly losing the will to live, Dirty Derek from the post room comes up to my desk. He's called Dirty Derek not as a comment on his personal hygiene, but because he has a range of outrageously filthy jokes for all occasions. Today, he's bearing a huge bunch of red roses, wrapped in pink tissue.

"For you, love," he says with a wink. "Someone must have had a good time last night."

"They're wonderful!" I exclaim as I examine the bouquet. "No card with them?"

"No."

I wouldn't put it past Dirty Derek to have lost it on the way up here. Dirty Derek taps his nose as he walks away. "Secret admirer."

I place the flowers on my desk. I can see that Crush is craning his neck to get a look at them. Even without a card I know exactly who these are from. They have *Marcus* stamped all over them. A few days with his new love, and already he is having a change of heart. Isn't this always the way? Every time he leaves me, I think it's for good — and then he comes crawling back. My throat goes dry. Now what to do? Should I call him and thank him? Or shall I sit back and wait for his next move?

While I'm considering my quandary, my mobile phone beeps and there's a text message for me. It's from Chantal. CHOCO-LATE EMERGENCY, it says. CU @ 6.

Great. I sit back in my chair and sigh with relief. The girls will tell me what to do.

CHAPTER EIGHTEEN

"What am I going to do?" Chantal wails.

She's just told us the story of her very rude rumpy-pumpy and robbery. Quite frankly, my red rose bouquet quandary pales into insignificance in comparison with Chantal's traumatic experience. We're huddled together in the corner of Chocolate Heaven on the squashy sofas. Our friend lifts her glass and sips her hot chocolate. Her face is white and she's shaking. "I was robbed in a five-star hotel. This wasn't some down-and-out city center dump. This was a first-class country-house hotel. I've spent enough of my life in New York to know a con when I see one. I'm supposed to be streetwise. How can I have been so stupid? So gullible?"

I don't add "so desperate."

Autumn doesn't look much better. She's clearly shocked by Chantal's terrible news. She takes our friend's hand. "You have to go to the police."

"How can I?" Chantal says. "If they started an investigation, then Ted would be sure to find out. How could I keep it a secret from him?"

"My God, Chantal, you're lucky this guy just robbed you," I tell her. "He could have murdered you."

"It might have been better if he had," she says bleakly. "Ted will kill me anyway if he ever gets a whiff of this."

"Then we'll have to make sure that he doesn't," I say in as reassuring a way as I can manage. "Did you get the guy's name from the hotel reception?"

"No." She hangs her head. "They wouldn't give me any information about him. He could have used a fake name, for all I know. I'd be surprised if this was the first time he'd pulled this sort of scam. I'd like to bet he's a professional conman. Christ, I was a sitting duck. I sat there with a bull's-eye painted right on my forehead." She looks as if she's about to cry and Chantal never cries. This is the first time I've ever seen her so emotional.

"Clive, Clive!" I shout. "We need more comfort food. In a hurry."

"I don't want anything to eat," Chantal protests.

"Don't be ridiculous," I say. "Chocolate isn't really food. It's medicine." Besides, Autumn and I could do with some fortification. I wish Nadia had been able to make it, but she texted me to say that she couldn't get away as she had no babysitter for Lewis. She'll be gutted to have missed this meeting.

"You have to stop doing this," Autumn says to Chantal. She's using her sincere voice. "You have to stop picking up men that you don't know. It's dangerous."

"I know." Chantal shakes her head. "That was the last time. I promise. I've learned my lesson."

A very expensive one, I think, but I don't say it out loud. Chantal doesn't need me to point out the bleeding obvious.

"We have plenty of money," Chantal says with a shuddering sigh. "I'll have to start moving some small amounts out of the account to buy replacement jewelry as soon as possible. It's the only thing I can do."

"Won't Ted miss it?"

"I handle all the domestic finances," she says. "He trusts me."

The irony of her comment isn't lost on us. "Can't you just say that you've lost it and claim it on your insurance policy?" Not strictly ethical, but if she was able to say that it had been stolen then surely she'd be covered anyway?

"For that amount of money, they'd probably want to bring in the police or investigators or something. Ted would also want to know why I'd taken my most expensive jewelry away on a business trip. I don't think that's a solution. I have to cover this so he doesn't even know that it's missing."

Clive comes over with replacement supplies of hot chocolate and a plate of walnut and coffee brownies which we take gratefully. "This doesn't look good," he says, when he sees our glum faces, and slips down onto the sofa next to us.

"Chantal has been shagged and shafted," I tell him, and then we fill him in on the gory details.

"Men," he says, with a wave of his hand. "They're pigs."

Which reminds me, I have yet to tell them about Marcus's peace offering.

"Did you tell them about the glorious boy who was hitting on you at lunchtime?" Clive continues.

And I have yet to tell them about my hot date with Jacob Lawson. I quickly fill in the gaps. "We're supposed to be going out next week."

"Fabulous," Chantal says. "Just wear

cheap costume jewelry."

I don't like to tell my friend that cheap costume jewelry is all that I have. "He seemed really nice," I say a bit sheepishly. "I hope he calls."

"I'm sure he will," Autumn says earnestly. She is one of life's optimists. Autumn's glass is never half empty.

"I have something else to tell you." They're all ears. "Marcus sent me a huge bouquet of roses today."

"I have them in water outside," Clive chips in. "So they won't droop." Though Clive did comment that he hoped something else of Marcus's would suffer from drooping.

"What did he have to say?" Chantal asks.

"Nothing. There was no card."

"How do you know they're from Marcus then?"

"Who else would send me three dozen red roses after cheating on me? It's hallmark Marcus. Classic. I just want to know what I should do. Should I call him? Should I wait for him to call me?"

"Promise me," Chantal says. "If I have to give up sleeping with strange guys, then you have to stop taking Marcus back."

"At least Chantal only lets guys shit on her once," Clive remarks.

"Yes, thank you for that observation." I

sigh deeply. "So you think I should do nothing?"

Everyone nods at me. That's very easy for them to say, but to me Marcus is more addictive than, chocolate — he just has fewer calories.

CHAPTER NINETEEN

As Autumn reached the door of her flat, there was a man coming out. He wore a black leather jacket and mirrored sunglasses, even though he was indoors. His nose looked as if it had been punched a lot.

"Hi," he said, and then headed down the stairs past her at a brisk pace.

A frown settled on her brow as she let herself in through the already open door. "Richard?" she called out as she entered the sitting room. "Who was that?"

"Oh, just a friend," her brother answered vaguely.

Autumn followed the sound of his voice through to the kitchen where he was standing at the sink, filling the kettle with water. "Tea?" he said. "You look exhausted."

"A friend of mine is in a spot of trouble," she told him. "I've been trying to help out."

"You always did attract all the lame ducks, Autumn."

"Does that include you?"

"Now then, that's a bit mean."

"Was he really just a friend, Rich?" She sat at the table while he made the tea.

"I'm allowed to have friends, aren't I? It's going to be very dull living with you if you won't let me bring anyone here."

"I was worried that it was one of the guys you owed money to. I don't mind you living here, Rich, but I don't want you bringing trouble to my door."

Her brother went to place the tea on the kitchen table, but she noticed that the surface was covered with a film of white powder. Autumn went to sweep it away with her hand and then realized with a sickening feeling exactly what the white powder was. It wasn't the residue of some cleaning product or a sprinkling of talc, it was cocaine. She was sure of it. Autumn wetted a finger and dabbed it in the powder. Goodness only knows why she did it. Despite working at the rehab center, her only experience of drugs was a few puffs of pot at the odd party when she was at university, just to be polite. She wouldn't be able to tell the difference between talc and cocaine. But it was clear from the expression on Richard's face that he could.

"Don't look at me like that," he said

petulantly. "I'm not some crackhead living on a sink estate. I'm not like the people you have to deal with. It's acceptable in our class of society, you know that. I run with a crowd who like to snort a little coke. It isn't the crime of the century. Everyone does it. Go to any of the nightclubs — it's the way the scene is. It's no worse than having a bottle of wine. It helps me to relax. Gives me a buzz."

She noticed that his pupils were dilated, his movements animated, and wondered how she'd missed the signs until now. "Is this why you've lost your job? Your flat?"

He sniffed pointedly and wiped his finger under his nose. "I ran up a few debts, that's all."

"How much are you using?"

"Hardly anything," he insisted. "It's purely recreational."

"I wish I could believe you."

Her brother shrugged. "You should try it. We have some great parties. You need to get out — meet some people."

"Do some drugs?" she said sarcastically.

"You could do worse than try a few wraps of Charlie."

"Think through the consequences, Rich. I see people every day who've ruined their lives with drugs."

"You have an addiction too," he scoffed. "I've seen the way you eat chocolate. Stuffing it into your greedy little mouth."

Autumn shrank back. "That's ridiculous. You can't compare chocolate with cocaine."

"Can't I? You're hooked, just as surely as I am. Can you honestly say you could give your drug up?" he asked with a smirk. "It makes you feel great, doesn't it? Nothing else gives you a high like it. The only difference being, sis, that your addiction is legal."

"And I don't have to put all that I have on the line to feed it."

Her brother narrowed his eyes. "Wouldn't you like to try some coke — just once? It could make you feel even better."

"It could also kill me."

"We all have to go sometime." He laughed bitterly. "I could eat meat every day and die young of heart disease. What a boring way to shuffle off this mortal coil. I'd rather live the way I do than spend my life all tied up in a straitjacket. Cocaine is a glorious addiction. I feel that I could rule the world when I'm using. I'm bursting with confidence and everyone loves me. Don't you want to feel like that?"

"But the reality is that you've lost everything — your career, your home."

She wanted to add "your self-respect" but

138

felt that would be pushing Rich too far. Cocaine seemed to be a drug that fed the addict's ego and distorted their reality. It made the user selfish, immune to their own problems and insensitive to the feelings of others. She wanted to help him. She wanted to stop him ruining his life. But who would help *her?*

CHAPTER TWENTY

Nadia had put Lewis to bed early. The bath and story reading had, tonight, been conducted in double-quick time — much to her young son's chagrin. She'd make it up to him tomorrow. This evening, she wanted to spend as much time with her husband as she could.

Dinner was a meager affair, thrown together with the remains of a bag of generic supermarket pasta, a tin of tomatoes and a tin of cheap tuna which was barely one step up from cat food. It wasn't the sort of meal she'd envisaged creating when she'd first become a full-time housewife. She'd had visions of whipping up nutritious Jamie Oliver–style feasts every night involving goat's cheese, couscous and rocket. Now, as she and Toby sat opposite each other, she was pushing her penne listlessly around her plate while her husband was making a valiant show of eating his with relish.

"Mmm," Toby said, wiping his mouth on the piece of kitchen roll that Nadia used as a cost-conscious substitute for napkins these days. "That was delicious."

They both knew that it wasn't.

"I'm going to get back into the office, love," he said next. "Crack on with some work."

And they also both knew that it wasn't what Toby was going to do in the office.

Nadia pushed her plate away. "We can't go on like this, Toby," she said. "I went through the bills today. We owe thirty thousand pounds."

"Don't be ridiculous. It's nothing like that."

Nadia went to the sideboard and pulled out a sheaf of bills. She put them on the table in front of her husband. "We've already remortgaged the house twice to clear our debts, Toby. I phoned the bank this afternoon, but they won't lend us any more money. I don't know where else we can turn."

She didn't tell him that she'd even been trawling through all those adverts for dodgy loan companies in the back of the newspapers. It was getting to the point where she could really see no other option and, if they went down that route, they'd never be able to climb their way out of debt.

"I'm onto it, Nadia. It's not a problem. Just don't nag me."

"I'm not nagging, dammit! I'm trying to get you to face reality." She felt close to tears. "I don't have money for food, Toby. Lewis needs clothes. He grows out of his shoes every couple of months. We've got red bills for gas and electricity."

She'd sold most of Lewis's old clothes and a good proportion of her own wardrobe on eBay to bring in a few extra pounds. The house was sparsely furnished as it was, they had very few assets and there was simply nothing else to sell. All she had left were a few family heirlooms — a couple of carved wooden statues that had belonged to her great-grandparents in India — and nothing on earth would make her part with those. She couldn't sell her heritage for a few hundred pounds. Sometimes she felt it was the only link she still had with her absent family. She could never bring the girls from the Chocolate Lovers' Club back here now, she'd be too embarrassed for them to see her threadbare home. When she'd first met Toby, she had a great job in publishing and they might not have been exactly flush with cash, but they could manage, could pay their way. How had it all gone so wrong?

"I could go back to work, bring some money in," she said. "That would help us."

"We've been over this a hundred times. The money you earned would be spent on child care. What would be the point?"

It was something she'd already worked out for herself, but even if she cleared a few pounds, it would be worth it.

"I could go back to my family," she suggested. "Tell them that we're having difficulties. They might help." Even Nadia knew that it would be a long shot. From the day she'd decided to marry Toby they'd completely ostracized her. It would be humiliating for her to ask them for any favors, but she was running out of places to turn. Better to go begging to her family than get in bed with a loan shark — but it was a close-run thing.

"That would be great," Toby said sarcastically. "Go and tell them that your husband can't provide for his family. They'd just love that."

He was right. They might help, but they'd gloat over his misfortune. Her father was a successful businessman with a small and very profitable chain of jewelry stores. He would like nothing more than to have it proved right that Toby Stone had been the wrong choice of husband for his eldest daughter.

Her husband shook his head. "I don't want them to get their claws back into you, Nadia. Especially not your father. If that happens then I've lost you."

"If you don't stop this gambling, you could lose me anyway."

"If that's the way you feel, then there's no point discussing this." Her husband stood up and headed toward the door.

"I want to help you, Toby. I want us to get through this together, but if you can't even see that it's a problem, then I'm fighting a losing battle."

"I have things to do," Toby said and left the room.

Nadia picked up the plates and carried them into the kitchen as the tears began to fall. What on earth was she going to do? Opening the kitchen cupboard, she searched until her fingers curled around what she was looking for. She pushed aside the packet of McVitie's chocolate digestives. If only they were enough to blot out her pain — but sometimes, chocolate simply wasn't the answer. Hidden at the back, behind a little-used flour crock, was a small box of tablets. Watching the door, she pulled out the packet and popped one of the tablets from its foil bubble. She'd started taking these

144

for supposed postnatal depression a year after Lewis was born. Nadia had gone to the doctor and sat there in floods of tears. Her normally acerbic GP had been amazingly sympathetic and had readily written out a prescription for antidepressants to get her through the day, sleeping pills to get her through the night. But she hadn't been able to admit to her doctor what her real problem was. She hadn't told anyone. No one knew that her husband was addicted to gambling. She swallowed the antidepressant with a glass of water, but it was getting to the point where the tablets were no longer helping.

CHAPTER
TWENTY-ONE

"Is there something you'd like to tell me?" Ted said.

Chantal's heart stopped beating momentarily. Had Ted found out what had happened? For once, they were both at home together and they were getting ready for bed. The time of day that she'd come to dread the most.

"Your rings," he continued. She followed his gaze to her fingers. "You're not wearing your rings."

"Oh," she said, trying to cover her consternation. "I had a slight rash under them. Maybe some detergent got in there."

"Detergent?" Her husband laughed. "Honey, when did you ever come in contact with detergent?"

"Soap," she corrected quickly. "It could have been soap."

He took her hand. "They look okay to me."

"Thank you, Doctor Hamilton." She tried a light laugh, but it sounded uneasy. "They're fine now. I just wanted to leave my rings off for a couple more days to make absolutely sure." There was no other option; she was going to have to take some money out of their bank account pretty damn quickly to buy some convincing replacements.

"I thought there might be something you wanted to tell me." There was a twinkle in his eye, but she could tell that his words were serious. Of course there was something she wanted to tell him! She wanted to tell him that she couldn't go on picking up strangers to find sexual satisfaction. Christ, she wasn't even forty — she still had needs. Didn't Ted? There was no way she wanted to face the next twenty or more years in a union that had become completely sexless. It wasn't just the sex she missed — although, goddammit, you surely missed it when it wasn't there — it was also the loss of emotional closeness that she mourned. She didn't think that a relationship could survive that.

"Do you ever think that maybe our lives are too shallow?"

She looked up at him. "Shallow?"

"You know . . ." He gestured at their

expensive surroundings. "Don't you ever wonder what all this is for? What the point of it is?"

"It looks great," Chantal said. "We like nice things."

"And that's why I go to the office every day and work my ass off?"

"That's what everyone does."

"But they do it for a purpose. They do it to provide for their families, their loved ones."

"We don't have a family."

"What if we did? Would that be such a bad thing?"

"I'd rather open a vein."

"So this is all for us?"

"Is there a crime in that?"

"It's not a crime, but is it a way to live?"

"You like all this stuff as much as I do."

"Do I?"

Frankly, she had no idea what her husband did or didn't like anymore. Chantal sighed to herself. She was tired and feeling down. Perhaps Ted was depressed. Maybe he needed to go to the doctor and get some happy pills. Maybe that would perk up his libido too. This wasn't the time to get into a discussion about it — she had too much else to think about right now. They'd avoided an all-out confrontation about their situation so far; it could wait a while longer.

Ted stripped off his shirt and went into the bathroom. He still found an hour each day to go to the gym at his office despite working his "ass off," so his body was fit and toned. The sad thing was that she still loved and desired him — she only wished that it was reciprocated. Every women's magazine these days was filled with tips on how to improve your love life, but none of them ran articles about how to kick-start one that had fallen down and died completely.

It was so easy to let your physical relationship slide. First the kissing became less frequent, then — apart from a perfunctory peck on the cheek — it pretty much stopped. Then the cuddling disappeared and the regularity of lovemaking slipped further down the calendar as daily life interfered. The less you kissed and cuddled, the easier it was to avoid intimacy altogether. When they were first together, she and Ted used to make love nearly every night. Then it was once a week, which then eased off to once a month. Now she couldn't remember when they had last lain together entwined. Six months? Longer? When had Ted last slipped his arms round her waist to give her a hug? Even a friendly one would do. Some of the sexiest words in the English language were, "I want to make love to you," and they'd been absent from her husband's vocabulary for years.

Ted came out of the bathroom and slipped between the sheets. He used to sleep naked, Chantal thought, but now he wore shorts and a T-shirt in bed. Even contact between their bare skin seemed to offend him.

Chantal took her turn in front of the mirror, cleaning away her makeup, washing the grime from her skin. She tried not to think of what she'd been doing last night or how stupid she'd been. When she'd finished, she joined her husband in bed.

Ted was lying on his side, already breathing deeply. Chantal curled in behind him. Perhaps they could rescue their relationship — she sincerely hoped so. She loved him and she didn't want to let this go. She stroked her fingers along his back. They should talk about the things that were bothering him. It was wrong of her to dismiss his feelings, even if she did feel that his concerns were somewhat misplaced. She knew that. It was just that whenever she tried to get him to talk about his feelings, he just shut down, pushed her away. The Brits were the ones who were supposed to have the "stiff upper lip," the penchant for suffering in silence. Maybe Ted had picked up too many bad habits from working here for so long. If only it were that simple. But there was no doubt that he'd buttoned down his feelings over the past few years. If she was honest, maybe she didn't want to hear what was wrong. What if he was finding the pressure of work too much and wanted to give up his job and become a painter or a novelist? Could she handle that? Would it rock the boat too much if she kept probing, pushing, prodding at Ted until he spilled the beans? She had a feeling that this wouldn't be an easy problem to solve and sometimes it seemed like too much hard work to start peeling back the layers of the onion. Chantal propped herself up and looked across at her husband. They couldn't carry on like this. Whatever the problem, they had to address it.

"Ted," she said softly. "I need you to hold me."

"I have an early start tomorrow, Chantal," he replied.

Despite her good intentions, she felt herself bristle. "And it would be too taxing to hug your wife?"

"Go to sleep," he said, and pulled the covers over his shoulders.

But she knew that now she would stay awake staring at the ceiling.

CHAPTER
TWENTY-TWO

I don't think I've ever seen the sunrise in London before and I'm not sure that I'll be in a rush to do it again. Somehow I've managed to get myself to the office for six o'clock on Saturday morning and we're now all lurking around on the pavement waiting for the minibus to arrive. The banter is far too perky for my liking, so I hang on the edge of the group trying to avoid speaking until my voice has woken up. There's a stainless-steel bench outside the office and, quite honestly, I could just lie down on it and go back to sleep.

"Hi, Gorgeous." Crush comes up to me. "Glad you could make it."

I think this is a comment on the fact that I can't normally manage to get in for nine o'clock on a weekday. I grunt because I can't think of anything to say in my defense. He hands me a cup of Starbucks coffee.

"Thanks," I say, amazed that my vocal

cords are actually working at this hour. Breakfast hadn't really occurred to me. It's so early and my brain is so unused to this time of day that I haven't even remembered to bring chocolate. Am I going to be stuck in a van for the next five hours without food of any kind? How will I survive?

"I bought some of their sunrise muffins and some double choc-chip ones too," he tells me.

I could really love this man.

"Did you like your roses?"

"Yes," I say with a sigh. "But it doesn't mean that I'm going to take him back." I don't tell him that I've been instructed on pain of death not to — and that, technically, Marcus hasn't asked. I have to remember that one bouquet of flowers does not a marriage proposal make.

He sips his coffee studiously, a frown on his brow. "You think they were from Marcus?"

"Who else would send me flowers?" I'm not Jennifer Lopez, for heaven's sake. My string of admirers are thin on the ground. "Who else but my cheating ex-boyfriend would have reason to?"

Crush shrugs, but the frown stays. Then the minibus turns up and the sales team cheers. I feel my heart sink to my boots.

■ ■ ■ ■

Five hours later and we're in the depths of Wales somewhere — a place with an unpronounceable name and a river that looks far too ferocious to be found in Britain. This is a river that should be in a remote and exotic place. The water looks black and there are humongous rocks sticking out of it, and it seems to be rushing by at an alarming rate.

I spent the entire journey sitting next to Martin Sittingbourne, our oldest and most tedious sales rep. He has told me all about his aging mother who lives with him, and her habit of putting her false teeth in the goldfish bowl, his wife's hot flushes and her struggles with hormone replacement therapy, his children who are both at university and are both wastrels, his neighbor who he can't stand because of the size of his leylandii hedge. I know that his dog — Mr. Monty — currently has worms and a bit of a problem with his prostate gland. I'm just glad that Martin Sittingbourne's prostate must be fully functioning, otherwise I would have heard all about that too. I don't think that I spoke at all, other than to say "mmm" in the appropriate places. Even the succor of my double choc-chip muffin failed to turn it into a pleasant experience. Crush occasionally looked over and grinned at me. He knows exactly what Martin Sittingbourne is like and I could see that it was amusing him greatly that I was his current victim. It would have been so much nicer sitting with Crush — but that isn't really a compliment, given the quality of the competition.

I couldn't wait to get out of the van, but now that we've all disembarked and I've seen the crummy hut and the ridiculously inadequate size of the dinghy-thingy that we're supposed to be going down this raging river in, I want to get back inside and head straight back to London. I hadn't realized that I was allergic to the outdoors, but I can feel myself hyperventilating just looking at it.

"All right, Gorgeous?" Crush wants to know.

"Fine," I say brightly. "This looks great."

"It's brilliant fun," he informs me. "I've whitewater rafted in Nepal and Peru and down the Colorado River. You'll love it."

I could really hate this man.

One of the organizers is handing out bright orange overalls. He gives me the once-over and then hands me my overall which I take into the cold, damp changing room. Peeling off my jeans, I readjust my underwear. I've taken the precaution this time of leaving the lacy lilac frillies at home and have opted instead for sensible white pants. I try to ease the orange overalls over my legs . . . my goodness, they're tight. On the one hand I'm pleased that the overall-handing-out operative thought me a suitable size to squeeze into these; on the other, I'm in danger of cutting off the blood supply to my vital organs. With much huffing and puffing, I lever all of my fat bits into the suit, trying not to lose flesh as I struggle to zip it up. I'm not sure that I want to check this out in the cracked mirror as I feel like a cross between a garbage man and a Jaffa orange. By the time I've strapped on my life jacket, I can hardly move.

Waddling outside, I join the group who are already loading themselves into the raft. They look a lot more keen than I do. Their overalls look a lot more roomy too. I'm given a helmet and a paddle — both of which I receive with a degree of enmity. Why do we have to do team-building exercises like this? Why can't we just do bonding down at the local bar? Or why can't we go to a health spa for the weekend to get to know each other better while we have pedicures? Although I *so* would not want to see Martin Sittingbourne's feet. I try to blot out the image and the rushing noise of the river. Why does this water look so much wetter than any other I've seen? Who would willingly want to do this? I look over at Crush and he's smiling back at me. I bet this whole bloody thing is all Aiden Holby's bloody idea.

"Come on, Gorgeous," Crush says. "You're next to me."

That makes me feel better, but I don't know why. I perch precariously on the side of the inflatable. This does not feel safe.

"Jam your foot into that strap," he says, pointing to something which doesn't seem anywhere near up to the job on the bottom of the raft. "It will stop you from falling out."

I can feel my eyes widen with fear. I didn't imagine that I might actually fall out of the damn boat. This adds a whole new realm of terror to the experience that I hadn't previously considered. I wedge my foot into the strap, so far that I'm going to have to have it amputated to remove it.

Then, without a by-your-leave, we're pushed away from the safety of the bank into the raging torrent. The raft bobs innocuously on the swell — I hate it already. I should have taken some Kwells or Kalms or

any other seasickness tablets beginning with
K.

"Stay behind me," Crush shouts. "I'll try
to shelter you from the worst of the water.
Just dig in with your paddle when it gets
rough."

Does he mean this isn't rough? And, sure
enough, with a whisk as vicious as any
fairground ride, we're taken by the current
into the middle of the river and the dinghy
starts to buck frighteningly.

"First of the rapids coming up," Crush
shouts.

I don't think I needed to know this. The
breeze picks up and I can feel the wind on
my face quicken as the flow of the river ac-
celerates. I start to scream. Before anything
has actually happened, I scream louder than
I've ever screamed before. Then we're
tossed about on the waves which are churn-
ing around the rocks. I'm getting very, very
wet. Crush's plan to protect me from the
worst of the water has failed, it seems.

"Dig in with your paddle," he shouts.

Before I can do anything, I'm hit in the
face by a wall of water which knocks me flat
on my back in the middle of the dinghy. I'm
like a turtle which has, well . . . turned
turtle. My legs and arms flail in the air.
We're bounced through the rest of the

rapids and then the boat starts to slow. The team is hooting and hollering. Are they mad? Crush is laughing. He reaches down into the bottom of the boat and hoists me up by the straps of my life jacket and hangs on to me until I can regain my equilibrium enough to perch back in my place.

"Was that not fantastic?" he says jubilantly.

It was not.

"Great." All my insides have been mushed about. But before I've time to even think about recovering my senses, the breeze is quickening on my face again. Now the screaming starts in earnest, even before the rapids appear on the horizon.

"Hang on. This will be tougher," Crush tells me.

Oh joy.

The first wall of water hits me straight in the mouth. Which, of course, is wide open due to the screaming. While I'm coughing and spluttering and trying not to drown internally, the next wall of water hits, my foot comes loose from the safety strap and I'm knocked straight out of the dinghy. I feel myself being engulfed by the river. I can swim, but I can't even work out which way up I am at the moment. I'm spinning around in the water and I now know what my duvet cover feels like when I put it on prewash. Feeling myself bob to the surface, I open my eyes, blinking rapidly at Crush's face which is right in front of mine, and suddenly feel two strong hands clamp on to me and start to drag me out of the water. My overall is snagged on a rock and is resisting my rescue. Crush pulls harder and, as I'm hauled back into the dinghy, there's a terrible tearing noise.

"Thought you were a goner there, Gorgeous," Crush says.

My helmet has slipped down and is over my eyes. My life jacket is halfway over my head, and my lovely orange overalls are rent asunder. They have completely given way under the strain of containing all my fat. I'm lying over the edge of the dinghy, coughing my head off, my lungs full of water, my heart full of disappointment, my knickers full of fish, my bottom bared to the world.

Crush's face is close to mine and he's grinning broadly.

"That is the closest you are *ever* going to get to my bottom," I say tightly, before I cry.

CHAPTER
TWENTY-THREE

I ache all over. Even my hair aches. When the minibus comes to a halt outside the office, I go to move and groan with feeling.

"Come on, Gorgeous." Crush gives me a hand out of my seat as if I'm some old granny.

I've slept all the way back from Wales — emotionally overcome by my near-death experience. No one else fell in the water, so the sales team is all feeling very smug and they keep patting each other on the back and doing high-fives and all manner of comradely things. I hate them all. Especially the ones who got a good look at my bottom. They're the ones I despise the most. On Monday I'm going to phone the agency and get them to move me to another job as soon as possible.

They all high-five each other again and then fade away into the darkness, leaving just me and Aiden Holby standing on the pavement in the chilly night.

"What are you going to do now, Gorgeous?" he asks.

"Go home and have a long, hot bath."

"I thought you might have had enough of water for today," he observes.

"Very funny," I mutter.

Gently, he runs his thumb over my cheek. "I'm glad you were okay," he says.

"Okay" meaning that I was injured, shocked and deeply humiliated, but not actually dead. He'd have had a lot of paperwork to fill in for the company if I'd croaked it. Serve him right if I had.

"Do you want to get a cab together?" Crush asks. "I ought to make sure you get home safely. Who knows what disasters could befall you between here and Camden?"

"You can get off your white horse now," I say crisply. "I'll be just fine. Don't trouble yourself."

"No trouble. I live out your way."

"Do you?"

"Belsize Park."

And before I can either agree or disagree, he's hailed a cab and is bundling my bruised body inside. I give the driver my address and we trundle off into the night and toward my flat. I don't really know what to say as

I've never been in such an intimate situation with Crush before. Not that being in the back of a slightly scruffy black cab is intimate, but you know what I mean. We're sort of close to each other and alone and all that kind of thing. I've been frozen to the core all day after my dunking, but now I'm surprisingly warm. While I'm still tongue-tied, Crush turns toward me and says, "You did enjoy today?"

"No. I didn't."

He laughs out loud, clearly thinking that I'm joking. "We should do it again sometime."

We *so* should not! "I'd love to."

The cab pulls up outside my flat and we sit there with the engine idling away. "Well," Crush says. "Time to say good night."

"Yes." Should I invite him in for a nightcap? Or does that sound like I'm trying to get off with him? Which I'm not. My flat's probably in a complete state, and I'm not sure if I've even got any milk — but there's a twenty-four-hour shop on the corner. I could get some. Or we could skip the coffee and just eat some Green & Black's chocolate caramel bars; there're always plenty of those in the fridge.

While I'm trying to work out all the necessary permutations, Crush sighs and he leans toward me. And I wonder for a moment if he's going to kiss me. What if I've got smelly breath from swallowing fish in the river? Which I surely must have done.

"Where are we off to next?" the taxi driver — with impeccable timing — wants to know.

Crush, his lips close to mine, reels off an address. Then he kisses me. On the lips. Just a small kiss — but very nice, nevertheless. Not a romantic kiss, but a bit more cozy than perhaps two colleagues should be.

"I . . . I . . . I'd better be going," I manage to stammer.

He looks deep into my eyes. "You're a lot of fun, Lucy Lombard," he says with a sexy smile.

"Thanks." I get out of the cab and then stand on the pavement while I watch it drive away. Crush looks out of the back window at me until he's out of sight.

Well! I walk up to my flat. What am I supposed to think about *that?* If I hadn't got water on the brain then I might be able to work it out. I unlock the door and dump my stuff on the floor. My answerphone is blinking and I press play.

First message: *Hi, Lucy. This is Jacob Lawson. I hope you remember me.* My God! He's phoned! I wasn't sure if he would. *I was calling to say that the chocolate evening is on*

Tuesday. If you'd still like to go, please give me a call. My number is blah, blah, blah. That's me putting in the *blah-blahs,* not Jacob. Would it seem too keen to phone him back straight away? It's only midnight, after all. Surely he wouldn't be in bed at this hour. Oh well, maybe not. A chocolate extravaganza on Tuesday night! I do a little happy dance in the middle of my sitting room. What a clever girl I am, bagging such a great date! It would mean missing my yoga class and all that Downward Dogging again, but it would be in a good cause.

Second message: *Hi, Lucy.* This voice needs no introduction. *It's me. I was thinking about you today.* There's a big sigh down the line. *I've forgiven you for trashing my clothes and my sofa and my rug. The saffron mash in the shoes was a nice touch.* I wonder if he's found where the smell is coming from yet. He might not forgive me for the prawns when they kick in. *I miss you, Lucy. I know what I did was wrong. And I wondered if you could forgive me too.*

I sink down onto my sofa and stare at the phone. All my euphoria about my date with Jacob dissipates. Marcus has called. And he's very nearly begging for my forgiveness. What now? I'm going to have to head for the kitchen and eat chocolate until I can come to a decision. Can I forgive him? Are our misdemeanors on the same scale? Marcus tore my heart apart. I just did unpleasant things to his wardrobe and soft furnishings.

CHAPTER
TWENTY-FOUR

So, it's Sunday lunchtime and, once again, it's me who's called a meeting of the Chocolate Lovers' Club. I've texted all of the girls and they're on their way. Even Nadia, who has managed to persuade Toby that he'd like to babysit for their son for a few hours.

Even more of me aches today and I've got bruises all over my body. A hot cup of coffee and a swirly-whirly dark- and white-chocolate marbled brownie are providing some succor. The sun is out today — too rare an event in any of the British seasons — and the faint warmth coming through the window is soothing.

Chantal is the first to arrive and she swings through the door with the air of a woman on a mission. Flopping down next to me and without preamble, she asks, "What do you think?"

Her hand is held out for my inspection. On her ring finger, right where they should be, are her wedding and engagement rings.

"You got them back?" I clap my hands in glee for her.

"Don't be silly," she tuts. "Life is never that simple. The wedding ring was £7.99. The engagement ring £19.99. It's pure, unadulterated glass." She holds the ring up to the light. "The original was worth over ten thousand pounds."

I nearly choke on my coffee.

"It makes me wonder why we bothered to pay that much. Does this look so different?"

To the untrained eye, I guess it doesn't.

"I bought them from some cheap accessories shop on Oxford Street." I didn't think Chantal had ever heard of Oxford Street. She's more your Knightsbridge kind of person. "Think Ted will notice?"

"Not if you keep him at a distance."

"Honey," she says with a brittle laugh, "believe me, that is *no* problem these days." Chantal admires the bauble more closely. "We have enough money in the account for me to 'borrow' some for a while. I'll make it good as soon as I can. Maybe I'll take some extra freelance assignments. Thirty grand should buy me all my babies back — or good quality look-alikes. Ted will never know."

I'm glad that I don't have another mouthful of coffee, otherwise it would definitely be sprayed all over the table. Fancy having enough money in the bank that you could withdraw thirty grand and your husband wouldn't even bat an eyelid. I need a husband like that. But then I'd like one who slept with me occasionally too.

Autumn is the next to arrive. She doesn't bound in with her usual enthusiasm, but sidles in and slips quietly into a chair. Our friend looks exhausted.

"Autumn, what on earth is wrong?"

Shaking her head in a world-weary way, she says, "My darling brother is staying with me at the moment. He's having a spot of bother. Let's just say that he isn't the easiest of houseguests."

If he's getting on Autumn's nerves then he must be a complete nightmare. "Anything you want to talk about?"

"No." She gives us a tight smile. "I'm hoping it won't be for long. It's just nice to get away for a while. What are you having?"

"I'm going to go along the cappuccino and chocolate-coated nuts route," Chantal says decisively, and she sets off to the counter to make her selection. Autumn trails along in her wake.

When we're all feeling much better — our sugar levels having been restored by our favorite comfort food — I confront my friends with my current Marcus dilemma. "He called and asked me to forgive him. Yesterday," I say. "While I was being tortured by whitewater rafting in Wales."

"No," Chantal says without even letting her brain ruminate on it for a moment. "You will not take him back this time, Lucy. No. No. No."

"Perhaps he's changed," Autumn tries to pacify her. "This time."

"It's five days since she caught him banging someone else. How can he have changed?"

I think Chantal has won that point. Autumn looks chastened, but then she herself would admit to finding good in even the worst of the Bond-film baddies.

"And Jacob phoned me for a date," I chip in. Maybe I shouldn't tell them about the kiss in the cab with Crush — I feel that would overly complicate matters.

"Go for it, girl," Chantal instructs me. "Move on. Let Marcus take a hike. Don't you dare phone him."

Right. So that's me sorted. *Don't phone, Marcus. Don't speak to him. Don't thank him for the lovely flowers.* And, especially, *Don't let him darken my door again.* Easy-peasy. Except why does my heart feel so full of

171

dread when I think of a future without him?

Before I can ponder further on the landscape of my life, Nadia joins us. She looks flushed and flustered and as if she's rushed here. Our friend pulls off her coat and a miniature truck falls out of her cuff and onto the floor. I hand it back to her and Nadia sighs wearily while stuffing it into her handbag.

"Had trouble getting away," she explains. "But boy, do I need this."

"Let me," Autumn says, standing to go and get Nadia's order. "What would you like?"

"Anything," Nadia breathes. "Anything at all. I'm just so relieved to be here."

"I know just the thing," Autumn says, and goes off to see Clive.

"We were admiring Chantal's new jewels," I tell Nadia. We fill her in briefly on Chantal's humping and heist experience as she missed our last gossiping session. Her eyes widen as the tale unfolds.

"What a jerk I was," Chantal says ruefully. "So now I'm having to appropriate thirty grand out of our joint account to replace them."

At that, Nadia bursts into tears.

"Everything will be all right," I say, giving her a hug, but feeling puzzled. I'm not sure that Chantal's problem — tricky as it might be — warrants this emotional response. "You know Chantal. She'll sort it."

"That's not why she's crying," Chantal observes. "What's this all about, hon?" She picks up a napkin and wipes Nadia's tears away. "Is Lewis okay?"

At that, Nadia bursts into tears again.

Autumn returns with a cappuccino and a heap of goodies for Nadia. "She wouldn't have left Lewis if there had been anything wrong," Autumn notes as she sits down again. "Ssh, ssh," she says soothingly to Nadia. "Things can't be that bad."

"They are," Nadia says bleakly. Autumn pushes her coffee toward her and Nadia duly sips at it as she sniffs her tears away. We all sit and wait for her to get herself back together. Eventually, she tries a smile at us. "I wasn't going to tell anyone about this," she says. "I'm so embarrassed."

"Honey," Chantal says, "I've just been fucked and fleeced by a guy who I picked up at a hotel. It doesn't get much more embarrassing than that."

That breaks the tension and we all laugh at our friend's expense, which gives Nadia enough confidence to speak.

"We're in debt," she says. "Toby and me. Deep debt." She avoids looking at us and studies her coffee, pushes her chocolates around the plate. "We're behind with the mortgage. Our credit-card bills are spiraling out of control. I don't even have enough money for food." Tears roll down her face again.

"Is Toby short of work?" I ask gently.

"It's not that," she says, wiping at her cheeks. "He's got more than enough work, if only he would concentrate on it." Nadia takes another shuddering breath. "He's addicted to online gambling. There," she tries a brave smile, "that's the first time I've said that out loud."

Shocked, we all look at her sympathetically while she composes herself again.

"He spends hours on the computer every night trying to win, but it's just pushing us deeper into trouble," she goes on. "I can't even talk to him about it. He thinks he can gamble his way out of it — that the next big win is just around the corner. But this has been going on for years and it's simply getting worse."

"Oh, Nadia." Autumn hugs her tightly.

"In the meantime, I've run out of places to turn," Nadia continues. "We've remortgaged the house twice already to pay off our debts. Then we just start all over again. Now the bank won't lend us any more money.

I'm even thinking of going to a loan shark. I don't know what else to do."

"When you say 'we,' I think you mean Toby," I note.

"What a jerk," Chantal says.

"I love him," Nadia tells us flatly. "We're in this together. I don't know if his gambling is some sort of illness, but I know that he can't control it by himself. I want to help him. I *have* to help him."

I don't want to sound judgmental, but I have to ask the obvious question. "Can't you go back to work?"

"That's what I want to do," Nadia says, "but Toby won't hear of it. He says we'll just spend any money I earn on child care and I haven't got anyone else to look after Lewis. He hates the thought of putting him in a nursery all day. I even thought about going back to my family to ask for help, but they wouldn't understand."

Or perhaps they'd understand only too well, I think.

"You can't work," Chantal says. "Not in the state you're in. You need to get yourself straight first, then you can think about getting a job again. How much do you owe?"

Nadia's hands are shaking and I wonder how she's managed to hold all this in to herself. She laughs without humor. "Thirty thousand pounds," she answers. "That's what made me cry. It seems ironic, somehow, that it's the same amount as you're planning to spend on jewelry."

I think all of us can see the irony in that — even Chantal, and you know what Americans are like with irony. Well, this has certainly put my Marcus quandary into perspective.

"You can have it," Chantal says. "You can have the money."

All our heads swivel toward Chantal.

"It's the only practical solution," she says, fixing her stare on our surprised faces. Trust Chantal to be so practical.

Nadia is speechless.

"But there are conditions," she continues. "You go home and cancel your Internet connection. Today."

"Toby wouldn't stand for that," Nadia says.

"Tell him you won't stand for his gambling any longer," she says. "This isn't going to be easy, Nadia. You're going to have to show him some tough love until he can admit that he needs help."

"Won't he simply go to other places to get online?"

"I guess so, but at least this will make it harder for him."

"The funny thing is," Nadia says, "I checked out some of his favorite gambling sites and they all have direct links through to the Quit Gambling help line. Which should tell him something." She shakes her head sadly. "We can't be the only family who's been blighted by this addiction."

Chantal bends to get her handbag. "I'll write the check out for you today," she says. "I was going to draw out the money in smaller amounts to keep it under Ted's radar, but what the hell. Your need is greater than mine." Chantal holds out her glass ring proudly. "I'll have to stick to my fakes for now."

Nadia's lip is trembling again. "I don't know what to say."

"Then you *have* to get a job," Chantal says. "Whatever Toby's objections. You need it for your own self-confidence and security. I'm not worried about the money — you can pay me back whenever you can. I'm a good loan shark." She flashes Nadia a warm smile. "I take tiny installments."

"You can't do this, Chantal," Nadia says. "It's too much."

"That's what friends are for," she says dismissively as she signs the check with a flourish. "Bank this, first thing tomorrow morning." She pushes the check across the table.

"I insist."

"I can help to look after Lewis when you get a job," Autumn offers. "My hours are quite flexible. Then your child care expenses won't be so high and you'll be leaving him with someone you know."

Nadia gives in and cries again. "I don't deserve you all," she sobs.

I think we're all a little damp-eyed. "What can I do?" I say. "I can't babysit. I haven't got oodles of spare cash. I feel useless." In fact, I have a negative bank balance myself, though not to the extent of Nadia's. My overdraft pales into insignificance, by comparison. "What can I do to help?"

"You're lovely, Lucy," Autumn says. "You're the reason we're all here together."

We all hug each other round the table.

"You can get us all more chocolate," Chantal suggests.

"Now that's what I call a very fine idea," I say.

CHAPTER
TWENTY-FIVE

News of my whitewater rafting and bottom-baring team-bonding exercise has clearly spread like wildfire through the offices of Targa. It's not even ten o'clock, and yet every time I innocently pass by a desk — any desk — I'm sniggered at. By lunchtime I'm not going to be able to hold my head upright in this place. At this rate, I'll have eaten all my emergency stash of chocolate by lunchtime too. I head to the vending machine, where I am accosted by Helen from Human Resources.

"Lucy!" she shrieks in the false, over-friendly tone much used by the harridans in that department. They approve the time sheets that go into my temp agency every month and, as such, have supreme power over me, so I have to pretend that I like them. I widen my mouth in what might be considered a smile in some parts of the world. "God!" she carries on. "I heard all about your whitewater rafting disaster!"

I'm sure.

"I heard Aiden Holby rescued you!"

You heard right.

"Did he really haul you out of the water? Is it true that your overalls came completely off? Did he really have his hands all over your arse?"

Yes. Sort of. No, he just looked.

"He is so hot!" Helen continues, unaware that I haven't yet spoken. I sigh and punch in my beverage request to this Star Trek flight-deck abortion that is our coffee and tea machine. Eventually, having cracked the computer code, a feeble dribble of brown liquid oozes out into a plastic cup. "I wouldn't kick him out of bed either. But you'd better be careful," she says, laughing. "He's dating Donna from Data Processing. She'll be furious if she finds out what's been going on."

Dating Donna from Data Processing? My breath stops in my chest. Crush is seeing another woman? And I wonder how on earth she'll find out about our little accident when this is such a well-kept secret? It's not exactly as if I planned to hurl myself into a raging torrent just so that Mr. Aiden Holby could prove how much of a macho man he is, did I? But Donna from Data Processing would have every right to be distressed if she knew he'd been trying to play fast and loose with me in the back of a black cab. What a bastard. Toying with my emotions when all the time he's been going out with someone else!

Helen braces herself to punch in her required drink combination, so I take the chance to skulk away while she's otherwise engaged.

I'm sitting at my desk drinking whatever it is I've summoned up from the vending machine while gnashing furiously on a Toffee Crisp when Crush comes and perches on the edge. His hair is all messy and I like it when it looks like that. It makes him look as if he's just fallen out of bed. But I don't want to like it today.

"Have all your bruises gone now, Gorgeous?"

"I'm busy," I say briskly as I rapidly scour my desk for something that I can look like I'm doing. "And don't 'Gorgeous' me."

"Ooo," he says. "You're a prickly old pear this morning. Hormones?"

"Fuck off."

"Stuffing chocolate in at that rate is a sure sign a woman is premenstrual."

"Oh, and you're an expert, are you?" I stop "stuffing" chocolate in. "You're way off

181

the mark. Way, way off."

"So, if you're not hormonally challenged, why are you sulking?"

"I'm not sulking either."

"Now that *is* something that I'm a bit of an expert in," Crush says. "And you *are* sulking. In fact, I've never seen such a sulky puss."

I say nothing, but try to rearrange my face into a neutral expression.

"Does this have anything to do with your introduction to whitewater rafting?" he asks.

I stay silent, but start to tap at my computer keyboard with a vengeance.

"I know that the story is entertaining the office this morning, but personally I thought you did very well. Two out of ten for skill," he says earnestly. "But a whopping nine out of ten for artistic interpretation."

"Get lost," I say.

"Not until you tell me what's wrong."

I stop typing and lean on my desk. "Why didn't you tell me you were seeing someone else?"

Crush looks puzzled.

"When you kissed me in the cab," I say. "I didn't know you were seeing someone else."

"Would it have mattered?"

"Yes. I wouldn't have let you."

"You didn't *let* me," he counters. "You just

182

sat there and looked blank. Attractively blank."

I can't really argue with that as it's a pretty accurate summation.

"And I'm not actually *seeing* anyone."

Hah. I have him there. I fold my arms about my chest. "What about Donna from Data Processing?"

"Ah. Donna." He strokes his chin. "We did have a date — about three weeks ago. Fairly disastrous. Though she didn't fall in water or bare her arse, so maybe not that disastrous. We said we must do it again. We probably won't."

"Oh." I don't really know what to say to that. Looks like Helen's information isn't all that accurate. You'd think those Human Resources harridans would at least get their stories straight.

"So is that what the problem is? You want a date with me?"

"I do not," I splutter.

"We can organize it if you like."

"I've told you, I'm already seeing someone else."

"Ah. Yes," Crush says. "Looks like I've missed the boat then. Or should I say raft?" He laughs uproariously at his own joke.

"Go away," I say. "Go and annoy another minion."

He starts to wander away, still chuckling. "By the way, Gorgeous. You've just typed *isith firip tiggle splink plart.* Do you want me to find you some real work to do?"

My cheeks are flaming. I can't stand that man. And to prove it, I fish in my handbag until I find Jacob Lawson's ever-so-tasteful card and I punch his number into my mobile. "Hi, Jacob," I say when he answers. "This is Lucy Lombard returning your call. I'd love to see you tomorrow if you're still available."

CHAPTER
TWENTY-SIX

A date at the Savoy Hotel is much better than going to my skanky yoga class. I bent the plastic this afternoon in honor of the occasion and bought a slinky frock — black, strappy, figure hugging. One that I could ill afford. I have on my sexy, black vamp shoes and a fake-fur shrug. Even I think I'm looking cool when I totter into the reception of the hotel to meet up with Jacob. I'm a match for Scarlett Johansson — even without the bee-stung lips.

My date's already waiting for me when I arrive even though I'm on time for once. I have a lot of qualities, but punctuality isn't one of them.

"Hi." Jacob pecks me on the cheek and hands me a single red rose. That's so romantic a gesture that I nearly swoon. No one has ever done that for me before. Particularly not Marcus. "You look wonderful," he says.

"Thank you." He's not looking too shabby either. Jacob has on a black suit with a black open-neck shirt. He obviously works out and has a hint of a tan that's not natural for this climate. Even though he's blond, there's a faint air of the Italian gigolo about him — but in a good way.

"Our table awaits." He takes me by the arm and guides me into the Thames foyer, overlooking the slate gray ribbon of the river, where we're shown to a table by the piano. The pianist is gently tinkling away at a romantic ballad. "Some Enchanted Evening," if I'm not mistaken. A bottle of pink champagne is already chilling in an ice bucket. There's a selection of exquisitely tiny cakes, chocolates and truffles laid out on a tiered stand for our delectation.

"Good evening, Mr. Lawson," the waiter says. "Nice to see you again."

Jacob flushes slightly, which is very cute. So this is one of his regular haunts. Strange. I wouldn't have had him down as a Savoy man. Jacob seems more suited to Fifteen or Oscars — the places where minor celebs hang out. I look round at the opulent splendor: beautiful crystal chandeliers glitter above us, stained-glass mirrors decked with flowers decorate the walls. Autumn would love those. A huge display of orchids

186

graces the center of the room. The piano is providing relaxing background music. There's a gentle buzz of conversation — no braying laughter or pounding beat. This is a class establishment. And my date hangs out here regularly. Mmm. What a dark horse.

The waiter talks us through the selection of confectionary. There's a white chocolate mousse cake infused with fresh mint and topped with raspberry purée, organic truffles made with my favorite Madagascar beans flavored with jasmine tea, passion fruit and limes sundried on trees in Iran. Even the descriptions are sending me into an ecstatic trance. Our glasses are filled. Jacob hands me one and we chink them together. "To us," he says.

"To us," I echo dreamily.

This is the sort of meal I like — no piddling about with starters and a main course, just straight on to the desserts! Then we start on the chocolate and, quite frankly, I'm transported to paradise. Chocolate, champagne and a cool guy — what more could a woman want? And in that order. I could *seriously* get used to this.

Jacob murmurs appreciatively as he tucks into the chocolate cakes. "This is the worst of my vices," he says. "It means that I have to work out in the gym too much."

"You said you worked in the entertainment business?"

"Here, try this." He hands me one of the cakes. "Isn't that wonderful?"

"What sort of things do you do? Are you an agent?"

"Oh," Jacob says, "my job is very boring. Long hours, endless demands. You don't want to hear about that."

"I'd love to."

"I deal with the service side."

"Keeping the talent happy?"

"That kind of thing." He nods. "Now enough about work. I'd much rather talk about you."

The trouble is, my job is crushingly boring too. Did I say "crush"? I didn't mean to. I will not think about Crush or Marcus or anyone else tonight apart from this lovely man by my side. I wonder what they'd think if they could see me now. They wouldn't believe it. Even I could do with pinching myself to make sure it's real. This is the most romantic evening I've had for a long, long time.

"Thank you, Jacob," I say sincerely. "This was a lovely idea."

"It's my pleasure," he says. "I thought I'd spotted a fellow addict when we met in Chocolate Heaven."

How right he is.

"Now try this," Jacob instructs as he hands me another tiny cake, his fingers curling over mine. "Beyond divine," he says in an affected camp voice and he kisses his fingers in a theatrical gesture.

I laugh at his joke and then bite into the soft chocolate cream and the barely there sponge. My hot, hot date asks, "Is that good?"

"Oh, yes." It truly is beyond divine. Clive would have a full-on orgasm if he tasted some of these creations. Then Jacob leans across, and his lips cover mine with sexy, gentle kisses. I have to admit I'm coming pretty close to the edge myself.

CHAPTER
TWENTY-SEVEN

Nadia, as instructed, had banked the check from Chantal first thing on Monday morning. She'd opened a separate account for the money, in her name only. Toby wouldn't like that, but she'd yet to tell him about any of this. Which meant that she'd yet to disconnect the Internet from their computer, but she had organized for that to happen starting today. Chantal might think it was best to go in with both guns blazing, but she preferred the softly, softly approach — even though she'd have to admit that she'd probably been far *too* soft in the last few years. This gambling addiction would end — she would make sure of it — but she would try to do it with the minimum of pain.

Nadia had never imagined that the girls from the Chocolate Lovers' Club would come through for her in the way they had. What had started out as a bit of fun for her and a shared interest in all things chocolaty had turned out to be a lifesaver. Now she didn't know what she'd do without them. The relief that Chantal's loan had given her was incalculable. It sounded like such a cliché, but she felt as if a weight had been lifted from her shoulders. Her friend looked glamorous and aloof, but inside her there was a heart of solid gold. It was humbling to think that she hadn't even hesitated in handing over her money to Nadia. Now she could pay off all of their bills and start with a fresh sheet again. This time, she would be in control of their finances. She was going to cut up all of their credit cards and deal in cash only. It was the only way they were going to get out of this terrible situation. All she had to do now was tell Toby.

She'd been flicking through the job ads in the paper this afternoon and there were plenty of positions she could apply for. Toby would go ballistic about that too, but they didn't have any choice. Chantal was partly right, though — she was in no fit state to work. But it wasn't her physical condition that was a problem, it was more an emotional issue. She hadn't worked in over three years and her self-esteem was in a fairly bad place. If she didn't address that now, then she wouldn't have the guts to get back into the workforce. The only proper adult conversation she got these days was with the girls and — on rare occasions — with Toby. All her other chitchat was with a person under three feet tall. Her social circle had grown woefully small since she'd become a stay-at-home mum.

She was going to keep a few grand back from Chantal's money to help with child care for the first month or so — and it would be fantastic if Autumn really *could* help her out. Though her friend didn't quite seem her usual upbeat self at the moment. Nadia hoped that she wasn't struggling with a problem alone, as she had. There was never a truer proverb than "a problem shared is a problem halved." As soon as she was sorted out she would make sure to find time to help Autumn with whatever it was that was bothering her.

Toby was due in from work soon and she'd already bathed Lewis and put him in his pajamas, so that his daddy could take him straight to bed while she made dinner. Maybe she was a bad mother, but she'd bribed him with a handful of chocolate fingers into getting ready for bed early. It felt good to be able to go to the supermarket, queuing up at the checkout, knowing that there was money coming into the account.

Tonight she'd made an Indian dish that was one of Toby's favorites — murghi rasedar, chicken in a delicious fried onion sauce. It was one of her mother's recipes, what she called her "everyday" chicken. Nadia had bought the poultry and the fresh herbs and spices she needed. She wanted him in a good mood before she started telling him the news that his gambling days were numbered.

When he came through the door, he kissed her warmly. Every now and then there were glimpses of the old Toby with whom she'd fallen in love. He was still in there somewhere — she only hoped she could reach him before it was too late. They'd met when Toby was fitting a new bathroom in her friend's house — not the most romantic of starts but that didn't mean they'd loved each other any less. Despite all of her family's opposition, she'd chosen Toby over them. There was no way she was going to give up on him lightly. She hoped that he'd feel the same way about her.

Toby swung Lewis up into his arms. "Who's Daddy's best boy?"

"I am," Lewis said proudly. "Today I drew a picture of an angel with a blue heart."

"For me?"

Lewis raced off to show Toby his handiwork. Nadia had been given a viewing when she'd picked her son up from nursery school. Then she'd been told it was a horsey. It looked like neither. She hoped that Lewis would develop talents in other areas, as his grasp of celestial beings or the equine form seemed to have a few shortcomings.

"Do you want to read Lewis a story and put him to bed?" she asked.

"Yeaaaaaaaah!" Lewis shouted.

"Do I have any choice?" Toby said with a laugh.

It was good to see that he was in a mellow mood tonight. "I'll finish making dinner," she said. "Don't be long."

"Race you to bed, Tiger," Toby challenged his son. "Last one there's a sissy!"

They charged up the stairs with Lewis shouting, "Sissy. Sissy. Sissy."

She should really remind Toby that this was supposed to be quiet time; a calm routine before going to bed. Nadia smiled to herself. Toby really was a great dad in a lot of ways. Maybe if they started to go out on more family days then he'd find it easier to quit the online casinos that currently had him in their thrall.

■ ■ ■ ■

After they'd eaten, Nadia cleared the plates away and they sat at the table together enjoying a cup of coffee.

"Lewis loves it when you're home in time to tuck him in bed," she told Toby.

"He's a great kid," Toby said. "Even though I'm biased."

"He is," Nadia said. "And I want us to work together to start making his future secure."

Toby's face darkened. "If this is about my gambling . . ."

"It is, Toby. I've given up a lot to be with you." The love and affection of her family being at the top of the list. A great job coming a close second. On some days it seemed as if her sanity had gone too. "I won't stand by while you squander what we've got. I'm putting plans in place to get us clear of all these debts. I've taken a loan." Her husband didn't need to know that it had come from her friend Chantal. "We can clear everything and start over."

Toby went to protest, but she cut him off. "I'm clearing the debts. I've organized someone to look after Lewis while I go back to work. Autumn is going to help us out."

Her husband sat there with his mouth wide open, a startled look on his handsome face. "I want you to help me, Toby. It's not worth me doing all this if you carry on throwing our money away on blackjack and roulette and whatever else you do online."

Still he said nothing. She took a deep breath. "I disconnected the Internet connection today, so you won't be able to go online at home."

Toby blinked rapidly.

"And I'm going to cut up all our credit cards, so that we can't start running up debts again. If you want me and Lewis to stay around then you have to agree to get help. There are organizations that can help you and *I* want to help you."

When she finished what she needed to say, she looked up to see that her husband was crying silently. Nadia went to the other side of the table and put her arms around him.

"I'm sorry," Toby wept. "I'm so sorry."

"We'll get through this," she said softly. "We'll get through this together."

CHAPTER
TWENTY-EIGHT

Chantal was online in their comfortable study at home. Ted hadn't yet come home from work, but she'd been finished for hours. There was some salmon to grill with asparagus spears and a side salad to accompany it; supper would take moments to throw together once he arrived. A bottle of good Sauvignon Blanc was chilling in the fridge. She'd bought a small, rich chocolate torte when she'd popped briefly into Chocolate Heaven on her way home which they'd have for dessert. She'd kicked off her shoes and was enjoying a cup of Darjeeling as she picked absently at a packet of Munchies to keep her going until dinner. The theory was that if she was acting like the model wife, then Ted might not examine their bank account too closely and find the gaping hole in their finances. She shook the thought away. There was no way that she could have spent that money on jewelry — no matter how important — when Nadia had looked so damn desperate. Her friend was clearly going through agony. Chantal hoped that handing over the check would help Nadia to curb her husband's gambling addiction and get the family back on track. She was aware that if Nadia didn't get this under control, then it might be the last Chantal saw of her money. But if it could help her friend to get herself out of the mire, it was a risk worth taking.

Gazing at the screen in front of her, Chantal realized that Nadia's husband Toby wasn't the only one with a serious addiction. It had been a week since the debacle with the guy at the hotel; you think she'd still be smarting in the aftermath but no, she was sitting here surfing the Internet for a glimpse of firm male torsos. She couldn't help herself, but she was thinking about sex every waking minute. Every sleeping minute she was dreaming about it. Last night Daniel Craig was drizzling melted chocolate ice cream all over her — and she wasn't even a Daniel Craig fan. The night before, it had been Russell Crowe's turn. She felt as if she was slowly losing her mind. Her need for physical release seemed to increase in direct proportion to the lack of sex in her life. How did nuns manage? How did people who lived alone manage? Did their sex drives gradually tail off so that a nice cup of hot chocolate at night would suffice instead? It wasn't happening to her. The less Ted wanted her, the more she needed him. And if she couldn't have him then she damn well needed to get her quota of sexual pleasure elsewhere.

The girls had been right, of course. It was dangerous to pick up strangers in bars. Madness. She'd promised them — and herself — that she was going to stop. And she would. It just seemed as if she'd hit on an idea that might be the solution to her problem.

She'd entered "male prostitutes" into the Google search engine, but all it came up with were academic works dealing with the history of male prostitution and related subjects — not the hot sites that she'd anticipated so eagerly. "Gigolos" had thrown up a million references to the dreadful film *Deuce Bigalow: European Gigolo* and a variety of products that all came with their own batteries in plain brown wrappers. Being a gigolo, it appeared, was a fast-fading profession.

After much surfing, it seemed to Chantal that "male escorts" was the correct term for today's stud for hire. "Straight male escorts" had narrowed it down from the reams of Web pages with gay sites emblazoned across them featuring ripped and toned guys available for your pleasure — if you were another guy, of course. Though she had to admit that some of the hunks listed on them looked quite enticing. Now she'd found one of the few sites that actually seemed to cater exclusively to women. It had a terrible title — Macho Males — and the banner heading was a naked guy with a snake twined round his shoulders, holding an apple over his important little places. But, cheesiness aside, it looked professionally put together. The site purported to be an upmarket service for businesswomen, but Chantal doubted it. Mind you, the kind of women who were able to pay around two hundred pounds an hour for an escort, plus the cost of a hotel room, had to be able to lay their hands on a fair amount of cash.

Chantal toyed with the keyboard. Should she register for this? Would there be more safety in hiring a guy for a few hours from an agency than picking up someone in a bar? Surely that would protect her from the kind of situation that she'd just been involved in — he wasn't likely to rob her afterward, was he? She wondered how many women used this kind of service these days.

Career women who didn't have time to juggle a home and children or a needy partner? Men had been playing this game for years — taking their pleasure with women as a business arrangement. Was it so unusual that the oldest profession was now available for women to take advantage of as well?

Logically, this was the most sensible thing to do. This wasn't some casual pickup with all the risks that entailed. It was a professional arrangement. He couldn't turn her down, he wouldn't make off with her handbag afterward. He'd been vetted by an agency. The escort, she assumed, would be clean, personable and, more importantly, he'd know the score. Chantal had long since managed to divorce her emotions from her sexual feelings — another trait that used to be viewed exclusively as male. But paying for sex? Could she really do that? She ran a manicured nail over her lip, deep in thought. How many other women were sitting at home doing exactly the same thing? The businesswoman in her wanted to know how many hits this kind of site got every month. Was it a growing business, or would most women still balk at doing something like this? How about her? How did she feel?

Chantal tried to think clearly, but she

couldn't push down the pleasant flutterings in her stomach that all this was giving her. She made her decision. She could try this just the once and then, if it didn't work out as planned, she could just walk away from it. She could do that. It could be that simple.

She scrolled down the list of escorts, all posing provocatively in color photographs, in a section romantically named *Look Before You Buy*. Chantal groaned inwardly at some of the names the escorts had given themselves — Candyguy, Hotjohnny, Kingsizekip, Musclemark. Her finger stayed on the button and she scrolled past them all. Then her eyes strayed to one of the guys called simply Jazz. He had dirty-blond hair, a pronounced six-pack, and was well past jailbait age. She'd guess that he was in his early thirties, more mature than the average offering — though some of them looked as if they were lying about their age and exaggerating other assets too. Spending some time with Jazz could be fun. There was a buzz about doing this — it felt adventurous and wicked. Was this the sort of feeling that hooked Nadia's husband to go back to gambling time and time again?

Before she thought better of it, she pressed the button next to Jazz's name. A blank e-mail template with Jazz's contact details popped up. What should she say? Did she have to give any details about herself? Chantal shrugged at the screen and typed, *I'd like to see you as soon as you can make it.* It didn't need to be any more complicated than that. Should she put her own name? Of course she should. Her e-mail address was a bit of a giveaway, anyway. She added *Chantal* to the bottom of the mail and pressed "Send." Now all she had to do was wait for Jazz to reply. She smiled to herself and switched off the computer. This would have to be her secret. There was no way she could tell the girls about this — they'd kill her.

CHAPTER
TWENTY-NINE

It had been a difficult day for Autumn. The dull-eyed teenagers had been more difficult than usual during her class. One girl had tried to slash another with a shard of brightly colored glass over some imagined misdemeanor and Autumn had struggled to break up the ensuing cat fight. She earned herself some deep scratches down her arms for her pains. Then there were the reams and reams of paperwork to complete that followed such an incident. Some days she wondered why she did this. The teenagers all took the piss out of her cut-glass accent — sometimes good-humoredly, other times not. If this didn't matter to her so much, she could resign tomorrow and go to teach well-behaved little ladies in some posh prep school. But then what would be the point of that? At least at the rehab center she felt as if she occasionally made a difference to one of her clients' bleak lives — even if it was only to offer them a few hours' respite.

Now, all Autumn wanted to do was go home too, put her feet up, open the box of chocolates that she'd bought from Chocolate Heaven specifically for times like these and listen to some of her New Age music — soothing sounds to wash the cares of the day away. Although her flat was in a smart area, it wasn't very chic inside. Autumn preferred the homely look, and most of the furniture had been castoffs from one of her parents' homes. Not that she minded. The pieces were either antiques or held special memories for her from childhood. Perhaps they didn't match wonderfully with the ethnic pieces she'd collected from her various travels around the world, but it suited her style, such as it was.

She was just about to leave when Addison Deacon came into the room. He was wearing a black T-shirt, his jacket slung over one of his broad shoulders. He slipped onto a stool behind her. "I heard you had a tough day," he said.

"Not one of my best."

"Don't take it personally," he advised her. "Some days the universe simply conspires against you."

"Yes," Autumn agreed earnestly. "It does." She felt close to tears. There was a lump in her throat and her usual optimism had been swamped by a wave of world-weariness.

"You look all in," he commented.

"I'm very tired," she admitted.

"Too tired for dinner?" he asked. "It doesn't have to be anything fancy. We could pop into that little Italian place at the end of the road for a quick pizza and a glass of passable Chianti."

Autumn smiled. "That sounds very nice."

"It's a date then." Addison stood up. "Are you ready now?"

"I . . . er . . . I have to call my brother first," she said. "Richard's staying with me at the moment. He'll worry if I'm not home soon." She couldn't bring herself to tell Addison that it was actually she who was worried about leaving Richard alone in her home for too long. She was fretting herself sick at the thought of what he was getting up to during the day — and half of the night. "Do you mind?"

"Is everything okay?"

The tears were too close to the surface for her to begin an explanation without breaking down. Perhaps when she was on the other side of a few of those passable glasses of Chianti, she might take Addison into her confidence. There was a reliable air about him that made her think he was the sort of man she could trust. Unlike her darling brother. "It's fine," she said by way of reply. "I'll just give him a quick call."

Richard's mobile went unanswered. Strange. There was very little that could keep her brother from answering his phone. Autumn tried the landline at the flat and that too rang until it switched to answerphone. "Richard," she said. "If you're there, pick up, please." But he didn't.

Autumn nibbled at her lip. "I think I should go home," she said to Addison. "I'm sorry."

"Are you sure?" Now he looked worried too. "Is something wrong? Should I come with you?"

It was tempting, but the fewer people who knew about Richard's problems the better. She shook her head. "Can we do this another time?"

"Sure." Addison stretched as he stood up. "If there was a problem you would tell me, wouldn't you, Autumn?"

"Of course," she said. "Of course I would." But she couldn't meet his eyes. "I have to go."

"Me too." He waved a hand at her. "See you around."

"Addison," she said as he neared the door. "Don't stop asking me."

His face broke into his customary wide grin. "Okay," he said. Then: "Don't keep turning me down."

She laughed. "I won't."

The door was standing ajar when she reached the flat. Autumn felt the hackles on her neck rise. She pushed away a wave of irritation. It had been the same every night since Richard had arrived — a variety of unknown and shifty-looking men visiting her flat to see her brother. They were knocking for him at all hours of the night. Even though she was supposed to be sleeping, Autumn could hear the gentle tapping on the front door in the wee small hours. Every day she felt she was getting more and more tired from disturbed nights; even upping her chocolate intake had failed to provide a lift to her energy levels. She was going to have to sit down and address some of these issues with Rich if he was going to continue living here. She just couldn't cope with the way things were. There was no way that she could trust him, and now that meant that she was turning down the offer of a perfectly pleasant dinner with a nice man — the first man to have asked her out in months — so that she could rush home to babysit her brother. This couldn't continue. Autumn wondered what was really going on in Richard's life and whether he was taking steps to get his act together or whether he was simply coasting. The more she worried for him, the more unconcerned about his plight he seemed.

In the living room, a table lamp had been knocked over. She went to it and righted it. The whole place just didn't feel right. An uneasy feeling prickled over her skin.

The selection of chocolates sitting waiting on the coffee table seemed to be mocking her; the mocha-colored box with its silky brown ribbon somehow looked out of place now. This was her sanctuary and yet it no longer felt like her own home. Having her brother here and the constant to-ing and fro-ing of his string of acquaintances made her feel as if she was being violated. Was that being melodramatic? Had she simply spent too much time living alone to be able to cope with existing in close proximity with another human being? She just couldn't imagine putting her feet up and relaxing with Rich skulking around. Perhaps another human being other than her brother might not be so taxing. Her thoughts went again to Addison. Perhaps she should have confided some of her worries to him, after all.

As she went through to the kitchen, she

was greeted by a pile of dirty dishes stacked in the sink. There must have been a dozen used mugs in the bowl. Exactly how many people had been here to see Rich today? He'd clearly heated up some soup for lunch. Two empty Heinz cans sat next to the cooker, two dirty pans were still on the hob and two dishes discarded on the table. More depressingly, there was a half-empty bottle of vodka on the table too and two tumblers. But where was her brother now?

"Rich?" she called out. "Richard!" There was no answer.

His bedroom door was closed and she wondered if he was in there asleep. She went to the door and listened carefully, but she couldn't hear any sounds. Gingerly, Autumn opened the door. Sure enough, Richard was curled up on his side, his hair flopping over the side of his face, his arm flopping over the edge of the bed. Autumn stepped back. There was a girl next to him. She was a tiny little thing and was wearing just her underwear — a skimpy pair of pink pants and a white cotton camisole. The girl was stretched out on her back, arm flung above her head. Autumn sighed with relief. Thank goodness she hadn't opened the door and caught them doing anything else other than sleeping. Then she noticed something odd about the girl. Even in the gloom of a bedroom that had the curtains closed against the daylight, she looked unnaturally pale. Contradicting all of her best instincts, Autumn tiptoed inside the room to look more closely at her. A trail of vomit had spewed from the woman's mouth onto the duvet cover. Autumn could hear her heart hammering in her chest. This didn't look good at all. She gently shook the girl's arm but there was no response. This time she shook harder, but there was still no movement.

"Rich!" she shouted in panic. "Rich! Wake up!"

Her brother snorted in the bed and tried to sit up. He stared in Autumn's direction, his eyes unfocused. He looked like a man who was drunk — but Autumn instinctively knew that it wasn't alcohol alone that had left him in this state.

"What the hell are you doing here?" he wanted to know. His voice was slurred. "Get out."

"Richard," Autumn whispered. "Your friend's been sick. I've tried to wake her, but she isn't responding."

"She's fine," he said dismissively, and sank back to his pillow.

"She *isn't* fine," Autumn snapped. "Richard, wake up. I need you to help me."

Her brother forced himself to his elbows. "She'll be fine," he said again. "Make her some black coffee."

"What's her name?" Autumn wanted to know.

Richard sounded affronted. "What difference does that make?"

"Tell me." She rubbed at the girl's hand.

"Er . . ." Her brother struggled to search through the filing cabinet of his brain. "Rosie," he said uncertainly. "It's Rosie — I'm sure it is."

Clearly she was a long-standing acquaintance. "Rosie," Autumn said, holding the girl's shoulders. "Come on, sweetheart." Her eyes were rolling in her head and her body felt lifeless. "What's she been taking?"

"A bit of booze, a bit of coke." Her brother sounded bored by her line of questioning.

"She doesn't look well."

Richard sighed and rolled over. He looked at Rosie's face and then sat bolt upright. "Shit."

Her brother's reaction was enough to tell her that all was *not* well. "That's it, Rich, I'm phoning an ambulance."

He grabbed at her arm as she went to leave the bedroom and held her back. "You can't," he pleaded. "You can't bring it here. If the paramedics see her like this, they'll know it was me who gave her the gear."

"She's in desperate need of help. Surely you can see that?"

"I know. I know." Her brother leaped out of the bed. He was wearing only his shorts and he released Autumn long enough to hurriedly pull on his jeans. "I can take her in the car. We can leave her at A and E."

"You're in no fit state to drive," Autumn said. "And we can't just leave her anywhere."

"If we stay with her, then they'll be asking questions. They'll want to know who gave her the drugs. They might call the police, Autumn. There's stuff in this flat that I wouldn't want them to see."

"She needs *immediate* medical attention. If we don't get her to the hospital *now* she could die."

"For fuck's sake, Autumn. Don't lay that one on me."

"I'm trying to help you, Rich."

"You could drive her."

"I haven't driven in ten years. More. This isn't the time to start again."

"Shit," Rich said. "If someone sees you they might be able to trace the car anyway."

"What exactly have you been doing, Rich?"

"Let's get her into a cab," he said, avoiding the question. "We can drop her right at the door." Her brother was sweating profusely. He pulled a crumpled T-shirt over his head. "Trust me, it's the right thing to do. You have to protect me."

"Get her dressed," Autumn said, and she went into the bathroom. She ran cold water onto a flannel and took it back to Rosie.

The girl was now sitting on the edge of the bed, propped against the pillows, and her brother had somehow managed to put her back into her little flirty skirt. He was currently fastening up her blouse. Autumn was relieved to see that some color had come back into her cheeks. She wiped round the girl's face with the cold flannel and her eyes flickered to life. "Good girl, Rosie," Autumn said, cupping the young woman's elfin face in her hands. "Stay with us. We're going to take you to the hospital."

Rosie murmured a reply but it was unintelligible. Her brother paced the floor. "Help me to get her downstairs," Autumn instructed.

"I'll carry her," Richard said. He was suddenly a lot more sober and coherent. He swept Rosie into his arms and Autumn led the way as he staggered behind her.

"Wait here while I hail a cab," Autumn said. She thought that if they stood there with a sick-looking woman who couldn't even stand up, then it was highly likely that most cabs would drive by. Against the odds, it was only moments before one pulled up next to her and Autumn opened the door. "Can I go to the Chelsea and Westminster Hospital, please?" she shouted to the cab driver, then she waved to Rich who came out with Rosie in his arms.

"She doesn't look too good," the cab driver noted.

"She isn't," Autumn said. "She's had way too much to drink." She shot Rich an accusatory look. "We need to get there as soon as we can."

"You young people love your binge drinking," the driver observed with a shake of his head. Nevertheless, he put his foot down and minutes later they pulled up outside the hospital.

"Take her in while I pay the driver," Autumn instructed.

Richard hoisted Rosie over his arm while he took her to the door and set her down. The girl's legs buckled beneath her, but she managed to stay upright. "You'll be fine now," he said, holding onto her hands and trying to make contact with her flickering eyes. "Tell them what you've taken, but don't say where you got it from if they ask." He eased her toward the door. "There's a good girl, Rosie."

Her eyes focused briefly and she said hoarsely, "It's Daisy." Rich let go of her and she stumbled and weaved her way into the hospital.

Autumn came up behind him. "You haven't just left her alone like that?" she said. "We've got to make sure she's okay."

She went to push past him into the hospital reception, but Richard held her arms. "She's fine," her brother said. His voice was strained with anxiety. "She can walk and she was just talking to me. In fact, she probably doesn't even need to be here. We caught her just at the right time."

"How do you know that?"

Her brother avoided her eyes.

"My God," Autumn gasped. "You've been in this situation before."

"She said she was a regular user," her brother whined. "Maybe she wasn't. Maybe she took too much. Maybe the booze didn't agree with her."

"And maybe you're lucky she didn't die in your bed!" Autumn said.

Richard hung his head.

"Don't ever put me in this situation again, Rich," she said sharply. "You have no idea how badly I feel about doing this. If anything happens to that girl, I'll never be able to live with myself." It was terrifying to think that if she hadn't followed her instincts and had gone instead to have dinner with Addison, this girl might not have made it. Christ, couldn't she leave Richard alone for a minute without him doing something stupid?

"I'll call her later," he said sulkily. "Make sure she's all right."

"You're all heart." At this moment she couldn't even believe that they were related to each other — their principles were so entirely different. And in trying to protect her brother, she had compromised herself.

"Can we go home now?" Richard asked dolefully. "I'll hail a cab."

It had started to rain and the day was chilly and gray. It suited Autumn's mood. "You can walk," she said. "It will do you good." All she wanted to do was get home and eat lots and lots of chocolate, and she didn't give a fig what her brother thought about that.

CHAPTER THIRTY

I'm leaping around the living room with Davina McCall. She seems to be making a better fist of it than I am, but then she's probably being paid a squillion pounds to feature in her own exercise DVD, whereas I am not. I'm doing this under the utmost sufferance. The amount of chocolate I've consumed recently is beginning to settle on my hips and that is not a good look. This morning, the waistband on my skirt nearly garroted me. Why is it that weight never settles on my boobs, where I could do with a bit of extra help? Why are calories preprogrammed to go straight to the lower half of your body?

I could do all of these exercise classes at my gym, but I find the place so demoralizing that I can't bear it. All the women who do the classes there can keep up with the instructors and I can't. I *so* don't get my money's worth out of that place. My reasoning is, if I do all of these exercise DVDs at home then I can eventually get in shape enough to risk a class at the gym. Seems fair to me. I have an extensive selection to choose from. I can *Pump It Up!* with the sickeningly fit women from the Eric Prydz music video — which, if you ask me, is more porn than Pilates and the most depressing exercise workout known to man. They are all so athletic and lithe I'm sure it has the reverse effect on my psyche. Why bother to do any exercise at all if you don't have a hope in hell of ever looking like that? Poor mortals like me can only get halfway through all those pelvic thrustings. I'm in severe danger of dislocating both of my hips every time I try it. Anyway, their leg warmers are *so* eighties. When I get fed up with them — and it doesn't take long — I can also salsa with Angela Griffin — *"How I danced away two stone in just two months!"* Of course you did, dear. I can do the *Ultimate Challenge, Ultimate Results* pain fest with Nell McAndrew. Or I can pretend I'm punching Marcus's lights out and do my Tae Bo with Billy Blanks's DVD — *Get Fit, Lose Weight, Have Fun, Be Strong.* Build the body of a heavyweight boxer.

See, Davina? When I get sick of you, I can just move on. I can throw you in the cupboard and pick out another one. If only it were so easy with boyfriends. . . . Uh-oh. This is the fat-burning section, and this is the bit that kills me the most. I'm glad that the hairdressing salon beneath my flat has closed for the night as it must sound like there's a herd of elephants dancing on the ceiling. I thump around doing my star jumps, my knee lifts and my lunges, huffing and puffing, red in the face and sweating. My hair is plastered flat to my forehead and, frankly, I have damp patches in places that you don't want damp patches. This is why I prefer yoga. It may not be so good for burning up the calories, but you don't get yourself all worked up into a lather either. There's a certain serenity about it. I already know that, come tomorrow morning, I won't be able to move my thighs, they'll be so tender. I stop to have a quick, restorative bite of Twix to keep my energy up.

"Come on!" Davina urges me from the screen. "Just eight more! Eight . . . Seven . . ."

Smug bitch. I hate all her slick black exercise gear — particularly when all I have is ratty old track bottoms and a cast-off T-shirt with a Ben & Jerry's Cherry Garcia stain forming an attractive pattern down the front. I huff and puff a bit more. I bet they recorded this DVD over the course of several days so that she only had to do five minutes at a time and, here she is, pretending that she's struggling along with the rest of us. There's not a hair out of place and that sheen of perspiration on her brow has probably just been sprayed on by her personal assistant. She's not fit — she's got a damn good editor, that's all. Call me a jealous old tart, because I'd actually like to be Davina — rich, successful, not too shabby in the looks department *and* able to do sixteen sit-ups without going purple. I finish the last bite of Twix. Still, at least, Davina is the shape of a real woman — as am I — and isn't one of these stick-thin, lollipop heads whose BMI is more akin to a shoe size. I *really* hate those.

In the middle of all this torture, my doorbell rings. "Get lost," I gasp at the door. It will be someone trying to sell me cheap double glazing, cheap gas, cheap electricity or one of those cheap restaurant loyalty cards. I don't need any of them. I need nothing in my life but chocolate. The doorbell rings again. No one of any note ever visits me, so there's really no point in me even opening it.

Then Davina decides to increase the speed of the fat-burning section, punishing me further, and I decide that it might be a good idea to have a quick breather after all. I take my bottle of water and glug some down as I go to the door in the vain hope that I might be able to speak to my caller. When I open the door, Marcus is standing there. If I wasn't speechless from exercising, I'd be speechless anyway. He's leaning on the door frame, looking very cute and not a little repentant. His brown eyes are limpid pools of sorrow.

"Hi, Lucy," he says.

"Hi." No other words will come out. I pant attractively at him.

"I thought we could talk," he says. "You haven't returned my calls, so I decided to pop round."

"I'm busy, Marcus." We both take in my appearance. It doesn't compare well to the immaculately groomed and petite Joanne who is my current love rival.

"It looks like hard work," my ex-boyfriend says.

"I'm trying to keep fit."

"Very admirable." Marcus purses his lips at me in a pitiful manner. "Have you eaten?"

Before I can think of a lie, I shake my head and say, "No." One measly Twix hardly counts as eating.

"You could let me buy you Chinese and

apologize for my appalling behavior."

I could. But wouldn't that get me back on the same old treadmill that I've spent so long trying to get off? I sigh in lieu of an answer.

"Why don't I come in and wait for you while you jump in the shower?"

Is he saying that I smell? I try to sniff surreptitiously at my underarms while my insecurities go into overdrive.

Marcus smiles widely at me. "What do you say?"

I'm not strong enough to fight this on my own. I am a feeble bar of Dairy Milk to Marcus's searing blowtorch charm. Less than five minutes and I'm already melting. I can hardly stand the thought of Marcus sitting around in my living room while I'm naked and wet in the shower in the next room, so I say, "Go down to the Lotus Blossom." I sound weary. We've eaten there many times before. I used to think of it as "our place." "I'll come down in a few minutes."

Reluctantly, Marcus eases himself away from my door. "Don't be long, Lucy. We've got a lot to talk about."

Have we? When he's gone, I lean against the door myself for a minute. Should I phone the Chocolate Lovers' Club for some backup? None of the girls live near Camden and, if my usual track record is anything to go by, I'll be in bed playing hide the sausage with Marcus before they even arrive. No. I have to do this alone. I have to be strong. I do *not* have to sleep with Marcus. I do *not* have to let him sweet-talk his way back into my life. If I had any sense, I'd carry on bouncing around like a demented loony with good old Davina McCall and leave Marcus waiting, all alone, in the restaurant. If I had any sense. That's what I'd do.

CHAPTER
THIRTY-ONE

Marcus is already sitting at a table drinking a Tsingtao beer when I arrive at the Lotus Blossom twenty minutes later. I join him and order a beer for myself. Why not just replace all of those calories I tried so hard to work off in one fell swoop? The restaurant is busy and we're seated near the window, squashed in between another couple who seem to be arguing and two blowsy middle-aged women laughing raucously. This cannot, in any way, compete with my wonderful, grown-up, sophisticated date with Jacob Lawson at the Savoy Hotel and I take some small comfort in that fact.

I ran round the shower in a frenzy after Marcus left, but I've deliberately down-played my appearance. I forced myself not to glam up for him. He doesn't deserve it, I tell myself. The hair is still damp — no styling products have graced it. I've gone for the natural look and a cursory flick of mascara is all that adorns my eyelashes. I'm in my old jeans and I've just pulled on a plain black jumper. I hope he appreciates how little effort I've made for him.

"You look great," Marcus says huskily.

Damn. The funny thing is, whenever I used to go out with Marcus, I never felt that I looked good enough for him. Now I just don't care. Not really. Well, not very much.

"Shall we order?" he says. "Do you want your usual?"

I'm annoyed that he thinks he knows what my "usual" is and also that I'm so predictable. "That's fine," I say, and wait to see what he requests.

"I'll have satay beef and the lady will have chicken chow mein. And we'll have some special fried rice and some prawn crackers."

Bum. It's probably fair to say that I *might* have ordered that. Marcus smiles at me. He's really on his best behavior tonight and I wonder why he can't be like this all of the time. One of those heaters with candles in them is plonked on the table between us.

"I've been thinking about you," Marcus says.

"I've been thinking about you too," I reply. "I do hope that we haven't been thinking the same things."

My ex-boyfriend has the courtesy to look

suitably mortified. "You have every right to be angry with me."

He's right. I do.

"I just wanted you to know that it wasn't serious with Jo."

"But it was serious enough to discard our relationship for it?"

"That was the only night we spent together," he continues. "That *fateful* night." He looks like he might laugh ruefully about it, but my warning gaze tells him that I still don't find this funny. "We haven't seen each other since."

"Whose idea was it, Marcus? Did she dump you, or did you dump her? From where I was standing, it looked like *I* was the one you were in a rush to get rid of."

He takes my hand. His fingers feel like those of a stranger. Are these the same hands that not much more than a week ago could bring my body to the very heights of ecstasy? Now I don't know whether I ever want them near me again.

"I can't believe I behaved like that," he says.

But the sad and awful thing is that I *can* believe it. I can believe it all too well.

"We ended it by mutual agreement," he says.

"How jolly civilized."

227

The waiter brings us our food and we busy ourselves with dishing it out. I could go on forever like this with Marcus. We always seem so happy and then, out of the blue, as soon as some woman bats her pretty eyelashes at him he forgets all about me and love and commitment, and goes chasing after her. In the meantime I sit around on the sidelines, licking my wounds and waiting until he comes back. He's so handsome and he's great fun when he wants to be, but this could be my pattern for the rest of my life if I allow it to be. I can't even summon up the necessary energy to find out how this particular fling started.

"I only want you, Lucy," he says. "You know that."

"You know," I tell him flatly, "I don't. How would I know that when all of your actions tell me otherwise?"

"If you want commitment then I can do that."

If I want commitment. When was that ever in doubt? "What if one day when I'm older and grayer and it isn't so easy to pick up the shattered pieces of my life, what if you still can't say no to other women? What if you do find one that you like better? What happens to me then?"

"That won't be the case." Sincerity positively shines out from his eyes. "It would never be the case."

How I would love to believe all of his sugar-coated lies. Usually the food is good here, but my chow mein tastes bland and loaded with MSG. It's weighing heavily in my stomach, just as Marcus's spiel is weighing heavily on my heart. This week has shown me that I can actually feel better about myself when I'm without Marcus than when I'm with him.

"You had your revenge." Marcus smiles good-naturedly.

I wanted him to be spitting blood, not sitting there taking it on the chin, but then I wonder if he's identified the origin of the whiff that by now must be permeating his flat. How on earth can I drop the question casually into the conversation? Smelled any rancid prawns recently, Marcus?

"We can go over old ground," he says, "but what I'd rather do is forget all about it. Move on."

"I have forgotten about it. I have moved on." The surprise registers on Marcus's face. I push my unfinished meal to one side. It was a mistake to come here. It was a mistake to listen to what Marcus had to say.

I sit back in my chair. "I'm seeing someone else now. Someone who treats me like a princess." I think back to my night with Jacob. He was lovely. Polite. Presentable. Romantic. He wants to see me again. Since our chocolate evening, he's texted me a dozen times a day. Nothing slushy, but perky messages that have warmed my heart. We've got a date arranged for Monday night — a poetry reading at a new bookstore. I look at Marcus. Is he really any great shakes? Would he even think to arrange fab dates like that for me? Would we be sitting in a cheap Chinese restaurant in Camden if he truly wanted to win my heart back? Shouldn't he have made more effort? One bunch of roses and a bit of chicken chow mein and he thinks that's enough to make up for his betrayal? I can't help feeling that he's complacent about my love.

"You're right," I say as I stand up. "It isn't worth going over old ground. I think I might be falling in love and, as much as I enjoyed our relationship, I believe it's better if it ends now."

Marcus's jaw drops open, but he doesn't speak. Which is unusual for Marcus. Then he finally finds his voice and stammers, "Who . . . who is this guy?"

"He's called Jacob," I tell him frankly. "I loved you very much, Marcus." I reach out and stroke my ex-boyfriend's cheek, touching him for the last time. "So very much. But now I'd rather take my chances with him."

CHAPTER
THIRTY-TWO

Wait until I tell my fellow members of the
Chocolate Lovers' Club that I managed to
resist Marcus all by myself! Not only that,
but I left him sitting in the restaurant looking very bemused. I make that: one to Lil'
ol' Lucy, nil to Manky Marcus. It's the first
time I've ever refused to have him back and
I don't think he could believe his own ears.
Hah! I'm not sure I could believe mine
either.

I could text all the girls to tell them my
news, but I'm at Targa this morning and —
surprise, surprise — I'm actually busy working, so haven't found the time. One of the
management team has given me a dozen
different sales reports and my fingers are
smoking away typing them out and putting
new figures in. I've gone for hours without
tea or a treat. Well . . . *an* hour. No wonder
I'm feeling delirious. I haven't seen Crush
this morning, either — he hasn't been out

to annoy me once. I caught a glimpse of him only briefly when he was hunched over his desk looking stressed. But then everyone at Targa looks stressed.

My cell phone rings and I pick it up. It's a number I don't recognize.

"Lucy?" the voice at the other end says.

"Yes?"

"This is Felicity from Office Goddesses. How are you?"

"Fine, thanks." I never hear anything from the agency from one week to the next. Even though I threaten to call them and change my job on a regular basis, I never actually do it. I'm part of the furniture here now. A particularly useful office chair, perhaps. Or one of those great-looking stainless-steel filing cabinets.

"We've some good news," Felicity burbles on. "Your contract at Targa comes to an end on Friday and we've got a great new job lined up for you."

It takes a moment before her statement registers in my dullard of a brain. Friday is tomorrow. Which means I have only one more day here. I hear myself gasp.

"Are you okay?" Felicity wants to know.

"Why? Why?" I say. "No one told me about this."

"They didn't?" Now it's her turn to sound

surprised. "I wonder why."

I wonder that too.

"Well," Felicity says, "the person whose job you're covering is returning to work and you're on a weekly contract."

Tracy Whateverhernameis is coming back? Why has no one mentioned this? I aim a glower in the direction of Crush's office.

Felicity blah-blahs on about how cool my new job will be, that I'll love the challenge, that all my colleagues will be wonderful people and all other kinds of bollocks. I won't like it. I like it here. Somehow I write the name and address down and then I utter some sort of pleasantries and hang up. I gaze into the middle distance in a state of shock. I'm leaving. I'm leaving here tomorrow.

I need chocolate. But first I need to speak to Crush. When I march into his office, he looks up at me and there's a sheepish/startled/scared shitless expression on his face. "You knew about this," I say.

Crush holds up his hands. "Only yesterday, Gorgeous."

"I thought Tracy Whateverhernameis was still on maternity leave."

"Apparently, those fine young ladies in Human Resources calculated it incorrectly." He raises his eyebrows at me. Perhaps this is them exacting cruel revenge on me for the fact that Crush likes me better than their friend Donna from Data Processing. "Now Tracy's coming back on Monday."

"But doesn't Targa normally find a reason to give the bullet to everyone who gets pregnant?"

"Only the women," Crush says with a shrug. "Apparently the company must be developing a heart."

"Shouldn't I stay for another week?" I venture. "Help her to slip seamlessly back in?"

"Tried that one," he says. "Budget won't allow it."

My lip starts to tremble.

"I also asked them to find you a job in another department — no go. And to interview you for any other jobs we might have — nothing available."

"There's always someone sick here," I try. "Or pretending to be."

"Human Resources assures me we're all in rude health at the moment. Or pretending to be."

We both look blankly at each other for a bit. "That's it then?"

"If there was anything I could do, Gorgeous, believe me I would." Crush looks as miserable as I feel. "I'm going to miss your cheery little face around here."

"That's the worst thing about being a temp," I sigh. "I'm completely disposable."

Crush stands up and also gives a hearty sigh. He comes and puts his arm round my shoulders, squeezing me gently. It's nice and warm nestled here against his chest. "You're irreplaceable," he says.

"I could give you my phone number," I suggest. "If anything comes up, maybe you'll give me a ring."

"I could give you *my* phone number," he echoes. "Maybe you could give *me* a ring and take me out to dinner one night."

I can feel myself flush and I must gape at him insanely, because Crush flushes too. Then in a vaguely embarrassed and jokey way, he adds, "Then we could see if anything comes up. Ha. Ha."

Has Crush really just asked me out? Or asked me to ask him out?

"Ha, ha, ha," he says again.

And as I don't know what else to do, I go, "Ha, ha, ha," as well.

CHAPTER
THIRTY-THREE

The mood is somber among the members of the Chocolate Lovers' Club.

"Do you think those bitches did it on purpose?" Chantal wants to know.

"I'm not sure that the humans in the Human Resources Department are that resourceful," I admit as I sip on my cup of tea. "But I'm also sure that they would have done it if they could have."

We've all gathered together on Saturday afternoon — a busy time in Chocolate Heaven. Both Clive and Tristan are working flat-out to keep the queue of customers down. Their freshly made chocolate desserts, having recently warranted an appearance in the glossy weekend supplement of one of our national newspapers, are on the current "must-have" list for the Notting Hill set. We have, of course, road tested them all. Clive's chocolate and hazelnut mousse tart is a particular personal favorite. To taste that is to be a woman forever changed. Maybe a small slice of that would lift my spirits today. Better make it a large slice, to be on the safe side.

We're all ensconced in the shabby chic sofas at the back of the shop and have no intentions of moving for anyone. Clearly, we have a lot to discuss and repel any pretenders to our sofas with steely gazes. The customers come and go briskly today, minds intent on shopping, their chocolate break snatched as a quick energy boost to propel them on with greater purchasing power.

"I can't believe I'm starting a new job on Monday." The lightning speed of my departure from Targa has yet to sink in. I even went to the gym this morning to fit in a yoga class to see if that would de-stress me. But no amount of ohming or backward-bending could clear my fuddled brain.

"It could be good to have a new challenge," Nadia says.

"But what am I going to do if I can't see Crush every day? He's the only thing that makes my mundane working life worthwhile. Who am I going to tell off for nicking my chocolate supplies?"

Crush and the sales team gave me a box of chocolates to mark my departure — Cadbury's Milk Tray — not quite my number one favorites, but nevertheless very thoughtful. No doubt they will still be consumed with gusto. Crush also gave a little speech thanking me for my contribution to the department. No one sniggered, which I view as a positive thing and, if I'm not mistaken, there might have been a tear in his eye. I'm going to miss him.

"A little more stability in both your career and your personal life might not go amiss, Lucy," Autumn points out. Quite unnecessarily, to my mind. "All this confusion can't be good for your aura. It makes you vulnerable to psychic attack."

Oh good. Something else to worry about. I bury myself in the comfort offered by my bar of white vanilla and olive oil chocolate, enjoying every luxurious morsel. This isn't strictly pure chocolate as it's made with cocoa butter rather than cocoa solids (these things matter to the aficionado) but it's so great that Clive is allowed to keep it in his repertoire. It's like a grown-up version of a Milky Bar — but I'd never dare say that within earshot of Clive. I let its velvety texture melt slowly on my tongue and let out a long, steady exhalation of breath. Joy is returning to my life.

"At least you've got your date with Jacob

to look forward to," Nadia offers. "He sounds great."

"He sounds too good to be true," Chantal says, introducing a cynical note to the proceedings. "Sorry, Lucy, but I'm off men at the moment."

"Jacob's taking me to a poetry reading," I say with a little glow of pride. "Imagine. I didn't think men did that sort of thing anymore." I sort of hoped that he'd want to see me this weekend. It's the worst thing about being a single person — Saturday and Sunday now drag whereas they used to hurtle by when I was part of a couple. I dropped lots of hints to Jacob, but he said that he was busy all weekend. Great, another workaholic.

"I think he sounds wonderful," Autumn says as she picks at her chocolate and marmalade muffin.

"Do you want me to see if he's got a brother for you?"

Autumn shakes her mass of curls. "Brothers are bad news," she says enigmatically.

"Still having trouble with Rich?"

She puts down her muffin and leans forward. "I wasn't going to tell anyone," she says, "but I don't know what to do." Our friend checks around us in a conspiratorial manner. "I think Rich is dealing."

We must all look at her in a puzzled way as she continues, her voice hushed to a whisper, "Cocaine." She pauses to let that sink in.

Ohmigod. Autumn's posh brother is a *drug* dealer. I can hardly believe it. When she said dealing I thought she meant stocks and shares and stuff like that.

"We had a terrible situation just a few days ago," Autumn continues. "A young woman nearly overdosed in my flat. It was someone Rich brought back. He hardly knew her. We managed to get her to the hospital in time . . ." Autumn trails to a halt. Tears sparkle in her eyes.

"But you nearly didn't make it," I prompt.

"The scary thing is, I nearly accepted a date . . ."

"A date?" I almost jump out of my chair. "Who with?"

"A guy at work," Autumn tells us. "He's really nice. But if I'd gone, then this girl might have died."

I want to tell Autumn that she has to live her own life and let her brother make his own mistakes and all that kind of stuff, but I know that she's simply not the sort of person who could do that. Maybe I should remind her that she hasn't had a date in all the time I've known her, and that opportunities like this shouldn't be allowed to pass, no matter whose life is at risk.

"I can hardly bring myself to speak to Richard after what he did and the fact that he's dragged me into his sordid world," Autumn continues. "She's all right now, thank heavens. I made him call her to find out — which he wasn't very keen to do. What I find hard to come to terms with is that I went along with him to help to protect him. How could I do that?"

"You were put in a difficult situation, Autumn," I sympathize. "What else could you have done?"

"I should have gone to the police myself," she says. "He needs to stop before he gets too far into this."

To my mind, he already sounds like he's in over his head and sinking fast. "You need to sit down and talk to him," I say. "Urgently."

"I've tried to, but Rich is denying everything."

"You have to find some hard evidence," Chantal says — ever practical. "Then you can confront him with it."

"I hate confrontation," Autumn says miserably. "I spend most of my life trying to avoid confrontation. What if I find some evidence? Do you think I should go to the police then? He's still my brother."

"Perhaps there's another way," I say. "Can't you sell him the benefits of rehab as opposed to going to jail?"

"I keep trying," Autumn says. "All he does is throw back in my face that I'm addicted to chocolate." She puts down her choc marmalade muffin and looks at it with disgust.

"Chocolate and cocaine are worlds apart," I remind her.

"Are they?" she says. "I can't give this up any more than Rich can give up his drugs."

"Eating chocolate doesn't hurt other people. It doesn't destroy lives. If that's all he can pin on you, Autumn, then I'd say he was clutching at straws. All that chocolate is to any of us is a bit of comfort in a harsh world."

"I find it so sad that someone with Richard's privileged upbringing can stoop so low," our friend says with a shake of her head. "When I spend my days dealing with teenagers who are trying to get themselves out of the gutter, it's hard to stand by and watch my own flesh and blood who's seemingly hell-bent on ending up there."

I give Autumn a hug. "We're here for you. Whatever you decide to do, we'll try to support you." I want to know more about the guy and the date that never was, but it seems as if I'm the only one, so I keep my lip zipped.

She sniffs gratefully.

Chantal sighs. "Tell us some good news, Nadia. We could do with cheering up."

"I do have some good news," she says proudly. "I paid off our debts this week and Toby has managed to stay out of the Internet casinos so far. We're going to go to Hyde Park this weekend, kick a football around, take the Frisbee. Do some normal family stuff. I can't thank you enough, Chantal." Nadia squeezes her hand.

"You'd have done it for me if the situation had been reversed," she says.

"Well, you've given us a fresh start," Nadia says. "I intend to make the most of it."

"Glad I could help."

"Have you any news?" I ask Chantal.

She shakes her head. "No. Having no sex is still the new having lots of sex at my house. Nothing has changed."

But I wonder if I'm the only one to notice that Chantal has a very enigmatic look on her face.

CHAPTER
THIRTY-FOUR

Fantastic. I look at the front of Jesmond &
Sons and wish that I hadn't bothered to get
out of bed this morning. My mood turns as
gray as the morning sky. When you're a
young, funky, feisty go-getter, the last place
you'd want to be working is a bookshop.
And Jesmond & Sons isn't one of those
trendy high-street bookstores with a coffee
bar and staff called Philippa and Camilla —
like the bookstore I'm going to with Jacob
tonight. That would be fine. I could do *that*
kind of bookshop. No. This is a crumbling
back-street establishment that looks as if it
has one customer every half century. Their
sign announces that they're specialists in
secondhand military history books and also
— that famous oxymoron — books on
military intelligence. So not even a few dog-
eared romance novels to keep me amused.

I gird my loins, wishing that I'd worn my
sober black suit this morning and not my

bright pink number, and before I decide to throw up my hands and run away, I cross the road to the bookshop. A bell tinkles pleasantly as I step inside the door, heralding my arrival. The smell of musty books assaults my nostrils and all I can see in the gloom are shelves and shelves of dusty tomes. Motes of dust filter down in the chinks of sunlight where I've disturbed the air by opening the door — probably the first person to do so this year. A man shuffles toward me. He's wearing a brown checked shirt, a red tie, a green cardigan and blue trousers.

"Hi," I say in my best singsong voice. "I'm Lucy Lombard. I've been sent by Office Goddesses." I extend my hand.

"Ah," he says, examining me over the top of his spectacles. "Yes. Lovely." He takes my hand and gently presses it. His fingers are the texture of soft dough and, come to think of it, there's a faintly yeasty smell about him. "Pleased to make your acquaintance, Miss Lombard."

Doesn't look as if I'm going to be commonly known as Gorgeous here then. "Are you Mr. Jesmond, the owner?"

"No, no," he says with a self-deprecating smile. "That's my father."

This guy must be a hundred and five if

he's a day. "I'm the youngest of the Jesmond brothers." And the last surviving one? I wonder. We walk the three steps it takes to reach the desk by the window. "Ever worked in a bookshop before?" he asks.

"No," I say politely. "This is my first time."

"Nothing too hard," Mr. Jesmond assures me. "I'm sure you'll soon get to grips. Don't worry."

I smile appreciatively. Normally, as a temp, I'm dumped in a corner, given a pile of work that I usually don't have a clue what to do with and then I'm left alone to get on with it.

"Well then," Mr. Jesmond says. "Shall I show you the ropes?"

"That would be great." I try to maintain my fake upbeat mood.

"This is the desk," my new employer says. "On it is the till." The till appears to be nothing more sophisticated than a wooden box. He gestures at the shelves. "These are all the books."

Strangely, I'd managed to work that out.

"When a customer buys a book, you put the money in the till and then, only if they require it, write them out a receipt." He picks up the relevant pad and shows it to me. "Then," he says, as if this is the tough bit, "you write down the title and the amount in the bought ledger account." Again the relevant book is pointed out.

"Wow," I say. Are there still businesses left that don't rely on computerized systems? I had no idea. I'd hazard a guess that Jesmond & Sons has only just dispensed with quill pens and an abacus. This could be one of those places from a bygone era that they reconstruct in museums called Life in Our Times.

"Do you think you'll be able to manage?" Mr. Jesmond seems very concerned that the job is beyond me. Perhaps my pink suit is giving off the wrong vibe.

"I'll give it a stab," I say. I just hope that the morning rush doesn't knock me clean off my feet before I'm fully *au fait.*

"Normally I can cope on my own," Mr. Jesmond says proudly, "but I need someone for a few weeks. If it works out, I could well want you here for longer. After all, I'm not getting any younger," he says. "I'm having to go to hospital. *Tests.*" The last word is whispered. He points downward. My eyes follow his finger to the blue polyester trousers. *"Waterworks."*

That is definitely too much information.

"Shall I put the kettle on?" I ask, hoping that whatever his condition is, it doesn't preclude him from drinking tea. It's always a good opening ploy, to see what the attitude is to tea breaks. "Then I can make a start on familiarizing myself with the stock."

"What a marvelous idea," he says perkily. "The kitchen's upstairs."

So, I climb the dark, narrow stairs and tucked in one corner there's a minute kitchen area with gray, cracked tiles, a dodgy-looking hot-water geyser and a few scabby mugs. This place should come with a health warning. There's a vague smell of drains and it could definitely do with a rub-round of lemon cleanser. Choosing the least cheesy-looking mugs, I give them a good rinse with boiling water before I make the tea in them, then take them down into the shop.

"The stockroom's at the back," Mr. Jesmond says. "I'll get on with a few chores while you settle yourself in."

When he's gone, I look round the shop, not sure what to do. This place doesn't exactly run on the same frantic lines as Targa. At least there, I do have a lot of work that I *could* be getting on with, should I choose to. Here, I could turn into a desk potato through no fault of my own. I put my tea down on the desk and go over to the bookshelves. There's a thick white film of dust at the front of each one. I glance through the books — World War One, World War Two, a wide variety of other wars . . . I had no idea there have been so many of them, nor that so many books had been written on the subject. There are volumes on espionage, tactics, battle campaigns and the armed forces; whole sections are devoted to military science, military life, weapons and sundry warfare. They all look terribly dry to me. Probably contain very little gratuitous sex. No smoldering heroes to lust after. But maybe this sort of book would attract a military-style, rufty-tufty type of customer. The thought brightens my mood but, frankly, I've had more than enough of stock familiarization and I retreat to the desk.

Fishing the box of Milk Tray that was my present from Crush and team out of the depths of my handbag, I hold the box in my hands while I examine them. What a lovely thought it was for him to buy me these, and I get a little pang of longing for my former boss. Mr. Jesmond is very nice, but he's not exactly sex on legs. Perhaps I should ring Crush and just thank him again? But maybe he'd guess that I'm really just bored and that I haven't gone to a great job where I've hardly had a second to breathe and I'm not missing anyone from Targa — particularly not him.

Oh, I *so* need some chocolate to get me through the day. I open the box and enjoy the rush that the scent gives me. I'm going to make these last all day. It's now 9:30 a.m. My, I've been here thirty minutes already. Doesn't time fly when you're having fun? I'm going to have to fill my day by thinking about my date with Jacob tonight and eating my chocolates. If I have one chocolate every half an hour, then I'll need eight to get me up to lunchtime. I spend a few minutes picking my selection. It has to be the Turkish Delight first, then the coffee crème . . . orange crème . . . and the hazelnut whirl. Mmm. Maybe these chocolates are my favorites, after all.

I lose the urge to be picky and simply line up a random selection of eight delights in a row in the middle of the desk. I could phone Crush and goad him by telling him that I've got a Turkish Delight that I don't have to share with him. My fingers linger over the phone again and I eat said Turkish Delight while I contemplate it further. When Mr. Jesmond comes back into the shop, I'll see if he wants one too. I eat the coffee crème, and that leaves only six chocolates, which doesn't seem nearly enough. So I up my quota and decide on one every fifteen minutes to pass the morning more quickly. Then I can do the same to get me through the afternoon. What a great idea. I eye up the Dairy Milk. But that's going to leave me perilously short of chocolates. They might not get me through until six o'clock. If Crush had really cared about me, then he should have bought me a bigger box.

CHAPTER
THIRTY-FIVE

At 5:30 on the dot, I sprint upstairs to the
tiny toilet cubicle — also in need of some
serious bleach — and strip off my businesslike white shirt, swapping it for a romantic
little number in floral chiffon as is fitting for
a poetry reading. I haven't got time to rush
home for a shower, so I have a French wash
instead, squirting myself liberally with some
sexy Anna Sui fragrance. Hope Jacob
doesn't want to get *too* up close and personal tonight. Well, I *sort of* hope that. I
touch up my makeup, eat a handful of those
breath-freshening mints and slick on some
lipstick.

Tomorrow, I'm going to bring a whole
heap of cleaning products in here and give
this place some elbow grease. My chocolate
clock to mark the passing of the day was all
very well, even though it made me think of
Crush more often than was healthy, but I
had literally *nothing* to do. We didn't have

one single customer. All my dreams of hunky military types remained just that. Now, I'm generously putting this down to the fact that it was Monday and it was raining for most of the afternoon, but still . . . How on earth does the Jesmond family make any money from this place? They could simply shut up shop and have an Internet site. I wonder if Mr. Jesmond Junior has ever heard of the Internet? The very least I can do for the dear old boy is get his shop spick-and-span. Having so much time on my hands is making me start to think of Targa with fond memories, as you do with boyfriends you had in your teens. Somehow you forget all the things you hated about them and only remember their good points. That's how I'm currently feeling about my last position.

"Good night, Mr. Jesmond," I shout as I sprint out the door. "See you tomorrow."

"Have a nice evening, Miss Lombard."

I've asked him ten times to call me Lucy, but he can't quite compute it. Bless. Dashing across to the bus stop, I manage to jump on a bus that's just departing and that will whisk me toward Jacob.

The bookshop where I'm meeting my date is one of the newfangled "lifestyle" stores that has coffee shops and sells wrapping paper and greetings cards too. There's a blackboard outside with the details of the poetry reading written on it in pink chalk. I swing inside and follow the signs to the third floor. Chairs are set out for the reading and there's a crowd milling around the table bearing wine and nibbles. In the middle of the throng, I see Jacob. He's wearing a slate gray suit this time and he looks as fabulous as he did when I last saw him. My heart pitter-patters a little faster and it's nothing to do with the fact that I've recently run for a bus.

He smiles when he sees me and heads toward me. Then he kisses me rather shyly on the cheek. "Hi," he says. "Glad you could get away from your job in time."

I don't tell him that I've been waiting for the moment I could leave since the minute I arrived at Jesmond & Sons this morning.

"Let me get you something," Jacob says.

"Red wine," I answer. "That would be nice."

The poetry book that's being launched is an anthology and I notice that there are several of the contributors mingling nervously with their guests. You can tell that they're poets as they're wearing mainly velvet clothing with lots of scarves and some of them have on jaunty hats. Jacob brings me a glass of wine and a small plate with a selection of canapés on it, which I struggle to balance. "I hope I brought the right ones."

"They look lovely. How thoughtful of you."

"Ulterior motive. I was hoping you'd share the smoked salmon with me."

He keeps his eyes locked on mine as I offer him a bite and he covers my fingers with his while I finish the rest. The ground goes soft beneath my feet and my breathing is sounding borderline asthmatic. Jacob smiles at me, amusement playing at his lips. This man knows exactly the effect he's having on me and what's more, I don't care. When we've finished our canapés, Jacob picks up a copy of the book and flicks through the pages.

"Do you read a lot of poetry?" I ask.

"Yes." He nods enthusiastically. "I'm a big fan. The more romantic the better. I love all the heartrending stuff. You?"

I shrug. "I don't usually get the time. This is a rare treat for me."

"Then I'm pleased that you could come." He has the most fabulous eyes, and they're all twinkly in the bookshop lights. Could this be the start of a new relationship for me? I wonder. I've always wanted a sensitive and cultured boyfriend and, to date, they've almost exclusively evaded me. Most men's idea of sensitivity is wearing a ribbed condom. Really special, and special guys don't come along that often in one's lifetime.

"It's about to start," Jacob says, which is just as well as I think I was going to pass out with sheer joy.

The readings don't last for long. Half a dozen of the velvet-clad poets stand at the front of the audience and read out a couple of verses. They're mostly amusing or romantic, nothing too heavy. Jacob holds my hand throughout the event, which makes me hot. It feels strange to have the touch of unfamiliar skin on mine after all the time I've spent with Marcus, but I have to admit that it's also rather nice. I find myself drifting off from the poetry readings and wondering what it might be like to feel more of his skin against mine.

We all clap politely when they've finished and Jacob says, "Will you let me buy you the book?"

"Thank you. I'd like that." So we queue and buy the book, which a couple of the poets sign for me. Jacob hands me the little brown carrier bag with my autographed anthology tucked inside.

"I'd like to take you to dinner," he says, and my heart swells. "But I have to go to work now." It sinks again like one of my more tragic soufflés.

Glancing surreptitiously at my watch, I see that it's eight o'clock. This is far too early to be going home.

"It's a meeting that I couldn't reschedule," he says apologetically.

"Oh. That's fine," I say, my heart sinking. "We all have to work."

"I'll call you soon," Jacob tells me. He kisses me softly on the lips, which makes my knees go weak. "I promise."

And I resign myself to hot chocolate and an early night when I was really thinking about hot sex and a wild night. Oh, well.

CHAPTER
THIRTY-SIX

Chantal had told Ted that she'd be away on an assignment overnight. Her husband would never know the difference, anyway. She rarely called home when she was away and he never asked her where she was going. If he ever needed her, he simply called her on her cell phone. The hotel she'd chosen was one of the best in London — her own personal favorite for the occasional drink — but she'd never had cause to stay here overnight before. When she had meetings in London it was easy enough to go home whatever the hour. The hotel was modern, minimalist, clean and businesslike — which suited her purpose.

She'd called a cab, which had come to collect her shortly before Ted was due home. Now it pulled up outside the St. Crispin's Hotel, which was near the busy area of Covent Garden. Chantal had decided to arrive early to give herself time to prepare for the evening. She'd have a long, hot bath, a glass of champagne, the chocolates she'd brought to calm her nerves. She was paying for this escort service by the hour, but she thought she might as well make a night of it as she was also paying handsomely for the room. People were bustling by on their way to one of the many theaters or to dinner — happy couples, arm in arm — and she suffered a pang of loneliness which twisted her insides when she thought that her life should have come to this.

Hoisting her small overnight case out of the cab, she paid the driver before entering the hotel. Checking in, Chantal could feel her palms sweating when she said, "I'm expecting a guest later." She wondered what the woman behind reception would think if she knew that she was, in fact, hiring her guest by the hour.

"And the name?"

Chantal had a moment's panic. She didn't know this guy by anything but his agency name, and that sounded ludicrous. "Mr. Jazz," she said after some thought. "Mr. Jazz."

"We'll call you when he arrives, Mrs. Hamilton. Can I help you with anything else?"

"No. I'm good, thank you."

As she made her way to the elevator, she heard a voice behind her. "Chantal!" the woman cried. "How are you?"

Chantal spun round. Her mouth went dry. Amy Barrington was the last person she wanted to see. "Amy," she said brightly. The woman was a casual acquaintance who they'd met at several dinner parties over the years. Her husband, Lucian, was in the same line as Ted and they occasionally played golf together. Amy Barrington was known for her great taste in gossip. "Good to see you," she lied.

"Fancy meeting you here." Amy kissed her on both cheeks. "You're staying here?" Her eyes went to Chantal's case.

"Just for the night."

"No Ted?" Amy looked around her.

"I'm here on an assignment," Chantal explained. "I'm meeting someone who I'm going to be doing a feature on."

"And you have to stay overnight?"

"Sometimes it's easier." Chantal knew that Amy Barrington wasn't convinced.

"Come into the bar," the other woman urged. "Sit with us while you wait for her. Lucian's just ordering some drinks."

"I can't," Chantal said, backing away. "I have to go to my room and prepare my notes."

"Oh." Amy was clearly put out. "Just one little drink."

"Sorry, Amy. Another time. You and Lucian must come to the house for drinks one evening."

"I have my BlackBerry right here," Amy said.

"I'll get Ted to organize it with Lucian." Chantal waved her good-bye. "That would work for me."

"Have a nice evening," Amy said. Then her eyes narrowed slightly. "But then this isn't pleasure. You said it was business, didn't you?"

Chantal was wired and edgy after her encounter with Amy Barrington. It was a mistake to have brushed the woman off like that. She should have had a quick drink with them in the bar, played nicely and that would have been the end of it. Now she felt guilty and as if she'd been caught out in an infidelity, which was not what this was. It was a business arrangement. There was no emotional attachment to it. What she did with this guy would have no bearing on her relationship with Ted. It was true that Ted might not view it in that light, but as far as she was concerned, that was the score.

The room was huge, tastefully furnished

in different hues of cream, with dark wood furniture. She wandered around admiring the artwork, trying to stave off the feeling that she was rattling around alone. There was a bottle of Krug nestling in an ice bucket on the coffee table, ready for later. Chantal unpacked her cosmetics in the bathroom and studied herself in the mirror. The face that stared back at her was cool, calm and collected, but that wasn't how she felt inside. She lay in the oversized bath, inhaling her vanilla bath soak and working her way through the line of chocolates she'd laid out on the edge of the bath. She was trying to regain her composure, but it was proving elusive. The water grew cold, so she popped in the last chocolate, stepped out and toweled herself dry.

What to do now? The guy was due in fifteen minutes. Should she get dressed again? Or should she put on the black and pink silk shortie kimono that she'd brought with her? Was it worth making any effort at pretense when they both knew exactly what he was here for? She decided on her fresh black lacy underwear and the kimono. No cash was to change hands. All she had to do was book the appointment and the escort agency would deduct the fee from her credit card. If it was such a simple and efficient arrangement, Chantal wondered why she felt quite so nervous.

Moments later, there was a firm knock on the door of her room. It could well have been room service, but she knew that it wasn't. Not that kind of room service, anyway.

The guy that she'd chosen from the Web site stood in front of her. It was good to see that he hadn't exaggerated his details. He was incredibly handsome. In fact, he looked better in the flesh, so to speak, than he had on the Macho Men Web site. He was tall, tanned and toned. That would do for her.

"Hello," he said with a warm smile. "I'm Jazz."

"Come in," Chantal said. "I've been expecting you."

He was wearing a smart suit with a shirt and tie, highly polished shoes. It was a good look for him. If you'd have passed him in the street you would have assumed that he was a successful businessman — maybe a slick City trader, just like her husband. His face was kinder than she'd imagined and there were fine lines radiating from the corners of his eyes, showing that he smiled a lot. There was no way that you would guess he was a male hooker. Jazz set the small attaché case he was carrying on the coffee table and she wondered what it contained.

"Champagne?"

"That would be great," Jazz said. He was supremely confident and relaxed. "Let me open it."

Jazz twisted the wire and then, expertly, eased the cork from the bottle.

"I'll pour," Chantal said, and her hand trembled as she let the champagne froth out into their glasses. Christ, she should have taken some Valium or something to help her chill out. Or drunk half of this bottle before Jazz had arrived. "This is the first time I've done this," she admitted. No good pretending to know the etiquette of these things when she didn't have a clue. "I'm hoping you'll lead the way."

She turned to see that he'd taken off his jacket and was loosening his tie. He took the glass of champagne from her and chinked it against hers. His eyes glinted with mischief, promise and even desire. Chantal took a deep breath. That was something she hadn't expected to see. She smiled to herself. This could well turn out to be a lot of fun.

"I want you to enjoy yourself," Jazz said. "Just leave everything to me."

CHAPTER
THIRTY-SEVEN

It was seven o'clock the following evening before Chantal returned home. After her assignation with Jazz she'd gone straight into the London office of *Style USA* and had chatted to the editor about some ideas for future articles. She'd taken a long lunch at Oscars with one of the other journalists from the magazine to catch up on office gossip — who was sleeping with whom, who *wished* they were sleeping with whom, who was about to be fired, who didn't realize they were about to be fired. Chantal couldn't help but smile to herself. If only her colleagues knew *her* dark secret.

After her lunch, she'd gone along to Chocolate Heaven and had indulged in some green tea and a bar of Clive's wonderful Samana Penisula chocolate made with rare cocoa beans from the Dominican Republic. This was one of Lucy's favorite chocolates, but then her friend had a lot of favorites when it came to chocolate. It was a shame that none of the other girls were here today, but Chantal wasn't able to linger long enough to text them for a get-together. Besides, if she saw them today, she knew that she'd have to tell them all about her wild night with Jazz. The glow on her cheeks was a dead giveaway that something — or someone — had tickled her fancy. Sometimes those quaint British sayings fitted the situation so well. Feeling strangely happy, Chantal had then commandeered one of the sofas in Chocolate Heaven and spent some time talking on her cell phone to a handful of home owners about the potential of future articles while she enjoyed the rich, spicy taste of the chocolate and the gentle ache of her body.

She'd felt more alive than she'd done in years. The tips of her fingers, the hair on her head all zinged with an energy that she hadn't realized was missing. She was fabulously and fully sexually sated. Jazz had stayed with her for three hours. Three long, luxurious hours where he'd pleasured her — to use an old-fashioned word — time after time. And what she'd paid for was good old-fashioned romancing. That had taken her by surprise. All of Jazz's attention had been entirely focused on her body, her desires. He'd managed to push buttons that she didn't even know she had. How many women could say that they got the same service from their husbands? He'd been the ultimate professional, the perfect gentleman. It was hard to see this arrangement as a fairly sleazy business contract. Jazz had seemed to enjoy himself too; either that or the man was a damn fine actor. She closed her eyes and a stream of sexy images washed over her. His attaché case had contained a range of potions, lotions and toys to set the scene for a very naughty evening. He'd drizzled chilled champagne all over her body and had lapped it up with his hot tongue. The thought of it made her shiver with delight.

Chantal sighed contentedly as she walked through the front door and dropped her overnight case in the hall. Ted, she hoped, would be back from the office soon. Tonight's supper would be a quick pasta dish, so they didn't eat too late. She'd brought home a small box of Clive's milk- and white-chocolate brownies, which were sublime, for her husband. They were a type of peace offering, she supposed, and a pang of guilt nipped at her conscience.

"Hi." Her husband made her jump as he popped his head out from the kitchen door.

"You're home early," she said.

"I couldn't take any more at the office," he said. "They had their pound of flesh today."

She unbuttoned her jacket. "I could have come home earlier too, if I'd known," she said. "You should have called. I've just been hanging out at Chocolate Heaven, fixing up some features." Chantal held up the box of brownies.

Ted smacked his lips appreciatively. "How did your assignment go?"

"Great." She nodded too vigorously. Suddenly the glossy varnish of her tryst cracked and peeled away. It made her feel sick to think where she'd been last night and what she'd been doing. How could she pay someone to have sex with her? How could she do that to this man standing in front of her? She should confront this issue with him and find out what was at the root of their problem. Normal, red-blooded males didn't just stop having sex with their wives for no reason. Booking appointments with prostitutes wasn't the solution.

For years, Chantal had wondered whether her husband, too, was having affairs, but she was sure that he wouldn't have the time even if the inclination was there. He was either at the office, eating dinner or asleep.

The corporate treadmill he was on at Grenfell Martin simply didn't allow time for the pleasure of a mistress. She was sure of it.

Chantal went over and kissed Ted on the cheek, hoping that, for once, he wouldn't flinch away from her. He didn't exactly flinch, but neither did he respond. There was no reciprocal kiss, no hug, no stroking of her cheek. Instead, he turned back into the kitchen. "I've started to make a salad for supper," he said. "Hope that's okay."

"It's fine," she replied, noting that a weariness had crept back into her tone. "I'm just going to throw some pasta in a sauce. Give me five minutes to freshen up."

"There's a message in the study for you," her husband said over his shoulder, as he picked up a red pepper and continued slicing. "Some guy phoned last night while you were away. He said he'd got some information that you might find useful."

Chantal stole a piece of red pepper from the chopping board and nibbled at it as she started to make her way upstairs. "Yeah?"

"You met him at the hotel in the Lake District, apparently."

Chantal's blood turned to ice. It could only be one person. And he'd called her here, at home. Her heart started to pound in her chest. He must have gotten her number from her cell phone which was in the handbag he'd stolen. She wondered if she could speak and if her voice would sound normal. "Did he leave a name?" It sounded strained to Chantal's ears.

Ted mused for a moment. "No," he replied. "Just a number."

"What else did he say?"

"Not much." Her husband's expression gave nothing away. "He said it would be to your advantage to call him as soon as you could. Wanna do it now while I make supper?"

"I'll call him tomorrow," she said, as nonchalantly as she could manage. "It can't be that urgent." But she had a feeling that it was.

CHAPTER
THIRTY-EIGHT

Jacob texts me to say that he had a great time and would I like to see him again on Friday. This time he has tickets for a charity event in aid of breast cancer. I text him back to say that I'd love to go. It means that I have to wait four whole days before I can see him again. Still, I have my high-powered job at Jesmond & Sons bookshop for the militarily inclined to keep me occupied until then.

This morning I've brought in a carrier bag full of cleaning products. I have lemon-scented Cif, Mr. Muscle, Mr. Sheen, Windolene, Spring Fresh Bleach and a new packet of J Cloths. If I've nothing else to do then I might as well give the bookshop a bit of a spring-clean. Now I'm sitting having my first tea break of the day and enjoying a mint chocolate Green & Black's bar while I contemplate where I should make my start. I'm also thinking about Jacob and how much I enjoyed his company, although because I'm at work I am, of course, thinking about him less than the job in hand.

"We have got a cleaner," Mr. Jesmond Junior assures me as he eyes my bag of household products suspiciously. "Mrs. Franklin comes in once a fortnight, regular as clockwork. You don't have to worry yourself with this."

It's nowhere near enough and, looking at the state of the place, I think she must curl up in the corner and go to sleep while she's here. "I'd like to do it," I say brightly. "It will help me to get my bearings too."

"I have to go out today," he tells me with a worried frown. "Will you be able to manage on your own?"

"I'll be fine," I answer.

"What if we have a sudden rush?"

If a coach party arrives wanting armfuls of books on military history then I'll fly into a blind panic. But I think I'm pretty safe. "Everything will be shipshape by the time you return."

The voice goes down to a whisper. *"Hospital."* And again, Mr. Jesmond points to a part of his blue polyester trousers that I'd rather not look at.

An hour later and we've had another cup of tea and I've shared my Twix with Mr.

Jesmond, but I still haven't launched into spring-clean mode. I'm just working myself up to it. Mr. Jesmond takes his hat and his coat from the stand, fusses about as he prepares to leave. "You will manage?" he asks for about the twentieth time.

"No problemo," I reply for the twentieth time. "You won't know this place when you get back."

I ignore the look of terror on his face and sigh with relief when he closes the door behind him. Sinking back into my chair, I wonder whether I should phone Crush — a quick, friendly call, just to see how he's getting on without me — but then I think that he might be getting on very well without me. Tracy Whateverhernameis might be a fabulously efficient personal assistant, excellent at typing, filing things, getting coffee and other personal assistant–style duties. I bet she doesn't have a great stash of chocolate like me though. I turn away from the phone, thinking if Crush was missing me, he could have called. I gave him my mobile number and what have I heard from *him?* Not a sausage.

The clock is ticking loudly in the silence, so with an unenthusiastic puff, I haul out my hoard of cleaning products. Turning myself into Kim and Aggie from *How Clean*

Is Your House? seemed like a good idea when viewed from a distance. Now the moment of truth is upon me, my initial verve appears to have deserted me. Still, better to do this than have another day of sitting at the desk twiddling my thumbs.

I've brought rubber gloves and an old apron specifically for the purpose and, as my first step, I don those. There's a line of bookshelves down the center of the shop, laid out widthways, one after the other, so I decide to work my way from the front to the back. I'll try to dust and polish all the bookshelves today so that Mr. Jesmond can see I've made an impression, and then tomorrow I'll turn my attention to the kitchen, loo and I'll possibly even venture into the stockroom — even though there seem to be intermittent scrabbling sounds coming from its depths.

I get a bowl of hot water from the manky kitchen and dampen a J Cloth. There's a tall stepladder on wheels which Mr. Jesmond must use to reach the top shelves and I pull it to the front of the first big set of bookshelves, preparing to clean the first section. *Weapons and Warfare.* Climbing up the ladder, I grab armfuls of books and bring them down to put them on the desk, trying to leave them in some semblance of order so that I don't have to do too much sorting out of the titles when I put them back. Clearly, Mr. Jesmond has his system and I have mine. The books are thick with years of undisturbed dust and, whatever else Mrs. Franklin does, it doesn't involve brandishing a duster in anger. Before I've unloaded even half of the shelves, the air is thick with black particles and my eyes are itching and my nose is running. Wiping the shelves with my damp J Cloth, I hope to stem the toxic cloud of dust mites. Then I dry the surfaces and give them a polish with Mr. Sheen. That looks much better. There are actually beautiful mahogany shelves under all the grime. I stand and admire my handiwork. It's nice to get stuck in and do some physical labor — every now and again.

I decide to take all the books off the first shelf at once rather than do it in sections as was my original plan. I could accidentally knock dust onto my newly cleaned area if I do it piecemeal, and then I'd have to do it all over again — turning it into a Sisyphean toil. I'm sure that was the name of the guy who was forced to push the boulder uphill for all eternity by some other bloke (who's probably now working for the management at Targa), but my knowledge of Greek mythology is distinctly shaky.

The next half hour is spent bringing down more piles of books and stacking them up on the desk, which is almost completely obliterated. I do hope that the coach party doesn't arrive now — ha, ha! All these steps must be good for my thighs; all this humping of books, good for my biceps. Before long, I'm going to need some more chocolate to recuperate.

Another half an hour and the bookshelf is empty. All the books are heaped on the desk and on the floor in front of it. I'm feeling a lot of empathy with Sisyphus. The only place I haven't thoroughly cleaned is the very top of the bookshelf. I hitch up my apron, take my damp cloth and climb to the top of the steps again. It's a bit of a stretch to reach the top and I'm hanging onto the ladder while I lean out. Then my mobile phone rings. It's buried amid the mountain of books on the desk and I'm sorely tempted to leave it chirping away. But then I realize that it could be Jacob or it could be Crush and I try to dive for the phone before it switches to voicemail. Hurtling down the stepladder as fast as my little legs will carry me, I dash across the floor dodging the piles of books and lurch for my phone, which I manage to grab with one hand just as it cuts off.

In my haste, I somehow knock into one of the stacks of books, which then knocks into another and then another, then the pile of books knocks into the stepladder, which sways alarmingly. Dropping my phone, I make a lunge at the stepladder to stop it from toppling over. I fail miserably and watch as it hits the first bookshelf, that too starts to wobble, and I make a grab for that to try and keep it upright. It teeters and totters, slipping from my grasp. The sides are so nice and shiny where I've just polished them and I simply can't get a grip on anything. The weight of the shelf clearly reaches its maximum topple allowance and it groans as it leans over and knocks into the next shelf, scattering books and dust to the four corners of the shop. That bookshelf, in turn, topples and groans and I hear myself groaning as I lunge forward again as that one too clatters into the shelf behind it. On and on it goes until all six of the towering bookshelves are upended, lying drunkenly on the floor like a Saturday-night binge drinker. Books lie splayed out, pages open, like dogs do when they want to show off their undercarriages. Dust as thick as smoke fills the air. The clock's ticking loudly in the ensuing quiet.

I walk back to the desk, climbing over the

detritus of damaged books until I get to my phone once again, huffing to myself as I look at the *Missed Message* display. Punching the buttons, I bring up the message. There's a voicemail from Marcus. I can't even bear to listen to it now. Then my fingers hover over the keys. Maybe I will. *Lucy*, he says. *I'm missing you desperately.* How often have I longed to hear these words? *I know that you said you were seeing someone else, but please call me. Please.* How am I supposed to respond to that?

There's another groan from the back of the shop and something else that shouldn't, crashes to the ground. This is all Marcus's fault.

While I'm still in my catatonic daze my phone buzzes. There's a text. This time, it's from Chantal. SERIOUS CHOCOLATE EMERGENCY! MEET ME AT NOON. Staring at the wreckage around me I think that I might very well have my own serious chocolate emergency to contend with.

CHAPTER
THIRTY-NINE

"The guy from the hotel called me," Chantal explains. "At home. Ted took the call."

We all gasp collectively. Chantal's robber is phoning her. Ohmigod. Our friend is pale faced and looks strained. There's a tremor in her voice.

"I guess he got the number from my cell phone when he stole it."

"Bloody hell, Chantal." That's my useful contribution.

She stirs her coffee and then lifts the cup to her lips. Her hand is shaking and she puts the coffee back on the table. Chocolate Heaven is always busy at lunchtime, but we've somehow managed to bag the sofas and have got them all to ourselves. I think Clive should put a RESERVED sign on this corner just for us, but we've yet to get him to agree. We've all managed to get here within half an hour of receiving Chantal's frantic text and we're all in a cozy, conspiratorial huddle with a heap of chocolate muffins between us. Except the subject matter isn't quite so cozy, it seems.

"Did he tell Ted who he was?"

"No." She shakes her head. "He just left a number and said we'd met at the hotel in the Lake District."

"Thank goodness."

"The inherent threat was there though, Lucy. I feel as if it was his warning to me that he could just as easily have spun Ted some line about what had happened. I was lucky."

"Couldn't you just tell your husband everything? Honesty is often the best policy," Autumn suggests.

"Not in this case," Chantal says flatly. "How could I fess this up to Ted? He'd divorce me."

We all exchange worried glances.

"Did you call him yet?" Nadia wants to know as she wipes away a hot chocolate froth moustache.

"I rang him this morning," Chantal says. "It was horrendous. He sounded so flaky, I wondered how I'd even considered letting him come near me, without even . . ." She tails off, but we all know exactly what she means.

Autumn shakes her curls. "Promise me

that you won't do this again," she says. "Sex with strangers is fraught with danger. You should think about getting your chakras cleansed to dispel the negative energy."

She should get her head examined, is what I think!

Chantal has the good grace to look embarrassed. Her cheeks flush bright red. "He says that I can have all of my jewelry back —"

"That's good news, isn't it?" Autumn chips in.

Chantal gives her a weary look. "If I give him the thirty thousand pounds it's worth. He must have had it valued."

"People like that have fences," I say, proving that I had a misspent youth watching gangster movies. My friends look at me blankly. "Not garden fences. Fences for stolen goods. Shifty guys in back-street pawnshops who'll move their ill-gained booty for a cut of the loot. Chantal's jewelry will probably be melted down or will be winging its way to some dodgy dealer in the depths of Europe if she doesn't comply."

"This is not making me feel happier, Lucy," Chantal says.

"Sorry."

"Thirty thousand pounds is an awful lot

of money." Autumn tells us what we already know.

"That will buy his silence too," Chantal adds.

"Bloody hell." I'm just chock-full of sparkling advice today. Maybe it's the vision of all those destroyed books and bookcases that are blocking my mental processes. I cannot possibly tell them about my earlier employment mishap. There are far more pressing matters than me having totaled a bookshop and more than likely being out of work. Besides, I might cry and I have to stay strong for Chantal. She needs us now.

Nadia looks shamefaced. "But I've taken all your money, Chantal," she says. "What will you do?"

Chantal's face takes on an expression of grim determination. "I'll have to find some more."

"You have to take it back. I can get a loan . . . or something." Even Nadia doesn't look convinced.

Chantal puts a hand on her arm. "I wouldn't hear of it," she says. "Your need is still greater than mine. I got myself into this goddamn stupid mess. I'm the one who has to get me out of it. I'll find the money somehow."

"But you can't buy your own jewelry

back." Autumn looks horrified. "It belongs to you. This must be the time to go to the police."

"No," Chantal says firmly. "I can't do that."

I have to agree with her. Watch any film about handing over ransoms and the minute the police get involved, it all goes to pot. The baddies always get away with the loot. There'll be blood up the walls and dead bodies everywhere. Metaphorical, if not literal. It seems that Chantal has the chance to get her jewelry back and she has to take it. "Can you realistically get the money though?"

"It's going to be tough," she confesses, wringing her hands together. "Getting thirty grand out of the account without Ted noticing took some skill and dexterity. Another thirty?" Chantal shrugs. "I don't know. That would pretty much clean us out. We have paintings that might have to take a hike. Maybe I could tell Ted that I've sent them for restoration, put them in the attic, eaten them. I'm a resourceful woman. There must be something I can conjure up. And fast. I have to call the sleazeball back today and let him know what I want to do. He wants me to meet him at a hotel to exchange the cash for my jewels." Chantal huffs expansively. "Yeah, sure."

A lightbulb pings on in my brain and I shoot upright in my seat. "No. No. You must do it," I say. "Arrange to meet him — not in London though. Somewhere out of the way. Out in the country, maybe." My friends look at me expectantly. "I have a *great* plan," I say excitedly. "Chantal, we are going to get your jewelry back."

They stare at me agog, and even I wonder why I'm behaving like someone out of *Ocean's Eleven*.

CHAPTER FORTY

Mr. Jesmond had to be taken straight back to hospital suffering from shock after he'd seen the state of his bookshop. He'd returned expecting everything to be "ship-shape" and instead his ship had been well and truly scuppered. The agency tell me that he's okay now, no permanent damage, and they've sent him some fruit and flowers which they're billing me for. I think that's only fair. They've also sent two girls to his bookshop free of charge for the next week to sort out the mess. One of them used to be a librarian, so I think everything will work out okay. Except that now I haven't got a job or even an agency. Office Goddesses — clearly coming to the conclusion that I was an Office Demon — invited me to leave their books even though I explained how it had all happened and how I'd started out with only the best of intentions.

This morning, I registered with another

agency and I'm hoping that they don't take up references from Office Goddesses otherwise I am up shit creek sans the proverbial paddle. I've spent the morning with a big sheet of paper spread out on my living room carpet hatching out a cunning heist plan for the members of the Chocolate Lovers' Club — *Operation Liberate Chantal's Jewelry.* I'm chewing my pen, pacing the floor and scratching my head in the manner of all Hollywood master criminals. I'm thinking of getting a white, fluffy cat. Not having planned my own robbery before, it's proving somewhat tricky, but I think that I've now got everything in place. I wanted to meet the girls at lunchtime to go over my idea, but everyone's busy today. The Aggrieved herself, Chantal, is on an assignment. A very secret one, by the sound of it, as she was rather cagey about telling me where she was. Nadia has a job interview and Autumn is trying to improve the tortured lives of the druggies of this world — her own brother included. Now it's fast approaching lunchtime and I have nothing to do and no food in the house, unless you count heaps of chocolate, and as I have eaten little else these last few days, I think it's time that I had something more nourishing and wholesome. Fruit, veg, lentils —

some farty food. I'm sitting here eating my own fingernails and wondering what to do.

I could go to the gym and work out — but I dismiss that thought straightaway. I don't need to punish myself today; losing my job was punishment enough. I need something or someone to give me a bit of love or comfort. There are some times — only very, very occasional — when chocolate just isn't quite a good enough substitute for human sympathy. I could give Crush a call, but then I'd have to tell him about the Jesmond bookshop incident and that I don't now have any discernible work, and he'd laugh his head off and it would be all round the Targa offices before teatime. Maybe I'll call him when I've got my career back on track again. Sometime in the next millennium, then.

I could also call Jacob and see if he's free. But guys get spooked about that sort of thing, don't they? If you've only had a couple of dates and then you start phoning them out of the blue they think you're turning into a bunny boiler or want to marry them or, at the very least, meet their mother.

Or I could call Marcus. Just for old times' sake. Even though, technically, it was his fault that I've lost my job. My fingers hover dangerously over the buttons on my mobile.

It would be a shame after five years in a relationship if we couldn't even remain friends, don't you think? That would be a total waste of our time together. If you don't forgive someone their misdemeanors, doesn't it leave a black mark on your own soul? I'd like to avoid that, and if one small call to Marcus would do it, then I think it would be worth the risk. I press in his number and take deep breaths as I hear it ring. I hope that he doesn't read too much into this. He shouldn't. Besides, he called me first.

Marcus looks so handsome and my heart squeezes when I see him, even though I've firmly instructed it not to. He's wearing a charcoal gray suit, a white shirt and a deep pink tie. I like a man who is easy enough with his masculinity to enable him to wear pink. I'm waiting outside his office, and when he swings out of the revolving door, he takes my hand and kisses me on the cheek.

"It's good to see you," he says, while I can only wonder why I've chosen to ring my ex-boyfriend at a time of crisis. Particularly when he's the cause of my crisis. I guess familiarity sometimes doesn't breed contempt, it breeds comfort.

Still hand in hand, we head for a café with

tables outside in the shadow of St. Paul's Cathedral. The tattered pigeons peck around our feet, strutting their stuff as we each order grilled vegetable and mozzarella paninis and a glass of red house wine.

"I thought I'd *really* blown it last time," Marcus admits. "Thanks for giving me another chance."

"This isn't another chance," I tell him firmly. "I called you because I've had a truly terrible week and I wanted to be with someone I'm . . . *comfortable* with. Nothing more."

Marcus grins at me in his heart-stopping way. "Comfortable?" He laughs. "It's a start, I guess. I'll settle for that."

The waitress brings our food and drinks. Marcus slugs back a gulp of the warm red wine and bites decisively into his sandwich. When he looks back at me, he's suddenly serious. "I don't know what's wrong with me, Lucy. Really, I don't. When we're like this together I think that nothing can compare to our relationship. I love you — you have to believe that. But then, when we're all settled and get too *comfortable,* I start to think about marriage and kids and cozy domesticity for the rest of my life, and I panic. That's what makes me do the things I do. It's as if some sort of safety valve blows. Every time that I do it, I know that I've made a monumental mistake —"

"But it doesn't stop you from doing it."

He shakes his head.

"The thing is, Marcus, if I keep taking you back after you've made one of your 'monumental' mistakes I'm going to end up as one of those sad women who writes to agony columns. *'Dear Cathy, My husband can't stay faithful to me. I still love him. What can I do?'* Or I'll be on some talk show, sobbing into a handkerchief with a caption that says in capital letters LUCY'S HUSBAND CHEATS ON HER!"

"So, you *can* see yourself married to me?"

Now it's my turn to laugh. "I used to be able to, Marcus. I'd love to get married and have children, I can't deny that. I'm happy being single, but I don't want to be on my own forever. With you, I have the worst of both worlds. I'm in a constant limbo, never quite knowing whether I'm back on the singles scene or in a relationship."

"I want to get married and have kids too," he says. "Eventually. Our industry has a terrible track record, though. Without exception, every guy in our office who's been married is now divorced. Some are onto their third or fourth wife — their third or fourth set of kids. They spend their weekends on the motorway shuttling between families for their two-hour access visits, then spend their afternoons hanging round McDonald's. I don't want to be like that. Is it so wrong that I want to make absolutely sure before I sign up for the whole package?"

When put like that, it's hard to argue against.

"We're still young, Lucy," Marcus continues. "Do we need to rush this?"

"We've been together for five years." Mostly. "If you don't know now, then the chances are that you never will." I sigh and finish my wine. "I feel as if I'm getting too old for all of this emotional turmoil."

Marcus looks stricken. "What can I do to prove that it's you that I want to be with?"

Stop sleeping with other women would be a good start, I think. But I don't voice this. Instead I sigh wearily and say, "I don't know." I'm too exhausted to deal with a relationship discussion today. This isn't what I'd planned. But then what exactly am I doing here? "I think it's all a little late for this conversation."

"Don't say that."

I make to stand up. "I should go."

"Don't!" Marcus begs. "Stay. Please stay."

Reluctantly, I settle back in my seat.

Then he becomes animated. "I know." He clasps the sides of his head as if he's had a brain wave. "Move in with me. Move into my place. Permanently."

My face must register the shock I'm feeling. All I wanted from Marcus was a glass of wine and a few jokes. *Maybe* a bit of flirtation and *possibly* some begging. But this was definitely not on the cards.

"Seriously," he says, and an excited note trills in his voice. "We can do this, Lucy. Let's give it a try. Now. I'll blow out work this afternoon."

I'm rooted to the spot. Is this really coming from Marcus the workaholic? Bunking off work? He must have had a personality transplant.

"We can move your gear in straightaway," he continues. "Why wait?"

I can feel my eyes blinking rapidly and my mouth has dropped open as if it plans to speak, but it's currently refusing to say anything. Marcus wants me to move in with him! Could we do this? Can I give my straying boyfriend yet one more chance? He's never asked me to move in with him before. This is certainly a step change. I've never been a live-in lover and the thought of it seems so tempting. That would surely mean that he's beginning to embrace the concept of "forever." You don't ask someone to move in with you if you're planning to have a parade of different totty through your flat every night, do you? If I'm around all the time, when would he get the opportunity to be unfaithful? Perhaps taking our relationship to this new level could be just the thing we need. I suddenly feel feverish and a shiver of anticipation or fear or something travels through my body. Could we *really* do this?

Just as a response is formulating in my stunned brain, Marcus claps his hand to his forehead.

"We can't," he says with a miserable puff of air. "We can't."

"Why? Why?" I was just getting used to the idea. "Why not?"

"All the floors are up at the moment in the flat."

"The floors?"

"I've got a problem with the drains or something," he says. "The whole place stinks. Dyno-Rod has been in, but they couldn't find the source of the smell. I've had to get a team of builders in. They've ripped up the floors in all of the rooms, but they can't find a thing."

My cheeks turn the livid color of Marcus's tie. "Really?"

"It smells like rotting fish," he continues. "You wouldn't want to be there. Not yet. I'm considering moving into a hotel myself until they find out what's wrong. But as soon as they're finished . . ."

I press my lips together and consider what to say next. So nearly, I was caught up in Marcus's enthusiasm. So nearly, I was thinking about what to pack. So nearly, I was forgetting all about Jacob and how much I like him. So nearly, Crush was simply my boss. So nearly, I was forgetting how truly awful Marcus has been to me.

"It's prawns," I say.

Marcus looks suitably puzzled.

"The smell," I confirm. "It's prawns. They're in your sofa and under your mattress."

My ex-boyfriend looks horrified. "You put them there?"

"I did."

He stares at me for a moment, not speaking. His jaw is working away as it does when he's anxious. "You did it at the same time as you filled all my suits and shoes with mashed potatoes?"

"Yes."

Marcus rubs a hand over his brow. "I suppose I should laugh about this."

"That would be one way of handling it," I

say, my face on fire.

"But I can't," Marcus tells me. "It's cost me thousands of pounds so far. The sofa's being replaced next week because the lipstick stains wouldn't come out of it. Remember? Where you wrote MARCUS CANNING, YOU ARE A CHEATING BASTARD in very large red letters on the white leather?"

I remember.

Marcus is clearly shell-shocked. "Did I really deserve this, Lucy?"

"At the time, I thought you did."

"And now?"

"Now, I'm sorry."

Marcus stands up. "I have to go back to work."

"Marcus," I say. "I *am* sorry. I just wanted us to be friends."

He doesn't say anything. He simply walks away from me.

The waitress comes to tidy away our plates. "Would you like anything else?"

"Can I see the dessert menu, please?"

She brings it and I order not one, but *two* whacking great slices of chocolate fudge cake.

CHAPTER
FORTY-ONE

When I meet up with the good ladies of the Chocolate Lovers' Club the very next day, I have finalized the details of my master plan. We've all managed to get together after work and, if this were a pub, we'd be having what is commonly known as a "lock-in." The CLOSED sign is on the door and it's just our select band enjoying the delights of Chocolate Heaven. Rain is lashing at the windows and Clive has lit some candles on the coffee tables to ward off the encroaching grayness. I tell you, if I were a billionaire, I'd pay Clive and Tristan to keep this establishment for my own exclusive use.

"We're going to get your jewelry back," I tell Chantal in a voice that sounds full of grit and steely determination.

They all laugh at me.

"And how are we going to do that, honey?" Chantal wants to know as she breaks a bite-sized piece off the edge of a chocolate chip cookie.

"Like this." I hand out a sheet of instructions to each of them.

Today I've been temping in some anonymous, gray office building where no one spoke to me. A truly terrible place and so, to make it more bearable, I spent the day finely honing the details of *Operation Liberate Chantal's Jewelry* and printing out copies for all of us.

They all scan the pages. Now they're not laughing quite so much.

"You're serious," Autumn breathes.

"Deadly."

"Do you really think we can do this?"

"I think we have to try," I say firmly. I'm comforting myself with a bar of single Madagascar, this time the milk chocolate rather than the dark. It's creamy, sweet and buttery like the chocolate I remember from my childhood. My mother used to be a chocoholic — it was she who started me out on this path. Then she decided that she needed to be size eight to have a fulfilled life and now lives on nothing but lettuce. It makes her completely miserable, but she does have the body of a malnourished child that she so desired. I think, at her age, I'd settle for fat and happy.

Normally, my scrummy Madagascar cures

all ills, but currently it isn't helping to quell my nerves. I am, however, committing sacrilege by washing it down with a cup of tea. That's not hitting the spot either. "There's no way we can let this guy get away with extortion," I say grumpily.

"I'm going to struggle to get the money for him in the timescale he's demanding," Chantal admits. "Maybe Lucy's right. Perhaps we do have to try this."

"Has he contacted you again?"

"This morning," she says. "I managed to stall him, but I think I'm running out of time."

We're even beginning to talk like heist masters. One of us will soon be saying, "Hang him on a meat hook!" in the style of Vinnie Jones. We all look around at each other nervously.

"Is this actually legal?" Autumn asks in a whisper.

"We're only taking back what belongs to Chantal," I say with a conviction that I don't necessarily feel. Perhaps our methodology treads a fine line. "I can't think of any other way."

"I'm in," Nadia says. "When are we going to do it?"

"As soon as possible." I look at Chantal for confirmation. She nods.

"I'll need plenty of warning as I'll have to make sure that Toby can look after Lewis. I don't want the extra expense of a babysitter if I can avoid it," Nadia tells us.

George Clooney never had these problems. Did he ever have his heist foiled because one of his *Ocean's Eleven* gang couldn't get a babysitter? I think not.

"Are you okay with your role?" I ask Autumn.

Her eyes are wide with fear. "I'll do it," she says. "For Chantal."

"Why are we going out into the countryside to do this?" Nadia wants to know.

"I thought it would be better off our own patch." *Lock, Stock and Two Smoking Barrels*–speak again. "Neutral territory." Though, come to think of it, I'm not sure why we *are* going all that way. Could we do this closer to home? Quite probably. But I won't mention it now though, as they might start to doubt the validity of the rest of my cunning plan.

"This is a lovely hotel," Nadia says as she glances at the name of the venue. "Toby and I got the brochure a few years ago. We thought we might have a few days there for our anniversary, but it was so expensive. I've always wanted to go there."

We all give her a look.

"Sorry," she says. "This isn't a picnic. I know that."

"We'll need some sleeping tablets too," I say, thinking out loud.

"I can supply those," Nadia says, and we all swivel our eyes in her direction, wondering what our friend is doing with a stash of sleeping tablets. I thought it would be Autumn who'd have access to the drugs. "How many do you need?"

"How many does it take to drug a conman?" I realize that this might be an inexact science.

"We don't want to kill him," Autumn interjects anxiously.

"I do," Chantal says bluntly.

"Tell me the name of the tablets," Autumn says. "I'll ask Richard for his advice. He knows all there is to know about prescription drugs as well as illegal ones." I knew her contacts would prove invaluable.

"Do you think the boys will be up for this?" I cast a surreptitious glance in the direction of Clive and Tristan.

"We can only ask," Chantal says. "Hey, guys," she calls over. "Wanna be involved in a robbery?"

Laughing, the guys then come over to sit with us, bringing a bottle of chocolate vodka and half a dozen shot glasses which they proceed to hand around. The smiles fade from their faces as they realize we are, indeed, planning "a job" and that they're required to be part of it. Six shots of chocolate vodka later and, surprisingly, they both agree.

"Call him," I instruct Chantal — also fortified by the vodka. "Call the bastard. Fix up the meet. Tell him to book a room as you don't want to do the exchange in a public area."

"Are you sure?" she says.

"It's our only chance."

Chantal takes a deep breath and flicks up a number on her mobile phone. We all lean in toward her, straining to hear the conversation. "It's Chantal. We'll meet at the Trington Manor Hotel," she tells him without preamble. "You know it? Fine." Our friend also sounds a little slurry. "Friday, nine o'clock. Book a room. I want to make sure we do the exchange in private."

"It's on," she says when she hangs up. Then she downs some more vodka.

"Friday, nine o'clock," I repeat, and we all nod in agreement. "We'll meet up here after work. It'll take us a couple of hours to drive there." Chantal is the designated driver, seeing as she has the poshest car. And Autumn and I don't actually have cars at all. Doing a heist on a bike just isn't the ticket. So that's it. We're sorted.

Clive pours us all another shot. We click our glasses together. And, despite the fact that I realize it doesn't have quite the same ring as *Ocean's Eleven* does, I say loudly, "To the Chocolate Lovers' Club Four!"

CHAPTER
FORTY-TWO

My new agency — Office Angels — has fixed me up with another job. This one is great. I'm working for a trendy designer with her own small fashion house in Covent Garden. Is that not cool? This is definitely more me than fusty old bookshops and sterile computer companies. I've been here for two days already and I haven't broken a thing. Really. All the mannequins in the showroom are still wearing their ten grand evening gowns as they should be. None of the gowns are ripped. None of the models have lost arms, or other body parts, inappropriately. The floor is highly polished oak and I haven't fallen over on my backside yet in the style of a circus clown. I think this really could be a turning point for me.

The designer's called Floella and she's a tiny Jamaican woman with a wicked temper and a penchant for Jimmy Choo shoes. She's just starting to make her mark on the fashion world and is now dressing a smattering of A-list celebrities. Already, I've whipped her filing cabinet into shape and have booked in an array of appointments for clients who want fittings for couture gowns. I know exactly how she likes her decaffeinated coffee — three drops of soy milk and a grain of sugar in the morning; unadulterated black in the afternoon. In making myself completely indispensable, I hope that she'll keep me on as a temp or even elevate me to the position of permanent staff.

Today, however, my mind is on other things. Tonight is the night of *Operation Liberate Chantal's Jewelry* and my nerves are already making me jittery. I've drunk about ten cups of nondecaf coffee and I've eaten the equivalent number of Green & Black's chocolate bars from my rapidly dwindling stash — taking great care not to get any chocy fingerprints or smudges on the evening dresses or on the bolts of fabric in the cutting room, of course.

"Lucy," Floella says into my daydream. "You need to drive these dresses to the Landmark Hotel for the fashion show later today."

Drive? Me? Is this in my job description?

"I'll give you a hand to load up the van."

Van? I have passed a test to say that I can

drive, but that was many, many moons ago. And it was in a car. Does she not realize that it's about five years since I've driven anything and I've never, ever been in control of anything anywhere near as substantial as a van? Clearly not. Living in London has meant that — like everyone else — I go everywhere by bus or Tube. What shall I do? I can't really fess up at this late stage that I'm not really *au fait* with this driving lark. Floella might pack me off back to Office Angels without a qualm. There's no choice. I have to do this.

With a feeling of impending doom, I go out to the back of the premises — somewhere that I've not yet had to explore — and there is a big — humongously big — white van. Oh good. I'm about to become white van woman. But part of my being indispensable means that I mustn't protest, so, alongside Floella, I load up a heap of dresses. They're all wrapped in tissue and plastic and we put them on specially designed rails in the van. The very *big* van.

"Take your time," Floella says, perhaps sensing how nervous I am. "My assistant, Cassie, is already at the hotel. I'll call her to say you're on your way."

"Right."

Then she disappears back into the shop

and leaves me at the mercy of the van. I climb in. My goodness. It feels more like a pantechnicon, sitting up here in the cab. I sit there trying to fathom how everything works, until I can put off my departure no longer. This looks a bit more tricky than the Vauxhall Corsa in which I had my last motorized outing. My hands shake as I jam the thing into gear and, very tentatively, ease it out into the back street behind the shop, trying very hard not to scrape it on the brick walls that are hemming me in on either side. Already my face is hot and my armpits are attractively sweaty.

I swing out into the London traffic and make my way toward the Landmark Hotel, letting all the cars weave around me while I keep a steady course. I don't swear — well, except to myself under my breath — I just maintain a death grip on the steering wheel and make slow progress toward my destination. By the time I've reached New Oxford Street, I'm actually starting to relax. My back isn't quite so ramrod straight and my knuckles have an element of blood in them once again. When I turn into Tottenham Court Road I take my eyes from the road, only momentarily, and someone walking along the pavement ahead of me catches my eye. It's Jacob. He's striding down the street, attaché case in hand, slipping through the crowd. And then I remember that I'm supposed to be going to a charity do with him tonight — it could even be the one that I'm delivering the dresses to. I'd completely forgotten! In my haste to organize the jewelry heist, my hot date had gone right out of my mind. How could I have forgotten this? Am I mad?

Stopping at a pedestrian crossing, I watch as Jacob approaches. This would be the ideal opportunity to cancel my date and explain my predicament, although I realize that I can't really tell him that I'm masterminding a robbery instead of attending a charity event with him. What would he think of me? I try to wind down the window, but I can't work out how to get the passenger side down. The driver's window opens as I press all the buttons, even though that wasn't what I intended. Nevertheless, I shout out of it: "Jacob! Jacob!"

Oblivious. I could ring him, but I don't want to get nicked for using my mobile phone while driving. The lights on the pedestrian crossing change to green and the traffic behind me starts to show its impatience with a cacophony of hooting horns. I start to move away, but then decide that I really do need to catch up with Jacob now.

What if I can't get hold of him this afternoon? He'll think that I'm terrible. Decision made, I slam on the brakes and slew the van to the side of the road. But then there's an almighty crash and the van is shunted forward from behind. "Oh, bugger!"

The hooting starts afresh. I jump out of the cab and rush toward the back of the van. Another identical white van is embedded deeply into the back of it. His bumper looks relatively undamaged, whereas my van is distinctly crumpled. The back doors have broken open and are both smashed in. There are two guys in the other van; they've both jumped out into the road and one is ranting at me.

"Can't you look where you're going, darlin'!" he says. "Fuckin' idiot!"

Jacob is walking past. He hasn't given our little accident another glance.

"One second," I say to the guy. "One second. I'll be back in just a jiffy."

I leave him openmouthed while I sprint after Jacob, shouting at the top of my voice: "Jacob!" We can sort out the insurance details when I get back — this is far more important. The guy drove into me, it's clearly his fault. "Jacob!" Is the bloke deaf? Has he got an iPod on? Whatever the reason, he doesn't turn to acknowledge me.

Instead, he swings into the reception of a big hotel. I chase after him, having to wait for a party of businessmen coming out of the revolving door before pushing through and into the hotel. Inside, there's no sign of Jacob. I scour the seated groups of men in reception, but he isn't in any of them. Then I see him, crossing toward the lifts, and I shout out, "Jacob!"

He looks up and seems startled when he sees me, as well he might. There's another handsome young man with him. He's tall and dark, wearing a beautifully cut pin-striped suit.

"Sorry, sorry," I say breathlessly. "I've just had an accident. When I saw you passing, I jumped out of my van."

"Accident? Van?" Jacob says. "Are you all right?"

"Yes, I'm fine. The van's a bit dented." A lot dented. "It doesn't matter," I tell him. My eyes fall on the other guy. What a stunner. "I'm sorry," I say. "You're going to a meeting. I don't mean to keep you."

"No worries," Jacob replies, but I see him glance apologetically at the other man.

"Could I have a quick word?"

He looks at the guy for approval. The man nods, rather curtly, as he checks his watch.

Jacob steps away from him and takes me by the elbow until we are out of earshot.

"I can't make tonight," I tell him. "I'm really, really sorry. I have something else planned."

"Oh." He looks genuinely disappointed.

"I feel dreadful," I babble on. "If I could cancel this, then I would. But I'd be letting my friends down."

"I understand," Jacob says.

"What about the rest of the weekend?" I ask. "Maybe we can meet up then. I'm free."

"I'm busy," he says with a rueful smile and I can't tell if he's spinning me a line. Does he think that I'm cooling off on him? That's certainly not the case.

"We could do something during the week." I'm sounding desperate and I don't want to.

"I have to work most evenings."

Most evenings, but not *all* of them. I don't know what else to suggest.

"Tuesday," he says, coming to my rescue. "I have a couple of hours around six. Do you want to meet after work at Chocolate Heaven?"

"Yes," I say, pouncing on what seems to be my one chance. Bang goes my yoga class again. "Tuesday's fine."

Jacob's colleague over by the lift is fidgeting overtly. "I have to go," he says. "We have clients waiting."

"See you, then." I lift a hand and wave at his disappearing back.

I dash out of the hotel and sprint down the road. When I get to the end, I can only see one van. Bugger! The bastards have driven off. They had better have put their insurance details under my windscreen wiper or something. Damn. I never thought about them doing this. You can't trust anyone these days. What am I going to tell Floella? How can I explain the crump in the back of her van? Will she take it better than Mr. Jesmond did the dramatic re-arranging of his shop? No. She'll more than likely have a fit with one of her Jimmy Choo-ed feet in the air.

The doors at the back are flung open and I'm probably going to have to find something to try to tie them together as I can't drive along with them flapping apart like that. I tut. This is not turning out to be a good day. I hope that tonight's festivities go a bit better than this has done. If bad luck comes in threes then I still have one more calamity on its way.

When I look into the back of the van, I realize what that calamity is. All of Floella's couture evening gowns have gone walkies.

There's not a single one left. The back of the van is a cavernous maw. The guys who crashed into me must have decided to help themselves to the dresses. Here's me thinking about my very own heist and, in the meantime, I've become the victim of one. I stare at the empty space and wonder what on earth I'm going to do now. Floella is not going to like this. She's not going to like it at all.

Feeling stunned, I walk to the front of the van. Then I see that there's a piece of paper under one of the windscreen wipers. My spirits lift. Perhaps the guys have left a contact address after all. Perhaps there's a perfectly valid reason why all the dresses are missing. Perhaps they've taken them somewhere for safekeeping. I pull the paper out with trembling hands. It's a parking ticket. A bloody, bloody, bastardy parking ticket. That's four bits of bad luck in one day. Surely that's my quota filled. Then I realize that I've kissed another job good-bye — this time a great one — and my tally racks up to five.

CHAPTER
FORTY-THREE

"So this is your little empire?" Richard said. He didn't sound impressed.

"Yes." Autumn had somehow managed to persuade her brother to come into the drug rehabilitation center and find out a bit more about the KICK IT! program she was involved in. With luck, it might make him want to KICK IT! himself. Autumn had arranged for him to drop into a class so that he could meet some of their clients too. It was politically incorrect to call them kids, even though that's what they all were. Damaged, messed-up kids. She thought that by bringing her brother in here, letting him get to know some of the kids whose lives had been blighted by their addiction, then it might well bring him back down to earth with a bump. He would see the end product of the harsh reality of drugs, rather than the glamorous images of cocaine that existed in the media world and in which he seemed fervently to believe.

"What a dreary place," he said, turning his nose up at the flaking paint on the walls. "I'd want to take *more* drugs if I was forced to spend my days in a hellhole like this."

It was true that the accommodation for the center was more utilitarian than attractive. The Stolford Centre was never destined to win any design awards. It was housed in an old red-brick school, built in the 1930s and now crumbling nicely. A substantial part of their budget was spent in simply keeping the place from falling apart. But the rooms were large and well lit, even though the central heating was clonky and the original wooden floors were pitted and dirty with age.

"Yes," Autumn said. "You're very lucky that Daddy can pay for you to go to a rehab clinic that's more like a five-star hotel, but that's not the case for the majority of drug addicts."

"Oh, don't go on, Autumn," he moaned as he trailed behind her. "I keep telling you, I'm not an addict. I'm a recreational user. I have this completely in control."

"Sure." Her brother had been cowed for a day or two after his close shave with Daisy, but now he was back to his most obnoxious self. "Isn't that how everyone who dabbles with drugs starts out? In control?"

"It's cocaine," he said petulantly. "That's all. You can get high for the price of a cup of cappuccino, these days. Even the government is downgrading the classification of drugs. They aren't the evil things they were. They're a lifestyle enhancer. We use them like after-dinner mints, darling. Just pop a few lines around with the coffee to give you a little buzz. There's no harm in it."

"I hate to contradict you, Rich, but you've lost your job and your home. The way I see it, you seem to be in a very bad place."

"Look, this is all very well, sis." He swept his arm around the hallway. "I really admire the fact that you want to do good in the world. I'm sure all of these spotty teenagers appreciate it. I'm sure they see you as a lifeline, but I'm not the same as them. I'm a long way away from a cardboard box on a street corner." He gave a sneering laugh which made the hackles on Autumn's neck rise. Only Richard could feel so smug about his current situation.

"That's because you have a sister with a smart flat in Sloane Square," she reminded him. "Where would you be otherwise?"

They turned into the art room, which was her domain. None of the clients had arrived yet, but the walls were decorated with their creative efforts. Some had made stained-glass mirrors with various creatures — cats, puppies, dragons — curled contentedly in one corner. Wobbly lines of lead beading betrayed the unsteady, inexpert hands of the artists. Others had been more adventurous, making colorful panels for doors that they would probably never see. Wonky suncatchers adorned the windows, sucking in the few rays of light that made it to this, the north side of the building, casting rainbows of red, yellow and green over the tidy workbenches. This is where she loved to be. This was where she was happiest. And if she could make some small difference, bring a bit of color or satisfaction to the lives of her charges, then it was all worthwhile.

Richard slung his arm round her shoulder and gave her a conciliatory squeeze. "This looks great, Autumn. You really do a good job."

"I try to," she said honestly. Though sometimes she wondered whether it was enough. "My students will be here soon."

On cue, a desperately thin girl with Goth clothes and a mop of dyed black hair complete with pink stripes came in — Tasmin, a sixteen-year-old crack addict. She'd been with Autumn for nearly a year and clearly had a talent for working with the glass. Tasmin had moved on from stained glass to use the kiln, searching out the most vibrant colors and blending them together to form delicate pieces. While the others were often champing at the bit to go home as they toiled to make a decent mosaic tile or a trivet, Tasmin would spend hours absorbed in twisting fine silver wires around the glass pieces she'd created and fired to make fashion pendants and earrings — pretty pieces of jewelry that she sometimes sold to friends for a few pounds. It gave Tasmin a great boost to her confidence and it thrilled Autumn too. She couldn't help but admire the girl's skill and determination. It was good to see one of her students doing so well. Tasmin truly had promise and yet every day was a struggle for her. With better education, Autumn was sure that Tasmin would have been quite academic — she was certainly bright, even though she sometimes let her quick wit and her foul mouth run away with her. Autumn just hoped that she could break free from her current social circle, the friends who seemed to be doing all they could to hold her back. On too many days, Tasmin turned up with bruises. None of the girls here really liked her. Underneath all the Goth makeup she was a very pretty girl: They were jealous of her looks and the fact that she'd found at the center that she had a talent for creating jewelry.

It was only a pity that Tasmin couldn't produce a diamond ring and a few bracelets, so that they wouldn't have to go through with their plans for tonight. Autumn felt sick with nerves when she thought of what her evening held for her. There was no way that she was going to tell Rich about it. The less he knew of her involvement in this hare-brained scheme, the better. She was supposed to have asked his advice about the number of sleeping pills that they might need to send their prey into a deep slumber, but they'd have to guess and hope for the best. Autumn's stomach lurched again. Lucy was convinced that they could pull it off together. Autumn was less sure. She just hoped that they didn't get caught.

"Hello, Tasmin."

"Hi, Miss." Autumn had tried to get her students to call her by her first name, but most of them still insisted on calling her "Miss."

"Meet my brother, Richard."

Tasmin glared at him suspiciously, taking in Rich's black cashmere sweater and his designer jeans, just as he was taking in her ripped fishnet tights and her Dr. Martens boots.

"I'd better go," Rich said uncomfortably. "I've got things to do."

Autumn wondered what they might be. At least her brother had agreed to come here, but it seemed that actually spending time talking to the kids was going to be a step too far. They weren't the easiest bunch of individuals to get close to — goodness only knows, it had taken her long enough. Now, very occasionally, Tasmin might bring her in a bar of chocolate since she'd discovered Autumn's particular weakness. It was the closest she ever got to open admiration or thanks.

Her brother kissed her on both cheeks. "See you later."

Autumn nodded. She longed to tell him to be careful, but knew that would only irritate him. Every time she wanted to talk to her brother, it felt as if she were walking on eggshells. She wished that Addison had been here to do it for her. He might have been able to convince Richard to get involved with the project somehow, where she had failed.

As Rich reached the door, a tall youth pushed past him, also giving her brother the wary once-over. This was Fraser, a heroin addict and small-time pusher from the age of fifteen. He ran a group of pickpockets who, in order to feed his habit, regularly relieved the shoppers on Oxford Street of their hard-earned cash. Despite his many problems and failings, he was a funny, likeable boy with a strong Glaswegian accent that she couldn't understand half of the time. She wasn't sure what he got out of her creative glass classes, but he was one of her most regular attenders. Perhaps it was something to do with the fact that he had a soft spot for Tasmin. Fraser was currently struggling with a suncatcher destined for his mum's kitchen window at her home back in his native Scotland. It was perhaps as well that Richard hadn't stayed around for long. There were things that she needed to discuss with Fraser that would be better kept from her brother's ears.

"Wotcher, Miss."

"Hello, Fraser." Tasmin, she noted, was busy taking her latest project from the kiln. Autumn beckoned him to one side. "I need to ask you a favor."

The boy leaned on the workbench next to her. "Ask away."

Autumn lowered her voice. "Can you teach me how to pick pockets?"

If Fraser was taken aback by her unusual

request, he didn't register it. Instead, he nodded confidently. "Aye."

"Good," she said. "I have to learn before tonight."

CHAPTER
FORTY-FOUR

I'm wearing my strappy little black dress and my killer heels in the manner of all femme fatales. I'm shivering from head to toe, even though I feel as if there's a furnace raging inside me. My cheeks are burning hot when I desperately need to look cool, calm and collected. I've had a bad day though and my poor old wits are rattling round my brain.

Needless to say, I was sacked from my lovely, lovely job as soon as I returned to the shop to tell Floella my sorry tale. I'm left with cheeks burning with shame and my ears ringing to the sounds of Floella threatening to "sue my bony white ass." For a moment, I experienced a surge of joy because, not in my wildest dreams has anyone ever called my ass "bony" before. Then she phoned the police and that soon wiped the smile off my face. I'm currently trying to stay out of reach of the long arm of the law, not run straight into it. As if I haven't enough to worry about. I kept out of Floella's way until the police arrived and I gave my statement to the boys in blue — who weren't overly interested in Floella's plight or mine — while trying not to look criminally inclined. I last saw her screeching down the phone at her insurance company as, thoroughly humiliated, I crept away. So — my brief interlude as a personal assistant to a soon-to-be famous fashion designer has come to an abrupt end and, as well as being a bag of nerves, I'm feeling pretty miserable too.

All the members of the Chocolate Lovers' Club are gathered at Chocolate Heaven on the night of *Operation Liberate Chantal's Jewelry* and we're all showing signs of anxiety. The shop is already closed and we're the only ones here. Chantal is pacing the floor, Autumn is chanting some sort of hippy mantra, while Nadia nibbles alternately on her nails and a chocolate chip cookie.

Chantal is dressed completely in black and — apart from the fact that the balaclava with little holes for the eyes is missing — she looks as if she's about to do a bank job. Nadia is wearing jeans and a thuggish-looking jacket. Autumn has gone for a floaty, cheesecloth number and her mass of titian curls are tumbling loosely over her shoulders. I suppose I should have remembered to tell her that if she possessed anything with a vaguely brutish air then she should have worn it. I suspect that not many thieves wear folksinger-style clothing. Still, it will have to do. Time is pressing on and we need to be too.

Our accomplices, Clive and Tristan, are lurking behind the counter looking furtive. As we approach, they put a small box of chocolates on the counter.

"There are twelve chocolates in here, Lucy," Clive tells me with a serious expression on his face. "Half are drugged with Nadia's sleeping tablets. We've used our house blend of rare Brazilian beans and have crushed the pills into the ganache. They're flavored with green and black cardamom pods which give a spicy, fresh taste with a hint of smokiness. So they should be undetectable."

Mmm. The chocs sound great. "How will I know which is which?"

"The clean ones have two ridges on the top. The dodgy ones have three ridges."

"Clean — two. Dodgy — three."

"That's right."

"Could I just have one to taste?" My hand

is slapped away.

"No," Clive says sternly. "Exercise restraint. And remember, don't get them mixed up. You're not the one we want flat out on the ground."

"I hope we've got the quantities right," Autumn says nervously. "I couldn't bring myself to ask Richard, he'd have been too suspicious."

"We used our judgment," Clive tells us.

"Based on what?"

"Blind ignorance," he tells me. "Hopefully, we've put enough sleeping tablets in the chocolates to knock anyone out for a while."

"What if you've put too many in?"

We all glance at each other anxiously.

"I'm sure it will be fine," I say. When I'm not sure it will be fine at all. "Thanks for making these, guys."

"I just hope we won't be enjoying prison food with you at some later date." Clive clasps a hand to his bosom in a dramatic fashion.

"We'd better be making a move," Chantal tells us. Her face is white and drawn. "Let's get this jewelry on you."

I stand stock-still while she kits me out with all the bling she's bought. A diamond look-alike necklace, two bracelets and a pair of earrings with what could easily pass as two-carat diamonds dangling from my lobes. "Does it look real?" I don't have a mirror to check out my appearance.

"I hope so," Chantal says.

"Pour plenty of drink down him," Nadia advises. "Then he won't notice."

We're hoping that there's a lot that our target won't notice.

"You look fabulous, Lucy," Autumn breathes.

"Thanks." I wipe damp palms down my dress. "Let's hope that someone else thinks so too."

"Wish us luck, boys," Chantal says.

Clive and Tristan come from behind their counter and they hug us tightly as if we're departing on a perilous journey. Which, in some ways, we are.

"Come back safely," Tristan says. I do believe there's a tear in his eye.

"We will," I say stoutly. "This will be a walk in the park."

"Before that we have a long ride in the car," Chantal says, looking pointedly at her watch.

As the ringleader, I'm supposed to instill confidence into my cohorts, so I throw back my head and square my shoulders. "Let's do it, then," I say.

CHAPTER
FORTY-FIVE

I don't know what sort of car Chantal drives, but it's something expensive and it smells like a new leather handbag. We're sitting in a tense silence, each of us lost in our own thoughts. I am clutching the box of doctored chocolates in my lap and I'm going over and over the role I have to play when we get to the hotel. Quite frankly, if I do it again, my head will more than likely explode. I bet the others are doing the same.

"Put something perky on the CD player, Chantal," I say. "This might be serious, but there's no need for us to be miserable."

Chantal slips in a CD and "Walking on Sunshine" rings out. In no time we're all singing along with Katrina and the Waves as the last of the day's sun starts to sink toward the horizon. How can we be gloomy with such a great tune belting out? I pull a family-size packet of Maltesers out of my bag — they have been kept nicely chilled by

Chantal's air-conditioning — and hand them around. The mood in the car lifts instantly. Clive would be distraught to see that we were using mass-produced chocolate as our comfort, but sometimes the old favorites just hit the spot like nothing else. A tube of Smarties can transport me back to my primary school in a flash.

We're onto "Mr. Blue Sky" by the Electric Light Orchestra by the time — an hour later — we reach Trington Manor Hotel. We collectively take a deep breath as Chantal swings in through the tall, wrought-iron gates, the tires of her car crunching on the gravel. It's nearly showtime and Chantal cuts off the Electric Light Orchestra in their prime.

Trington Manor Hotel is one of those five-star establishments with its own health spa in situ. I gaze in awe at the sheer splendor of the place. It is *so* out of my price league, you can't begin to imagine. I fantasize about going to places of this caliber — and not in this particular context. It was always my hope that Marcus would whisk me away to somewhere like this and propose to me. Ah, well. Another dream turned to dust. The night is starting to settle in as we drive up toward the palatial front door.

"My knees are shaking," Chantal confesses. "I feel as if this guy didn't just rob me. I feel as if he *violated* me, even though it was all my own stupid fault."

I give her knee a gentle pat. "We'll get your jewelry back for you," I tell her. "That will at least be some compensation."

"I hope we can pull this off," she says with a nervous tremor in her voice. This is the first time I've ever seen Chantal's confidence falter.

Turning in my seat, I address the girls. "We all know what we've got to do?"

Nadia and Autumn, in the backseat, nod vigorously. There's a huge artificial lake outside the front of the hotel and a veritable pod of verdigris dolphins leap from the splashing fountain at the center. We slow down to look for a parking space.

Then Chantal gasps in horror. "That's him," she says, pointing ahead of her. "That's him. Getting out of that white Mercedes."

We all gape. My word, he's a handsome beast. Tall, dark, athletically slim. Classic good looks. No wonder our friend was so keen to get him into her bed. Maybe she shouldn't be regretting that part of their encounter quite so much. From this distance he doesn't look like your typical villain. He looks like a babe. There's a black leather attaché case in his hand and he strides toward the hotel.

"I'd like to bet a hundred bucks that my jewelry's in that goddamn case," Chantal observes bitterly.

"Keep your money," I advise. If all this goes pear-shaped, she's going to need every penny she can lay her hands on.

"We could just run him over now and grab it," Nadia suggests.

"That would definitely get us arrested," I point out. "Besides, we don't know for sure that Chantal's stuff is in there."

Our target has parked facing the lake and we stay still until we've watched him go up the broad sweep of steps and into the hotel's reception, then Chantal slots her car in opposite his.

My role in this heist is to spend my time chatting him up in the bar, giving the rest of the girls time to go up to his room and retrieve Chantal's jewelry. At the moment, that doesn't seem too bad a prospect. The drugged chocolates are for emergency backup. The idea is that Chantal is going to be late for her rendezvous with him, but that I'm going to seduce him in the bar and be so charming that he'll be happy to spend time with me instead. I can do that. Piece of cake. How many men in the past have failed to fall for my feminine charms? Actually, let's not go there, otherwise my knees will shake even more than they are now. The ten tons of bling that I'm wearing are supposed to act as an extra lure.

"What's his name?"

"He's calling himself John Smith." Chantal raises her eyebrows at me.

"He could have had a sexier pseudonym."

"I guess so."

Consulting my checklist, I say, "Phone him and tell him that you're going to be late and that you want to meet him at the bar."

Focused, Chantal punches in the number and then says briskly, "I'm running late. I'll be there as soon as I can." She sounds as if she means business. If I wasn't her friend, I'd be scared of her. "Meet me at the bar. Then we'll go to your room to do the swap."

She hangs up. "I hope that bastard doesn't think there's anything else on offer."

Swiveling round in my seat again, I face Nadia and Autumn. "Are you two ready?"

"As we'll ever be," Nadia says solemnly.

"Autumn, we're on first," I remind her — not that she probably needs me to. Our hippy little friend has a look of grim determination on her face. Autumn has the unenviable task of picking John Smith's pocket to lift his room key — a skill she has acquired just this afternoon. I hope she's a good student and that her criminal client has taught her well, as there's a lot resting on this. While I'm at the bar with him, the girls are going to rifle through his room and then, if all goes well, hotfoot it out of there with Chantal's jewelry. Simple.

"I could do with some Dutch courage," Autumn says with a wavering voice.

I hand her another Malteser.

"Thanks." She munches it gratefully.

Then I decide that I need some fortification too and eat the rest of the Maltesers in double-quick time. "Good luck everyone," I say and, before my nerve fails me, I hop out of the car.

CHAPTER
FORTY-SIX

Autumn and I enter Trington Manor Hotel just in time to see the receptionist at the front desk hand over a plastic key card to Mr. John Smith. "Room 270," the woman says in a bright singsong voice. "It's up on the second floor. I hope you enjoy your stay with us, Mr. Smith." We hang back so that he doesn't see us.

This place is very opulent. The carpet must be four inches thick and we both sink deeply into it as we try to saunter in with a casual air. My vertiginous heels make me totter dangerously. Autumn fares better in her rope espadrilles. There's a scattering of color-coordinated sofas in tones of burgundy and midnight blue, shadowed by large bay trees in terra-cotta pots. We watch our target closely as he takes his room key and heads toward the lift. This guy looks every inch the sophisticated businessman — confident and poised. Who would have thought that he was a thief and a conman! But then looks — especially good ones — can be deceptive.

When our Mr. Smith is safely on his way to his room, I phone Chantal to let her and Nadia know the current status, a rush of adrenaline surging through my body. This is really quite exciting in a totally nerve-wracking way. It makes me realize that up until recent weeks, my life has been relatively uneventful. "He's checked in," I say, using a stage whisper, "and has taken the case upstairs."

I hang up. Turning to Autumn, I tell her, "I'll go through to the bar now and get myself ensconced. You loiter here until Mr. Smith comes back down. If you go over by that rack of tourist info and pretend to be interested in it, then you'll have a perfect view of the lifts."

Autumn nods at my suggestion. She looks worried half to death.

"You'll be great," I say reassuringly. Giving her hand a quick squeeze for support, I leave her in reception and go through to the bar area.

It's fairly quiet in here. On the far side of the room, the lone barman is aimlessly polishing glasses behind the curved mahogany bar. A pianist with more talent than enthusiasm tickles out some bland standards at a baby grand over in the corner — "My Way" is his current offering. It makes me remember my date at the Savoy with Jacob. And to think that I could be out with him now, rather than doing this. . . . I sigh and continue my perusal of the bar area. There's a small group of businessmen huddled together on two facing sofas enjoying a raucous laugh. A few couples are dotted around at the other tables. I walk across to the bar, my legs suddenly reluctant to move, feeling as if all eyes are on me. Trying to be as poised as possible given the circumstances, I slip onto a bar stool, choosing one that gives me a clear view of the reception area and Autumn, who's still lurking behind her potted plant and the tourist information. She's feigning being engrossed in some sort of pamphlet, but surreptitiously gives me the thumbs-up when I look toward her.

"What can I get you, madam?" the barman asks and I snap my attention back to him.

"I'd like a bottle of champagne, please."

"We have a good Duval-Leroy."

"That's fine." I have no idea whether it is or not.

"Just one glass?"

"Two," I say. "I'm expecting a friend."

The barman puts two champagne flutes in front of me and then disappears, only to return a moment later with my bottle of fizz. Popping the cork with an expert twist, he then lets the champagne froth into one of the glasses. He raises an eyebrow at me with his hand poised over the other glass.

I shake my head. "My friend hasn't arrived yet."

He leaves me to my drink and I take the glass, sipping self-consciously. Putting the drugged chocolates on the bar in front of me, I pat them affectionately. These babies are our insurance policy. I go over it in my mind: two ridges — clean, three ridges — doctored. Actually, I could really do with one of these yummy chocolates right now. Just a look wouldn't hurt, surely.

The lovely scent of vanilla and spices wafts out when I lift the lid. Mmm. These will go very nicely with this glass of champagne. My hand hovers over them, but I pull it back reluctantly. As Clive said, I must exercise restraint. Instead, I knock back my glass of champagne, enjoying the instant buzz that the bubbles give me. It seems a bit stupid now, but I haven't eaten all day — not even much chocolate — as a bad case of nervous tension had tied my stomach into knots. Consequently, the fizz goes straight to my head. My cheeks instantly flush pink and I'm sure my pupils dilate to cartoon dimensions. The barman comes and pours me another one before I can protest. I down that too and he refills my glass once again.

Sitting at a bar on your own is a soul-destroying experience and I'm glad that I'm not really waiting for a friend who isn't going to turn up, otherwise I'd be truly depressed. A few of the businessmen are giving me lingering glances and I try not to acknowledge them as I wouldn't want to be in the middle of being flirted with by someone else when our target arrives.

After what seems like an eon, the lift doors open and Mr. John Smith — him of the terrible alias and nasty postcoital habits — strides out. I crane my neck to make sure that I can see Autumn. She grabs another handful of tourist pamphlets from the rack and she's now striding out too, heading him off. Midway across reception, she bumps into him and he knocks all of her tourist information to the floor. He bends down to help her retrieve it, amid a flurry of apologies from Autumn. I can't hear what they're saying from here, but it looks as if Autumn has stage-managed this very well. My friend fusses with the literature, picking it up only to drop it again.

Eventually, he stands and hands the pamphlets he's collected back to her. He's smiling in a very charming way. Autumn has gone all coquettish. And I can only sit here and hope that she's achieved what she set out to. They part and Mr. Smith continues his journey toward the bar. Autumn continues toward the front door of the hotel. When she gets there, she holds up a key card in her hand and gleefully waves it in my direction. I try not to make my jubilant smile too obvious. She's done it. Autumn has picked his pocket. A bubble of relief bursts inside me and I chuck down some more champagne in celebration. This is going *so* well.

"What's a pretty thing like you doing sitting here alone?" a voice next to me asks and I spin round to see one of the businessmen leering in my face.

This is disastrous. I see John Smith taking up a seat at the end of the bar. It's him I need to be chatting me up, not this clown! "I'm waiting for a friend," I say through gritted teeth.

"Mind if I wait with you?" he says, lurching toward me.

"Yes," I say.

"Go on," he slurs. "Let me buy you a drink."

"I already have a drink. Thank you." Go away, Idiot Features!

I can see our target looking over at me. There's a frown on his brow.

"A little drink wouldn't hurt." Clearly there's some pride at stake here, as he knows that his colleagues are all watching him and are now tittering between themselves.

"Thanks, but no," I reiterate firmly.

He's gone crimson in the face and isn't looking too happy.

"You heard the lady." The voice comes from the end of the bar. It's a very Clint Eastwood type of statement and I'm surprised that it's coming from Mr. Smith. A chivalrous conman. Now there's a thing.

"What's it to you, mate?"

"The lady said no," Mr. Smith says calmly. "Leave her alone."

The guy looks like he might square up for a fight, but then one of his colleagues, perhaps sensing that the situation has gone beyond a bit of fun and could well turn ugly, comes across and pulls him away. The man looks embarrassed. "Sorry," the guy says. "He doesn't mean anything by it. It's just the drink talking." Maybe this is a regular occurrence.

I try to look forgiving, but my hand is

shaking. "That's okay."

He steers his colleague back to the group and they all laugh uncertainly.

This is it, I guess. Now or never. I lift my glass in a toast and tilt it toward Mr. Smith. "Thanks," I say. "For speaking up on my behalf."

"No problem." He's certainly handsome. If I wasn't here on *Operation Liberate Chantal's Jewelry* and didn't know all about his dark side, then *I'd* be seriously tempted to chat him up if I saw him in a bar.

"Perhaps you'd join me in a glass of champagne?" I suggest. "Then you can protect me while I wait for my friend."

He smiles at me, but hesitates. Panic pulsates through me. Supposing he doesn't bite. What then? I give him a flash of my whopping fake diamond ring. And I don't know if that's what swings it, but after a moment, he leaves his own seat and takes the one next to me instead. "I'm also waiting for someone," he says. "Business."

Don't I know it, buddy! I hastily splash some champagne into a glass and hand it to him so that he feels beholden to stay with me for one drink, at least. Will that give the girls enough time to go up to his room? I wonder. I have to keep him here for as long as I can. "Lucy Brown," I say. If he can have an unimaginative alias, then so can I.

"John Smith," he replies.

As we clink our glasses together, I see three little heads pop up by the window. My friends are staring through the glass, checking whether the next part of the plan is working. Now all I have to do is be witty, charming and alluring for as long as it takes them to search through his stuff. I'd better have some more champagne. Their heads disappear.

"To my knight in shining armor," I say.

We both laugh and I think, You bastard!

CHAPTER
FORTY-SEVEN

Chantal, Nadia and Autumn waited until the receptionist's back was turned and then they hightailed it across the lobby and jumped into the lift as the doors opened. Autumn clutched her booty. "It's Room 270," she said to the other members of the Chocolate Lovers' Club.

They were all nervously chewing their lips, the sound of Norah Jones and "Come Away With Me" singularly failing to soothe them.

"I hope that this doesn't take long," Chantal said, her breathing shallow.

At the second floor, the doors opened again and they cautiously peered out. No one was around. They kept close together as they went along the deserted corridor looking for Room 270. As soon as the room was located, they slotted in the key card and slipped inside. The room could have been in any hotel, anywhere in the world; it was clean, nicely appointed and utterly bland.

Mr. Smith clearly had made little use of the facilities on offer. The tray of tea-making accoutrements lay untouched, the television was still displaying *Trington Manor welcomes Mr. Smith* on the screen.

Chantal experienced a flashback to when she'd been in a hotel room with this guy. Her stomach turned at the thought of it. All she wanted to do was get her jewelry back and get out of here. John Smith's attaché case was sitting on the dressing table, beside the television. She went across and grabbed it, flinging it to the bed. They all gathered round expectantly. But when Chantal tried to click open the clasp, she found it was locked. "Goddammit!" She banged her fist on top of it.

"Here. Let me see if I can open it," Autumn said. "I had quite a few useful lessons from my client this afternoon."

Their friend pulled a metal nail file out of her handbag and worked it into the lock of the case. A minute later, the lid sprang open. Even Autumn looked surprised.

"Fantastic," Chantal cried, and she rifled inside the case. There was nothing there. No sign of her necklace, rings or bracelets. Just a copy of that day's *Financial Times* lay untouched, pink and perfect, in the bottom. At that moment, she could have wept. This was a stupid, half-baked idea and she should have known that it would never work.

"We have to search the whole room," Nadia said. "And quickly. I don't know how long Lucy will be able to entertain that guy before he gets suspicious."

"We'd better get a move on," Autumn agreed.

"What about the room safe?" Chantal suggested. "I'll check that." She opened the wardrobe doors in succession until she located it tucked at the back of one of the shelves. The mini-safe was, of course, also locked. She turned to Autumn. "I don't suppose safe breaking is part of your repertoire too?"

"Yes, although we only covered a few of the basics," her friend admitted without irony. "We ran out of time."

Nadia and Chantal laughed. Autumn grinned proudly.

"You are a dark horse, Autumn," Nadia said. "I hope they don't hear about your newly acquired skills down at the Green Party. You'd be blacklisted."

"Give me a few minutes with this," she said, "while you two go through the rest of the place."

So, Autumn concentrated on opening the safe, while Nadia and Chantal checked under the bed, under the mattress and the pillows, in all of the cupboards and the drawers, behind the curtains, on top of the pelmet and in the waste bins. They even checked whether Chantal's jewelry had been taped to the bottom of one of the chairs. But they could find nothing.

"It's *got* to be in the safe," Chantal said. "It can't be anywhere else."

"Come on, Autumn," Nadia urged. "Do your stuff." They both sagged back onto the bed and sighed deeply while they waited.

A few moments later, Autumn said, very quietly, "Bingo."

"Good girl!" Chantal exclaimed, and they both dashed to the safe where their friend was still crouching.

"Nothing," Autumn said with a disbelieving shake of her head. "Absolutely nothing."

"Where the hell can it be?"

"Could he have it in his pockets?" Nadia asked.

"I didn't feel anything when I was searching for the room key," Autumn said. "But maybe I struck lucky. I didn't have the time or opportunity to give him a thorough frisking. He could very well have them hidden about his person."

"Damn." Chantal sucked in her breath. "Now what do we do?"

CHAPTER
FORTY-EIGHT

"I'm giggling like a loon. I've hitched up my dress so that I'm exposing a fair amount of thigh and I've let my shoulder strap slip seductively down my arm. For the last twenty minutes or more, I've been trying to pour as much fizz as possible down Mr. John Smith's neck. We're onto our second bottle — at his insistence and expense. He seems to be holding his drink very well, whereas I am three sheets to the wind.

The businessmen have just departed and the couples have started to thin out too, everyone heading back to their rooms until there are very few of us left in the bar. We're on the point of exhausting general chitchat, particularly as I'm lying through my teeth to him. He thinks I'm a marketing executive for a computer company and I think he's a smarmy bastard. Mr. Smith is now glancing surreptitiously at his watch and I get the feeling that my charming company is starting to pale. Though I've noticed that he's clocked my fake diamonds more than once. I give him another flash of my twenty-one-diamond tennis bracelet — worth a princely £21. My mobile rings and I fish in my handbag for it. This had better not be my mother phoning to tell me about some row she's had with one of the neighbors or the new shade of her hair color or how hot it is in Spain compared to Britain or how little she's had to eat today. All of them form the usual topics of her conversation. And her timing is appalling. Why does she always seem to catch me in the middle of a crisis? I answer briskly. "Hello?"

"It's Chantal," my friend says in a whisper.

I turn away from Mr. Smith, so that he'll have no chance of catching even a snippet of our conversation. This had better be good news.

"We need more time," she tells me. "We've searched his room from top to bottom and the goddamn jewelry isn't here. It's not in the case. It's not in the safe. Can you check out his pockets?"

Looks like the drugged chocolates are going to be needed, after all.

"Will do," I reply. "Talk to you soon." I hang up and then give a nonchalant little shrug to Mr. Smith. "My friend doesn't seem to be coming." Seem comes out as "sheem." I try to appear coquettish. "Looks like I'm stuck here alone."

"Yes," he agrees.

I eye the chocolates on the bar and pull them toward me, flirtatiously. "I think we should eat her birthday present."

"I'm not a big chocolate fan," Mr. Smith tells me.

Is this guy a complete arsehole? Not a chocolate fan? My brain is having trouble computing that. But then my brain is having trouble computing much at the moment. Good grief, I shouldn't have got tucked into the fizz quite so enthusiastically. I feel dizzy.

"But these are not just any old chocolates," I slur at him. If only he knew. I open the box and take one out, holding it temptingly in front of him and I lean forward so that it's hovering invitingly just above my cleavage and my fake diamond pendant. I go into Marks & Spencer advert mode. "Oh no. These are a taste of chocolate heaven. Especially handmade from the choicest beans plucked from a single plantation in deepest, darkest Brazil. They're filled with a rich ganache flavored with the best green and black cardamom pods, which give it a spicy and fresh taste with just a hint of smoldering smokiness." I try a bit of smoldering smokiness in my own voice. Clive would be proud of me. "Every bite is like a shuddering explosion on your tongue."

"You go ahead," he says, unmoved.

"They'd go wonderfully with this champagne." To prove it, I glug some more down.

"Don't let me stop you."

"It's not nice to eat alone." I try a pout. God, I've always been useless at this sort of vamp stuff. It's probably why I've stayed with Marcus for so long. Why didn't I nominate Nadia to play this role? She's sexier than I am. Everyone seems to be sexier than I am, at the moment! I hold out one of the three-ridged, drugged chocolates toward him. "Just a nibble."

His fingers snake lightly round my wrist as he guides the chocolate to his parted lips. I feel myself gulp. He's bitten it. Both the chocolate and my plan.

"Mmm," he says. "That is good."

I eat one of the two-ridged ones. They are very good. I have no idea how long the sleeping tablets in the chocolate will take to work and I want to get him away from the bar in case he passes out here.

"Why don't we move over to the sofa?" I suggest. "Make ourselves more comfortable." John Smith looks uncertain again.

Perhaps he's thinking that he ought to hedge his bets in case Chantal doesn't show with the money she's supposed to be bringing him. I stroke my £14.99 fake diamond pendant lovingly and flash my equally bling bracelet one more time. His eyes brighten. "Your business colleague will see us just as easily over there."

"I ought to call her," he says, a frown darkening his brow. "She's very late."

"In a minute," I suggest. "When we're comfortable."

We cross the bar, taking the champagne in its ice bucket with us and I choose a sofa in the corner of the room, facing toward the door. Sitting next to him, I angle my legs toward him, giving him plenty of good body language. I splash some more champagne into his glass and then offer the chocolates once more. Thankfully, without me prompting, he picks out a three-ridged one. Then, inching nearer to me, he turns the chocolate and offers it to me. Now what? I can hardly refuse, can I? Leaning forward, I bite the chocolate in half and say, "Mmm."

I hope that isn't enough to make me keel over. Mr. Smith pops the rest of the chocolate in his own mouth. If it were me, I'd stuff another chocolate straight in, but I try to leave a suitable interval before I pick up another one of the chocolates. I'm feeling a bit sleepy already, I think. Why does that half a chocolate seem to be working more quickly on me than it is on our target? I select another one of Clive's lethal creations. The ridges are starting to blur together. Is this a three-ridged danger zone or is it a two-ridged okeydokey one? This is getting harder. My eyes slide briefly into focus. It's a three-ridger — I'm pretty sure.

Mr. Smith holds up a hand. "No more for me."

"One for the road," I say, and before he can protest, I post it into his mouth. A lovely warmth rushes over me and I hear myself ask, "Is it hot in here?"

John Smith loosens his tie. "Yes," he says. "I think it is." And then, without further ado, he falls backward against the cushions. I wait for a moment, but there's still no movement from our prey. His mouth falls open slackly. He looks for all the world like he's having a nap after a particularly heavy Sunday lunch. Glancing round quickly, I check to see if anyone else in the bar has noticed him sink into oblivion. No. The barman's busy serving someone at the other end of the bar. There are only one or two other couples left. All's well.

Shaking my head like a dog shaking water

off its coat, I try to bring my own eyesight back into focus. Drink and drugs are a very bad combination. Particularly when carrying out an important heist. Our target is snoring gently. I snuggle up next to Mr. Smith, looking as if we're getting cozy. Then, while no one's watching, I rifle through his pockets. I check them all, even the ones next to his private places, which makes me grimace, but I can't find any trace of Chantal's jewelry. Where on earth could he have put it? Perhaps while he's drugged we could take him somewhere and torture him until he coughs. Then, even though I'm severely drunk and possibly under the influence of drugs too, I realize that I've possibly watched too many Hollywood movies.

CHAPTER
FORTY-NINE

I might not come up with the jewelry, but Mr. John Smith's car keys are in his pocket and I take those so that we can give his Mercedes a quick going-over. For good measure I take his mobile phone and his wallet too. Then, making sure that no one sees me, I arrange John Smith so that he looks as if he's having a nice nap and that he hasn't been drugged, robbed and thoroughly scammed.

Trying not to weave too much, I make my way out of the bar and out of the hotel doors. The fresh air hits me in the face like a wet fish. I see the lights on Chantal's car flash at me and, unsteadily, make my way over to them.

Chantal, Nadia and Autumn are huddled in the car. "Any luck?" Chantal wants to know as I slip inside next to her.

"He's sleeping like a baby," I tell them. "Clive's chocolates have worked like a dream."

"You're looking a bit squiffy yourself," Autumn observes.

My eyes are, indeed, rolling. "I had to eat some of the drugged chocolate," I say. "To make it look authentic."

Chantal nibbles at a nail. "And the jewelry?"

"No jewelry," I admit with a defeated purse of my lips. "I searched all of his pockets, but nothing. Absolutely nothing." I hold up the keys to his car. "I did get these though."

The members of the Chocolate Lovers' Club give me a round of applause.

"I don't know how long he'll be out for," I say. "So let's go and check out his vehicle." We all jump out of the car and head across to Mr. Smith's Mercedes. I hand the keys to Nadia, who is distinctly more compos mentis than I am.

She unlocks the car and slides into the driver's seat.

"Pop the trunk," Chantal instructs.

Nadia presses some switch or other and the boot lid swings up. Inside there's a classy leather overnight bag. There's also a small selection of ladies' handbags, most of them bearing designer labels: Prada, Chanel, Dolce & Gabbana. This guy obviously likes to steal from posh women. Good job I kept my twenty-quid vinyl Next job well out of the way.

"Wow!" Chantal says. "Would you look at this!"

"It seems as if you're not the only one he's conned," Autumn says.

Our friend rifles through the pile of handbags and then pulls one out. "It's mine," she says. "It's my bag." She opens it and searches through the contents. "No jewelry," she spits out, disappointment in her voice. "But my cell phone is here and my wallet." Inside the wallet, amazingly, all of her credit cards seem to be intact.

"I can't believe this guy didn't go on a spending spree," Nadia says.

"I had them stopped straightaway," Chantal says. "He wouldn't have got very far even if he'd have tried. It was the one sensible thing I did."

We all gather round as, next, Chantal lifts the overnight bag out of the boot. Our friend gazes round at us all before she unzips it. Then we hear a crunch of footsteps on the gravel and we all freeze. "Shit," Chantal mutters under her breath.

A torch shines our way. I can hear my heart hammering in my chest. What if John Smith's constitution is particularly resilient to sleeping tablets? That's something that I didn't take account of in my plan.

"Everything all right, ladies?" a voice asks. Then a uniformed security guard pops his head round the side of the boot.

"Fine," Nadia says. "We're fine."

"Are you checking into the hotel?"

"Yes," she answers again. Seemingly she's the only one able to find her voice.

"Make sure that you take all of your valuables inside. Don't leave anything in your boot," he warns us. "I patrol round here regularly, but we have had a spate of thefts. Can't be too careful."

"Thank you," Nadia says. "That's good advice."

"Do you need a hand with your luggage?"

"No." Nadia shakes her head. "We can manage. We're traveling light."

Traveling light? Women? He's bound to know that we're lying.

"You have a nice stay then, ladies." Clearly he doesn't know anything about the fairer sex. The security guard nods to us all and then goes on his way.

When he's out of earshot, we give an audible and collective sigh of relief.

"That was close," I say, doing my best George Clooney again.

"Let's get a move on and get out of here,"

Nadia chips in. Seems as if it's infectious.

Nadia keeps an eye out for the security guard while Chantal unzips the bag. Inside, there's a selection of pressed shirts, clean underwear and socks. "This is my laptop too," she says joyfully. "I'm sure it is. I scratched the case last year." Her finger caresses a hairline scratch across the lid. "I'd know it anywhere." She hands it to Autumn.

There's also a small leather pouch in the holdall. Chantal grabs it and, with only a moment's hesitation, pulls open the thong and lets the contents spill out onto her hand. Not one normally moved to high emotion, she promptly bursts into tears when she sees her cherished jewelry glittering back at her.

"We did it," she says with a quivering breath. "We damn well did it."

We all hug each other and do a silent happy dance in the car park in the shadow of the big Mercedes.

"I can't believe it," she says again. "We got it back. Everything. It's all here." Chantal holds up her whacking great diamond engagement ring and kisses it to her lips. "Thank you, girls." She wipes away a tear. "Thank you so much."

"We'll take all these handbags and try to

reunite them with their rightful owners," Autumn decides.

"Good idea," Chantal agrees.

"I don't think we've finished yet," Nadia says.

We give her a puzzled look.

"Don't you think this car would look perfect as an extra centerpiece for that lake?"

"Yes," Autumn says without contemplation. "It would." Clearly her afternoon of criminality has turned her politically correct brain to one of darkness and corruption.

"What about our security guard friend?" I suggest.

"We'd better be quick before he comes back," Chantal says.

"Let's do it, then." Checking that the coast is clear, Nadia slips back into the driving seat. She puts the car into neutral and takes off the hand brake. Chantal slips her jewelry back into the pouch and puts it into her pocket. We all stand at the back of the car and lean on the boot, putting our weight behind it. With a little synchronized grunt from the good ladies of the Chocolate Lovers' Club, the wheels move and the car starts to roll toward the lake.

We stand back as it then creates its own momentum and sedately eases itself down

360

the slope on course for the water. It picks up speed as it heads to the bank and then it catapults itself into the waiting blackness. There's a hearty splash as the two tons of car hit the water, followed by a lot of gurgling noises as it sinks slowly into the lake. It comes to rest with its boot sticking up heavenward.

"I'd really like to cheer," Chantal says.

The car glugs some more from the depths of its watery grave.

"We'd better get out of here fast," Nadia says, "before anyone notices."

"Or before our conman friend wakes up," Autumn says.

"I doubt Mr. John Smith will be overjoyed when he wakes up and I, for one, would rather not be around to witness it. "I also lifted his mobile phone and his wallet," I tell them with a certain amount of pride. "Hopefully, it means that he won't be able to contact you again, Chantal."

"Is his driver's license in his wallet?"

I flick through the pockets until I find it. "Yes. His real name is Felix Levare."

"Could be another alias." Chantal takes it from me. "But I'll keep that as a little extra insurance anyway," she says.

There's a wad of cash in the wallet which I help myself to. "This can all go to a deserving charity," I say, then throw the wallet and the mobile phone into the lake after his car. They also splash satisfyingly and then sink without trace. I press the money into Autumn's hands. "Take it and buy some chocolate for your druggie kids."

She takes the cash and pockets it. "Thanks."

Chantal hugs me tightly. "This really was a fantastic plan, Lucy. Well done. You don't know how much this means to me."

But before I can say anything momentous to mark the occasion, Nadia's sleeping tablets from the drugged chocolate finally kick in, my knees buckle and I slip into a deep and dreamless sleep.

CHAPTER FIFTY

Chantal dropped Lucy off at her flat. Her friend had slept all the way home from Trington Manor, snoring loudly in the back of the car. Their criminal mastermind had roused briefly as they'd arrived home, but Autumn had insisted on seeing her into the flat and had then tucked Lucy safely into bed, still in her strappy dress.

Chantal smiled to herself as she traveled across London. She was taking Autumn home first and then dropping Nadia back at her car, which was parked near Chocolate Heaven. This evening had been so successful, she could hardly believe it. Nestling in her handbag was all her lovely jewelry, safe and sound. What could have been a terrible catastrophe had turned out to be a complete triumph for them. She was so relieved that she could have hugged herself, and she owed it all to the resourcefulness of her companions in the Chocolate Lovers' Club.

Who'd have thought that she'd ever be blessed with such great friends? She felt very grateful to them all. From now on she would look after her possessions — and herself — much more carefully.

It was very late when she finally arrived home, but the lights were still on downstairs, which meant that Ted was probably watching television or listening to some music. After parking the car, she sat with the leather pouch filled with her jewelry on her lap. This had been a sobering lesson for her and she slipped her wedding ring and her engagement ring on with a happy sigh. Chantal was glad that her husband wasn't in bed yet, as she was feeling far too buzzy to be able to sleep. She wondered how actors after a particularly pleasing performance ever managed to come down. Her legs felt unlike her own as she climbed out of the car.

"Hi, honey," Ted called from the lounge as she went in through the front door. "You're late."

"I had a long drive back from my assignment," she said, which wasn't a lie. Ted just didn't know what type of assignment it had been.

"Can I get you something?" he said. "You look tired."

"No, not tired," she told him as she rubbed her aching neck. "I'm wired."

"How about I make you some herbal tea?"

"A big glass of red wine would work for me."

"Sounds good," Ted said. "I'll join you."

She threw her handbag onto the sofa, noting how good that felt, and then sagged down after it, stretching as she nestled into the soft cushions. Her husband was listening to Andrea Bocelli and the soothing sounds of the tenor's rich voice washed over her.

Minutes later, Ted came back with a decent bottle of Cabernet Sauvignon and two glasses on a tray, complete with a plate of cheese and biscuits, olives and a small bunch of white grapes. "That looks good," she said appreciatively.

Her husband sank down next to her. "I missed you tonight, honey."

Chantal smiled across at him. "I missed you too."

"Drink your wine, then I'll give you a neck rub."

She wondered why he was being so nice to her, but she wasn't about to question it and spoil the mood. *He* was acting if he was the one who had a guilty conscience rather than her, she thought. Chantal sipped her wine, spread some deliciously ripe Camembert cheese over a wholemeal cracker and bit into it enthusiastically. She needed chocolate too — creamy, milky and comforting. When she'd eaten her cheese, she'd see what there was in the kitchen. All day she'd been too anxious to eat — Lucy said she'd felt the same — but now she was ravenous.

Ted pulled off her shoes and slipped her legs across his lap, stroking her bare feet.

"Mmm," she said appreciatively. "That feels *so* good." Chantal hadn't realized how much tension her body was holding until he'd started doing that. She put her plate on the floor and let her head drop back onto the cushions. Her husband's warm hands slid up inside the leg of her trousers and his firm fingers massaged her tight calves. He'd always been great at massage, but it was a long time since he'd wanted to do this for her. For months he'd been avoiding any form of intimate contact — rubbing her feet, her legs or her neck included.

"Slip off your trousers," he said, and she registered the husky note in his voice with surprise. His eyes were dark with desire for her.

Ted helped her as she eased her hips out of her trousers, his hands traveling up to caress her thighs. His thumbs toyed with the lace at the edge of her panties, then he hooked his fingers round the sides and slid them off too. Her husband lowered his head and covered her stomach, her hips, her thighs with hot kisses. Chantal felt tears spring to her eyes. It had been so long since Ted had wanted to make love to her and she realized how dried up, how unloved that made her feel.

Ted unbuttoned her blouse, kissing her skin as he slowly exposed her to him, and then he eased off her bra until she was naked beneath him. He stripped off his own clothes and lay along the length of her, their limbs entwined on the sofa. When he eased himself inside her, Chantal was more than ready for him, and she gasped with pleasure as she pulled him to her. Their lovemaking was soft and gentle and had never felt sweeter.

Afterward, she pulled the cozy chenille throw from the sofa over them and they lay in each other's arms as they drank their wine and listened to the soulful voice of James Blunt softly serenading them. She didn't know what had caused this change in Ted, but she knew that she very much liked it. Why couldn't it be like this permanently? This was always where she wanted to be, Chantal thought. Lying in her husband's arms. Not in some hotel room with a guy she'd only just met, getting her brains fucked out with no emotional connection, no love, no caring. She leaned against her husband. "I love you so much, Ted."

"I love you too, honey." He stroked her hair absently. Then he cleared his throat and said, "You're okay with the fact that we didn't use protection?"

She nuzzled his neck. "I'll go to the drugstore tomorrow and get the morning-after pill." His body tensed against her and she looked up at him. "What?"

"This is always about what *you* want, isn't it?" he said.

Chantal was shocked. "I don't know what you mean," she said. "Is this about me getting the contraceptive pill? We don't want me getting pregnant. We don't want a family."

He sat upright now. "Don't *we?*" he said sarcastically. "Or is it just *you* that feels like that?"

"We've never wanted children," she countered. "We've talked about it often enough." Though not in recent times, Chantal had to concede. "We hate kids. We hate our friends' kids. You get completely stressed when Kyle and Lara bring their boys to our home and they put chocolaty fingerprints over everything and nearly burst your eardrums with their incessant noise. You have to take a handful of Nurofen the minute they've gone."

"Things change," he said. "And we don't talk about anything anymore. This whole relationship is run on your terms. With you it's 'my way or the highway.' Perhaps I've had enough of that."

"But that's because you avoid me," she said, pulling the throw up to her neck, suddenly embarrassed by her nakedness. "You avoid conversations with me. You avoid me in the bedroom."

"What's the point?" Ted said. "Why do we need a sex life when there's no point to it?"

"Do you mean that we shouldn't have sex unless we're making a baby?" She was stunned by his crazy viewpoint. Chantal touched his arm, but he shrugged her away. "Is that why you don't sleep with me?"

He stood up and pulled his shorts and his jeans back onto his long frame. Her insides lurched when she thought of where she'd been minutes ago — in ecstasy in his arms — and how they'd come so quickly to this.

"I find your voracious appetite a turnoff," he stated frankly, avoiding her eyes. "It makes me sick when I think that there's never going to be a purpose to it."

"When did you start to feel like this?" she wanted to know. "Why didn't you tell me?"

"I tried." Her husband sighed loudly and she could hear the pent-up frustration in his voice. "But you just don't listen to things you don't want to hear. We're not in a marriage anymore. We're two people conveniently sharing a house. I want more than that. I want a wife who cares about me enough to consider my wishes. I want a family, Chantal. I want kids of my own. And you don't."

"Let's talk about this," she said. "I love you."

"Sometimes that simply isn't enough," he answered.

CHAPTER
FIFTY-ONE

"So you couldn't stay away, Gorgeous," Crush says. He has his feet up on his desk and his hands are behind his head. There's a wide grin on his face. Which, strangely, seems to have grown more handsome since I've been away.

I'm standing in front of his desk feeling like a schoolgirl in front of the headmaster — a smug bastard headmaster. "You're the only people who will employ me," I admit. There's a truth in that statement that's too horrible to acknowledge. Targa, politically incorrect stress machine, is my spiritual home.

The only good thing about being back here is that I've already managed to persuade Dirty Derek from the post room to return all the other rescued handbags from our heist back to their original owners, courtesy of Targa's postal account.

First thing this morning, I loaded all of

the bags into a black bin bag — taking long-ing looks at a particularly fine Prada number that's probably worth a bob or two — and took a taxi so that I could bring our haul in. Every single bag had some identification inside, so I had a good old nosey at the details of the other women whom Chantal's gentleman thief rogered and relieved of their handbags. There are a wide range of gullible women out there and I hope that, like our friend, they've learned their lessons too. Derek's packing the bags up even as we speak. I might well bring him some choco-late to say thank you for his help.

I did briefly consider, after our ultra-successful operation to liberate Chantal's jewelry on Friday night, becoming a full-time heist master. This is a talent I didn't previously know that I possessed and some-thing, I'm not too modest to admit, at which I excelled. Surely criminality is a growth industry? There must be plenty of jobs I can do in the dark recesses of the underworld. I could just see my name on my office door — LUCY LOMBARD, MAS-TER CRIMINAL. I'd have to get some Mas-ter Criminal–style accessories like a slob-bering Doberman, a facial deformity or two and maybe some form of insanity involving grave mental disturbance. I'd need a lot of high-tech gadgetry. Particularly a machine for feeding do-gooders to hungry sharks — always handy — and a team of shaven-headed, muscled henchmen too. It's nice to dream. This job is sounding more attractive by the minute. However, I've decided to give going straight one last go.

I turn my attention back to Crush. It's humiliating being back here so soon, especially when Mr. Aiden "How Smug Am I?" Holby seems to be taking great delight in my discomfiture. Crush has an extensive selection of those executive toys on his desk, including a Newton's Cradle — and I feel moved to knock his balls together.

"The others don't know what they're missing," he tells me. He even tries to sound sincere.

I don't inform him that "the others" are now missing neatly organized rows of rare volumes about war, and a few racks of hideously expensive evening gowns. I don't tell him that I've been blacklisted by every major agency in town, and that a tearful, begging call to the hideous, gorgon-headed monsters of the Human Resources Department first thing this morning was required to get me this job back. I also promised them a very large box of chocolates from

Chocolate Heaven. Every week for the next month.

"I knew that Tracy would crack before long," Crush says. "Motherhood and working don't mix. The minute you drop a few kids, your brain shrinks. She was even worse than you."

I think he's being ironic, but I'm never quite sure. "Well," I say, "I'm glad that your expectations of me are so low. I hope to be able to fulfill them."

Crush laughs. "Have you brought chocolate?"

"Is Russell Crowe one hot Australian?"

"Good," he says. "My blood-sugar levels have been dangerously low since you left." He makes a steeple of his hands and fixes me with his big brown eyes. "The office has been quiet without you, Gorgeous."

"You could have called me," I say, and then I want to bite my own tongue off. I don't want Aiden Holby to think that he's even featured in my thought processes while I've been away.

"I did," he tells me. "Seventeen times, to be exact. The owner of the mobile phone number you gave me was getting very pissed off."

"You called me?"

"No," he says. "I called someone called

Marcia. Who sounded very cute, but told me that she was, unfortunately, very married and that I must have got the wrong number."

My mouth is gaping open. "I didn't give you the wrong number?"

Crush fumbles in his pocket and pulls out a crumpled piece of paper which he then, slowly and methodically, straightens on his desk before passing it to me.

I read the number. One digit is wrong. I look at it aghast. I can't believe that I'm not even capable of writing down my own phone number correctly. What chance is there of me ever forming a deep and meaningful relationship if I can't be trusted with my own phone number? Staring up at Crush, I say, "I can't believe this."

"I can take a hint, Gorgeous," he states.

"It wasn't a hint," I say. "It was a genuine mistake. One of the digits is wrong."

"Ah, that old chestnut — the one-digit-wrong trick."

"Why were you calling me?"

"I wanted to take you out to dinner."

"Oh."

"Would you have come?"

"I, er . . . I, er . . ."

"Or are you still seeing someone else?"

"Jacob," I say. In fact, he phoned me twice

over the weekend. Once to tell me that the charity event on Friday night was a great success, even though one of the designers had suffered the misfortune of having all her dresses stolen from a van in the afternoon, and that someone else had been forced to step in to the breach. I tried not to hyperventilate too much while he was telling me. Jacob also checked that I was still available for "our date" on Tuesday evening at Chocolate Heaven, and that I hadn't been stupid enough to double book myself once again. He didn't say that, but you know sometimes how you can tell what someone's thinking. Then he phoned me on Sunday for nothing in particular, just to chat as he was between appointments. That guy works so hard. If this relationship continues, I'll have to make sure he cuts down his hours. I've been down this road before with Marcus.

As for me, I felt drugged all weekend following our successful jewelry heist. Despite a feeling of euphoria that we'd pulled it off, I had to lie on the sofa and eat lots of chocolate to recuperate instead of leaping around the room with Davina. A smile plays at my lips and I finally remember to answer Crush's question. "I would really have loved to come to dinner with you," I say. "I can't believe I'm such an idiot."

Aiden looks at me as if to say he can.

"But, yes," I admit hesitantly, "I'm still seeing Jacob."

Crush is suddenly businesslike. "Well," he says, sounding slightly piqued, "no harm done then, because I'm seeing someone else too."

We sound more like kids in the playground rather than the mature, consenting adults that we are, but I can't help feeling a nip of jealousy. "Oh?"

"Charlotte from the call center."

I've heard that she's a tart. Pretty, but a tart. Clever, but very definitely a tart. Destined for management, in fact, if she wasn't such a tart. "She's lovely," I say.

"*I* think so," Crush says, and there's a boyish pink flush to his cheeks that makes me want to scream. They're at it, I can tell. Call it women's intuition. I haven't been gone from here for five minutes and he's already shacked up and shagged up with someone else. If that man thinks I'm going to share my chocolate with him, then he's got another think coming.

He grins at me and says, "So what chocolate have you got today?"

I rub my toe into the hideous brown carpet. "A Twix."

He raises his eyebrows and with a pointed sigh, I delve into my handbag and fish out my Twix. When I open the packet, I reluctantly hand him one of the bars, which he tucks into straightaway. Can I refuse this man nothing? I'm weak willed and feeble-minded. If there was anything about me, I'd have told him to go and get his damn chocolate from Charlotte the Harlot. At least I didn't fess up about the Green & Black's Butterscotch bar and the Snickers that are lurking in there too. I'm not as easy as I look. Ha. "I'd better do some work," I say.

"There's another team-bonding event coming up," Crush informs me with a rakish expression. Oh, no. Wasn't the white-water rafting enough? If he's imagining my bare bottom sticking up out of that boat then I'd like to wipe the smile off his silly face. "You'd better just run through the arrangements and make sure that everything's set up for us."

"What is it this time? Dinner at the Ivy? A day at the Mandarin Oriental spa?"

"Go-carting!" There's a competitive glint in Crush's eye. Oh joy. Go-carting. "Coming with us?"

"Sure," I say with a nonchalant shrug.

"Fab." Crush sits back in his chair again,

folding his arms contentedly. And I could kick myself in the leg for being so stupid.

Chapter Fifty-Two

"How'd it go, miss?" Fraser wanted to know.

It was the end of the lesson and he'd hung around especially to talk to Autumn. He stood amid the debris of his creative efforts, shards of glass littered all over his workbench, the wonky suncatcher that had been his project for the last month gradually starting to take shape. Fraser was the most untidy of all her students.

Autumn pulled a bar of Cadbury's Dairy Milk out of the box of goodies she'd bought with the money Lucy had given her from the heist and held it out to him.

"What's this for?" Fraser wanted to know.

"A thank-you present from my friend — and from me."

"Share it?"

She was well aware that Fraser knew her weakness for anything involving chocolate — as did all her students. "I'd love to."

Breaking two squares from the bar, he

handed it back to Autumn and she did likewise. She smiled at him indulgently as she enjoyed the creamy taste on her tongue. Beneath the hard-nut exterior, his shaved head and his many piercings, there was a softer side to Fraser that Autumn liked to think that she encouraged.

"It went well?"

"It went very well," she said, with a hint of pride in her voice. "Thanks to your expert tuition."

"You got your friend's jewelry back?"

"All of it," she confirmed. "I can't tell you how grateful I am. During the course of one evening, I lifted a room key, picked a lock and broke into a safe."

"Nice one, Miss!" Fraser laughed.

"Yes," she said. "I quite surprised myself." Autumn shook her head as if she still couldn't quite believe what she and her other chums in the Chocolate Lovers' Club had managed to get up to on Friday night. Who would have thought that she — shy, mousy, politically Green Autumn Fielding — had these hidden talents. "Please don't let this go any further though or I'll lose my job. And I'd miss you lot too much if that happened." She hoped to goodness that Addison Deacon would never find out about her criminal tendencies. For some reason, it suddenly seemed important to Autumn that her colleague thought well of her.

"I wilna tell anyone," Fraser promised solemnly. "There's still *some* honor among thieves."

"I wouldn't normally condone such behavior," Autumn said, "but this was all in a very good cause. You and I might just have helped to save my friend's marriage." She tried to look sternly at her young charge. "Remember, though, crime doesn't usually pay."

Fraser shrugged. "I've found that it does, Miss. Sometimes."

"Well," she said with a sigh, "I think we'd both be better to stay on the straight and narrow from now on, Fraser."

"That's fine for you, Miss," he replied flatly. "You can go back to your wee comfortable life. I might have been clean for a few months, but I'm still an ex-junkie of no fixed abode. It can be hard to do the right thing."

"I know," she said softly. "But at least you're trying. If there's ever anything I can do for you . . ."

"You can clear up after me, Miss," he said with a cheeky grin. "I've made a fine mess an' I've got an appointment to be at."

"Go on." She nodded toward the door.

"Yer great!"

"I hope it's something legal," Autumn said to his retreating back. But he merely held up a hand to her in a friendly wave. Sometimes it was best not to know.

Autumn had duly tidied away Fraser's project and the rest of the classroom before she'd jumped onto her bike and taken her daily dice with death as she cycled home through the dense evening traffic to her flat. She'd hoped that she might have seen Addison again this evening, but there'd been no sign of him at the center since the night that he'd asked her out.

The light was shining out from the living room as she chained her bike to the railings, which meant that Richard was in residence. It was time that her brother started looking for a proper job again, instead of spending the day hanging around the flat doing who knows what. Coming home now made her heart feel heavy. All she wanted to do was put up her feet and have a mug of steaming hot chocolate. There were some of her favorite Charbonnel et Walker real chocolate flakes in the cupboard, the thought of which had kept her going all day. She wanted to be alone. As much as she loved him, she didn't want to listen to her spoiled brother whining on about how bad his lot was. He ought to try living like some of her kids at the center did — then he'd know that life was tough. If she'd been in his situation, living on the charity of his sister, she would at least have made some effort during the day — kept the place clean, maybe had dinner ready. But he did nothing. Nothing that made her feel he was in the slightest bit grateful for her help. Autumn tried to push down her mounting irritation. How could she feel that she could help her clients when she couldn't even turn her own brother around?

The door was open as she approached the flat, but that wasn't unusual these days. Richard had a steady stream of seedy visitors coming through her home at all hours of the day and night, and closing the door behind themselves seemed to be too much trouble. She took a deep breath before going inside. And when she saw the sight that greeted her, she forgot to exhale again.

The flat had been ransacked. The sofas had been slashed and the stuffing, like entrails, spilled out onto the floor. Both coffee tables were upended, the magazines that had been piled on them were now ripped to pieces and the shreds were scattered about the room. Her books had been pulled off the shelves and lay in higgledy-piggledy heaps across the carpet. All of the lamps were smashed.

"Richard?" she shouted. "Richard!" But there was no reply. The only sound was that of her heart banging erratically against her chest. Whoever had been here, it looked as if they were long gone. Even so, Autumn picked up a cut-glass lamp base that had been her grandmother's. It had parted company with its shade during the mayhem and she carried it as a club, just in case she was required to whack anyone. It felt cold in her clammy hand.

She picked her way through the debris, tiptoeing silently, legs shaking. In the kitchen, all the drawers had been wrenched from the units and their contents turned out; knives, forks, spoons lay in a muddled pile beneath the table. The cupboards were open too and the tins and packets of food had been swept out. Rice, lentils, flour and sugar crunched under her feet. Her precious Charbonnel et Walker hot chocolate flakes were there too and that very nearly made her cry.

What little there was in the fridge — a few yogurts, some tofu, a few tired carrots — had also been tipped onto the floor. Even the oven door swung open on its hinges. If she had been burgled, what on earth were they looking for that had made them turn the place upside down like this? And where the hell was her brother when all this was happening? Suddenly, her blood ran cold. Good grief, maybe Richard had been here at the time!

She dashed through to his bedroom, feeling the floor sway beneath her feet as she took in the enormity of what might have happened. This was obviously done by men coming after Richard for some reason. It was unlikely that it was her stash of chocolate that they'd been after, but it may have been a stash of an entirely different kind. Who knew what went on in the sordid side of her brother's life? She certainly didn't. Perhaps she'd expected to see Richard in here, but there was no sign of him. All the drawers and cupboards were open, the contents tossed about the room. There was some cash left on his bedside table — small change mainly, but nevertheless it hadn't been taken. Whatever they were after, it didn't look like it was money. More worryingly, Richard's mobile phone had been left behind too, and her brother never went anywhere without it. It was his lifeline. Her heart was in her mouth when she said out loud, "What the hell have you done now, baby brother?"

By now, Autumn knew that her bedroom also would have been subjected to similar treatment, but she plodded through there anyway. She wasn't disappointed. Her underwear was strewn over the bed. Her meager wardrobe graced the floor. She sat down on the edge of the bed, feeling numb, and let her lamp-base weapon drop out of her hand. So this was the "comfortable wee life" that Fraser thought she had, was it? She surveyed the jumble of a room again. Now what should she do? Should she call the police? Rich would be furious if she brought them in. She should wait and see if her brother contacted her. Maybe he'd turn up tomorrow all penitent with some implausible excuse, and she was worrying unnecessarily. It wouldn't be the first time.

The only thing she could do for now was bolt the door and hope for the best. There was no way that she wanted to come face to face with the people who'd done this, whoever they were — but she was assuming that they were business associates of her brother's. She'd spend the night on the sofa, armed with the lamp base in case they thought about coming back. Perhaps she should give one of the girls a call for backup? Autumn knew that Lucy would come over straightaway and spend the night with her if she asked her to. But it was better not to drag anyone else into this situation. She could cope alone.

Autumn shook her head. What could have happened to Richard? This looked as if it was serious. If he was into something bad — then exactly how deep was he? Hot tears coursed down her face and she rubbed them away with a pair of her pants that were at hand. She could only pray that he'd made a run for it at the first sign of trouble and was now lying low somewhere — perhaps at a friend's flat. If he had any friends left. All she could do was wait and see if her brother came back. It was a hope. But she realized that it might be a vain one.

CHAPTER
FIFTY-THREE

Nadia smiled at her son as he played at her feet and finished off the plate of chocolate digestives that they'd been sharing. Lewis's capacity for eating chocolate was nearly as great as hers — but then, he was so active that he burned off all the calories without any trouble, unlike her. That was the difference between being three and being thirty-three. His Farmer Giles farmyard set was spread out all over the living-room floor and Lewis crawled carelessly through it.

"This is a blue pig," he said to her.

Kneeling down next to him, Nadia took the blue pig which her son held out. It looked more like a cow to her, and it was also brown. Experience told her that she was more than likely the one who was right. Another one of the few benefits of being thirty-three. She must spend more time with Lewis, going through his colors. And his farm animals, come to that. It was

Lewis's fourth birthday this weekend, maybe that would be a good excuse for them all to take a ride out into the country and find one of those kids' petting farms which were so popular. That might help her son to sort out the pigs from the cows. She'd have to see if Toby was working on Saturday; he was very busy at the moment and, thankfully, taking all the jobs that were on offer. If that was the case, they could perhaps keep Sunday free and go then.

"Elephant," Lewis announced, holding up another hapless creature. It was a sheep.

"It's a sheep," she told him. "Sheep."

"Sheep," her son echoed.

"What does a sheep say?"

"Moo," her son said with absolute conviction. "Moo. Moo. Moo."

Clearly there was work to be done.

There were times when she was bored to death by being a full-time mum and craved the company of adults and intelligent conversation — or conversation of any kind — but she was going to miss the precious time she spent alone with Lewis teaching him the ways of the world or simply playing with him like she was now. A job offer had arrived through the post this morning. She'd been interviewed last week and was delighted that they'd got back to her so quickly. It was a part-time post, which certainly appealed, and it was during school hours, which meant that once he was at school full-time, she'd only need to get help looking after Lewis in the holidays. The job would be quite interesting — promotions work for a local newspaper. It wasn't on the level she'd been used to, but neither was it to be sniffed at. The pay was terrible though and, of course, that was always the catch with part-time work. More often the jobs were full-time posts crammed into short hours with worse financial rewards but, at the moment, beggars couldn't be choosers.

Nadia wanted to pay Chantal back as soon as she could, and it would be a hard job to do it on this salary — even though her friend didn't want any interest on the loan and kept insisting that there was no rush for the money. It was on Nadia's conscience, nevertheless, and she wanted to clear the debt as quickly as possible. Toby understood that too and had been trying really hard. He'd sent out a heap of invoices to clients and Nadia hoped it meant that some money might be coming in soon. Toby had already attended a couple of the Quit Gambling meetings and, although he said he hated it, she was thankful that he was still going along.

Nadia smiled to herself. If only her husband knew what they'd been up to on Friday night. Thank goodness they'd managed to get Chantal's jewelry back from that creep, and it had all gone according to plan. Toby thought that she'd just been out for a drink with the girls and she wondered what he'd think if she told him where they'd really been and what they'd been doing. He never imagined that she could be deceitful too. Still, it wouldn't hurt to have one secret from him. Goodness only knows, he'd kept enough from her in the past. Thankfully, that was all over now. Maybe she'd tell him one day and they could have a good laugh about it.

"Woof-woof," Lewis said with a frown. "Can't find Woof-woof."

She turned her attention back to her son. "He must be here somewhere." There was a black-and-white sheepdog with his tail chewed off that was Lewis's favorite in the farmyard set. Nadia searched through the jumble of animals. No Woof-woof in sight. Come to think of it, there were quite a few pieces missing. There was a rickety tractor with a trailer full of logs, a figure of Farmer Giles himself in a dodgy tweed jacket, several animal pens and bits of fencing, some Vietnamese potbellied pigs and a range of milk churns the like of which most working farms hadn't seen in fifty years. Where had she last seen them? "I think Woof-woof might be in your toy cupboard," she informed him. "You wait here while Mummy goes to look for you."

She stood up and stretched her back before going upstairs to Lewis's bedroom. The toy cupboard was a mess, as always. Nadia wondered whether a girl, if she'd had one, would have been more tidy than a boy. And then she thought back to her own messy bedroom as a child and guessed probably not. Maybe if she and Toby could get themselves out of debt in the next few years, then they could think about having another baby before Lewis was too much older. It would be nice to have a little girl too.

Scouring the shelves and shelves of toys, she pushed teddies, puzzles, cars and diggers to one side. She shook her head. "This boy could give some toys to FAO Schwarz," she said out loud. "No wonder we've never got any money." Some of these were definitely destined for the next car boot sale.

"Hurry up, Mummy," Lewis yelled from the bottom of the stairs.

"You count all the sheep," she shouted back. "They're the ones with the white coats and the black faces. I'll be down in a minute."

Tutting to herself, she renewed her search and within moments had put her hands on the box of missing Farmer Giles pieces, including the much-chewed Woof-woof. Nadia dragged the box to the front of the shelf and as she did, it snagged on a black strap. She pulled harder and the box tugged the strap further out of the cupboard. A compact black bag followed it. A black computer bag.

Nadia's heart was in her mouth as she reached in and lifted the bag from the cupboard. It was a laptop. A new laptop. What was it doing, hidden at the back of Lewis's toy cupboard? Instantly, she knew the answer and her stomach twisted into a sickening knot. She took it through to the office and, fumbling with the leads, she plugged it into their phone connection. With trembling hands, she switched on the computer and waited until it sprang into life. She clicked on to the Internet symbol and, sure enough, their broadband connection had been restored. Clearly, Toby was back online.

Tapping into the history, she soon found — as she suspected — that he'd been visiting the virtual casinos. Her husband had betrayed her. This time he'd been even more devious in trying to cover his tracks. After all that she'd gone through to borrow the money from Chantal and to clear all their debts, now he'd started gambling again in secret. He must have got hold of another credit card too — not that it was hard these days, for weren't all the banks just lining up to offer easy credit? It was only the paying it back that was difficult. She felt sick to her stomach. How soon would it be before they were up to their eyes in debt once more? Nadia logged off, closed the lid of the laptop and slid it back into its bag. She went through to Lewis's room and returned the computer to its hiding place. Inside she was crying, but she had to stay strong. There was no way she could go through this time and time again. This had to end. All she had to do was decide how.

Nadia picked up the box of Farmer Giles farm pieces and made her way back down the stairs with a heavy heart. Whatever happened, this mustn't affect her son. He was her life. Her only joy.

"Look what I've got for you," she said, a bright smile fixed on her face.

"Woof-woof!" he cried. "You've found him."

Unfortunately, Nadia thought, that wasn't all she'd found.

CHAPTER
FIFTY-FOUR

Ted had barely spoken to Chantal all week-end. After their *nearly* fantastic evening on Friday, he'd now moved into the spare room — something which he'd never done before. It was the cold shoulder in extremis. He'd stayed at the golf club even longer than he would normally, dinner had been eaten in virtual silence apart from a few mumbled pleasantries, and after that he'd stared at the television until bedtime, resolutely ignoring her. Chantal felt even more frustrated than usual. Well, two could play at that game. If he was going to punish her by withdrawing even further from her, then she'd just make sure that she got her pleasure elsewhere.

Chantal lay back on the sofa and sipped a glass of good Shiraz. Just thinking about Jazz and his firm young body made her aroused. It wasn't ideal, having to see a male prostitute to get her satisfaction — what woman wanted to be in that situation? But if that's what it took, then she would do it. There was no way at her age she was going to resign herself to managing without a sex life. She had to admit that it had shocked her to hear Ted's view of having children. Chantal was so sure that they'd been on the same wavelength there. Neither of them had ever wanted kids — they pitied their friends who were shackled with them. When had that changed for her husband? Mind you, if he refused to sleep with her, it was hardly going to be a problem that she'd have to address.

She wondered why Ted hadn't been able to sit down and discuss it rationally with her. Maybe it was because he knew that she would never agree to it. Her own family had been so dysfunctional that she'd never wanted to replicate that. She'd never wanted to bring any offspring into the world so that she could subject them to the sort of things that she'd experienced. In all her years she never remembered her mom or dad telling her that they loved her. An only child, Chantal was viewed as a necessary nuisance. Kids were something that you did back then — there wasn't a choice. It didn't mean that people were automatically transformed into wonderful, nurturing parents at the birth of their first baby. Her mother and father worked hard, which meant she was left alone in the house for long periods to find her own entertainment. Sometimes she studied. Sometimes she drank the Jack Daniel's in their cocktail cabinet and then topped up the bottles with tea. All through school she strove to be a high achiever, hoping that something she did would one day win their affection, their admiration, their love. It never did. Being a straight-A student hadn't been a cause for praise. She was a gifted musician, as was expected of her. Yet from the day she'd left home, she'd never once played the piano again.

Her parents were still alive, but they featured very little in Chantal's life now. Contact was restricted to the odd guilty phone call and an exchange of Christmas and birthday cards. No doubt, if they were more involved in her life they'd still find something that they didn't approve of. Even Ted, with his good looks, his charm, his great prospects, had failed to impress them when he presented himself as a suitor. What had they wanted for her? Didn't her own happiness come into it at all? Just imagine the sort of grandparents they'd make when they couldn't even be bothered with their own child. And why would Chantal want to have a kid so that she could pass on all of her own neuroses, to make them feel insecure or unloved at her whim? It had never been on her agenda. She'd talked about her own feelings toward children over the years and Ted had always agreed. He'd never once sat her down and said that he might actually *like* a family one day. Why hadn't he ever done that? Did he feel that if he expressed his own opinions on the subject, then he'd be in danger of losing her? Wasn't it just typical of a man to avoid discussing these critical subjects simply to avoid a scene? She'd always assumed Ted had felt the same. Now, it seemed, she had been wrong.

Neither of them was great at apologizing, so this standoff could go on for some time. To distract herself, Chantal had sent Jazz an e-mail, asking for an appointment this week. If her husband didn't want her, it didn't mean that she couldn't have some fun in the meantime. In her opinion, it was safer to have fun with Jazz than to risk picking up another sleazeball in a bar. She was giving this her full consideration when Ted strode into the room and tossed a piece of paper onto her lap. It was a reply to her e-mail to Jazz and it simply read, *Would Thursday evening suit you? Jazz.*

Her mouth went dry and she looked up at Ted.

"Jazz?"

Chantal let the paper drop carelessly to the floor. "He's a client."

Her husband's face was dark with anger. "I don't think so, Chantal."

"Believe what you like," she said coolly, even though inside she was shaking. "What does it matter to you?"

"It matters when there's also over thirty thousand pounds missing from our bank account."

She felt as if a lead weight had been dropped into her stomach. "I loaned that money to a girlfriend. She was in trouble."

"Care to tell me who?" Ted said.

"No," Chantal replied. "I don't."

"I spoke to Lucian Barrington this week. He said that Amy had seen you in the lobby of the St. Crispin's Hotel in town. She said you were acting unusually. That you brushed her off."

"The woman's a bore and a gossip. It would have been more unusual for me to be keen to go for a drink with her and Lucian as she wanted me to."

"She told Lucian that a young man called Jazz asked for you at the hotel reception desk and went up to your room."

Chantal stared ahead of her. She could continue to deny this, try to talk her way out of it, tell Ted that he was a client again, make a convincing case, but what would be the point? Maybe this was the time to come clean. Chantal pressed her lips together tightly and took a deep breath. "I'm guilty as charged," she said flatly as she turned to her husband. "I've been seeing other men."

"Men, plural?" Ted's fists were clenched and white.

"Yes." She lifted her chin defiantly, but inside she felt like throwing herself to the floor and sobbing. Somewhere inside she always knew that this day would come — the day of reckoning — but she never knew that it would feel quite so painful.

"Then I think that there's no more to say."

"Ted —" she started.

"Get out," her husband said. "Get out of my sight."

She stood up and walked toward him. Now that it was out in the open, she felt sick, felt as if she could throw up there and then. She wanted Ted's forgiveness and didn't know how to ask for it. "I don't want our marriage to end," she said, and touched his arm tentatively. Ted pulled away from her. "I want to get back to where we used to be. We should talk about this. We should talk about where we're going to go from here."

There was a look of pain and loathing on her husband's face. "The only talking that we're going to do, Chantal, is through our lawyers."

CHAPTER
FIFTY-FIVE

I texted all the girls to meet me at Chocolate Heaven for a quick drink and a bite of our favorite substance at the close of business. Jacob isn't coming for another hour and I thought it would give me and my fellow criminals a chance to catch up on the events of Friday evening while I wait for him — seeing as I unceremoniously passed out before we'd had an opportunity to celebrate in proper fashion. I'd also like the members of the Chocolate Lovers' Club to check out my new boyfriend. I want them to see that I am capable of attracting cool, gorgeous men who are also nice and not emotional fuck-wits.

I'm already tucking heartily into a heap of champagne truffles, working on the theory that less is not always more, when Chantal arrives. She flings herself on the sofa next to me and lets her head drop back with a heavy sigh. My friend looks more subdued than she normally does. Her face is tired and drawn. She picks up one of my truffles listlessly and pops it into her mouth. The usual gasp of ecstasy is missing.

"Problems?"

"Big-time," she says.

I thought that after she retrieved her stolen jewelry in such grand style she'd be walking on air for weeks. A cold panic spreads in my stomach, nudging the comforting glow of the truffles out of the way. "You haven't heard anything from Mr. John Smith, Gentleman Jewelry Thief?"

"No." She waves her hand dismissively. "My troubles are closer to home."

"Let me get you a drink," I say. The girl looks as if she's in need of a double brandy. "Then you can tell me everything."

"Hot chocolate, please," Chantal says, and I scuttle off to order it from Clive.

Minutes later, my friend is nursing a steaming mug of chocolate in her hands. She looks better already. Chocolate does, indeed, have healing powers. Women all over the world know this. When the chocolate has had time to work its magic, Chantal looks up at me. "Ted's thrown me out," she says, shrugging at my shocked expression.

"Thrown you out? Why?"

"He noticed the money missing out of the

bank account and he didn't buy my explanation."

"Nadia will feel dreadful," I say.

"Don't tell her," Chantal begs me. "She has enough to worry about. Besides, this isn't really about the money. There are other more . . . *pressing* issues too."

"You're still not sleeping together?"

Chantal laughs and she sounds slightly unhinged. "Would you believe it, we had a great time when I got home on Friday night. Mad passion on the couch. The first time in months." She cackles again at the irony of it. "Then I found out that Ted wanted us to have kids." My friend looks at me in amazement. "He knows how I feel about children. *Everyone* knows how I feel about children."

"Maybe he'll come around," I say soothingly. "Or maybe you will."

"I don't want kids," Chantal insists. "Never have. Never will."

"And Ted's absolutely set on it?"

"Yes."

"Then it's over?"

She nods. "Looks like it."

"What will you do? Where will you go?" I ask her. "If I didn't live in a shoe box you could come and stay at my place. I can offer you my sofa until you get sorted."

"I packed a case this morning, then I

phoned round all of my friends and contacts until I found someone who could rent me a flat for a few months." Chantal risks a smile. "I moved into a fully furnished, two-bedroom apartment in Islington this afternoon."

"Wow." I'm suitably stunned at the pace of this.

"I'm nothing if not resourceful," my friend admits with a rueful expression.

Before I can comment further, Autumn and Nadia bowl in through the door. They come and sit with us, fussing as they strip off their jackets and dump their handbags. Clive comes over, pad in hand. "How are my favorite girls?"

"Fine." I think "of mixed fortune" would be a more accurate answer but that would then involve lengthy explanations and we are women in want of chocolate. Our esteemed host takes our order and then disappears to minister to our needs. It has to be said that neither Autumn nor Nadia looks in great spirits today.

"Spill the beans," I say.

Nadia launches in first. "I've found out that Toby's gambling again," she says. "I'm leaving him."

Chantal and I burst out laughing.

"What?" she says darkly. "What's so funny?"

Tears are streaming down my face and I don't know if they are of sadness or hilarity. "It's not funny," I say, trying to bring my hysteria under control. "It's not funny at all."

"It is," Chantal says, clutching her sides. "I've just left Ted."

Now Nadia starts to smile too. "Impeccable timing," she says with a tired chuckle. "What a sad bunch we are."

When I've calmed down I ask, "Where will you go? What will you do?" It seems inappropriate at this point, but nevertheless, I say it anyway.

"I don't know yet," she admits.

"Move in with me," Chantal states. "I've just rented a great apartment and I have a spare room."

Nadia shakes her head. "I'm not sure that my meager budget will run to anything in your league, Chantal."

"That isn't an issue. Pay me what you can," our friend says earnestly. "I'd rather share with someone I know than rattle round that place on my own. We can be young, free and single together."

"Not so free in my case," Nadia corrects. "Remember Lewis?"

It's clear that Chantal hadn't factored a toddler into this cozy arrangement, but she recovers well. "That's fine," she says brightly, but her voice sounds ever so slightly strangled.

"Are you sure?"

"Positive. We'll manage."

They look at each other sadly. "I'd like that, Chantal," Nadia says softly and squeezes her hand. "It will give me some breathing space."

"Then it's settled," Chantal says. "I'll jot down the address for you. Move your stuff in when you're ready."

Clive reappears with a tray laden down with goodies which he sets in front of us. "You ladies look like you need this today," he says, and there's never been a truer word spoken. We all dive in.

"I've been left too," Autumn tells us quietly. "Richard's gone."

None of us laugh this time as we know how much Autumn worries about her brother.

"My flat's been ransacked," she continues, her voice cracking, "and my dear brother is missing."

"Oh, Autumn."

"I've not heard from him since." Our friend lets out an unhappy sigh. "I thought about going to the police to report him missing, but how would I explain it? Richard would kill me for involving them. I've no idea what to do other than wait."

None of us pipe up with any bright ideas either.

"Tell us that you're all right, Lucy," Nadia urges. "We need one of us to be doing okay."

"I'm fine," I say. "I'm happy. Marcus is well and truly out of my life and I have a great new boyfriend. Everything in the garden's rosy."

"Thank goodness," Nadia sighs.

"Jacob's coming along in a few minutes," I tell my best friends, "and I want you all to meet him. I'm not sure if he's the One, but I really, really like him."

"Good for you, girl," Chantal says. "You go for it."

I smile coyly. "I have great hopes for this relationship."

And, on cue, Jacob walks through the door.

CHAPTER
FIFTY-SIX

Jacob strides into Chocolate Heaven looking oh so cool. He's wearing a sexy dark suit, his blond hair is tousled in all the right places. A surge of pride goes through me. This guy is going out with me! Ha, ha!

When he sees me, he gives a casual wave and walks toward us. And, as he does, Chantal gasps. This time not in ecstasy, as I would expect; this time she gasps in horror. There's a check in Jacob's confident step and the sunny smile on his face fades slightly, but he continues toward us. Chantal is nibbling her lip nervously and her body language is registering extreme discomfort.

"What?" I say. "What's going on?"

A hush has fallen over our group. Autumn and Nadia look as puzzled as I do.

Jacob joins us. "Hi," he says, his voice overbright.

"Hi," I reply. There's an uneasy tremor in my voice and I don't know why. I feel I should get up and give Jacob a kiss or something, but I don't. So he stands there looking discomfited while I stay rooted to the spot. "Good to see you," I say. "These are my friends. Autumn, Nadia and — Chantal." I see my date and my friend exchange an anxious glance. Somewhere in my fuddled brain a lightbulb pings on. "But then I think you already know that."

"Hi, Chantal," Jacob says quietly. He tugs uncomfortably at the collar on his shirt.

"Jazz," she says.

"Jazz?" I look to her for an explanation, but she remains silent and Jacob speaks instead.

"I know your friend," he says. "In a business capacity."

But I get the feeling that he isn't one of her interviewees for *Style USA* magazine. Call it female intuition or put it down to too much experience of deceit with Marcus, but there's definitely something between these two — a spark, some chemistry, shared history. I don't know, but I'd certainly like to. "How?" I want to know. "How do you know each other? What type of business?"

"I think Chantal should explain that to you," Jacob says. His confident demeanor has vanished and he suddenly looks lonely and vulnerable.

Turning to Chantal, I say, "Tell me what's going on, please."

My friend is staring intently at her lap.

"You probably won't want to know me after this, Lucy," Jacob says sadly, "but if you do, I'd really like it if you'd call me. I've really enjoyed your company, our short time together. You're a lot of fun. I thought . . ." He clears his throat as he searches for the words. "I thought we might have had something special."

I'm speechless. So speechless that I say nothing as I watch Jacob turn around and walk away from me.

Everyone fidgets while I sit there in a catatonic state. "Well," I say to Chantal eventually, "are you going to let me into your little secret?"

She forces herself to look at me and then says, "Your boyfriend — Jacob, Jazz — is a male escort."

"A male escort? What type of male escort?" I'm trying to recall whether Chantal has been to any glamorous parties recently where she'd need someone to accompany her — someone who wasn't her husband.

"Lucy . . ." my friend says with a raised eyebrow and an exasperated tone.

Then I realize that she hasn't been to any

parties at all. I let this sink in for a moment.

"I've been hiring him," Chantal continues.

"Hiring him to do what?"

The other members of the Chocolate Lovers' Club shift uneasily in their seats.

Then there's a rush of blood to my brain and it all becomes horribly clear. "You've been *shagging* my boyfriend?" The question comes out hideously loudly, even though I nearly choke on the words, and a hush falls over Chocolate Heaven as the rest of the customers spin round to enjoy the commotion.

"Lucy," Chantal says in the voice of reason, "I didn't know he was your boyfriend. I had no clue that Jacob and Jazz were the same person. How could I have guessed?"

I can barely bring myself to breathe. "My boyfriend's a *rent boy?*"

"He's hardly that," Chantal snorts. "He's an escort."

"Who you pay for sex," I snap back.

My friend has the good grace to blush. "It isn't as sleazy as you make it sound. He's very professional."

"Good," I say. "Oh, good. I wouldn't like to think you were paying for substandard services."

"I'm sorry," she tells me. "Really sorry. I

know that you're fond of him."

"*Was* fond of him," I correct. "How can I face him now? How can I face him knowing what he does, knowing that you've . . . you've *slept* with my boyfriend when I haven't." I want to hang my head in my hands and weep buckets. Jacob seemed so lovely and our developing friendship, relationship . . . I don't know what to call it now . . . was really helping me to get over Marcus. I've never been an exponent of the "all men are bastards" theory, but at this moment I can see the attraction in it. How could I have been so easily deceived again? As the prime offender has made a hasty exit — and who could blame him? — I turn my anger onto Chantal. "I thought you were a better friend than this. I can't believe you've been seeing Jacob behind my back."

"I haven't been *seeing* him, Lucy," my friend insists. "I've been hiring him by the hour."

"What do you pay him?" I ask.

"Lucy," Chantal says. "Don't do this to yourself."

"I want to know."

"Two hundred pounds an hour." There's a sharp intake of breath from Autumn and Nadia. I would give a sharp intake of breath too — if I could actually breathe. That's a lot of money, by anyone's standards.

"Is he good?" I ask petulantly.

Chantal's face looks bleak when she answers, "Yes. He's very good."

"I *so* don't want to know that," I wail. "I so *do not* want to know that!"

CHAPTER
FIFTY-SEVEN

Chantal has tried to contact me about a hundred and seventy-nine times, but I'm not returning her calls. I'm having a mega sulk and, frankly, I think I have every right to. My mobile phone rings again and it's her number on the caller display, so I let it go to voicemail and stuff my phone back in my pocket.

"Hey, Gorgeous," Crush says as he comes up beside me. "Why the long face?"

I'm not in the mood for this either. Team bonding of the go-carting kind. Everyone else is bouncing around jovially, eager for the off, and here I am, alone in my misery, hating every minute of it. We're down in the Docklands and the track is set out on some of the wasteland surrounding the Millennium Dome. It's a fairly godforsaken place with the wind whipping across the acres of flat tarmac. Why couldn't they build a designer outlet mall here? That would have been a much better use of the space, in my humble opinion.

We've watched the drivers' briefing on a DVD in a boldly painted temporary building — which made this all look quite terrifying — and now we're waiting at the trackside for the fun and frolics to begin. The sales team is positively champing at the bit, while I will need wild horses to drag me into one of these silly-looking little machines. Why do grown men of all ages still need to play with toys to prove their manhood? It is a psychological trait far too complicated for me to contemplate at the moment. Needless to say, I'm dressed in some disgustingly unflattering red overalls that are too tight round my big, fat bottom, and a white crash helmet is currently flattening my hair which I spent so long styling in the hope of giving my battered confidence a boost. Why do all our team-bonding experiences require terrible clothing? Why do they not involve slimming, black designer outfits? Next time, I'm going to choose the team-bonding exercise and see how much more pleasant that will be. Ha. A week at the Chiva-Som Spa in Thailand would suit me.

I look at Crush and the words "Bog off" are not far from my lips.

He slings his arm round my shoulders. "Someone stolen your chocolate stash?"

"No," I say crisply. "I found out that my best friend has been bonking my boyfriend."

"Ooo." Crush's face takes on a look of concern. "Not good."

"No."

"This will cheer you up."

Of course it will. Dashing madly round a track in a pathetic-looking boys' toy for no good reason. I can't think of anything else that would soothe my wounded heart. But I might as well give it a go, as so far today a Mars Bar, a Bounty, a Turkish Delight, two packets of Rolos, an entire box of Thorntons Continental and three Green & Black's Hazelnut & Currant bars have failed to offer any kind of succor.

Mr. Aiden Holby gives me a friendly squeeze. "I'll make sure you have a good time, Gorgeous," he says with a big grin. "I'm going to whoop your peachy arse out on that track."

Hmm. So he thinks my arse is peachy? I smile in spite of my pain. "I'd like to see you try."

"Ten pounds says I beat you."

"You're on." We shake hands on the bet.

"I love a woman who doesn't know when she's beaten." Despite the fact that we're essentially in a work environment with the sales team all around us, he gives me a rather lingering kiss on the cheek. And then, out of the corner of my eye, I see Charlotte the Harlot from the call center sashaying her way through to the front of the track. Crush lets go of my shoulders when he sees her and his grin widens. My mood blackens once again. What is it with all this kissy-kissy, flirty-flirty, "Hello, Gorgeous" business? I'm not so stupid that I can't tell that I'm dropped like a hot coal when the girlfriend appears in the vicinity. Not so *gorgeous* then, am I? Huh! He's just another bloody alpha male who thinks he can toy with my affections. I'm sure steam must be coming out of my nostrils.

"See you on the track," he says, as he leaves me and goes to her.

"Be sure of it," I bite back under my breath.

Minutes later and I'm strapped into my go-cart, held in by a double harness, bottom perilously close to tarmac. The steering-wheel column is rammed between my knees in a very unladylike manner. Crush is sitting three go-carts ahead of me — being the boss, we have to let him go in the front. Already I can hear Charlotte calling Crush's name from the pit lane and I want to shout back that nothing's happened yet, he hasn't actually done anything! Silly bitch. If she keeps that up, it is *seriously* going to get on my nerves. Now I regret telling Crush the reason for my deep depression. If he blabs to Charlotte the Harlot then it will be all round Targa's office before lunchtime tomorrow and I'll have to leave. Again. At this rate, the only job open to me will be that of hooker-with-a-heart. I'll have to contact Jacob, Jazz or whatever name he goes by and get some tips off him for setting myself up in business.

I snap down my black visor and, before I know what's happening, the red light changes to green and we're off on our qualifying laps. I haven't driven for years and yet, within days I find myself in charge of a big, fuck-off van and now this spluttering, puttering piece of machinery. I feel as if I'm driving a high-speed lawn mower. My heart is in my mouth with nerves. I know that we have spent years advancing the cause for our equality, but let me tell you this — girls don't like doing things such as this. It is an indisputable truth that we like painting our toenails, we like doing our hair, we like having manicures. We do not like racing around in cars, and in that generic term, I include go-carts. It is not in our genetic makeup.

When we hit the first bend, one of the sales team spins off and I hurtle past him, a gleeful laugh building in my throat. Then I whip past another two go-carts, causing startled glances from the occupants. Before I know it, I'm up behind Mr. Aiden Holby, his bumper bar filling my vision. Crush is opening up a gap between us and I flatten my foot to the floor, squeezing every last inch out of the accelerator. There's no way that arrogant bastard is going to get away from *me!* We whiz round, the corners coming up with increasing alacrity, the wind rushing past my helmet. A few laps later and the red light comes on and we all putter back into the pits. Miraculously, I'm in second position behind Crush.

We hang around in the pit lane while the rest of the team completes their qualifying laps. Charlotte the Harlot takes the opportunity to drape herself all over Crush, which he doesn't seem to object to. I'm sure she keeps glancing pointedly in my direction. Slapper. I've had just about enough of this. When I'm ready to pull off my helmet and stomp home, we're given our grid positions and out we go, back onto the track. This time I'm right behind Crush on the grid at the off and, make no mistake, I have him in my sights. He's not going to get the better of me *this* time!

Crush turns round and blows a kiss to me. And I don't know quite what happens, but a red mist descends over my eyes, my heart pounds in my chest and very dark thoughts go through my brain. The lights change to green and we're off again. I'm like an athlete out of the blocks, hot on his heels. He barely makes it into the first bend in front of me. We flash down the straight. If Charlotte the Harlot is shouting encouragement to him, then I don't hear it — but, let me tell you, he damn well needs it. The nose of my go-cart is away from his rear end. I have a mind to ram him up the backside. I've no idea where the other drivers are on the track, other than that they're way behind us. This is a grudge match between the two of us. We both power slide round the next corner, wheels almost touching. There aren't sparks flying, but I feel there should be. My arms are aching already as I wrestle with the steering wheel. My jaw is aching too as my teeth are gritted together. Then we hit the next corner and I'm not sure what the sequence of events is, but I think I might have accidentally hit Crush up the bottom because next thing he's spiraling wildly off the track, spinning over the grass and thumping headlong into the pile of tires that borders the track as a safety barrier.

I punch the air in triumph, then I look over my shoulder and see that everyone is running toward Crush's mangled go-cart. Ooo. There's a man waving a black flag wildly in front of me, which I know from my drivers' briefing means that I have to come straight off the track due to bad behavior. I pull over into the pit lane and leap out of the cart. To be honest, I'm glad of the excuse to get out and see whether Crush is okay. Snatching off my helmet, I run down to where he is. One of the wheels is clearly bent and the front of the go-cart is staved in. There's a huddle of people gathered around him — people from work and, more worryingly, marshals from the track with grim looks on their faces.

"Aiden. Aiden," Charlotte is crying. In a very dramatic fashion.

My mouth has gone dry as I elbow my way to the front and I ask frantically, "Is he okay?"

Everyone turns toward me and the bleak expressions on their faces make my heart falter. A path opens and I'm kneeling in the churned-up mud at the side of the go-cart. Crush's helmet has come off and there's blood trickling down the side of his face. Tears flood to my eyes. This is my fault. All my fault.

Charlotte shoves me out of the way, giving me a black glare, and grabs at Crush's hand, which has fallen from the steering wheel and now hangs limply in the grass. She rubs at it furiously. "Aiden," she says, sounding distraught. "Aiden. Wake up."

But, from what I can see, there's absolutely no sign of life.

CHAPTER
FIFTY-EIGHT

Chantal shoved open the door of her new flat with her foot as she balanced her box of groceries on her hip. Then she tottered through to the kitchen and deposited it on her kitchen table, surveying the room with a satisfied smile. The flat wasn't too bad at all. It was fully furnished with reasonably good taste. Stylish on a budget was the look, but she could live with that. She would have to.

Today, she'd tried in vain to make it up with Lucy after their tiff over Jazz. As well as phoning her friend dozens and dozens of times, she'd also tried to speak to her husband to apologize again to him. His mobile went unanswered and his assistant refused to put her through to him, citing a continuing meeting which couldn't be interrupted and which Chantal was sure was mythical. Despite leaving a plethora of messages, neither of them had returned her calls.

There was nothing in the cupboards or the fridge, so Chantal had stocked up with some of her favorite and most extravagant store-cupboard staples — including truffle-flavored olive oil from the Tuscan hills, a ripe Camembert that Ted would have banned from the house as it smelled like old socks, and a large carton of Clive's extra-special Chocolate Heaven drinking chocolate. They would all help to provide her with some comfort when she needed it. As no doubt she would. It was going to be strange living alone, after being with Ted for so many years, and she choked back a tear as she thought about it. However, a lot of this was her own making, so there was no way that she was going to get all maudlin over it. She was in a better position than a lot of women in her situation. Her job paid very well, so she was financially stable. If they did decide to divorce then she would get a kick-ass lawyer and take a large slice of her and her husband's combined wealth. Ted could think again if he thought that he'd get rid of her so easily.

Still, she hoped that it wouldn't come to that. Chantal didn't believe that all was yet lost. There might well be a way to effect a reconciliation between them. Though, at the moment, she couldn't quite see how when he was even refusing to take her calls.

She poured herself a large glass of Pinot Grigio even though the bottle hadn't been chilled and, breaking open a box of champagne truffles that she'd also bought from Chocolate Heaven, she took them both through to the living room. The place was much smaller than her sitting room at home, but it was cozy and comfortable, decorated in shades of rich cream and caramel colors. Flopping back on the sofa, she snuggled into the cushions, curling her feet beneath her. She toyed with the buttons on her cell phone. There was someone else she felt she should call too and, before she changed her mind, she punched in the number. The cell only rang twice before it was answered.

"Hi," the voice said.

"Jazz," she said. Her voice sounded uncertain. She took a deep breath. "Jacob. It's Chantal."

"I didn't think I'd hear from you again," he replied flatly.

She sighed into the phone. "Maybe I shouldn't be calling," she told him, "but I wanted to phone and say that I'm sorry. I told Lucy about our . . ." What should she call it? She settled on, "Our arrangement."

She heard Jacob sigh too. "Is she very angry?"

"I think you could safely say that," she admitted.

"So I won't be hearing from her again?"

"It seems unlikely," Chantal said. "She's not speaking to me at the moment either. I never thought in a million years that our paths would cross in our daily lives. Perhaps that was foolish of me."

"It's never happened before," Jacob told her.

"Then just call it bad luck," Chantal said. "I'm sorry that it messed up your relationship with her. I know that she liked you a lot."

"I liked her too." Even down the phone Chantal could tell that he was miserable. "But it's one of the hazards of the job," he continued. "As soon as someone finds out about how I make my living then the relationship inevitably ends. Not many women would put up with it. Sometime soon I need to make a career change." He laughed, but it lacked real humor.

"My husband found out about us too," she said. "He kicked me out."

"I'm sorry," Jacob offered. "I never meant to mess up your marriage either."

"Hazards of being a client," she suggested, and they shared a hollow chuckle.

"I enjoyed meeting you, Chantal," he said. "You're one hell of a woman. I wish all of my clients had been as —"

She cut him short before he could finish. There was no way she wanted to hear how she compared to his other customers. "Thank you."

"I suppose you won't be calling me again either."

"Not as a client. My days of illicit sex are well and truly over. But I'd like to see you as a friend."

"I'd like that too." There was a pause. "Besides, I haven't taken any bookings since . . ." His voice tailed off. "I'm not sure that I'm cut out for this work anymore. I'm taking some time out to think about things."

"I have a lot of contacts," she said. "If you're serious about that career change, I could help you out. I might be able to find you something more socially acceptable, but certainly less profitable."

Jacob chuckled. He was a genuinely nice guy and she wondered what had drawn him into the life he was living. Perhaps one day he would tell her. "So you're not working tonight?"

"No," Jacob said. "If you want to know

the truth, I'm sitting here alone feeling sorry for myself."

"I have a bottle of warm white wine open, a wide selection of frozen dinners and some great chocolate," Chantal stated. "It would make me happy if you'd join me — as a friend."

"I'll be right over," Jacob said without hesitation.

It crossed her mind that it would have been nice to be entertaining him in another capacity, but she meant what she said — no more playing with fire for her. Simple friendship could work too. After all, friends were often worth so much more than mere lovers. She gave Jacob her new address and hung up. That wasn't so painful, Chantal thought as she sank back into the welcome softness of the sofa. If only she could make it up with Ted and with Lucy so easily.

CHAPTER
FIFTY-NINE

I hate hospitals. The all-pervading smell of the disinfectant is making me feel even more nauseous than I already am. Aiden was whisked away from the go-cart track by ambulance accompanied by Charlotte the Harlot, and I trailed after him, a quivering mass of anxiety, on the Tube. By the time I got to the Accident and Emergency Department, Crush had already been admitted and there was nothing I could do but sit and wait until I was allowed to see him. Those five hours passed very slowly, I can tell you. If only I hadn't been so mad, so competitive, so reckless, so . . . Oh, I don't know.

Finally, after downing what feels like thirty-eight cups of vending-machine tea and what's definitely six Kit Kats from the chocolate-vending machine next to it, a nurse comes to see me and says, "You can go up to see Mr. Holby now."

"Thank you." Relief floods my body. "Is

he all right?"

"He'll live," she says brusquely.

My footsteps are as heavy as my heart as I trudge along, wandering through the maze of corridors trying to find where Crush has been taken. Eventually, I find the right ward and, when I announce my name, I'm buzzed inside. The lights are low as it's late — way past proper visiting hours — and I'm grateful that they've even let me in. Crush's bed is right by the door. He's lying prostrate, leg in the air in some sort of sling. His face is pale and his eyes are closed. There's a mummy-style bandage round his head. My lovely, favorite, favorite boss looks truly terrible.

Charlotte the Harlot is sitting next to him on a hard plastic chair. When I approach, she looks up at me. That woman does a great line in withering glares and that's coming from someone who knows.

"How is he?" I whisper.

But before she can answer, Crush opens his eyes and stares at me. "Ah," he says hoarsely. "The Dark Destroyer cometh."

So, no "Hi, Gorgeous" this time. I sit down in the only other chair, even though I'm not invited to. "I was worried sick," I admit.

"Since when did your competitive streak

become two miles wide?"

"I don't know," I say. "I'm not sure what happened, but I'm really, really sorry."

"You bloody well barged him off the track," Charlotte informs me needlessly. "That's what happened."

"It was little more than a playful tap," I protest guiltily.

Crush smiles. His lips are dry, and if it were me sitting there as his girlfriend, I'd be giving him soothing sips of water. I hardly dare ask the next question. "What's the diagnosis?"

"I'll never be able to play the piano again."

"Could you before?"

"No," he admits with a tired grin. I smile back at him. Charlotte turns up her death-ray glare. "I've got a mild concussion and a busted leg."

"Oh, shit," I say. "I'm really, really sorry."

"They're keeping me in overnight for observation."

"I'm really, really sorry," I say again.

"Want to sign my plaster cast?" Crush asks. He sounds a bit feeble. "I feel you should be the first."

"I don't know what to say."

"Good-bye would be a start," Charlotte intervenes. "Aiden's very tired. Exhausted."

I feel pretty wiped out myself. Crush's

hair is poking out from his bandage at all angles and I want to smooth it down for him. If Charlotte the Harlot is supposed to be his girlfriend, why isn't she looking after him better than this?

"Maybe we should do our next team-bonding exercise at a health spa," I suggest, to add a bit of levity to the occasion. "I know just the place."

"You'd probably try to drown me in the Jacuzzi."

"If there's anything you need . . ." I say.

"*I'm* perfectly capable of tending to Aiden's needs," Charlotte pipes up.

I despise her. I despise her with all of my being.

"Chocolate," he says. "Bring me chocolate. You owe me."

"I will do. I promise."

Crush winces with pain. "I'll hold you to it."

Charlotte's death-ray glare is clearly having an effect as I suddenly feel very weak myself. "I'd better be going then," I say. "I'll phone tomorrow and see how you are."

I stand up and I want to kiss him on the cheek, but if I did that, Charlotte would leap over the bed and karate chop me. "Bye, then."

"Bye," Crush says quietly.

"Bye," Charlotte the Harlot says too enthusiastically. She gives me a sarcastic little wave.

I can hardly bear to leave my boss like this. But, turning away from him, I head for the door. As I get there, Crush calls weakly, "Lucy . . ."

I look back toward him.

"I would have beaten you," he says. He's smiling again and there's still a mischievous twinkle in his eye.

"No way," I tell him, and walk out the door.

CHAPTER SIXTY

Nadia was surprised that the estate agent's board had gone up outside her house within an hour of phoning them to put the family home on the market. But now that she'd decided that this was the only way of moving on, then there was no point in wasting time in taking steps to end her marriage. It might be drastic, but it was the only way she could see of putting the brake on her husband, who seemed intent on dragging them deeper and deeper into debt with his blind devotion to gambling. He couldn't tell her any more clearly that the bright lights and the empty promises of riches mattered more to him than the welfare of his wife and son. This way, if they sold the house quickly, then she might just get some equity back out of it before Toby squandered that too.

She'd hired a transit van complete with two burly men to help her move. Lucy was coming along for moral support too and, once again, she had to thank her friends from the Chocolate Lovers' Club for their kindness. The last of the boxes were being loaded into the van and they were nearly ready to leave. Lucy had just called to say that she'd gotten off the Tube and was on her way; five minutes and she'd be here. Thank goodness. All Nadia wanted to do now was get away before Toby came home. She'd decided it was the best idea to move her stuff out while her husband was at work. It seemed less painful that way. How could she possibly have left if Toby had been there watching her taking the small boxes away that represented the dividing up of their life together? If it had to be done, it was much better this way.

"Come on, Lewis," she shouted to her son. "Mummy wants to put you in the car."

"Where are we going?"

"Remember, Mummy said that we're going to live in a different house from Daddy for a while."

Lewis nodded to her, but it was clear that he didn't understand as his little smile didn't falter. "Is Daddy coming too?"

"No," she said. "It'll just be the two of us. We're going on a big adventure."

Lewis didn't look particularly impressed.

438

Perhaps one day he'd understand why she felt she had to do this.

"Can Mr. Smelly come?"

"Of course."

Lewis had his favorite teddy bear tucked under his arm. He was called Mr. Smelly because he gave off the most appalling odor, due to the fact that she was only able to prize the mangled bear out of her son's vize-like fists once a year to be whizzed into the washing machine, and even that took a huge bribe with copious amounts of chocolate.

One of the burly men poked his head back inside the front door. "We're loaded," he said. "Ready when you are, love."

"I'll be right there," Nadia said. Just one final look around the house to see that she hadn't forgotten anything.

She could hardly bear to take it in as she walked sadly through the rooms. Shabby as it was, she loved this place. She'd built it up for them, for her family. Now, even though it was still filled with her possessions and her furniture, it was nothing but an empty shell. On her bedside table, there was a picture of her and Toby on their wedding day. She picked it up and put it in her handbag. She didn't know why. Maybe for old times' sake. Her parents had said that the marriage would never last, that arrangements based on suitability were better, that marriages only formed out of love never lasted. It looked as if they were right.

She'd thought about leaving a note for Toby, but she couldn't find the right words to express how she felt, so had decided against it. When she'd finally checked the house, she scooped Lewis into her arms and took him outside. Firmly, she closed the front door behind her. The guys were sitting waiting in the van. Lucy, she saw, was striding up the road toward her and Nadia gave her friend a wave. Opening the car door, she put Lewis down so that he could hop into his car seat. Then, with shaking hands, she concentrated on the business of strapping him safely in.

Moments later, Lucy came up behind her, puffing with the exertion of walking up the hill. Her friend kissed her warmly.

"Everything okay?" Lucy asked.

"As well as can be expected," Nadia replied. "We're ready to go. I'm not taking much — mainly clothes, and toys for Lewis. Chantal says that the flat she's renting has everything."

"I'm sure that Chantal wouldn't compromise on her creature comforts," Lucy assured Nadia. "You've probably got an ensuite Jacuzzi and sauna."

Nadia forced a smile. "That would be nice."

"It'll be fine," Lucy said, squeezing her arm. "*You'll* be fine."

"I've given the driver instructions on how to get to the flat," Nadia told her. "The van will follow my car."

"Want me to drive?"

"Please." She felt far too emotional to be able to focus on the road. Her friend took the car keys from her and slipped into the driver's seat. Nadia climbed into the passenger seat beside her. Her hands were fiddling with the buttons of her skirt. Lucy gave them a pat. "Ready to go?"

Nadia nodded. Hot tears burned at the back of her eyes.

"Sure you've got everything?"

She nodded again. Then, as Lucy slipped the car into gear, there was the noise of screeching tires coming from the road behind them. Looking in the sideview mirror, Nadia could see another van slewing to a halt right behind them, and there was no doubt as to who the driver was. It had barely stopped when Toby jumped out and ran to Nadia's side of the car, snatching open the door.

"Daddy!" Lewis shouted joyously from

the back.

Toby was breathless when he spoke. "One of the neighbors called me to say you were leaving," he panted. "Don't do this, Nadia. Please don't do this."

Nadia felt distraught. "I have to go, Toby," she said. "I've tried everything else."

"I'll change," he promised, crouching down beside her. "I'm begging you. Please don't go. Don't take my son away."

We should be discussing this alone, Nadia thought bleakly, not forcing Lewis and Lucy to be our reluctant audience.

"You've put the house up for sale," he said, gazing disbelievingly at the FOR SALE sign that had just been erected. "When did you do that?"

"This morning," Nadia told him.

"Where are you going? How will I contact you?"

"I've got my mobile," Nadia said. "You can call me anytime and I'll keep in touch." Letting go was much harder than it seemed.

"When will I see Lewis?" His face bore an agonized expression. "How can you do this to me?"

"How could you do this to *us?*" Nadia retorted. "I'm not doing this lightly, Toby. I still love you. Despite everything."

"Then come back." To her horror, her

husband started crying. "Come back and we'll work it out."

"I can't," she said.

"I've given up the gaming sites," he said, "just as you asked. What else can I do to show you that I care?"

"But you haven't," she said sadly. "You haven't, Toby. I found the laptop. I know that the broadband connection has been restored. You've got another credit card and you're gambling again — behind our backs. I can't let you drag us down with you. I'm doing this to protect Lewis as much as myself."

At this, Toby looked resigned.

"I have to go," Nadia said quietly. "Let me go."

Toby slowly stood up. Then, after a moment's hesitation, he closed the door on the car and said, "I love you."

"Drive," she said to Lucy.

Without discussion, her friend slid the car back into gear and pulled out into the road. The removal van followed them. It felt like a funeral procession. Nadia didn't look back, but she knew that her husband was still standing on the pavement, watching them leave.

CHAPTER SIXTY-ONE

"The worst is over," I say to Nadia, even though I'm not sure that it is. Platitudes are always best, I find, on these occasions. Harsh reality is best left for another time altogether. "I brought chocolate," I tell her. "For you and Lewis." The little boy is playing with his teddy bear.

"Thank goodness." She allows herself a shuddering exhalation of breath.

"In my handbag. Help yourself."

My friend immediately buries her hands in my bag.

I've never been to Nadia's house before — none of the members of the Chocolate Lovers' Club have, as far as I know — and, somehow, it suddenly brings her situation home to me and how much she must have struggled to keep a roof over her head. As we drive away, I can see how shabby the area is, but that doesn't mean property prices are anywhere near a reasonable level, they're just marginally less extortionate than some. Where Nadia is moving to with Chantal is considerably more upmarket, but I would imagine that's the last thing on my friend's mind at the moment.

This puts all my troubles into perspective. I'm still worried sick about Crush, but I phoned the hospital this morning and the Ward Sister said that he'd had a comfortable night, though I couldn't speak to him because the doctor was examining him. Maybe I'll try again later. When Nadia asked me to help her move into Chantal's place, I was keen to show solidarity and give my support to her, but I also hope that by helping my friend, I might win back some brownie points with God and, therefore, still be on for a place in heaven, rather than burning in eternal damnation for deliberately ramming my boss off the go-carting track.

It's a bright, sunny day — the sky a vibrant cornflower blue. Which doesn't seem fitting for the task in hand. My friend's face is showing the strain. It doesn't look as if she's slept in days. And the rub of it is that, sometimes, it's easier to be left than it is to leave. In reality, I should have dumped Marcus a dozen times during our relationship, but I never quite got to the point where I could call it a day. I was like a Labrador with a soggy tennis ball — completely unable to let go. And I really admire Nadia's courage and strength in doing this. It must be terrible for her.

Lewis is sitting quietly in the back of the car, cuddling his bear, and I wonder what's going through his head at this moment and how much of all this he understands. Nadia pulls out a chocolate frog that I've bought for him, takes off the wrapper then hands it over to him.

He grasps it keenly with both hands. As emotional comfort, chocolate works for all age groups, I find. "Choc-choc," Lewis says, his eyes brightening instantly.

"What do you say?" she prompts.

"Thank you," he dutifully replies, chocolate already filling his mouth.

"Do you remember Aunty Lucy?" Nadia says.

We've all met Nadia's little boy before, but to be honest it was only on the rare occasions when his mum couldn't manage to get out of the house without him. The Chocolate Lovers' Club has always been Nadia's escape from all things domestic — including her son. "Hello, Lewis."

"Hello." I can see him smiling at me in the rearview mirror, a big chocolaty ring round his mouth, and I wonder how Chantal is going to cope with her smallest lodger. Let's face it, by her own confession, she's not the most maternal person in the world. We'd better wipe Lewis's mouth clean before we arrive.

An hour later — the traffic was hell — and we pull up outside Chantal's flat. It's a big old house that looks as if it's recently been converted into flats. The apartments occupy a prime position just off Islington High Street. Frankly, I wouldn't mind moving in here myself. It makes my tatty place above a hairdresser's look more than a little downmarket. A flutter of nerves has set up in my stomach as I haven't seen Chantal since our "altercation" about Jacob, Jazz or whatever the hell his bloody name was. I'm feeling a bit less animosity toward her as, after all, this is once again down to my truly terrible taste in men. I can see now that it wasn't *actually* her fault . . .

Glancing over at Nadia, I can see that she's feeling more than a little anxious too. I give her hand a squeeze. "There could be worse ways to start a new life," I tell her. "I'm sure Chantal will look after you both."

"She's been so good to me," Nadia agrees. "How did I ever deserve friends like you?"

"Yeah," I say. "We're great, but just wait

447

until we call in the debt." Using humor to deflect a potentially emotional scene is one of my favorite pastimes. It works and Nadia laughs.

While we're still sitting there, the transit van pulls up behind us. "Come on," I say. "Let's start getting you unloaded."

We buzz Chantal's flat and she comes down to greet us, kissing Nadia warmly. Then she looks at me and asks, "Do I get a kiss?"

I shrug and allow her to wrap her arms round me as she gives me a big hug. "I'm sorry," she says.

"Me too."

"Jacob sends his best wishes too," she tells me.

"Oh, no," I say in despair as I pull away from her. "You're not still seeing him! Jeez."

"I *am* seeing him," Chantal says, "but not in that way. Just as a friend. He's very good company and, amazingly, I'm managing to resist his charms — even as a paying client. I'm also helping him to find a new job. He's trying to change his lifestyle, Lucy. I think he deserves some credit for that."

"Well, I guess there's a lot of it going on." I find that I can't muster any energy to feel angry. Jacob, for all his faults, was a very nice guy. "I wish him well too."

"He'd like to see you again, Lucy," she goes on. "He really thought a lot of you."

"I don't feel *quite* that magnanimous," I tell her with a laugh.

"Maybe one day you'll feel differently."

But before I can give that further thought, there's a little voice behind us. "Hello."

Chantal's eyebrows rise. "Oh. Hi."

We've forgotten to clean the chocolate from round Lewis's mouth and I notice that it's all over his hands too. I *so* hope that Chantal's sofa isn't cream and is a deep, dark shade of chocolate brown. Lewis cheerfully hands Chantal his teddy bear. "This is Mr. Smelly," he tells her.

Chantal holds the bear at arm's length. "I can see why."

Nadia is chewing nervously at her lip. She comes to take hold of her son's hand. "You're sure you're okay with this, Chantal?"

If Chantal is having second thoughts about taking in Nadia and her son as lodgers, then she doesn't show it. Her bright smile doesn't falter as she takes Lewis by his revolting, sticky hand and leads him indoors. "I'm sure we'll manage just fine," she says.

CHAPTER SIXTY-TWO

Tonight, I need my yoga class more than ever before. I'm in the Cobra position — arching my back for all I'm worth and trying to look serene. Inside, I'm a mass of anxiety. I relax out of the pose, i.e., collapse in a great panting heap on my mat. It's at times like this when I know I should have stayed at home with a bit of Keanu Reeves and some chocolate instead. That would have been the thing to do.

"Slide back on your mat," my yoga teacher intones. Persephone is a tiny little thing who flits about the room like a fairy. "Go into the counterpose of the Child." I curl myself into a little ball and try to still my racing brain.

I have a lot on my mind. Crush is out of hospital, but not yet back at work. I'm missing him terribly. The office feels very empty without him. Charlotte the Harlot is studiously ignoring me whenever I catch a glimpse of her in the corridor at Targa. Thankfully, I never have to darken the door of the call center, so our contact is minimal. I've spoken to him a couple of times on his mobile phone — ostensibly relating to office matters — and he sounds okay. Our conversations are a bit stilted, but I think that's because I insist on apologizing every five seconds. I begged the harridans in Human Resources to give me his home address, citing the fact that I needed to send him some work to do, and they eventually capitulated despite reciting all the data-protection laws at me. So, today, I've been online and have ordered a massive hamper of chocolate to be delivered to cheer him up. I did slip in a small order for myself too — to cheer *me* up.

The other thing is that we've got a big office bash looming — the European kick-off meeting, which is always followed by a truly humongous party. The powers-that-be fly in from all over the world, spend the day moaning about the dwindling profits of Targa and then blow most of them by plying all of their staff with free booze for the night. I missed it last year because I was working somewhere else, but this year I've not only been dragged into organizing bits of it — the mountain of paperwork on my desk is truly alarming — but I'm also going along to the do afterward. I'd rather have all of my eyelashes pulled out with a pair of tweezers than go, but then I wouldn't miss it for the world. Plus, you have a duty to be there, otherwise everyone else will be talking about you.

"Now we'll try a shoulder stand." Persephone burbles on about the best way of achieving perfection in this posture and I tune out. I've done this a million times and I'm still crap at it.

My next quandary is who to go with. Partners are invited to the party and I know that Crush will be there, complete with crutches and Charlotte the Harlot. And there's no way that I can face the pair of them on my own. I'd take along one of the girls from the Chocolate Lovers' Club, but if I took another woman with me, then before you could say "butch" it would be all around the office that I was a lesbian. I'm already on the fringes of being an acceptable employee, so there's no way I can risk another label. Chantal would, I'm sure, have exhorted me to take Jacob with me. But — call me bitter and twisted — I know that I couldn't have afforded him. He would have been able to stay for about half a glass of champagne, then my budget would have run out and he'd have been off to another booking.

I lie back on the mat and then work on hauling the bulk of my body into the air above me, with much grunting.

"Let the hips fly!" the teacher urges.

My hips are filled with concrete and they complain bitterly about their treatment. With gritted teeth, I try to arrange my limbs in the required places. My bottom is refusing to part company with terra firma. I heave and shove and push and pant and then I'm there. I'm in a shoulder stand — albeit a rather floppy one.

"Good, Lucy," Persephone says with an intensely sincere nod. "Very good." My yoga teacher's a liar, but she tries to be extra encouraging to those of us who struggle with the inexplicable mysteries of the East. Tessa, in front of me, looks like some kind of inverted ballerina. Her toes are delicately pointed toward the ceiling, her stomach isn't sagging into her breasts, her face isn't turning purple with exertion. I hate her. But there's nothing to say that one day, with a bit of extra practice, I couldn't be as good as her. Yeah, right.

Then I commit the ultimate yoga class faux pas. My mobile phone rings and, in my haste to answer it, I crash out of my shoulder stand, risking damage to life and limb or, at the very least, a broken neck. The mood of the class is somewhat shattered.

"Sorry. Sorry," I mutter as I dash toward the door, my "I'm Every Woman" ringtone still playing loudly.

Several members of the class tut in my wake and Persephone looks at me as if to say, "You'll never reach spiritual enlightenment." But then *I* could have told her that.

Out in the corridor, I lean against the wall panting heavily and answer my phone. "Hi."

"Hi, Lucy." There's a hesitation and then, "You called me?"

I did, and I'm already wondering whether I've made a huge mistake. My heart is pounding inside my chest and I know that it's not entirely down to my exertions in the shoulder stand.

"Marcus," I say. "Would you like to come to a party with me?"

CHAPTER
SIXTY-THREE

Autumn was listening to her new CD featuring the pan pipes of Peru, bought primarily because a pound from every CD purchased went toward saving the indigenous peoples of South America from a life of abject poverty. She wasn't actually sure if she liked pan pipes, but what was a little compromise in musical taste when it was all for a good cause? To take her mind off the slightly annoying, breathy noise, she hugged a cup of her favorite Green & Black's Maya Gold hot chocolate to her chest, feeling good about supporting the noble efforts of the Mayan cocoa bean farmers, and flicked through a useful guide to recycling that the local council had produced — unheeding of the extra paper and resources that the glossy leaflet used, of course.

The one good thing about the music was that it took her mind off how quiet the flat was, now that Richard had gone. In truth, she'd rather have her brother here being intrusive and obstreperous than have no idea where on earth he might be. He'd been missing for two weeks now, and her anxiety levels were increasing by the day. No matter what he did, Richard would always be her baby brother and she'd always feel protective toward him. Worryingly, Autumn had heard nothing at all from him — not even one phone call. Now she was wondering how he was managing — whether he had money, whether someone was holding him against his will, or whether he was slumped in a heap somewhere in a back alley, unknown and unloved. If he didn't turn up before long then she really would have to go to the police. He'd always been unreliable, but he'd never gone missing for this amount of time before without any contact whatsoever.

Autumn tried to turn her attention back to the sound of the Andes and the benefits of washing out tin cans, but her heart wasn't really in it. Addison had been in the center today, but he hadn't popped into the art room to see her. He'd given her a friendly enough wave as he'd passed by the door, and although he was accompanied by someone in a smart suit who looked important, he normally would have found time to say hello. Maybe she'd blown it there, but she couldn't worry about that now; she already had enough to contend with. It was a shame though, as she thought she might really like him.

Before bedtime, she luxuriated in a long, hot bubble bath trying not to think of the people in drought-stricken countries who would never be able to enjoy this simple pleasure. Just as she was sinking into the lavender-scented foam for the last few minutes of bliss, Autumn heard a key rattle in her front-door lock. Her heart leaped into her mouth and she shot upright in the water, fumbling for a towel. No one had a spare key to her flat, as far as she knew. The hinges of the door creaked slowly open.

Climbing quietly out of the bath and wrapping herself in her bathrobe, she looked for something to arm herself with, but there was nothing much apparent. She could hardly loofah an intruder into submission or BIC-razor him to death. Autumn scanned the bathroom frantically. The only thing that came to hand was the loo brush and, with a wrinkling of her nose, she pulled it from its holder. She could hear someone stumbling around the living room — maybe more than one person — and she hoped that it wasn't the same heavies that had ransacked her flat

457

before, as they'd done a great job and she'd really only just got the place straight again. Now she was wishing that she'd changed the locks and put some more security devices on the door — chains, bolts, maybe a spy hole or two, that kind of thing. How much use was a loo brush going to be against people like that? It might not be environmentally friendly but, at this very moment, Autumn wished that she had one of those rapid-fire machine guns on hand.

She crept toward the sitting room, loo brush held high like a gladiator's pugil stick and, flattening herself against the wall, risked a tentative look through the door. There, flopped into one corner of her sofa, was the familiar frame of her brother. She felt like sinking to the floor with relief. Richard was massaging his forehead with one hand, but halted when she stepped into the room.

"Hi, sis," he said wearily. "What are you planning to do with that? Viciously scrub my U-bend?"

"Does it need it?" Autumn replied, feeling consoled and irritated in equal measures.

Her brother looked terrible. His face was gray and there was an unhealthy sheen of perspiration on his brow. He'd lost weight and his jacket hung on his wasted body. His once-bright eyes were now dulled, and the gaunt hollows that surrounded them were as dark as bruises.

"I was trying to sneak in without waking you," he said.

"You go missing for weeks and then you try to sneak in without me knowing? I've hardly slept a wink since you left." Though she didn't look like she'd been the only one. "My God, Richard, I thought you could be dead! I didn't even know you had a key."

"I had one cut for myself," he confessed.

"You could have told me. I thought you were an intruder," she said. "You nearly scared me half to death. I suppose you know that some of your business colleagues took it upon themselves to rearrange my flat while I was out?"

Her brother hung his head. "Sorry about that," he said. "Didn't mean to drag you into this messy business."

"Then stop dealing drugs from my flat."

"Don't lecture me now, sis." His eyes met hers. "I'm not here to stay."

Autumn sat down opposite him and dropped the loo brush onto the carpet next to the chair. "You're still in trouble?"

Rich nodded. "It's bad."

"Where have you been?"

"It's best that you don't know."

"Were these people holding you against your will?"

"In a manner of speaking," Rich said. "Let's just say that they won't yet realize that I'm not still enjoying their hospitality."

Autumn had suspected as much. "So you've managed to give them the slip?"

Rich shrugged his shoulders wearily and she took that as a yes.

"Where are you going this time?"

"As far away as I can," her brother said. "I have to get out of the country and I have to do it sooner rather than later. I leave tomorrow."

"So soon?"

"I've booked a place at a rehab clinic in Arizona. I'm in a mess. I need to get my shit together, Autumn."

"Are you going to the Cloisters?" It was the place where all the celebrity junkies went. Her brother's silence told her that she was right. "How exactly are you funding that?"

Rich looked at her sheepishly. "I popped along to see Mater and Pater before I came here."

As always, their parents would have been only too anxious to pay for yet another period of cold turkey for their son. Autumn sighed. She could just picture her father

460

handing over his credit card while Rich made the booking. They'd both gotten everything they ever wanted from their parents, except their precious time. She wondered how different their lives might have been if they hadn't had parents who were phenomenally wealthy but were never around to nurture them.

"Will going abroad stop these people from hounding you?"

"I don't know," Richard said. "I owe them a lot of money, Autumn, and I have some of their merchandise."

"Is it here?" she asked. "Is that why they ransacked my home? Am I safe staying here?"

"You'll be fine," he said. But she didn't like the way he kept his face turned away from hers. "They were looking for the stuff, but I don't have it anymore."

"Then can't you tell them that?"

His voice hardened. "They're not the sort of people that you can reason with."

"Then where did the money go? With Mummy and Daddy's vast wealth, can't you get them to settle your debts?" It wouldn't be the first time, or probably the last, that they'd bailed Richard out for one reason or another.

"I don't think even they would give me

461

that much," he said with a sigh.

"Isn't it worth a try?"

"It's very complicated," he said, but he still wouldn't look up at her.

"It must be if you have to skip the country." And, even though she wanted to believe differently, Autumn knew that the rehab clinic was merely an excuse to get away.

"I just came to collect a few things and to say good-bye." His voice caught in his throat.

She went and sat next to him, wrapping her arms round him as tears welled in her eyes. "I wish I could protect you," she said.

"You've done all you could for me," her brother said. "And, for that, I'm truly grateful, sis. I know that I'm a pretty useless brother, but I do love you."

"You will be able to come back?" she wanted to know. "You won't have to stay away for long?"

"I'm not sure," he said. "It could be some time before the heat is off. I should probably try to make a new life for myself elsewhere."

"One that doesn't involve drugs."

"It goes without saying," Richard agreed and, for a moment, she thought that he sounded sincere.

"Then we'd better get your things together," Autumn said as she took a deep, steadying breath and stood up. Even though the last thing in the world she wanted was to watch her brother walk away from her.

CHAPTER
SIXTY-FOUR

Marcus has persuaded me that we should spend the afternoon together. He said we should take time to "get to know each other again" before the Targa party and, to be honest, when he suggested going up onto Hampstead Heath this Sunday, I couldn't think of a reason not to. The only other pressing engagement I had is one to leap around with Davina McCall — who has been sorely neglected of late. My theory for this lack of exercise is that I'm coming out in sympathy with Crush who, of course, is having to forgo all manner of physical pursuits at the moment as he's still on crutches for the next few weeks. I wonder, darkly, whether he's still managing to have sex with Charlotte the Harlot — or is that off the menu too? That, I think, would be one positive benefit of my overexuberant driving style. For me, at least.

Before I have time to dwell on this any

further, the doorbell rings and when I open the door, Marcus is standing there. I haven't seen him for ages now, but he still has the ability to turn my knees to jelly.

"Hey," he says and his sexy smile widens.

"Hey, yourself."

"Ready?"

"I'll just get my sun hat." Not that I'm in danger of getting sunstroke, but the weather has been unseasonably warm for the last few days and it shows no sign of letting up. Hurrah!

I follow Marcus down to his car where, in an unusually chivalrous move, he opens the door for me while I lower myself inside. I catch him looking at my legs and pull my dress down to cover my knees.

"You look great," he says sincerely.

"Thanks."

There are two bikes strapped to the back of the car and we set off for the short drive up Rosslyn Hill toward Hampstead. The Heath is busy, as always, when we arrive. Sunday afternoons, particularly, are rammed. We should have left the car behind and cycled up here — which probably would have killed me — as parking is a bitch. But, somehow, we manage to bag one of the coveted spaces and, instantly, Marcus sets about unloading the bikes from the back of the car, while I stand around and try to look useful.

The bikes are ready and leaning against the car when Marcus pulls a kite out of the boot. It's a big, traditional-shaped diamond one and it's white with I LOVE YOU written in big black letters with a red heart. Underneath in black marker pen, in Marcus's hand, he's added LUCY and two kisses. He gives me an uncertain smile as he says, "For you."

"I don't know what to say." And I don't, as I really hadn't seen this coming. I thought we would simply be friends again and hadn't planned for the possibility of a romantic reunion. Really, I hadn't.

"Then don't say anything," he tells me. "Let's just have some fun together today. Like we used to."

Marcus straps the kite to his back and we set off, me hitching my skirt to get onto the bike. I could do with tucking it up into my knickers really, but decorum prevents me. It's ages since I've cycled and I'm a bit wobbly as we head off onto the Heath. Marcus puts a steadying hand on my saddle and we make our way through the tracks out onto the grassy, wide open spaces. Puffing loudly, we reach the summit of the Heath and then, howling with laughter, we career back down the hill, feet out, letting the pedals spin freely, bumping along on the grass. I feel I should be singing "Raindrops Keep Falling on My Head" à la *Butch Cassidy and the Sundance Kid*. Halfway down, when I can stand the hilarity no longer and am in mortal danger of losing control of my bike and crashing, we stop to get our breath back as we admire the magnificent view with the whole of London spread out before us. The warm wind is whipping about our ears and I think it was a good idea for Marcus to bring the kite. We lock our bikes to the nearest bench and then Marcus sets up the kite, unwinding the string and laying it on the ground. Then he takes my hand and says, "Ready?"

I nod, and then hand in hand, we run like mad things across the hill, trailing the kite behind us.

"Faster," Marcus urges. "Faster."

But I'm still giggling like a loon and, unaccustomed as I am to running, can hardly keep my footing, let alone go any quicker. The kite lifts in the air, soaring up to the cloudless sky, its tail of red ribbons fluttering beneath it.

"Fantastic," Marcus says and watches it in awe.

"You are a top kite flyer," I tell him.

He puts his arm round my waist and pulls me close to him. "Take it," he instructs.

"I've never flown a kite," I say.

"Then it's about time we remedied this terrible deficiency in your social development. You're never too old to learn to fly a kite." He puts the reel into my hands and cuddles in close behind me as he guides my fingers to feed out the string, letting the kite go higher and higher until it's so far away I can hardly read the words I LOVE YOU, LUCY. I feel a tug on the string and, as Marcus lets his arms linger around me, I also feel a far too familiar tug there.

"Keep tight hold of it," Marcus says. "I have to make a quick phone call." And he steps away from me while he speaks in a lowered tone into the phone. I wonder who he's calling and, I hate to admit this, but I feel a pang of jealousy. Whatever it is that attracts me to Marcus, it just never seems to want to go away, and yet this time I really thought that I was over him.

When Marcus comes back to me he's wearing a smug grin. "Feeling hungry?"

My stomach rumbles. Food is never far away from its mind. "A bit peckish," I admit.

"Good," he says, and turns me to face the other way. Over the hill, there is a line of three booted and suited butlers marching steadily toward us. Wearing pin-striped trousers and morning coats in true Jeeves mode, one of them is carrying a hamper, one bears a picnic rug and one follows up with a champagne bucket complete with a bottle.

"Oh, Marcus," I say with a tearful laugh. My ex-boyfriend does like to do things in style.

"I thought we'd have a picnic." So he reels in the kite, while the trio of butlers set up our picnic on the Heath. When they're finished, they bow lightly to us and then march away again into the woods.

Marcus throws himself onto the tartan blanket that they've spread on the ground, then holds out his hand for me to join him. He pours me a glass of champagne and toasts me with his own. "To us."

And even though I'm not sure that there is an "us," I echo his sentiments. "To us."

Marcus starts to undo the leather straps of the hamper.

"This is a lovely idea," I say. "Thank you."

He stops and sighs at me. "You're worth it," he says. "I just wish we could be like this all the time."

"We could," I tell him. "This may not be the time to mention it, but it was always you that messed it up."

"I'm determined to put an end to that," he says sincerely. "You have to trust me. I've changed. I've had time on my own to think about things." He fixes me with an earnest gaze. "I didn't even dare to phone you, Lucy. You wouldn't believe how elated I was when you called. Believe me, I'm not going to blow this last chance."

I don't point out that I hadn't actually planned to give him a last chance. All I wanted was a date for the Targa party so that I didn't look lame.

"This is what I want," he continues. "*You're* what I want."

I open my mouth to speak, but nothing comes out.

He puts a finger to my lips. "Don't say anything now," he says. "Let's just enjoy this picnic, enjoy today." And he starts pulling out plates and napkins and cutlery.

You might expect such a grand hamper to be filled with smoked salmon, a cocktail of olives — ciabatta bread, perhaps. But no. Marcus knows that my taste in food runs to the far side of Philistine. Instead, the hamper is packed with pork pies, hot pizza wrapped in foil, Walkers crisps, Pringles, my very favorite muffins from Chocolate Heaven and, in its own little cooler, a tub of Ben & Jerry's Chocolate Chip Cookie

Dough Ice Cream. He holds up the tub and I duly give an appreciative little gasp. "Oh, Marcus!"

Marcus's smile is confident now and he knows that he has me, once again, in his thrall. And I realize that I'm powerless to resist him. There's nothing I can do; this man has a GPS navigation system that takes him straight to the center of my heart.

CHAPTER
SIXTY-FIVE

"If you start going out with Marcus again," Nadia says, "you know that we'll have to kill you."

"It was just a date," I insist and bury my face over my glass of hot chocolate to hide my discomfort. I'm vainly hoping that the steam might work as some sort of mini face-lift while I'm here, since all this emotional turmoil is taking its toll on my skin as well as my heart.

An emergency meeting of the Chocolate Lovers' Club has been convened. It's lunch-time and we've all managed to get here at short notice. Not that we ever take much persuasion. If we ever miss more than a few days, then Clive and Tristan begin to wonder if we've all died of some hideous disease brought on by the absence of chocolate. Hardly the case for me. Vast amounts of chocolate are being consumed as I contemplate this latest development with Marcus. I just had to get some impartial advice. But I'd forgotten that the members of the Chocolate Lovers' Club are not impartial when it comes to Marcus. We have a plate of walnut brownies between us and Nadia picks at one.

"A date," I say to myself more than anyone else. "Nothing more."

"Involving an elaborately staged picnic and a kite with I LOVE YOU, LUCY painted on it?" Chantal chips in.

"Okay. It was quite a romantic kind of date." I squirm under their collective scrutiny. "But that's it."

"So you're not seeing him again?" Nadia asks.

"Not really," I tell her, and then decide to fess up before I'm rumbled. I'm well aware of the penalties that can be foisted upon you for telling lies. "Not in the *seeing him* sense of the word. I'm having dinner with him tonight, but only because we need to be on friendly terms again before the Targa office party. After that it's *so* over."

"You could have taken one of us," Autumn very helpfully suggests. "I would have loved to have gone. I don't get the chance to dress up very often." Do they make evening dresses in cheesecloth? I wonder. "Plus, it might well have taken my mind off my lovely brother's sudden departure."

Autumn has just come back from Heath-row where she's been waving good-bye to her brother Richard for the foreseeable future. Despite putting a brave face on it, we can all tell that she's really down. Her eyes are red from crying and she won't tell us the full story of where Richard has been and what he's been doing. We know that he's off to a rehab clinic though — so that's got to be a good sign, hasn't it? She's also stuffing in brownies without a thought for the starving masses — a sure sign that she's distracted.

"I can't go with another girl. They'll all think I'm gay." I lower my voice just in case Clive or Tristan are eavesdropping on our conversation — which, of course, being gay, they normally are. "It's not that I have anything against being gay," I say. "I just don't want to be it. And I'm at that funny age. Start having long gaps between boy-friends and they all think you've turned into a muff-muncher."

Autumn looks shocked. "You can't say that!"

This is exactly why I can't take a girlfriend to the party, because this is the sort of politically incorrect terminology that would be bandied around the office about me, and

I'd never be able to show my face there again. "Would you have wanted to spend the evening being looked at as if we had far too much knowledge of each other's bikini lines?"

"No," Autumn admits.

"Me neither."

"You could have taken Jacob," Chantal suggests.

I *knew* she'd say that. "Don't even go there." I shake my head vehemently. "After what happened, I just don't fancy Jacob anymore."

"Neither do I," Chantal says, trying to make light of the situation. "Well, not too much." She smiles across the table at me. "He's had a change of career and he still asks about you, Lucy."

"Well, give him my best wishes. I hope whatever he's doing now works out for him."

We're still a little tense with each other after the revelation of our mutual acquaintance with the aforementioned Jacob, and I don't really want to know what Chantal is or isn't up to with him, but I'm trying not to let it affect our friendship. And there's no doubt that Chantal *is* a good friend. She and Nadia have settled into a cozy routine in their new flat and seem to be getting along great. Today, they've brought Lewis with them and he's sitting cuddled up quite comfortably next to Chantal on the sofa. When Nadia and I were at the counter choosing our brownies, she told me that Chantal was insisting on reading Lewis's bedtime story to him every night and that she'd spent most of Saturday showing him how to do finger painting. Not a bad turnaround for someone who professes to hate kids. I smile to myself and think that Chantal and Lewis look quite at home together. Nadia's son has his own plate of chocolate chip cookies to keep him amused (it's good to see that we're breeding the next generation of chocolate addicts) and he's flicking quietly through a book, even though his eyes are rolling with tiredness.

"Be careful." Nadia pats my knee. "We don't want you falling under Marcus's spell again. Next thing, you'll be sleeping with him, in the *sleeping* with him sense of the word," Nadia says, mimicking me. "Then the whole emotional-roller-coaster thing will start up all over again. Take it from one who knows."

"But he seems so different this time," I say defensively. "He's never been quite so attentive before."

"Lucy, sweetheart," Chantal says. "Tread very carefully. It's about time you had some luck, but Marcus doesn't have a great track record. He'll only hurt you again, and no one deserves to get their heart broken that many times. Especially not by the same guy."

"What do you think, Autumn?"

"I think we should have some more chocolate," she says, avoiding the question, and picks up the plate to take it to the counter.

So a unanimous thumbs-down from my dear friends. I know that I should trust their instincts — let's face it, they can't be any worse than mine. But if they could have seen Marcus yesterday and how fabulous he was, then they might just think, like me, that maybe, just maybe, he's changed.

CHAPTER SIXTY-SIX

I've bought a killer dress and killer heels for the office party. And both are *killing* me. The evening has hardly begun and I'm already developing bunions and hammer toes. My dress is so figure hugging — to use a euphemism for flipping tight — that I can hardly breathe. I don't know who I bought the dress to impress, but I do know that I wanted to look my absolute best tonight. And it's not just because this is going to be Crush's first appearance back at Targa and I am, for some reason, very nervous about seeing him. Or the fact that he's going to be coming along with Charlotte the Harlot.

Marcus and I have been dating again for the last few weeks. He has been a model boyfriend and, frankly, it's scaring me. He's so attentive that he's almost morphed into a stalker. We've been joined at the hip since our brilliant day at Hampstead Heath and his courtship of me — if that isn't too old-fashioned a word — has been relentless. I've been for more romantic meals than I've had hot dinners. Even I'm getting slightly fed up of us gazing wistfully at each other over a shared chocolate mousse. Davina and I will have to jump around together for the next five years to work off all the calories I've consumed in the name of love. Perhaps that's why my killer dress is a little more asphyxiating than it was when I first purchased it.

It seems strange for us to be a couple again after I'd fervently and absolutely declared that we were no more. But is it really love? There's definitely a part of me that can't relax into it this time. Maybe my trust in Marcus has been eroded too much over the years, but I feel as if I'm holding something back. Can this "honeymoon period" really last? Then again, after all that business with Jacob and his "alternative" career, who *can* I trust? Is it better to stick with Marcus and be damned? At least I'm aware of all his faults. And, who knows, maybe this time he truly has changed. I'm planning to give up trying to analyze my relationships, as it never works, so I'm just going to go with the flow.

The party is being held at a vast banquet hall near the office, decorated in the corporate colors of navy blue and silver. I was responsible for tracking down balloons, streamers, party poppers, jaunty hats and customized crackers in said hues, and my feet are killing me because I've been here all day supervising the blowing up of balloons and the hanging of streamers. The place is looking great. Helen, Human Resources' chief harridan, has booked a Blues Brothers tribute band and a well-known club DJ — who I've never heard of — to provide the entertainment. Marcus and I are standing at the edge of the crowd. I'm anxious that this should all go well and he's holding my hand tightly for reassurance. We're imbibing pink champagne with gusto. I know why I'm throwing the booze down my neck as if it's going out of fashion, but I'm not sure why Marcus is.

"Did I tell you that I love you?" Marcus says, lightly squeezing my fingers.

"Not for the last ten minutes," I answer with a smile.

"Well, I do," my boyfriend tells me. "You look fantastic."

I try to breathe in my dress. Then, just as I'm going for a major exhalation, my efforts are arrested as Crush makes an entrance, hopping in on his crutches. Taking a gulp of my champagne, I note that he has scrubbed up particularly well tonight. He looks great in his dinner suit and even manages a nod toward suave and sophisticated despite being hampered by surgical appliances and the fact that, because of his plaster cast, one leg of his trousers is ripped to the thigh. Of Charlotte the Harlot, there's no sign. Crush scans the room, looking as if he's searching for someone — perhaps the old bat herself. Instantly, he's surrounded by a crowd of well-wishers, slapping him on the back as if he's just rowed the Atlantic single-handed. I choke on my champagne, managing to get the bubbles out of my nose, and Marcus slaps me on the back too, but in a different way.

"I ought to go and say hello to my boss," I tell him when I've finished spluttering. "See how he is."

"That's the guy you barged off the go-carting track?" Marcus queries.

"The very same."

There's a frown across his brow. "He's younger than I imagined," my boyfriend says. "And better looking."

It's not as if I ever described Crush to him as an old fart, but perhaps I didn't exactly tell Marcus quite how dishy Mr. Aiden Holby is.

"Come and meet him," I say to Marcus.

"Maybe later," he replies, the frown deepening. "You go. I'll just wait here."

"Okay," I say. "I won't be long." And, leaving Marcus hanging out by the canapés, I go over to Crush. By now his merry band of well-wishers has dispersed slightly and, when they see me approaching, the remaining few make themselves scarce, as they're all only too well aware that I'm the one responsible for his current predicament. I bet they're worried that there might be a scene.

Crush gives me one of his winning smiles. "Hi, Gorgeous."

"Hi, yourself," I say. "How are you managing?"

We both cast an uneasy glance at his crutches. "I'm an expert on these now, but I'll be glad when the plaster comes off," he says with a sigh. "It itches like hell."

"I'm really sorry."

"Don't start that again," Crush warns. "It's done. We'll both look back at this and laugh. One day." But there's a twinkle in his eye and I know that he doesn't hold this little accident against me. "Thanks for the regular supplies of chocolate," he says. "Much appreciated. I've had a very tasty convalescence."

"It was the least I could do." We haven't

482

had the opportunity to talk properly over the last few weeks. Our conversations have been kept mainly to work issues and I've been sending parcels of documents and chocolate to him at home by courier — but that's all.

"Where's Charlotte?" I ask before I can help myself.

"She's coming later," Crush tells me. "With someone else."

"Oh." I feel myself flush.

"Couldn't stand life with a poor old cripple," he says.

"I'd call that very shallow," I say, snatching the moral high ground.

"The minute our dizzy social whirl was curtailed, I didn't see her for dust."

"I'm sorry . . ."

"Stop apologizing, Gorgeous," Crush says firmly. "That definitely wasn't your fault."

"I would have stayed with you," I offer, flushing a deeper shade of mortified.

"I know you would." His eyes sparkle again. "Maybe we can have a dance later, so that you can make it up to me. It will have to be a *very* slow one though."

I giggle nervously. "I'm actually here with Marcus," I say, glancing back over my shoulder at him. He raises his glass of champagne in our direction. "Marcus, my boyfriend."

"Ah," Crush says, and he looks more than a little disappointed. "You're back together then?"

"Yes. Yes. Well, sort of. I had no one else to come with . . ." I don't quite know how to explain this. I can hardly tell Crush that the only reason Marcus and I are back together is that I couldn't face being here alone watching him and Charlotte getting down to it. Instead, I sigh inwardly and mumble, "And we're . . . Yes. We're back together."

"Another time then."

"Oh. Yes. Of course." I'm babbling and can't stop. "I should get back to Marcus."

"I'd better hop to it then," Crush says rather sadly. "Have a great evening."

"Thanks," I reply stiffly. "You too."

He leans forward and kisses me on the cheek, whispering, "You look beautiful, by the way." With an ungainly hop, he then turns on his crutches and lollops away, leaving me touching my skin where his lips have been.

CHAPTER
SIXTY-SEVEN

I am gloriously, fabulously and thoroughly drunk. My killer shoes have gone, I know not where, and I am currently feeling no pain. No pain at all. If success can be measured by degrees of drunkenness and debauchery, then the office party has been a *huge* success. Even the harridans from Human Resources are happy.

The Blues Brothers tribute band is in full swing and so am I. Marcus and I are on the dance floor strutting our funky stuff to "Mustang Sally." As I jig about, I notice that Crush is sitting by the edge of the dance floor with his broken leg up on a chair. Our eyes meet and he gives me some sort of rueful, regretful look. He looks a lot more compos mentis than I am and I have a brief window of sobriety in the depths of my drunken stupor. For one mad moment, I think that it would be nice to be sitting there quietly with Crush rather than lurching about to the band and I give him a warm smile. As he returns it, Marcus snatches my arm and flings me round again. My boyfriend spins me in some sort of exuberant *Strictly Come Dancing* twist and I twirl wildly away from him on unsteady legs. My feet feel suddenly very slippery on the floor and my balance goes all to pot. My legs get themselves in a lovely tangle and, with more enthusiasm than grace, I find myself heading straight for Crush. Tripping over my own toes, and with an unhealthy thud, I land sprawled out on his lap.

Crush does a magnificent job of breaking my fall, despite being physically incapacitated himself. His strong arms are round my waist, holding me to him, lest I fall to the floor and disgrace myself further.

"Thank you," I breathe.

"No problem, Gorgeous," he says as he grins down at me. "This is an improvement on your rafting technique. This time you get ten out of ten for artistic interpretation. Are you trying to break my other leg?"

"I have to be going," I slur. I'd like to reach up and stroke his face, even though it's ever so slightly blurred. Maybe even give those sexy lips a big, fat kiss.

Then I feel Marcus's arms pulling me up. "Thanks, mate," he says to Crush. But he says it rather crisply.

My boyfriend pulls me into the middle of the dance floor and, in a slightly more subdued fashion, we resume our bopping — but I can still feel Crush's eyes on me as the music comes to an end.

As we all look suitably exhausted by our exertions, the Blues Brothers sound-alikes slow the tempo down and move into the mellow strains of Van Morrison's "Have I Told You Lately That I Love You?"

"This one's especially for Lucy Lombard," the sunglass-wearing singer announces and there's a ripple of polite applause while I turn forty shades of red.

Marcus pulls me into his arms and holds me tightly as we stagger round drunkenly. We're both being a support for each other, as far as I can tell.

"Thank you," I say. "That's very nice."

"I love you," he tells me earnestly. "Do you love me?"

This isn't the time to voice any doubts about our renewed relationship or to discuss the finer points of what "love" actually means, and I can't fault how Marcus has behaved recently. He's clearly been reading the *How to Be a Great Boyfriend* manual. So I say, "Yes," and he nearly squeezes the life out of me.

There's a catch in his voice as he tells me, "You don't know how much I've wanted to hear that again."

Van the Man's lyrics drift over me as we stagger round in ragged circles and I try not to look over at Crush too much to see if he's still watching me. But every time I casually glance his way, he's steadily returning my gaze. As the music comes to an end, Marcus gives my arm a squeeze and says, "I'll be right back."

He leaves me standing alone on the dance floor as the other couples start to drift away. I turn to leave and think about going over to talk to Crush, but then the singer says, "Can I have your attention, please, ladies and gentlemen!"

Looking back at the stage, I see that Marcus is standing next to him, looking flushed.

"May I present Mr. Marcus Canning!"

To my abject horror, Marcus takes the microphone. This had all been going so well — what on earth is my boyfriend playing at? He didn't tell me he was going to do this. In fact, I don't even know what he's going to do! I want to hiss at him to get down and stop making a spectacle of us both, but he's too far away. Then he says, "This one is for Lucy too," and he starts to sing. I had no idea that Marcus *could* sing

— other than holding a passable tune in the shower.

I'm standing on my own in the middle of the floor while the rest of the Targa employees have formed a circle around me. They sway in time to the music while Marcus launches into an amazingly good rendition of the Commodores' "Three Times a Lady." This man has been watching far too much *X Factor.* I keep my eyes fixed firmly on Marcus and daren't even risk a peek in Crush's direction. Who knows what he'll be thinking about this! I'm not even sure what *I'm* thinking.

When Marcus has finished, which seems like hours later to me, he must have sung the twelve-inch version — everyone around me breaks into wild applause. I join in. He really was very good. But I'm also applauding because I'm glad it's over. Marcus takes a bow and then signals for quiet. When everyone is hushed again, he says, "Lucy Lombard, will you do me the very great honor of becoming my wife?"

More applause, while the impact of his words hits me full in the face and I suddenly sober up rather quickly. I'm sure that my mouth has dropped open, but it's failing to speak. It seems to be a recurring pattern with Marcus. I can't believe he's just asked me to marry him. In front of all this crowd! He stands expectantly on the stage and my poor, champagne-addled brain can't compute this. Marcus, the cheating, lying, commitment phobe, has just proposed!

Around me, the spontaneous applause turns into a rhythmic clap and the crowd starts to chant, "Yes! Yes! Yes!" Marcus is still looking at me hopefully. My fellow employees finally run out of steam in their exhortations and the room falls quiet. You could hear a pin drop. I remain catatonic with shock.

My boyfriend licks his lips nervously. "Lucy?"

Then, by some miracle, I find my voice and say, "Yes."

All the partygoers erupt in a cheer. Marcus jumps off the stage and runs toward me, falling to his knees at my feet. The cheer escalates. Out of his pocket, he pulls a huge, sparkling engagement ring. Honestly, it's bigger than the disco glitter ball hanging from the ceiling above us. There's a princess-cut, whopping emerald in the middle and a circle of diamonds surrounding it. Marcus slips it onto my finger. It's a bit tight, but it goes on with a push. "I hope you like it."

"It's fabulous," I say. And it is. It's not the

solitaire diamond that I'd always envisaged for myself, but it's truly lovely and it must have cost Marcus a packet. My mouth is dry as I say, "Thank you."

Marcus grasps me in a bear hug. I can't help looking over his shoulder at Crush, who raises his hands and gives a couple of desultory claps, but his smile is sad.

"I love you," Marcus whispers in my ear.

I hardly know what's happening. But I do know that the good members of the Chocolate Lovers' Club will kill me stone dead for this. I should be elated, but I'm in too much of a state for any kind of response to kick in. This is what I've wanted, isn't it? This is what I've always wanted.

The band launches into a raucous, rock 'n' roll version of "I'm Getting Married in the Morning" and everyone else joins in, leaping around the dance floor like mad things.

Marcus, drunk with joy, twirls me round and round. And, as I spin giddily, my brain whirling, I can see that Crush has gone.

CHAPTER
SIXTY-EIGHT

As soon as Marcus has slipped the ring on my finger, we have to do the rounds of showing everyone my new sparkler. Even the harridans from Human Resources are suitably impressed — although they do go as green as my emerald when they coo their congratulations through gritted teeth. There's still no sign of Crush, and I assume that he must have left immediately after Marcus's unexpected and rather startling performance. I felt that I wanted to say something to Aiden, but I wasn't sure what. Maybe it's just as well that he's departed.

My new fiancé — how strange does that sound? — then rushes me out of the office party and into the street. It's one office do that I'll certainly remember for a long time.

Outside the hall, there's a rickshaw taxi waiting, all decorated with white balloons, and the driver is resplendent in a smart white suit rather than the usual garb of scruffy jeans and T-shirt. Marcus helps me inside and we set off. Now we're being cycled through the streets of London, glasses of champagne in hand. Cars are tooting at us and not in a "Get a move on!" way. The evening is warm, but there's a cool breeze rushing over us as we travel. Marcus has given me his jacket, which is now round my shoulders. My hangover seems to be kicking in early as my head is throbbing and I'm feeling vaguely nauseous. He pulls me toward him and I snuggle against my boyfriend — fiancé — even though I still feel strangely detached.

"I didn't know that you could sing," I say.

"I had lessons," he says.

"Just for me?"

He nods.

"I'm impressed."

"I hoped you would be." Marcus slips his arm around me. "My repertoire is very limited though. In fact, that's the only song I *can* sing."

I laugh. "Well, it was very nice of you to go to all that trouble."

He looks into my eyes and strokes a finger down my cheek. "I wanted to make sure that you said yes."

And I wonder, Is that why he chose such a public arena in which to propose? Or was it simply Marcus being Marcus?

"I thought we'd get married as soon as possible," he says. "I can't see any reason to wait, can you?"

And, to be honest, I can't — even though the very thought of it makes my stomach lurch. *I'm going to be married. To Marcus.* Perhaps if I say it enough then I'll eventually start to believe it.

"I like the idea of a winter wedding," Marcus continues.

Winter isn't that far away. "Spring weddings are nice," I counter.

"I thought we'd have a *huge* celebration," my fiancé says. (No, still can't get used to that word.) "No expense spared. I want all our friends and family there to see me declare my love for you."

Personally, I'd always fancied sneaking away for a quiet wedding on a white, sandy beach somewhere, far from all the usual hassle. "We could just have a small affair, very personal."

"No way," Marcus says. "Now that I've decided to do this, we're going to do it in style!"

I suppose I should ring my errant parents and tell them my good news, but I can't make myself do it just now. Anyway, it's late. Tomorrow will be soon enough. They've only met Marcus a couple of times, but I know that they really liked him. Plus I've never told them how often he's broken my heart over the last few years. What the eye doesn't see, the heart doesn't grieve over — right? I don't like to give them any reason to worry about me. Still, I shouldn't be thinking such negative thoughts now. This is a time for rejoicing. I should phone the members of the Chocolate Lovers' Club too, but I'd rather tell them face-to-face. I know that they have their doubts about Marcus's sincerity, but I'm sure they'll be absolutely thrilled for me — once they know that it's what I want.

"I love you," Marcus says softly. "I want to tell you that, every single day of my life."

He lays his body against mine and kisses me deeply. A sigh escapes my lips. I want to relax into this, but for some reason a wave of panic keeps rising within me. I'm going to be married. *I'm going to be married.* As I close my eyes and try to surrender to Marcus's tender assault, I can't help but see a vision of Crush's sad face.

CHAPTER
SIXTY-NINE

The wooden blinds are down and the CLOSED sign is on the door of Chocolate Heaven. It's the evening after the office party and I'm still dealing with the aftermath. I've spent all day showing off my engagement ring at Targa and doing very little work. Crush didn't appear in the office today and he hasn't returned any of my telephone calls — which were all urgent and work-related, of course — but apparently Helen the chief harridan from Human Resources tells me that he'll be back at work on Monday. All the members of the Chocolate Lovers' Club are sitting in a huddle around me, Clive and Tristan included.

"Well?" Nadia says. "Spill the beans. What's the great announcement you've called us here for?"

I take a deep breath. "I'm getting married."

There's a stunned silence around the table

— which I'd sort of expected. There was also a stunned silence when I phoned both of my parents. People get married all the time, but clearly my closest friends and my relatives didn't see it in the cards for me.

Finally, Clive breaks the ice by clapping his hands together. We all jump. "I'll get champagne," he says.

We all look up at him blankly.

"We *are* celebrating?" he asks hesitantly.

Nadia looks at me. "*Are* we celebrating?"

"Of course!" I cry. "I'm getting married."

"To Marcus," Chantal observes.

"Doesn't this prove that he's changed?" My friends exchange worried looks that say they are unconvinced. "It was wonderful," I tell them. "He proposed at the office party. He got up on stage and sang a song."

"Marcus did?" Nadia looks flabbergasted.

"Then he had a rickshaw waiting to take us round London. It was very romantic."

Autumn grasps my hand. "It sounds absolutely wonderful, Lucy," she says. "I'm so pleased for you." She then gives what I can only call a glare to the others. "We *all* are. Aren't we?"

"We're delighted," Nadia says with a sudden change of tone. I think there might have been some kicking going on under the table. "Let's have a look at the ring then."

I hold out my sparkler.

"Wow!" Chantal says. "Someone who flashes that amount of cash must be serious. It's beautiful." I admire it again myself. It really is growing on me. Chantal comes over and hugs me. "Congratulations, Lucy. Take no notice of Nadia and me. I guess that being so recently estranged from our husbands has turned us into cynical old bags."

"She's right," Nadia agrees. "You and Marcus have as much chance of making this work as anyone does these days."

I think that's a compliment.

"I'll get that fizz," Clive says with a sigh of relief.

Tristan stands too. "I wish you'd have let us know, I'd have baked something special. You are going to let us do the wedding cake, aren't you?"

"That would be great," I say, even though I hadn't given a thought to wedding cake. Both Clive and Tristan disappear happily into the back of the shop.

"Have you set a date?" Autumn asks.

"Not yet," I reply. "Marcus wants to get married as soon as possible, but I don't want to rush things. I want it to be right."

My friends exchange another look. This time they're telling me that I should be whipping Marcus down the aisle without delay. But, frankly, I need some time to adjust to this new state of things. If, after all this to-ing and fro-ing, I'm finally going to be a bride, then I'd like to take it at a slow pace and enjoy it.

Clive appears with a bottle of champagne and some glasses. Tristan follows behind him with a chocolate fudge cake. I don't know which makes my heart lift more. Actually, yes I do. They set the cake out in front of me. "Practice run," Tristan says, handing me a large knife. "Come on. Cut the cake."

Doing as I'm told, I make a dramatic performance out of pushing the knife through the thick, fudgy icing. Everyone claps. I feel as if there's a tear in my eye. I could certainly get used to all of this attention. Tristan takes the cake from me and, expertly, slices it into large pieces. He has the measure of us well enough by now to know that we are not small-slice women. Then he hands it around.

"This is wonderful," I say, taking the first bite. "Perhaps I should have a chocolate fudge cake for the wedding."

"Sounds good to me," Nadia says.

"Was Crush at the party?" Chantal asks.

"Yes." Suddenly the cake is cloying in my mouth.

"Is he pleased for you?"

"I don't know," I mumble. "He didn't say anything." That tear is definitely in my eye now. I put my cake down. How can I tell them that I can't bear to think of the sad look that was on his face when I said yes? How can I tell them that Crush's reaction is bothering me far more than it should in this situation? All I have to do is get through the weekend and then I can find out what he's thinking when he comes back to work on Monday. "I'm sure he'll be thrilled," I lie. "Why shouldn't he be?"

And I have to ask that question of myself — why shouldn't he be? Wouldn't I have been delighted for Crush if he'd announced that he was going to be married to Charlotte the Harlot? And the answer is, *No, I would not.*

CHAPTER SEVENTY

We're in Marcus's car, speeding out into the countryside. Maroon 5's *Songs About Jane* is blaring out of the stereo. Fancy loving someone so much that you write a whole album of songs about them — even though the relationship went hideously wrong in the end. (Don't they all?) Perhaps that will be Marcus's next grand gesture. Instead of just singing soppy tunes, he'll be penning them too. Having set the bar so high with our last few outings, I wonder what he's going to do to maintain this state of heightened romance. Is the rest of my life with him going to be one big anticlimax? I push the thought to the back of my mind.

"This is a great place," Marcus says over the track. "You'll love it. I know you will."

We're going to look at a wedding venue that Marcus has set his heart on. The route looks vaguely familiar, but Marcus won't tell me where it is — he wants it to be a surprise. I'm praying that this is the only surprise. I'm hoping that when we get there, the place isn't decked with LUCY AND MARCUS balloons and there aren't already two hundred guests assembled and waiting for us to exchange our wedding vows. You can never be too sure with Marcus these days. He's making me very nervous. I wish I'd washed my hair and had lost a couple of stone just in case. To ease my anxiety, I'm comfort-eating a bar of Clive's extra-special milk chocolate and I pop a square into Marcus's mouth.

"I love you." My fiancé's hand slips along my thigh. "Not far now."

Before long, we turn into a narrow lane and, even before we sweep through the grand wrought-iron gates and head up toward the lake and the dolphin fountain, I know exactly where we are.

I stare out of the window in horror. "This is it?" I gasp.

"Beautiful, isn't it?" Marcus says, mistaking the tone of my gasping for one of appreciation.

Trington Manor certainly does look stunning in the daylight, but I can't get married here, the scene of our infamous jewelry heist. What if someone recognizes me?

"I've booked us in for lunch," my fiancé

says. "But I thought we'd have a look round first."

I don't want to look round. I already know this place far too well.

"They have their own chapel in the grounds," Marcus tells me as he parks in front of the splendid house. I must admit that I didn't suss that out for our raid. "It's small," he continues. "We could squeeze in about a hundred people."

"A hundred!" I think I'm going to be stuck in gasp mode for some time.

"Darling," he says with a patronizing laugh, "I've roughed out a list and we'd want a minimum of a hundred there. As it is, some people might have to come just to the reception."

I don't know that I have a hundred friends. Just three would suit me: Chantal, Nadia and Autumn. I could live without my parents being there either. That makes ninety-seven guests for Marcus. He jumps out of the car like Tigger on speed. "Come on, Lucy. Let's look around."

I haul my weary arse out of the car. Why is nothing ever straightforward in this life? In *my* life?

Marcus takes my hand, pulling me up the steps and into the reception area of the hotel. I'm thanking God that it's sunny and

I'm wearing sunglasses. The only thing that's missing is Mr. John Smith's Mercedes which, in the intervening period since my last visit, has been lifted out of the lake. Unfortunately, though, the receptionist is the same one who was on duty the night of our jewelry heist — I'm sure it is. I hope to goodness that she doesn't recognize me. So I hang back, keeping my sunglasses firmly in place and trying to let my hair flop over my face while Marcus tells her that we have an appointment with the wedding planner.

Supposing Mr. John Smith is also paying a return visit in whatever his new car is? That would just be my luck. I glance nervously into the bar. Why didn't we wear wigs when we did our heist? Or comedy moustaches? That was a serious flaw in my planning. But then, I didn't bank on coming back here in a rush either. And I certainly didn't foresee having my very own wedding here but a short time later.

The wedding planner arrives. She's called Michelle and she takes us out onto the grounds to see the chapel. It's a glorious, bright sunny day and the garden is fragrant with all kinds of native wildflowers that I can't name. There's a fabulous view over the best of British countryside and a mellow stone terrace from where it would be perfect for our guests to enjoy it. We cross the lawn to the chapel and Michelle burbles on about a range of packages, the sort of food available and the hotel accommodation for the myriad guests Marcus is intent on inviting.

"We put a beautiful flower bower up to the door of the chapel for weddings," Michelle says, but I tune out. I am *so* not going to get married here, even though it is undoubtedly a wonderful venue. The chapel dates back to the fourteenth century and is made of thick, rough stone. Inside, it is so idyllic that it almost takes my breath away. The sun through the stained-glass windows casts a dapple of rainbow patterns on the stone floor. Even with my sunglasses on, it looks great. I risk a peep over the top of them. This would look gorgeous decorated with white flowers. I can just see myself drifting up the aisle in a simple white satin dress. A hundred people in here would definitely be cozy . . . but I'm not going to have my wedding here, so it really doesn't matter.

Marcus squeezes my hand and asks, "Do you love it?"

"Yes," I say, "but —"

Michelle whisks us out of the chapel and back to the main house. "I'll show you the banquet hall," she says. "It's set for a dinner that we're holding tonight. That holds two hundred."

"Fantastic," Marcus says.

Two hundred? We'd have to rent guests to make up that number.

Michelle throws open the doors to the banquet room and I nearly gasp again. Arched stone windows with leaded lights make up one wall, creating a light and airy atmosphere. Dozens of tables are swathed in crisp white linen; they sparkle with highly polished crystal glasses and silver cutlery. The room is laden with arrangements of pastel pink roses and highly scented lilies — they're on the tables, on the sills of the windows, standing on tall iron pedestals. It looks absolutely perfect.

"I thought we could have something just like this," Marcus says.

"Yes," I say, "but —"

"Let's go and have lunch." Marcus pulls me excitedly to the door. "We can discuss it some more."

We say our good-byes to Michelle and head to the bar. "What do you want to drink?" Marcus asks as we wait to be served.

"Wine," I say flatly. "I need wine. Lots of wine."

Marcus smiles indulgently at me. Then

the barman comes over. "Hello again," he says to me.

So much for my superb sunglasses disguise. I take them off and stuff them in my bag. "Hi." I give him an uneasy smile and stare out of the window so that he doesn't try to engage me in further conversation.

"A large glass of dry white wine and an orange juice," Marcus says, and while the barman busies himself, my fiancé turns to me. "Have you been here before?"

"Never," I say, hoping that I'm not too scarlet. "He must be mistaking me for someone else." How can I tell Marcus that last time I was here, my friends and I were conducting a robbery? Albeit a robbery of something that technically belonged to one of us in the first place. I'm not sure how the law — or my fiancé — would view that. Maybe Marcus and I could have a laugh about it, but maybe he wouldn't find it funny at all. "Perhaps I've got a twin."

"God forbid," Marcus says.

The barman sets down our drinks and, thankfully, moves away. Marcus clinks his orange juice against my white wine and we sip in unison. Well, Marcus sips, I glug. "It's a great place, isn't it?"

"It's fabulous." Truly, it is. This would be a wonderful place for a wedding. In different circumstances. "But we can't possibly get married here."

My fiancé looks puzzled. "Why not?"

"Er . . . Er . . ." This would be a good time to come clean. But I don't. Instead, I say, "It's far too expensive. My parents wouldn't stump up for this — I wouldn't even ask them to — and I certainly don't have any spare cash that could pay for this." All of which is true.

Marcus takes my hand in his. He twiddles my engagement ring around with his fingers. The circle of diamonds catches the light. "I don't want you to worry about a thing," he says with a tender smile. "I have enough money. I'll sort everything out."

"Marcus . . ."

"You do like it here?"

"Yes," I say, "but —"

"I'm so glad," my fiancé tells me with a satisfied smile. "Because I've already booked it."

CHAPTER
SEVENTY-ONE

Ted had finally answered one of Chantal's telephone calls and, even more surprisingly, he'd agreed to meet with her. He had insisted that she be the one to select the venue for their rendezvous, so she'd chosen to go to Chocolate Heaven because it was the place where she felt most comfortable. If she was going to have to face Ted in difficult circumstances, then she might as well do it fortified by some of her favorite foodstuff.

Chantal sat in one of the window seats and Clive brought her over a piece of chocolate torte and a cappuccino while she waited anxiously for her husband.

Clive patted her hand in a motherly fashion. "Chin up. You're looking great, darling," he said theatrically. "He won't be able to resist you."

"I hope you're right," Chantal replied, and at that moment, the door swung open and

Ted walked in. He smiled tightly when he saw Chantal and walked over to her table. She stood up, but before she had an opportunity to embrace him, Ted slid awkwardly into the seat opposite her. His handsome face looked tired and drawn. Maybe he'd lost some weight.

"What can I get you, Ted?" Clive asked, and her husband looked taken aback at being addressed by his first name. "Sorry," Clive said. "I should have called you Mr. Hamilton. But I feel I've known you for years. Chantal talks about you so much."

Ted looked even more taken aback by that revelation. "No problem," he said. Chantal hoped that Clive's overt style of schmoozing was working. "I'll take the same." He flicked a finger toward Chantal's coffee and torte.

"Sure thing." Clive winked at her behind Ted's back and mouthed "Hunk!" before he turned away.

She smiled in spite of her tension and sat down again. "It's good to see you, Ted."

Her husband visibly relaxed and he shrugged out of his jacket, draping it over the back of his chair. At least he planned on staying around for a while. "It feels strange meeting like this," he admitted.

"It does," she agreed, and stared down at

her coffee so that she didn't have to bear the intensity of his gaze. "But I'm glad that you came."

"Me too." He sat back as he took in their surroundings. "So this is where you spend all those hours with your girlfriends?"

Chantal nodded and sipped at her cappuccino.

"It's a nice place," he said, just as Clive arrived with his order.

"Why, thank you, Ted!" Clive was sounding more camp by the minute and, if she wasn't mistaken, he was flirting with her husband.

When he'd gone, she laughed and said, "I think Clive's a little bit in love with you."

"Is he the only one?" Ted asked, suddenly serious.

"No," she replied. "I still love you very much."

Her husband stared out of the window. Now he was the one struggling with eye contact.

"I've missed you," Chantal said. She'd decided that she wanted her marriage back and had come here today in a conciliatory mood, not caring about keeping score, about who had done what to whom and who'd done it first. If they had a chance of getting back together, then they needed to put all that behind them.

Ted turned toward her again. "I've been dating other women," he said. "Since you've been gone."

"Oh." It hadn't occurred to her that while she'd been out of his life, Ted might have moved on in his own way. "Anyone serious?"

"No." He shook his head. Then he sighed deeply and Chantal felt her insides flip. "I don't want to be single again," he continued. "It's terrible out there. I'm too old to be on the dating scene. Women are . . . well, they've changed. They're so . . . *difficult.*" He risked a laugh. "I guess I didn't realize quite how lucky I was."

This is good, Chantal thought. Very good.

"It doesn't mean that I still want to be married to you though," he admitted, and her heart, which had enjoyed a momentary uplift, sank slowly again. "I realize that you're not the only one to blame for our breakup. I know that I have to take my share of the responsibility too. We drifted apart and some of that is my fault, I know. It's just your solution to the problem that I'm having trouble dealing with."

Thank God he hadn't found out that she'd actually been paying Jacob for sex. That was something she didn't think he'd ever forgive. It was a secret that she was going to have to take to the grave with her. If Ted ever discovered what she'd been doing, then she'd be heading there sooner than she hoped.

Ted distracted himself by attacking his chocolate torte with his fork. "This is good," he said.

"The best." As our marriage once was, she wanted to add.

"I've slept with one of the women I've been seeing," he went on. "I thought it might help."

"Did it?"

"No. It just made me realize that it's you I want to be with."

This *has* to be good, Chantal thought.

"I'm just not ready for us to be together again," he said. "I need some time on my own to get my head together."

"We can do this on your terms, Ted," she said, knowing that she sounded desperate. "We'll work this out whichever way you want."

"This hurts like hell, doesn't it?" His voice was gruff with emotion.

"It sure does." She wanted to touch him, to show him that she cared, but she didn't dare to reach out. What if he brushed her away as he had done so often in recent times?

"Where are you living?"

"I've rented a flat in Islington," she told him. "It's not home, but it's fine for now. I'm sharing with my friend, Nadia. She's the one I lent our money to."

Ted said nothing in response to her admission.

"They were up to their necks in debt. I helped her out. Now she's left her husband and she's moved in with me. She has a young son, Lewis. He's four."

"And he's living with you too?"

"Yep."

Ted's eyebrows raised. "You're voluntarily sharing your home with a small child?"

"He's a great kid," she said with a warm smile. "He's teaching me a lot. I've seen every animated movie Disney has ever made. I know all the songs from *The Little Mermaid*, *The Lion King* and *Mary Poppins*. I can do finger painting. I can recite more nursery rhymes than I ever knew existed. I can also, with a great deal of effort, now touch my nose with my big toe."

That made Ted grin. "Impressive."

"I never thought that having kids could be so much fun," she said, even though she knew she was moving onto an emotive subject. "I guess whenever we saw our friends' kids they just used to drop into our lives and disrupt them. With Lewis being around all the time I've kind of grown accustomed to him. It's not so hard once you work into their routines."

"So now you're an earth mother?"

"I'm just saying that I don't find the idea of kids quite so abhorrent as I did." Chantal didn't tell Ted that she spent an hour most weekends going round the apartment with a pot of paint, eradicating the crayon marks and the mini-size chocolate handprints that miraculously appeared throughout the place. Some things were still hard not to be anal about. "Why didn't you ever talk to me about how you felt?"

"Do guys talk about these things?"

"Maybe they don't," Chantal said. "But they should."

"I think we need to take this slow," Ted said. "There's a big gap between us and I don't know if we can breach it."

"We should try."

Ted polished off the last morsel of his cake and drained the dregs of his cappuccino. "Let's go out for dinner," he said. "Later in the week."

"I'd like that."

He gave her hand a brief squeeze. "I'll call

you tomorrow."

Chantal felt like crying. Perhaps if she started dating her husband again, he'd rediscover what he'd once loved about her.

CHAPTER
SEVENTY-TWO

Marcus has booked the wedding for Valentine's Day: February 14 is D day. The *D,* in my mind, stands for "Dread." It's a date that shouldn't be filling me with terror, but it is. Normally, my only worry is whether I'm actually going to get a card from Marcus or not.

I'm currently gazing out the window, trying to get my brain to focus on which flowers I should choose for my wedding bouquet, when Crush hops into the office. The sales team stands and gives him a round of applause, which he acknowledges with a cheery wave. I sink further into my desk, pretending to bury my head in my work. Sales forecasts have never been so fascinating. My heart is pounding just reading them. What is wrong with me? Then I see a pair of crutches hop into view and Aiden's voice says, "Hello, *Mrs.* Gorgeous."

My heart pounds some more. Crush's

eyes travel to my engagement ring. I take my hands from the desk and sit on them. "Hi."

"How are we today?"

"I'm okay," I say. Still trying to work out a way of not getting married at Trington Manor, even though Marcus has already paid the not-inconsiderable deposit — but Mr. Aiden Holby doesn't need to know anything about that. "More importantly, how are you?"

"Soon be back to my old self," Crush assures me.

"I can't wait," I tease him.

"I've missed you." He lowers his voice as he tells me. "It's good to be back and I never thought I'd hear myself say that about this place."

"The office has been very quiet without you."

"Is that a good thing or a bad thing?" he wants to know.

"A very bad thing." We exchange an easy smile.

"I've enjoyed my daily chocolate deliveries," he says.

"You're welcome. I hope they've made you feel better." Then in a rash moment, I add, "Just let me know if there's anything else you need."

"You'll have to go and get my coffee for me," he warns. "On the hour, every hour. I can't hop and carry cups at the same time. I've had to drink everything standing up in the kitchen by the kettle since this happened."

"That makes me feel terrible," I tell him. "The least I can do is be your coffee-machine slave until you're fully back on your feet."

"Mmm," Crush says. "I think I like the sound of that. Are there any other areas in which you'd consider becoming submissive to my demands?"

"Don't push it." I'm not sure that I can cope with this jokey chemistry thing anymore — now that I'm an engaged person. Is this kind of behavior acceptable in the modern workplace environment? Should I be actively discouraging Crush from flirting with me now that I'm officially a fiancée? It would certainly make my working day at Targa a lot more tedious if I did. Not that it's likely to develop into anything more. I've been here for ages and it's all been very innocent and aboveboard so far. Apart from one minuscule kiss. Why should that change now?

Perhaps it would be safer to consider quitting here and getting another job, so that I put myself out of temptation's way. But then I remember that I have been briefly and disastrously employed by a large number of establishments in London and Targa is, quite honestly, the only company that will put up with me and my slovenly work ethic. I wouldn't want to move too far away from Chocolate Heaven either. Apart from the crap pay and the fact that the work is dreadfully dull, this is actually a great job. Plus I'm sure this whole "Crush" thing is simply invented by my rather bored brain in the absence of anything else to do here. As soon as I'm busy organizing my wedding then I'll hardly give him a passing thought. Aiden Holby isn't that cute. Not really.

Crush looks as if he's going to hop off to his office, but then he stops and says, "I suppose I should offer congratulations on your forthcoming nuptials."

I look at him from beneath my lashes. "Thanks."

"That was quite a performance from Marcus."

"Wasn't it?" I attempt a laugh and fail.

Crush stays where he is and he clears his throat. "Is it what you want?"

"Yes," I say. My chin juts out all of its own accord. Why can no one believe that I'm getting married? Can no one see me as a responsible, domesticated woman? Or maybe it's Marcus they're having trouble visualizing in that role. . . . "Why wouldn't it be?"

"Then I hope that you'll be really happy together."

"I'm sure we will."

He turns and hops halfway toward his office, before he comes back to my desk. "There's just one thing I wanted to tell you." He stands in front of me, distractedly tugging at a strand of his hair. "I just wish I had asked you out while I had the chance. It might have reduced my life expectancy considerably, but I think you and I could have had a lot of fun together, Lucy Lombard."

Then he hops away. Just like that. Leaving me in a total state of confusion and reaching for the nearest Green & Black's bar.

CHAPTER
SEVENTY-THREE

The only problem with the countryside was that it smelled awful. Nadia's nose wrinkled in distaste as Toby swung the car into the car park of Medley's Open Farm.

Lewis, strapped into his car seat, bounced happily. "Are we there yet?"

"Yes, sweetheart, we are."

Instead of Toby taking Lewis out on his own this Sunday, they'd decided to have an outing as a family. The last thing she wanted was for Toby to become a McDonald's dad, though she was absolutely sure that Lewis wouldn't object to more regular trips to the golden arches. He'd missed being with them on Lewis's birthday, which she felt terrible about, and she hoped that this would help to make up for it. As arranged, she'd picked her husband up from their house just before ten o'clock and now, an hour later, they were in the depths of the Bedfordshire countryside, surrounded by endless fields, rolling hills and the pungent fresh scent of nature, i.e., manure.

The atmosphere in the car had been relaxed between them and, in some ways, it had felt just like old times. There was no doubt that she still loved her husband and he'd told her often enough in the last few weeks that *he* loved *her.* All he had to do now was prove it by his actions. She unloaded a wriggling Lewis from the car and he ran ahead of them to the entrance of the children's farm, brimming with excitement. They might be miles out of London, but the prices were no less astronomical. It was a treat that they couldn't really afford, but if it was going to help her son to feel that his family hadn't completely broken up then it was worth the struggle to pay for it. Also, Nadia viewed it as educational, seeing as Lewis's identification of farm animals hadn't improved despite hours of encouragement from Chantal. Toby handed over the cash and they were each given piggy stamps on their hands and a small bag of animal feed.

Their first port of call was the animal barn. A group of pygmy goats in a large pen set up a round of hopeful bleating as soon as they saw a new batch of happy feeders arriving. Nadia and Toby crouched down and helped Lewis to cup the feed pellets in his hand while the goats nudged each other out of the way to gently nuzzle them from his fingers. Lewis was beside himself with joy.

"This is nice," Toby said quietly. "We should have done this sort of thing more often."

Nadia couldn't disagree with him. Getting out of the city on the weekends felt great.

Once all of the feed had been hoovered up by the goats, they moved on to the animal cuddling area. Rows of big straw bales were set out for the children to sit on and Toby lifted Lewis into place alongside the other kids. Their son sat mesmerized while a clutch of beautifully behaved rabbits and guinea pigs hopped or trundled over his legs. Occasionally, one of the more laid-back rabbits lingered to sit on his lap or to have a chew on the top of one of his wellies. Lewis was in seventh heaven and Nadia wondered, once again, why they'd decided to make their life in London. What were the benefits these days? Unless you had an appreciation of graffiti art and litter, that is. Wouldn't it be better if they upped sticks and moved to somewhere like this? They couldn't downsize very much from a tiny, three-bedroom terraced house, but maybe they could release some small amount of equity by moving to a cheaper area. She wondered what Toby would think of the idea. Then Nadia realized that she was thinking of them very much in terms of a family, forgetting that their home was, in fact, already up for sale.

While her son was preoccupied with stroking an extremely tolerant, flat-faced, fluffy white rabbit, she asked, "Any news on the house?"

Toby scuffed his feet into the muddy floor, exactly the same habit that Lewis had when uncomfortable. "There's been quite a lot of interest. A few viewings, but no offers."

Nadia shrugged. "It's early days yet."

"Nadia, I don't even want to be doing this," Toby said frankly. "There's no need for it. I'm going to crack this thing once and for all. I've given the laptop to a mate to keep it out of my way. The Internet connection has gone. I haven't been near one of those damn casinos since you left."

"I'm pleased," she said sincerely.

"This is an illness," her husband told her. "They said so at Quit Gambling."

"It might be an illness," Nadia said, "but it's not like a cold or chicken pox. It's not an illness that you catch. It's one that you *choose* to get. You can also choose to give it up."

"I'm going to get over it," Toby said. "I promise you."

Nadia slipped her arm through his and squeezed tightly. "I hope so."

"I see Lewis like this and I don't want us to split up."

"Neither do I," she said. "But until I can be sure that you can put your son and your wife above your love for the online casinos, it has to be like this."

Plus they needed to sort something out soon. Chantal had been a wonderful friend, but Nadia knew that she couldn't live on her charity forever. She was very pleased for Chantal that she and Ted seemed to be working slowly toward some kind of reconciliation, but she also had to consider the fact that if Chantal moved back home, then what would happen to her and Lewis? There was no way that Nadia could afford to rent the place in Islington by herself.

When the rabbits started to lose their charm, they took Lewis to look at the newborn piglets, squeaky and wriggling in their pen. Toby put his arm round her as they leaned over the metal gate and left it there as they then went to feed some warm milk to greedy lambs with babies' bottles and robust teats, which the lambs sucked on zealously.

They stopped for lunch, eating a picnic of ham sandwiches and brownies that she'd made that morning. They weren't a patch on the ones from Chocolate Heaven, but Nadia had an appreciative audience nonetheless. She and Toby lounged in the meager rays of sunshine while Lewis clambered on the wooden fort and poured sand into his own wellies with a red plastic bucket. The sun was gradually warming through to her bones, relaxing all the tension in her neck, soothing aches and pains that she hadn't even realized she had. Perhaps it was something in the country air, but she couldn't remember a time when she'd seen Lewis so happy or had felt so contented herself.

"We have a donkey ride and egg collecting from the hen house to fit in this afternoon. Plus cow milking if you're up to it," she laughed. "I hope after these farmyard frolics that our dear son will now be able to tell the difference between a sheep and a cow."

"If I'm going to milk it, I hope *I* can tell the difference between a cow and a bull."

Nadia giggled.

Her husband twirled her hair between his fingers. There was a careworn frown creasing his brow and he spoke hesitantly. "I don't want this day to end."

"Me neither," Nadia said.

CHAPTER
SEVENTY-FOUR

Autumn was carefully applying the lead beading to the suncatcher that Fraser was still struggling with. Ostensibly, she was supposed to be helping him, when in fact, she was actually doing the whole thing for him while her student lounged against the workbench and looked longingly at Tasmin across the art room. The girl was studiously pretending not to realize that she was being observed while she worked.

"Are you paying attention, Fraser?"

"No, Miss." At least he was honest. "It's very hard to be focused when you're in love."

"I wouldn't know," Autumn said, and there was a note of regret in her voice. She nodded toward Tasmin and lowered her voice. "Does the object of your affection feel the same?"

"Not yet," Fraser said with his usual bravado. "Not yet."

Oh, to be young and so optimistic, Autumn thought. She always admired the kids who could keep positive despite some of the dire situations in which they found themselves. Perhaps she could learn something from Fraser by taking a leaf out of his book for once. She thought back to the night of *Operation Liberate Chantal's Jewelry* — it wouldn't be the first time that her student's life skills had come in handy.

Though she was feeling low about Richard having departed for America, somewhere at the center of herself, a core of calmness had settled. The turbulence of the last few months was definitely noticeable by its absence. She loved Richard — he was her brother, what else could she do? — but there was no doubt that her stress levels rose considerably when he was around. No amount of chamomile tea, chanting or chocolate could help her to deal with him. He'd e-mailed her since he'd been at the rehab clinic, but his messages were noncommittal. He said he was doing fine, but it was impossible to read between the lines. She had no idea whether he really was fine, other than putting himself out of immediate danger. If only she could visit him. All she could do from this distance was hope that he got his act together and put his life back on track.

Today, the sun was streaming through the windows, bringing a rare warmth to the run-down classroom and banishing the dreariness of their surroundings. Autumn felt selfish for thinking it, but it was good not to have to worry about what she might be going home to. She'd changed the locks on the flat, just in case, and had put some extra security bolts on the door. But she couldn't help believing that now that her brother had gone, she wouldn't be troubled by any further break-ins. Still, it helped her to rest more easily at night instead of lying there listening for every little noise.

The door to the art room opened and she looked up to see the figure of Addison Deacon filling the doorway. She smiled at the sight of him. He hadn't been at the center much over the last few weeks and she'd missed seeing him. No one else lifted her heart like he did when he popped in for his friendly chats. Her colleague's cheery beam was already in place.

"I have chocolates. I have flowers," Addison said as he held out a small, exclusive-looking box of chocolates and a bouquet of white roses. "I have a table booked at the little restaurant at the end of the street. I have checked that they have plenty of their very special tiramisu. I have a bottle of red wine breathing. Though I'm holding *my* breath that you'll say yes."

Autumn flushed and looked around at her charges as she took the gifts from Addison. "These are lovely." She inhaled the delicate scent of the roses, even though in truth it was the chocolates she had her eye keenly fixed on.

"You probably won't get a better offer, Miss," Fraser informed her without being asked his opinion. If even the kids realized that her love life was as dry as the proverbial desert then it was definitely time to do something. Most of them couldn't see beyond their next hit. "Addison's cool."

Grinning at her suitor, she said, "I don't think you'll get a better reference."

"Then you'll say yes?"

"Oh!" Autumn put her hand to her forehead. "I have a staff meeting tonight. In fifteen minutes." Then she frowned. "I thought you'd organized it?"

"I did," Addison confessed. "It's a meeting for just you and me."

"Then how can I turn you down if it's purely business?" she teased.

"I wanted to make sure that you'd warned your brother that you'd be home late."

"Richard's gone away," she told him.

"He's living in America for a while. I don't have anyone to report to now."

"Then you have no excuses."

"I don't need an excuse," Autumn said. "I'd love to have dinner with you."

"Great."

"Cool," Fraser added with a satisfied nod.

"I just need to finish up here." Autumn turned her attention back to the suncatcher. Fraser took the soldering iron from her hand.

"There are more important things in life than stained glass, Miss," he informed her. "I'll finish this. Then I'll tidy up."

"That's another offer that I can't refuse," Autumn said with a grateful laugh.

"I'll get Tasmin to help me," her student said, and treated her to the most lascivious wink she'd ever seen.

God help the poor girl, Autumn thought. She wouldn't stand a chance when Fraser turned the full force of his not-inconsiderable charm on her.

Addison held open the door, grinning happily at her. She was going to relax and enjoy this, Autumn decided. Love, it seemed, was in the air.

CHAPTER
SEVENTY-FIVE

Marcus has given me my key back. He says that he doesn't want to wait until we're married for me to move in with him, and that I should do it as soon as possible. So, on Saturday I've hired a man and a van to move all my worldly goods into Marcus's apartment. It's so much more salubrious than mine. Particularly now that he's gotten rid of the rotting prawns — something that I'm sure will become one of our fun dinner-party stories in years to come. Though I think that, eventually, we'll look for somewhere bigger together. If we're going to start a family — also eventually — then it would be nice to have a place with a bit of a garden.

Picking up the key from my bedside table, I toy with it in my hand. It's not yet five thirty a.m. and, unusually, I'm wide awake. The traffic on the Camden Road is rumbling by already, heavy lorries shaking my windows out of their frames. I've tossed and turned for most of the night. There are a thousand different things going through my mind and I just can't settle back to sleep, even though I could have at least another hour's sleep before I have to get up for work. I could take myself off for an impromptu gym session — but that seems far too energetic for this time of day. I could even take a slow jog along the Grand Union Canal, but I might get mugged for my iPod — the latest craze around here. I'd stay in bed and just veg out but, to be honest, I'm thinking far too much about Crush while I'm lying here — and not in a work-related fashion. I've got funny feelings in places that you shouldn't have funny feelings in when dwelling on your boss. That's not good, is it? This whole wedding thing is making me very jittery — as if I'm just realizing how big a commitment it is. Duh. Rationally, I've always known that marriage is a big deal, but it's only now sinking in emotionally.

I slide out of bed and am giving myself a good, hot drowning in the shower when I decide to go over and see Marcus and get myself a decent dose of reassurance before I head into work.

Slipping the key into my jacket pocket, I walk up the road to the Underground sta-

535

tion and jump on the Tube for the journey across town. We didn't see each other last night because Marcus was working late and I was packing up my stuff, but he called me about midnight to tell me that he loved me. You'd think that would be enough for me really, but well . . . I just want to see him today. It's nearly six thirty a.m. and he should be getting up soon to go for his run anyway. Maybe I could just slip into bed beside him if he's still asleep, and persuade him that we could do another form of exercise to get all hot and sweaty. . . . I march quickly up the road to see if I can catch him. When I get to Marcus's apartment, I quietly open the door and peep inside.

Marcus is already up and having breakfast. What he's *actually* up to, I can't even begin to describe. But, to eat, he's having yogurt and crushed summer berries with a sprinkling of granola. He's eschewed the normal medium of a bowl for his breakfast delights and, instead, is up on the table, straddled across the same young woman who he was with last time I caught him out in an infidelity — which, humiliating though it was, wasn't quite so graphic as this. She's spread-eagled beneath him, groaning in ecstasy. The yogurt he's licking off Joanne's extraordinarily perky breasts, the berries are crushed all over her washboard stomach and, quite frankly, I wouldn't want granola where she has it. But, let's just say that I didn't think anyone outside of porn movies ever really had completely bare bits and pieces.

I watch for a moment with a kind of detached horror as my fiancé's bottom bobs up and down. The other members of the Chocolate Lovers' Club were right all along. Marcus will never change. If I marry him, this is what I have to look forward to for the rest of my life. While I'm considering my plan of action, I notice that the groaning has stopped. Marcus and Jo are staring at me and I'm not sure who has the widest, most terrified eyes.

"I thought we'd have breakfast together," I say steadily. "But I see that you've started without me."

Marcus jumps up and there's a squelching noise. I notice that his rapidly shrinking willy is covered in yogurt and the thought goes through my mind that at least he won't be troubled with thrush. Normally, Marcus only has a piece of toast. I wonder who went out and bought all the ingredients, and then I realize that only a woman would buy granola.

I stare at the woman in question and wonder what happened to the concept of sisterhood. If women stopped doing this kind of thing to other women, there would be a lot less pain in this world. Men, I'll admit, are probably a lost cause, but we could stop cheating on other women with their husbands, boyfriends, fiancés. Jo props herself up on her elbows and gives me a defiant look which, frankly, I'd like to wipe off her face — preferably with a cricket bat. "Who'd have thought that I'd be seeing so much of you," I say. "And so soon."

Marcus's breakfast dish looks rather rattled.

"I can explain," Marcus says as he tries to dismount from the table with some dignity. Difficult to pull off.

"I'm all ears."

"This was the last time," he says earnestly. There are raspberries crushed on his knees. "The last time ever. I was having one last fling before settling down. As soon as you moved in, I was going to be completely and utterly faithful."

Jo doesn't look as if she knows about this particular part of the arrangement and she glares darkly at my fiancé. Perhaps she'll be sneaking into his flat and filling his clothes and his shoes with leftovers and leaving stinking prawns in his soft furnishings. Because, for sure, I won't be troubling myself to do it again.

"You called to tell me you love me while *she* was here?"

Jo clearly doesn't know about that bit either. Marcus chews his lip.

I stare at Marcus as if I'm seeing him for the first time. He looks ridiculous — yogurt on his knob, smears of berry juice all over his chest and legs, breakfast cereal in his hair. I burst out laughing. Marcus laughs too — nervously.

"Oh, Marcus," I say, clutching at my sides. "I can't believe you've done this again." I double over and belly laugh right the way up from my boots.

"I love you," he says bleakly, and then he continues to laugh along with me, although it sounds forced.

When I finally wrest control of my voice once more, I say softly, "I'm not laughing with you, Marcus. I'm laughing *at* you."

Slipping my engagement ring from my finger, I put it delicately into the bowl of yogurt that's lying by Jo's feet. Then, picking it up, I tip the bowl upside down on Marcus's head. Yogurt drips slowly down his face. He licks it from his lips. Perhaps he can get Jo to do it for him when I'm gone. "This really is the very last time you do this to me, Marcus."

Then I walk out the door, closing it quietly behind me. Taking my key — so recently reacquired — I post it through the letterbox.

Out on the street, I can hear my ex-fiancé's voice shouting out the window after me, but his pleas are lost on the breeze. Heading toward the Tube, I'm gripped with hysterical laughter once more. Tears stream down my face as I cackle my way up the road. When I get to the Tube, I can't make my legs take me any further and I drop to the floor by the ticket machines, curling myself up into a ball in the corner. I laugh as the commuters push by me to purchase their Travelcards, unconcerned at the plight of the unhinged woman at their feet. I laugh and laugh and laugh. I laugh at the ridiculousness of the situation. I laugh at how very stupid I was, to ever believe that Marcus was a reformed character. I laugh at the thought of Marcus's cock covered in yogurt and how it was possibly one of the saddest sights I've ever seen. I laugh because I'm alone once again and I don't know how I'll manage. I laugh because now I won't need to think of a reason not to get married at

Trington Manor. I laugh so much that I cry and cry and cry.

CHAPTER
SEVENTY-SIX
***

By the time I get to the office my mood is more somber. The unhinged hilarity has died down and I've eaten three Crunchies on the trot to up my sugar levels, which has made me feel much better. Marcus has called me thirty-six times so far and I've ignored all of his voice messages which, frankly, run to the predictable: *I love you, I can explain, she means nothing to me.* That sort of thing. Why do men always think it's better to disparage the woman they're caught with by saying, "She means nothing to me"? Is that supposed to make us feel better? If you're going to risk fucking up your relationship, then at least do it with someone who means a lot to you! *I don't see why this little setback means that we can't still get married* was another one that nearly set me off laughing hysterically again.

Crush is already in his office when I finally make it into Targa, so I pop over to the coffee machine and risk the complications of technology to order him a white coffee with two sugars. Then I take it into his office along with the Twix I've bought him.

Mr. Aiden Holby is sitting back in his chair with his plaster cast up on his desk. I put the coffee and chocolate down in front of him.

"Lifesaver," he says, rubbing his hands together. As he starts to open the Twix, he asks, "How are you today, Mrs. Gorgeous?"

"*Ms.* Gorgeous," I correct, and hold out my now unadorned ring finger.

"Ooo," Crush observes. "So soon?"

"Diamonds are forever," I tell him. "Emeralds, it seems, are very shortlived."

"Want to tell me about it?"

"Not really."

"Red eyes and blotchy cheeks," he remarks. "Never a good sign in a girl. Found him up to his nuts in another woman?"

"Pretty much."

"When?"

I look at my watch. "Nearly an hour ago," I say. "I'm *so* over it already." A pain shoots through my heart. I'll never eat yogurt again. Or summer berries. Or granola. Thank God Marcus hadn't smeared his bitch in chocolate.

"I'll take you out to lunch," Crush says

decisively. "Somewhere special. We'll pretend we're talking about work. You can claim it and I'll endorse your expenses. Fair enough?"

I nod.

"I've got some news I want to tell you too."

"Is it good?" I don't think I could stand any more bad news today.

Crush wiggles his toes at the end of his cast and studies them intently. "It depends which angle you're coming from."

This sounds like something I don't want to hear, but if there's a free lunch in it then I might as well go along. "I'd better go and do some work," I say. Or at least look like I'm working. My productivity rate might not be that great at the moment.

"I'm glad you're not getting married," Crush says. "For purely selfish reasons."

"Which are?"

He makes a steeple of his fingers and gazes at me over them. "If anyone's going to marry you, then I really think it should be me."

"That's not even funny," I say, and bang the office door on my way out.

CHAPTER
SEVENTY-SEVEN

Lunchtime takes an interminable amount of time to come around. I amuse myself by entering the sales figures into the computer and then completely losing them. I rip my tights on a splinter under my desk and make a complaint about the appalling state of health and safety in this company to Helen the chief harridan in Human Resources. She retorts by saying that my temporary contract might not be renewed at the end of the month, so it should make no difference to me.

To top my morning, I also ignore another forty-three begging phone calls from Marcus. I've turned off the ringtone and put it onto vibrate mode, so that I can now see my phone hopping round maniacally on the top of my handbag, but at least I can't hear it. I hope he's getting repetitive strain injury of his dialing finger. And I hope his knob drops off.

Finally, when I'm convinced that Crush has forgotten all about our lunch date and am about to lie down and weep, my boss appears in front of my desk and says, "Are you ready, Gorgeous?"

Grabbing my coat, I follow him to the lift, noting that he's become remarkably agile on his crutches over the last few weeks. My heart goes out to him and, when we're alone in the lift, I smile warmly at him.

"What?" he says, with a worried frown.

"I'm just smiling at you," I say. "I'm being nice."

Crush sucks in his breath and shakes his head in the manner of a dodgy builder. "Not sure I can cope with that, Gorgeous."

I whack him playfully with my handbag — maybe a little *too* playfully — knocking his crutch out of his hand and making him topple over.

"Oh, shit!" I dive to help him.

"That's better," he says, with a satisfied grin as he sets himself upright again, brushing down his suit. "That's the Lucy I know and love."

"Shut up," I warn him, "or I'll slam your leg in the cab door."

When we do get into a cab, I make sure that I'm extra careful to help Crush in first and *not* slam his leg in the door. You know what they say about true words being spoken in jest.

The cab whisks us off to one of the trendiest restaurants in town — the Tower. It's in a converted warehouse or something on the South Bank, overlooking the river, and is run by one of these trendy TV chefs — not the one who swears a lot, the other one. It's the sort of place where I don't want to be found shooting my peas — or my *mélange de petits pois* — across the plate and onto the floor or generally making a spectacle of myself. We take a lift to the fourth floor, and we're shown to a table by the window. Crush lays his crutches down by our feet.

"This is lovely," I say, and I wonder if he brought Charlotte the Harlot or Donna from Data Processing here. Bet he didn't! The view from our aerie is spectacular. Busy tourist boats are chugging up and down the gray strip of the Thames. Today the sun is shining, making the water shimmer and sparkle like silver. I've lived in London for years and have never done the whole tourist bit — maybe I should next summer. Goodness knows, I'm going to have time on my hands from now on.

The menu is fabulous and mine doesn't have any prices on it, which I didn't think anyone did anymore, because of equality and all that. But I bet there's nothing under a fiver on it, not even a glass of water. Still, Targa's footing the bill and I get precious little else out of them. We order and then Crush says, "Let's get some champagne. I need lots to drink and I suspect you do too."

The waiter brings us a bottle of something hideously expensive and it fizzes out into our flutes. Crush clinks his glass against mine. "This feels like a date, Gorgeous," he says with a nervous laugh.

I echo it and say, "You're right, it does." Then I glug my champagne gratefully. "Can I ask you a question?" I launch into it before I change my mind. "Did you start calling me Gorgeous because you couldn't remember my name?"

"No," Crush says. "Because you are gorgeous."

"Oh."

He looks at me expectantly.

"That's all right then," I add magnanimously.

He laughs again and, to my surprise, works his hand across the table and takes mine. My heart starts up a rap beat. "Confession time," he says. "It was me who sent you that ridiculously expensive bouquet to the office."

"You?"

He nods.

"And I gave all the credit to Marcus!"

"Yeah. I was pretty pissed off about that. I agonized for hours over a suitably cryptic message and then Dirty Derek went and lost the card. And lost me the girl too."

"Not *entirely* lost," I correct.

"I've been wanting to ask you out for ages," he says, with a rueful expression as he threads his fingers through mine. "I don't know why I haven't."

"Because you're a misogynistic commitment phobe?"

"Or I could just be shy and insecure."

We both laugh at that.

"And we've both been in relationships," he adds.

"Pretty disastrous ones," I remind him.

"I'll drink to that, Gorgeous," he says, and swigs his champagne.

"Well, I'm available now," I say, dispensing with any attempt at being coy. Clearly, the champagne is kicking in. "You'd better snap me up soon before I become a nun. Or a lesbian. Or both."

"I might wait," Crush muses. "That sounds as if it could be fun."

Sighing at him, I try out my best vamp voice. "Don't you think that we've waited long enough?"

"I'd planned to bring you here today to try to persuade you to leave Marcus," he admits, flushing slightly. "I'm glad that he saved me the bother."

I start to laugh, but not in the borderline insane way that I did this morning.

"Now all I have to do is convince you to hook up with me instead," he says.

"I don't know that I'll take much convincing." In theory, I know that I should be having some time alone to recover from my broken heart, but having already done it several times before, I've found that it doesn't work. If you ask me, you might as well throw yourself headlong into another relationship and be damned.

Crush purses his lips at me. "There is, however, one slight snag."

Why doesn't this surprise me?

"I've been promoted."

"Fantastic. Congratulations." We clink our glasses together again and both drink. The world is starting to spin ever so slightly faster than it should. "Isn't that good news?"

"I'm going to be International Sales Director."

"Wow! I feel as if I should be doffing my cap to you."

"Don't let me stop you," Crush says. "Doff away."

I snarf into my fizz.

"My first job is to set up a new marketing operation —"

"You'll be great at it."

"— in Australia."

The world screeches to a halt. *"Australia?"*

"It's not so far away," Crush says in a rush. "Not really."

It's miles, I think. Miles and miles. And miles. Just about as far as you can get without coming back on yourself. Even in this age of relative ease of air travel, where the world has become a very small place, a global village, Australia is still a Fucking Long Way Away. If EasyJet doesn't fly there for ten quid then it must be classed as a very remote outpost.

"It's for six months," Crush continues. "That's all, and then I should be back in the UK."

Six months. Anything could happen in that time. What are the chances of him avoiding the local attractions for twenty-six weeks? I can just picture him now, running along Bondi Beach in slow-motion with some big-breasted, bleached-blond *Baywatch*–type, surfboards tucked under their arms, hot sun beating down on their bronzed bodies. It's not a picture I like.

"The thing is . . ." Crush says, and I try

desperately to drag my attention back from this wholly depressing reverie. "The thing is . . . I'd like you to come with me, Gorgeous."

Now I'm on full alert. "Me? Come with you? To Australia?" My voice is louder than it should be in such a posh place — or any place, for that matter. "Me? Come with you? To Australia?" I repeat incredulously. This is why I was never top of the class at school. Slow mental faculties in times of crisis. Made exam time hell.

"All morning I've been thinking of nothing else. It would be a great idea." Crush squeezes my hand encouragingly. "The timing couldn't be better — in some ways. What is there to keep you here? You and Marcus are all washed up. You've got a crap job with no prospects. No commitments."

I'm not sure I like Mr. Aiden Holby describing my life in such disparaging terms. It sounds all too accurate.

"This could give us both a chance of a new start. We can allow our relationship to flourish away from all this rubbish." He makes a wide, expansive gesture. "What have we got to lose? We know each other well enough to realize that we could make a go of this, don't you think?"

I start to laugh again — and this time, the

hysterical edge has crept back in. Fueled by an excess of alcohol, I believe. "We could," I say breathlessly. As soon as I've said it out loud, I think, We could do this — we really could. As Aiden says, what is there to keep me here? The only people I'd truly miss are the girls from the Chocolate Lovers' Club. There's no doubt there'd be a big hole in my lives without them, but who else couldn't I live without? A big fat No One. And they have chocolate in Australia, don't they? They must do. Or I could get emergency packages of supplies sent by Clive. Or maybe I could even start up an antipodean branch of the Chocolate Lovers' Club.

"Is that a yes?" Crush sounds nervous, as well he might. "Will you come with me?"

"Yes!" The word bursts out of me with a giggle. "Yes, I will."

With some adjustment of his broken leg, Aiden leans across the table and draws me to him. "You don't know how happy that makes me." Then his lips find mine and he kisses me. In the middle of this swanky restaurant with everyone watching. There's a clattering of cutlery. I have a feeling that I've knocked my peas all over the floor, but I don't care. His lips are warm and soft and taste of champagne. A thrill runs through my body right down to my toes, stopping at some rather interesting places on the way. And I think that I'm very glad that I said yes.

CHAPTER
SEVENTY-EIGHT

We order another bottle of champagne and drink it too quickly. The bubbles float straight to my head and make my brain all swimmy. But I'm more dizzy with joy than with anything you can get from a bottle.

"When do you think you'll go?" I ask dreamily.

"When *we'll* go, Gorgeous," Crush corrects, and I get another rush in strange places. "As soon as this comes off." He glances down at his plaster cast. "Apparently, you're not allowed to fly with a pot leg. It should be removed next week. Then I'll probably leave the week after."

That's two weeks! "I need to get someone to rent my flat." I also need to buy shorts, T-shirts, factor 500 suntan cream and industrial-strength insect repellent.

"I'll pay for your flight."

"I wouldn't dream of it," I say, with more bravado than brimming bank account.

"You've probably got a lot to pay out for. I can manage it." I'll just max my plastic. I wonder, do debts follow you to the other side of the world? More than likely.

"We'll be based in Sydney," Crush tells me. He's starting to slur slightly and I think that we should go easy on the fizz, except that now the bottle seems to be empty. How did that happen? "I've never been there, but it's supposed to be great. Targa is renting a flat for me."

"For *us*," I correct and we both giggle childishly. "God, what will they say back at the office?"

"Who cares?" Crush says, and toys with my fingers.

"I think they'll be surprised," I tell him. "*I'm* surprised." Wait until Charlotte the Harlot hears about this! Ha, ha! What a result! Slim, beautiful person — nil. Chubby chocoholic — one!

"Will I be able to work out there?"

"I don't know," Aiden admits. "Maybe Targa can fix something up for you."

"I'll talk to the harridans in Human Resources." I'm sure they'll be delighted to organize something in Australia if it means seeing the back of me for a while.

Somehow we become sufficiently coherent to order dessert. We have a huge chocolate platter between us and I try to spoon the last morsel of the white chocolate mousse into Crush's mouth, but I miss and hit the end of his nose instead. We titter pathetically as he wipes it away with his napkin.

"Are you really sure you want to do this?" I ask in as sober a tone as I can muster.

"Share your dessert?"

"No, twit. Emigrate together." We collapse into fits of giggles.

"I'm sure," he says. "Are you sure?"

I get all emotional, when I reply, "I'm sure." A tear rolls down my cheek and Crush brushes it gently away with his thumb.

"I want to look after you." He stares at me all moony-eyed. "I want to cherish and treasure you."

"I want that too," I agree breathlessly. Taking his hand, I hold it against my cheek. "Let's not go back to the office," I suggest. Frankly, I'd like the cherishing and treasuring to start as soon as possible. "No one will miss us. Let's go back to my flat."

"That sounds like a very good idea, Gorgeous."

We somehow manage to pay the bill and lurch to our feet. Crush is very unsteady and he hops around while he tries to adjust his crutches into a comfortable position.

"Are you okay?"

He puffs out a slightly drunken breath as he tries to straighten up and look sober. "Fine," he assures me. "Fine."

I try to guide him as he hops out of the restaurant, moving chairs out of his way, creating a clear passage even though I'm weaving about all over the place. That second bottle of fizz was a bad idea. A very bad idea.

As soon as we're outside the restaurant and in a quiet corridor, Crush pulls me to him again. I lean against the wall for support and he presses his body along the length of mine, kissing me fervently. His hands travel over my body and I wish my clothing was thinner, silkier or, preferably, nonexistent. Everything inside me bursts into flame. I cleave toward him and, previously, I had no idea what cleaving meant. What little is left of my wits departs instantly. I cannot wait to get this man home.

"Are we mad for doing this?" Aiden breathes into my hair.

"Yes," I pant. "We're madly, badly reckless. But I think it's fabulous."

"Me too."

Crush, it's clear, wants me just as much as I want him. Why don't restaurants have rooms that they could rent out by the hour? That would be a very good service to offer. There must be other couples who feel like this after a very good lunch and too much booze. Couple! Crush and I are a couple! We're a *couple!*

Before we both explode, we manage to prize ourselves apart, rearranging our clothing, exchanging looks of lustful longing, and then continue our journey out of the restaurant. It's all going rather well until we get to the lift. There's a big OUT OF ORDER sign now slapped to the front of it.

"Bugger," I say. "What now?"

"I can manage the stairs," Crush says valiantly.

"We're four floors up."

A look of uncertainty crosses his brow. "I'm sure I can."

"Have you tried stairs before on those?"

"Not exactly," he confesses.

"Let's see if there's a service lift," I suggest. "It might mean going down with the vegetables, but it'll be better than trying to hop down this lot."

"I'll be fine," Crush says. "Absolutely fine." And, with that, he sets off down the stairs, hopping gingerly onto each step. My heart's in my mouth. He doesn't look very steady at all. I'm a bit dodgy on my own pins and I haven't got an unwieldy set of crutches to maneuver. I can hardly bear to watch.

We're half a dozen steps down when Crush has a nasty wobble. His crutches slip on the step, but he manages to correct his balance. He giggles while he catches his breath. "Bit close," he manages.

"Let me go in front of you," I beg. "I'll try to steady your crutches."

"There's no need."

"Trust me. There is." So we set off again with me walking backward down the stairs in front of him.

Crush hops toward me. He looks a bit steadier now, I think.

"Come on," I urge. "That's right. Easy does it."

"I'm fine, Lucy. Honestly. Watch where you're going yourself."

I have my arms spread out in case he falls. "Gently. Gently."

"The stairs narrow behind you," Crush says.

"What?" I turn to look and I don't know quite what happens, but somehow my ankle twists. I lose my balance and stumble. Crush instantly drops his crutches and lurches forward, trying to grab me. But he slips and misses me completely. Then I'm falling. Falling, falling, falling through the air.

CHAPTER
SEVENTY-NINE

Davina is jumping around like a mad thing. Whereas I am not. I'm lying on my sofa chogging my way through a box of Bendicks Gorgeous that's balanced on my belly and am pretending that by simply watching an exercise video I am absorbing the impact of it by osmosis. My broken leg, complete with shocking-pink plaster cast, is propped up on a heap of cushions. It feels as if a thousand ants are crawling up and down inside and it's driving me berserk. I can't believe that Crush went through all this without complaint. I, on the other hand, am chain-eating painkillers and whining on about my misfortune to anyone stupid enough to listen. I'm even phoning my mother every day to whinge — that's how bad it is. Somehow I feel it is getting my just deserts to have ended up like this after my spectacular fall down the stairs at the Tower.

There's a cheery knock at the door and then Aiden lets himself in. He, in an ironic twist, is now without the encumbrance of his plaster cast, although he's using a walking stick which lends him a very sophisticated air. My boyfriend comes over and kisses me. "How are you feeling this morning, Gorgeous?"

"Grumpy," I tell him as I ditch my chocolates — but not before he pinches one.

"Chin up," he says, and gives me another peck.

Aiden's plaster cast has been gone for over a week and now, of course, he has to be heading off to Australia as International Sales Director to set up the new marketing division for Targa. He's leaving today. Without me.

"Have you got enough chocolate to keep you going?" The fridge is bursting with the stuff. I'm bursting with the stuff. Despite having a red-hot boyfriend, it is currently my only comfort. Because of my temporary disability, Crush and I have yet to consummate our relationship — which is more than a little frustrating. We've indulged in some good, old-fashioned snogging, but sometimes it just isn't enough, is it? Particularly when he's about to disappear off into the wide blue yonder for six months. "I brought you some more." Aiden puts a wide range of assorted Green & Black's bars and boxes of chocolate on the coffee table. "Just in case you were running low."

I will be an eighteen-stone blimp with severe acne by the time I get back on my feet. But, in a bizarre way, despite all my current incapacities, I'm more contented than I've ever been. Improved self-esteem. Better self-image. Even a tiny upsurge in sadly depleted confidence. It may yet be very small, but there's definitely a little seed of happiness threatening to grow and blossom inside me. I put this all down to the final and all-time dumping of Marcus "The Bastard Boyfriend From Hell" and his replacement by the calming influence of Crush — who has been an absolute wonder these last few weeks. How did I manage without him all this time? How will I manage without him when he's gone? Flutter of panic. Reach for chocolate. Eat chocolate. Sigh contentedly. I just have to hold my nerve while he's on the other side of the world.

All of the girls from the Chocolate Lovers' Club have been round to see me this week, also armed with chocolate goodies in many forms and hearty commiserations. They brought me some of the chocolate-themed books from the library shelf at Chocolate Heaven to keep me entertained and a DVD of *Charlie and the Chocolate Factory* and *Chocolat,* both starring the inimitable Johnny Depp. I wonder if he's a chocolate fiend too? I could love him even more if he is. I'm currently working my way through *Friends, Lovers, Chocolate* by Alexander McCall Smith and saving Johnny Depp for later, when I get really down in the dumps. They're coming around again later to try to cheer me up.

"Nice flowers," Aiden says.

There's a huge pale pink Dutch bouquet on my sideboard. "They came this morning." This time they *are* from Marcus. The nerve of the man! I don't know how my bastard ex-fiancé found out about my broken leg, but one of our mutual acquaintances must have informed him. The card, along with the soppy sentiments he'd scribbled inside, went straight into the bin. *Kissy, kissy. I still love you. I'm so sorry.* Bollocks. Heard it all before, Marcus. Doesn't cut the mustard anymore. Have already got fab boyfriend to replace you. Ha! Still, I liked the flowers too much to ditch them. Frankly, it would have been a waste.

"From an old friend," I tell Crush, as I don't even want to utter Marcus's name, let alone credit him with such great taste in floral arrangements.

If my new man has his suspicions about their origins then he doesn't voice them.

"I don't want to leave you," Aiden says. He strokes my hair, tucking it gently behind my ear.

"I'll be fine," I tell him as I burst into tears.

Taking me in his arms, he says, "It won't be for long. As soon as your plaster's removed, you can follow me." That'll be weeks and weeks. I know from previous experience. He wipes away my tears with the edge of my T-shirt. "I'll have everything ready for us. Maybe it's actually better this way." And then he realizes what a stupid thing it was to say and we both laugh. "Perhaps it's not better *this* way, but you know what I mean."

I sink back onto the cushions. This whole arrangement has an air of unreality about it now. I'm still convinced that the minute Crush arrives on the other side of the world, he'll forget all about me. The movie with the blond beach babe plays in my head again.

"I can't stay long," Aiden says, thankfully truncating my film show, which I think was going to get a bit porny. "I've got a taxi coming to collect me soon and I've still got loads of packing to do."

"I hope it all goes well for you. I'm really going to miss you."

"I'm going to miss you too, Gorgeous." He comes and kneels in front of me and puts his hands on my hips. A minute later and we're in deep snog mode. Then, slowly, he unbuttons my shirt from the bottom upward and starts to place little hot kisses all over my stomach as he goes. "I want to remember you just like this."

"What? Fat, slovenly, miserable, incapacitated and utterly frustrated?"

"No," he says. "As lovely as always."

"We could make love just once," I say hopefully. "Here. Now. We could be quick."

"I don't want to be quick." Aiden frowns at me. "We've waited so long to get together, I want to do this properly."

"*Improperly* would work for me."

"We can wait."

He might be able to, but I'm not sure *I* can. "Come and lie down next to me." I shift up and Crush lies alongside me. "Just hold me."

And, of course, within seconds we're doing anything but just holding each other. Our lips are fevered and searching once more. An octopus would be proud of the way our hands are working. I have Aiden's

shirt undone, my blouse has gone for a bur-
ton and my bra's heading in the same direction. Juices are flowing. Nipples — and
other things — are very erect. Every place
that should be kissed has been kissed — and
maybe some that shouldn't be. All is going
swimmingly. Perfect, perfect textbook sex. I
sigh with joy.

"Oh, Lucy," Aiden murmurs in my ear.

This is bliss. Every nerve in my body feels
alive, zinging with wonderful sensations.
Aiden unzips my skirt. With much struggling he eases it down over my hips and my
plaster cast. I might be somewhat hampered
by my incapacity, but my power as a love
goddess has not diminished — oh no. All
that lies between me and ecstasy is a sexy
pair of flimsy pants — good underwear
choice this morning. Not that I'd imagined
this might happen. Ha, ha! Crush hooks his
thumbs into my underwear and, giving the
lie to my long-ago threat that he'd never get
his hands on my underwear or my bottom,
starts to slip them down.

"Wait, wait," I say. "Let me flip this way
and it won't be so tricky." Flipping is
something easier said than done. I swing
my leg over Crush and, I don't know what
happens, but maybe I swing it a tad too far.

"Oh, Lucy!" Aiden cries, and not in joy.

He loses his grip on me and I somersault off the sofa and land with an unhealthy crash on the floor. Darren will think I'm doing my Davina DVD again.

"Are you all right?" Crush wants to know. He's peering down at me and he's trying not to laugh.

"I haven't broken the other leg, if that's what you mean."

He helps me up from the floor, brushing down my skirt which is currently round my knees and, generally, rearranging my clothing. I feel as if the moment has passed. Sometimes you just know it.

"We should wait until you're not plastered," he says, presumably referring to my leg, not my alcohol levels. "I don't want to cause you another injury."

The only injury, once again, is to my pride. Crush buttons his shirt. "I have to go, Gorgeous."

"I could come to the airport."

"I'd really rather you stay indoors and don't go anywhere until you've had that thing removed." He points to my cast. "You can get yourself in enough trouble when you're able-bodied, I'd hate to think of the havoc you could wreak with a pair of crutches."

"You managed okay."

"That's because men are superior beings when it comes to . . . well, everything."

I give him a good bash with one of my cushions. "Remind me why I love you?"

"Because as soon as you're able, I'm going to whisk you away to a better life, like all good knights in shining armor."

I feel tears come to my eyes again. It's time for Crush to go. I bite down on my lip so that I won't cry. "I love you."

"And I love you too, Gorgeous."

"You won't forget me, will you?"

He takes my face in his hands and kisses me soundly. "How could I?"

CHAPTER EIGHTY

"My love life is nothing but a vale of tears through which I trudge wearily," I say, with the heartfelt sigh of a romantic heroine.

"Very soon," Chantal says, "your love life will be a spring field decked with wildflowers, through which you'll be gamboling happily."

"This is after I have my plaster cast removed from my broken leg?"

"Of course."

"Do they have fields of spring flowers in Australia?" I want to know.

"Stop whining, Lucy," Nadia instructs. "Eat more chocolate."

I'd be happy to comply, but I can't reach over to the plate of chocolate chip cookies with my busted leg up on a chair — this would require one of my more extreme yoga positions. Something which I'm not quite up to at the moment. Autumn puts an end to my predicament as, when she's finished signing my cast in black marker pen, she kindly hands one to me. Currently, I'm propped up against a pile of cushions in Chocolate Heaven.

"This is a temporary setback," Chantal reminds me. "You'll be off to the land Down Under in no time at all."

"Will I?" The way my life generally pans out, a happy ending is never a dead cert.

"Crush *is* texting you and phoning you ten times a day," Autumn says.

I smile contentedly and thank the God of Modern Technology that our communications can continue despite the fact that we're living in different time zones. I hug one of Clive's cushions to me affectionately. "He is."

"By the time you get out there, he'll be gagging for you."

From some of the more steamy texts we've exchanged, I think he is already. Our very interruptus attempt at coitus on my sofa clearly hasn't put him off.

"Anything more from Marcus the Bastard?" Chantal asks.

I shake my head. "No."

"Good. Let's hope you've heard the last from him."

"My sentiments exactly."

"He might well come sniffing around

again when he hears that you're off to Australia. Be on your guard!" Nadia warns in the manner of a wartime poster.

"I can't believe that you're going to be leaving us," Autumn says. "What will we do without you?"

Frankly, I can't believe that I'm going either. What will I do without my best girls? Who will I turn to in times of crisis? And, make no mistake, even though I'm going to the other side of the world, crises will follow me like a pack of hungry hounds. We've all been through so much together in the last few months. What will I do without my regular fixes with the members of the Chocolate Lovers' Club?

"You will keep in touch?" Autumn continues, a tear in her eye.

"Bloody hell," I say. "I'm not going yet. It'll be weeks before I get this thing off." The pink plaster cast receives my scorn again. "You're stuck with me for the foreseeable future. You'll all just have to get your lives together before I go. Then I want regular downloads in Australia." I nod at Autumn. "You'd better send me an invitation to the wedding if things work out with you and Addison. I can come back at a moment's notice."

Autumn blushes. "Lucy!"

"I know a good wedding venue that has a booking available for Valentine's Day," I tell her. "You can't get more romantic than that."

"Well, I'm trying to keep my life on the right track," Nadia says. "Toby's had nearly a month without gambling. And I believe him this time when he says he's given it up for good. I just want to make absolutely sure before Lewis and I go rushing back. As long as Chantal can put up with us . . ." She looks over at our friend.

"Believe me," Chantal says, "it's a joy. I come home every night to find a fabulous dinner ready for me and a glass of wine poured. Maybe I should divorce Ted and marry you, Nadia. You're a great catch."

We all laugh even though gay marriages are now legal and, technically, they could do that.

"Plus," Chantal adds, "I'm kinda used to having your little guy around. If you go back to Toby, I'll have to start buying those huge bags of chocolate buttons for myself!"

"How are things with Ted?"

"We're dating," she tells us with a shrug. "Once or twice a week. We've been to the movies. We've had intimate dinners in upscale restaurants. I'm gonna be as fat as a house before long." Chantal tugs at her waistband. Maybe it is a little more snug than usual. Then she sighs. "I can't help but feel that we're still skirting round the edges of the dance floor."

"Maybe you just have to give him time?" I suggest.

"That, I've got plenty of," she says. "Don't worry, I'll hang on in there until I wear him down. But I just want to say that I don't know how I would have got through all this without you girls. You've been great friends. The best."

And, because essentially she's still an American at heart, we all indulge her by holding hands around the table. "To the Chocolate Lovers' Club," I say. "Long may we reign."

"To the Chocolate Lovers' Club," my friends echo and we toast ourselves with our mugs of steaming hot chocolate.

And the truth of the matter is that the men in our lives may come and go — they may bring us pleasure, they may cause us pain — but whatever happens, we have each other and we have chocolate. No one can take that away from us.

Over at the counter, there's a tall business-man in a great suit making a selection of chocolates with Clive in attendance. He glances over at us and smiles.

"Wow," Chantal says. "He's a babe!"

We all scowl at her. She holds up her hands and says hastily, "Just looking."

"Autumn." I give her a nudge. "Is he your type?"

"He looks more likely to vote Conservative than Green Party," she says, lips pursed in thought. "Does he look like a man who'd wash out his cans to recycle them?"

"No," we tell her in unison.

"Then I'll stick with Addison," she says with a contented smile. "He's not so obviously Alpha."

"You'd better," I say. "There's not many that could meet your exacting criteria."

He smiles over at us again, then gives us a cheery wave before he leaves. We all wave back and then collapse into giggles.

Clive bustles over. "Looks like you have an admirer, ladies." Our dealer is bearing a plate of his finest chocolates. "He sent these over for you."

Clive hands the plate to me. "For me?" I ask. "Or for all of us?"

"For all of you. But he did ask who you were, Lucy."

"Me, specifically?"

"If you'd like it verbatim, he said, 'Who's the pretty blonde with the plaster cast?' "

"Yes," I say, "but did he ask because he

felt sorry for me because I'm a poor old cripple, or did he fancy me?"

"I don't know." Clive does his best exasperated "I'm a guy and I'm gay; you figure it out" look.

He marches away, leaving us with our booty. We all look at the heaped plate of chocs in amazement. "Mmm," I say. "Whoever he is, he has great taste."

I hand round the chocolates, and we all pick out our favorite. Nadia takes the Spicy Ginger one, infused with fresh grated ginger. A great chocolate for winter mornings with a strong cup of coffee. Autumn's next and she takes her time as she chooses the English Rose: a delicate classic flavor which Clive makes to perfection, filled with a ganache infused with distilled rose petals — bliss. Chantal selects the Earl Grey Tea with its distinctive bergamot flavor which releases in delicious waves, leaving a long, slow aftertaste, making it feel like two chocolates for the price of one. Now it's my turn. What shall I go for? As always, I'm spoiled for choice. My hand hovers over them — every single one loved and desired. Lemon and Thyme? Szechuan Pepper? I settle on one of the specialities of the house — Sea-Salted Caramel.

Snuggling back down into Clive's cushions, I pause for a moment and enjoy the buzz of anticipation. Then I pop the chocolate into my mouth, savoring the soft, chewy texture of the caramel and the creaminess of the milk chocolate, until Clive's perfect twist kicks in and the taste of the unrefined sea salt from Brittany cuts through. The caramel melts deliciously in my mouth. Now, I truly am in Chocolate Heaven and I sigh with pleasure.

Forget diamonds. Chocolate, I think you'll find, is a girl's best friend.

ABOUT THE AUTHOR

Carole Matthews is the author of eleven novels. In the U.K., her books are consistent bestsellers. In the U.S., *For Better, For Worse* hit the *USA Today* and *New York Times* Extended Bestseller lists. Matthews's previous novel, *Welcome to the Real World,* was nominated for the Romance Novel of the Year in the U.K. She lives in England.